Crimson Veil

An Otherworld Novel

YASMINE GALENORN

JOVE BOOKS, NEW YORK

THE BERKLEY PUBLISHING GROUP
Published by the Penguin Group
Penguin Group (USA) LLC
375 Hudson Street, New York, New York 10014

USA • Canada • UK • Ireland • Australia • New Zealand • India • South Africa • China

penguin.com

A Penguin Random House Company

CRIMSON VEIL

A Jove Book / published by arrangement with the author

Jove Books are published by The Berkley Publishing Group.
JOVE® is a registered trademark of Penguin Group (USA) LLC.
The "J" design is a trademark of Penguin Group (USA) LLC.

For information, address: The Berkley Publishing Group,
a division of Penguin Group (USA) LLC,
375 Hudson Street, New York, New York 10014.

ISBN: 978-0-515-15283-8

PUBLISHING HISTORY
Jove mass-market edition / February 2014

PRINTED IN THE UNITED STATES OF AMERICA

10 9 8 7 6 5 4 3 2 1

Cover art by Tony Mauro.
Cover design by Rita Frangie.
Map by Andrew Marshall, copyright © 2012 by Yasmine Galenorn.

ACKNOWLEDGMENTS

Thank you to all my usual suspects: Samwise, my number one fan and the best husband I could hope for. My agent, Meredith Bernstein. My editor, Kate Seaver. Tony Mauro, my cover artist. My personal assistant, Andria Holley; my fan mail assistant and Street Team leader, Jenn Price; and my social media assistant, Marc Mullinex. To my furry "Galenorn Gurlz." Most reverent devotion to Ukko, Rauni, Mielikki, and Tapio, my spiritual guardians.

As always, the biggest thank-you goes to my readers. Your support helps keep the series going. You can find me on the Net on my site, Galenorn.com, and on Facebook at facebook.com/AuthorYasmineGalenorn. You can also find an Otherworld Wiki on my website.

If you write to me via snail mail (see my website for the address or write via the publisher), please enclose a stamped, self-addressed envelope with your letter if you would like a reply. Lots of fun promo goodies are available. See my site for info.

The Painted Panther
Yasmine Galenorn

War does not determine who is right—only who is left.

BERTRAND RUSSELL

In war, there is no substitute for victory.

DOUGLAS MACARTHUR

Chapter 1

The sky was clear for once, though rain was forecast before morning. The moon glimmered, her faint sliver shining down over the cemetery. Soon she would be new, dark and hiding her face. A steady flurry of gusts shook the trees, their boughs shaking like tall sentinels sounding the alarm. It was the perfect night for a funeral. A funeral none of us wanted to be at.

We were gathered at the Seryph Point Cemetery, around the open grave. A small group we were, there to send our friend off to the afterlife. There was me, Menolly, and my wife, Nerissa. My sisters, Camille and Delilah, stood beside us. Derrick Means—my bartender. And Tavah, Digger, and Kendra—all from the Wayfarer. Chase had joined us, as had Mallen. We had asked the guys to stay home and keep watch over the house. As I said, we were a small group, but everyone in attendance had cared. Everyone was there because they wanted to be.

Chrysandra's casket rested in front of us, over the grave on the device that would lower her into the earth forevermore. Her body would return to the Mother, even as we consigned her soul to the long nights of eternity. At the service—which we'd held in our house—Morio and Shade had worked their magic to seal her body in her grave. Nothing save the most powerful necromancer could ever raise Chrysandra's remains. She'd be free from the threat of being raised as a zombie. She'd never come back as one of the undead. Her soul was long gone and her body would undergo its natural breakdown, undisturbed from the machinations of sorcery.

We had said our good-byes at the house. We had bade her farewell. Now we were simply here to stand witness to the final act. To the last chapter in our friend's life. Chrysandra Jones had been a waitress at the Wayfarer since I first came Earthside. She'd stayed on as I moved from bartender to owner. She'd helped me out, done her job and then some. But Chrysandra had been a private person. We still knew nothing of her family. It was like she'd left every trace of her past behind her, put it in a safe box, and buried it somewhere to keep it hidden. Even now, in death, all we had left of her were these—her mortal remains.

I'd gone through her effects, helped Chase clear out her apartment after the fire that had destroyed my bar and the lives of eight people caught in the flames, including Chrysandra. We'd torn the place apart, but there had been nothing to indicate that she'd had any life before she first came to the bar. I was beginning to suspect she'd been in the Witness Protection Program, but if so, they seem to have left her unsupervised. Whatever the case, Chrysandra had died as she had lived—a private person, a loyal employee, and a woman I considered my friend.

As Gage, the funeral tech, lowered the casket into the ground, I closed my eyes. I'd cried myself out. I'd cried when I realized she was dying, in such horrible pain that she couldn't even scream at the hospital. I'd cried as I sucked the life out of her burned and crisped body, ending that pain. And I'd cried till my bloody tears left irremovable stains on my sheets. Now, the tears were gone, and I just wanted to punish the arsonist responsible for Chrysandra's death, and the deaths of the others who had perished in the flames.

Gage glanced at me. The tech might as well be nameless and faceless, for all I knew him, though I knew he was a werewolf. He worked for the funeral home where we'd made Chrysandra's arrangements. We'd limited our transactions with them to buying her casket and paying for her care.

She had told me once she wanted to buried in a simple pine box, unprotected from the elements. She didn't want her body to outlast time. So we'd ordered a hand-carved coffin that was untreated, that would give her up to the earth as it broke down. We'd arranged for Gage to lower the casket, but we'd taken care of the service ourselves. The funeral director was a Supe, and he understood. He didn't try to push us into buying an armored casket that would last forever.

Silence hung heavy, like fog soup, as he slowly lowered the casket into the waiting grave. Delilah and Nerissa threw roses on the coffin as it descended into the ground. Derrick stared straight ahead, trying not to let anything crack his gruff demeanor, but I knew the werebadger was taking it hard. He and Chrysandra had gotten on, and I suspected they'd been on their way to a romance.

Tavah and Digger might be vampires, but they had also been her friends, and now they watched the proceedings bleakly. Camille stepped forward and gave me a nod. I took hold of her hand as we recited our prayer for the dead.

"What was life has crumbled. What was form, now falls away. Mortal chains unbind and the soul is lifted free. May you find your way to the ancestors. May you find your path to the gods. May your bravery and courage be remembered in song and story. May your parents be proud, and may your children carry your birthright. Sleep, and wander no more."

The words echoed in the night, punctuated only by the sound of the casket as it disappeared from sight. We stepped back and formed a circle around the grave, holding hands. And then, as a cloud passed over the face of the moon, Gage pushed the button on the portable stereo, and "Shuffle Your Feet," by the Black Rebel Motorcycle Club, echoed into the night. It was Chrysandra's favorite song, and it was the last time it would ever play for her in this world.

I recognized the strains of the Stone Temple Pilots echoing out from the crowded club. As much as I'd wanted to hole up with my sisters and wife at home after the funeral, I had an appointment to keep. Roman was waiting for me. With what had gone on this past week, there would be no downtime for any of us—not for the foreseeable future.

As I threaded my way through the room, the scent of blood hung heavy in the air. The Utopia was a new vampire club. Shikra, the owner, managed to keep on the right side of Roman's rules, albeit by a narrow margin, so all was good. No bloodwhores on the premises, but contracted private pets were allowed, and feeding on them was acceptable. I still was squicked out by the thought, but since the contract was a two-way street and nobody was here against their will, I couldn't impose my morals on the vamps frequenting the joint.

Hell, *I* fed on people—although they were the dregs of society. Life was full of gray. Black and white had ceased to exist for me the day Dredge took my life and turned me.

Roman was waiting for me, looking gorgeous as usual. He was wearing black leather pants, a shirt open to the navel, and a burgundy smoking jacket. His long dark hair was pulled back in a smooth ponytail, and his eyes were almost frosted over, he'd been a vampire so long.

The Lord of the Vampire Nation, son of Blood Wyne—the Queen of the Crimson Veil—Roman had chosen me for his official consort. He had also re-sired me, taking over as my sire to break a blood bond of which I had needed to divest myself. So while I was married to Nerissa and my heart belonged to her, I was bound to Roman in an unbreakable fashion. And to be honest, I didn't mind so much. He was ancient and dangerous, but seductive and passionate, and though I didn't love him, I was able to fully act myself with him. I was able to play, and not be afraid of hurting someone I loved.

He stood as I approached, holding out one hand. I took his fingers lightly as he guided me to the booth. Every move he made was smooth and deliberate. Roman did nothing lightly, nothing without a reason. He was a man of motives, and plans, and opportunities.

"Menolly, *love*. Sit."

There it was again. *Love*. He used the word casually, but every time it set off an uneasy feeling. I'd warned Roman not to fall in love with me. While I could sleep with him, I knew I could never return his love. I didn't want to become as calculating as he was. And . . . the fact was, I was more gay than straight. Nerissa held my heart, and I held hers, and I couldn't imagine loving someone else the way I loved her.

Roman motioned to the waitress. Only vamps worked at the Utopia; it was too dangerous to have living, breathing staff at a vamp club. But the fang girls and boys were out in droves tonight—FBHs who wanted to walk on the wild side. Full-blood humans here, Earthside, loved vampires as much as they feared us, just like they loved the Fae. We were dangerous and held the promise of sex and passion. Sadly, a lot of people over ES seemed to lack intensity in their lives and so they made up for it vicariously. A very few stepped over the line to actually take the risks.

"Two bottles of your best, warm." Roman normally disdained bottled blood, but when we were out together, he drank it to appease me. I objected to his bringing members of his stable along on our dates. It wasn't that the other women bothered me—in fact, I wanted him to focus on other women. It was the whole bloodwhores thing again.

I slid into the booth, leaning my head back and closing my eyes for a moment. The silence of my pulse echoed through my body. I had gotten used to having no breath over the years, but there were times I missed the involun-

tary sigh, the rush of air flowing out as I let go of the stress.
I missed catching my breath at something beautiful.

"Was it so hard?" Roman's voice brought me back to the
present.

I opened my eyes and gazed at him. "Rough enough."

He gave me a little nod. "I've seen so many people die
over the centuries, I suppose I'm used to it. But each time a
friend vanishes into the past, it still hurts." With a soft
murmur, he reached out and stroked my face, leaning in for
a gentle kiss. "Poor Menolly . . . it has been a harsh week
for you."

I stared at the table. Harsh was an understatement. My
bar had burned down and eight people had died in the fire,
and we were pretty sure that a daemon had a hand in it. In
fact, we were trying to break the white-slavery ring spe-
cializing in Supes he was running, but were having a hard
time figuring out how to go about it. We'd just met relatives
of our mother's, blood relatives at that, and had no clue
how they were going to figure into our lives.

And that wasn't the half of it. Back in Otherworld,
Elqaneve—the Elfin city—had been destroyed by the sorcerers, and we'd been there for the direct hit. Delilah and
Camille had struggled to make it out of the war zone. I
counted myself lucky that I'd been trapped and rescued
without having to run the gauntlet of fire and destruction
that the sentient storm had rained down on the city. And now,
Queen Asteria was dead, our father was missing and presumed dead, and the spirit seals were in jeopardy.

"Yeah, harsh is the word for it, all right. So did you draw
up a list?"

The waitress brought our blood. It was bottled, like beer,
only the bottles were red to mask the color for the patrons of
bars who might be a tad bit squeamish, and to differentiate it
from the alcoholic beverage. Couldn't chance a mix-up.

I cradled the bottle in my hands, then took a long swig.
A wave of thirst ran through me as I tasted the blood. If the
thirst gnawed too much, I'd want to go out hunting, and
right now, I didn't have the heart for it. Too much death, too

much anger and fear running rampant in my life. So I downed my drink to quench the aching emptiness.

Roman pulled out his tablet. He'd gone high tech when high tech was still a baby and his ease with the computer world confounded me the more I saw it in action. I hadn't known that little fact about him, not at first, but slowly had begun to realize just how savvy he was.

He tapped an icon, then another, and a document sprang up. As he scooted close to me, my skin tingled. He was old—one of the oldest vampires Earthside. Son of the Queen, his very presence exuded a magnetism hard to ignore. It made me want to run my hands over his chest, to slam him down on the ground and tear into him, fucking his brains out. And *that* was one thing about being Roman's consort that made it all worthwhile. My position gave me the outlet I couldn't have with Nerissa. Roman and I could play rough without hurting each other. In a way, it let me keep my love and passion for my wife safe and secure, keeping her protected from my inner predator.

"Later," he murmured, feeling it, too. "We'll play very soon."

"Count on it." I gazed into his eyes, the crackle of energy almost palpable between us. But then, bringing myself back to the task at hand, I took the tablet from him and scanned the document.

We really had no clue how many vamps frequented my bar, but there were some known regulars who had taken to hanging out at the Wayfarer since I'd become Roman's official consort. And that list ran to about forty names. As I looked them over, I recognized a number of them. One thing was for sure: Roman had rushed to pull this together, putting his best men on it.

The names had been highlighted with two colors. Green meant the vampire had been accounted for. Yellow meant they were missing and nobody had been able to get in touch with them. Out of the forty-two names, thirteen were highlighted in yellow. Their last known contact was listed, as well.

I winced. That meant thirteen more potential victims. "Can you sort these out from the others and e-mail them to my phone?" I'd given in and accepted that I needed to break down and get an e-mail address, as much as I hadn't wanted to go that route. Delilah had embraced her laptop. Camille had embraced her iPhone. I hadn't fallen in love with either one. Though I had to admit, I loved my iPod, especially since I could plug it into my car.

I handed him the tablet and he tapped away while I sipped the rest of my blood.

"I guess I should track them down." I toyed with the bottle. The thought of going on a hunt for missing vamps who might already be dead seemed like a colossal time suck. The legwork normally wouldn't bother me, but we were already facing so much chaos and trouble at home.

"I've already got my men on it." He punched one final button and I heard a little swoosh sound. The next moment, my phone pinged and the list was in my e-mail in-box.

I wiped a smear of water off the table where the condensation from my bottle had formed a ring. "Thanks. By the way, in addition to trying to figure out who burned down the Wayfarer—we're convinced it's arson—I have the privilege of having been slapped with a lawsuit. Don't know if I told you that. Add yet another thing to the week-from-hell list."

"What are you talking about?" Roman set down his tablet.

"I'm being sued for wrongful death or some such crap. One of the victims' families wasted no time in snagging a lawyer and slapping me with a lawsuit. Makes me wonder just how much they actually gave a damn about their daughter." Feeling terribly grumpy, I reached in my purse and pulled out the summons I'd received the night before and tossed it on the table. "Lovely, huh?"

Roman silently opened it, scanned it through—he read incredibly fast; his intelligence was at genius level—then slowly refolded it and set it back on the table, keeping his hand on it.

"Bullshit. I'll have my lawyer contact you and we'll put a stop to this nonsense." He shook his head. "Money-grubbing bastards."

"Chase said he'd find me a lawyer—"

"Nonsense. I have the best money can buy. You are my consort. No arguments." When Roman put his fangs down, he put them down. After a moment, he rubbed his chin, then placed one hand over mine. "I want to talk to you about something—two things actually. First, I want to pay for the rebuilding of your establishment."

Roman, pay for rebuilding the Wayfarer? That didn't go down too well. I cared about him, yes. I was bound to him, yes. But I still didn't fully trust him. Camille and Delilah assumed that I'd given myself fully over to his charm. While it was true that, since he was my sire, I *had* to answer to him, it didn't stop me from keeping my eyes open and I didn't have to agree to everything he wanted.

I shook my head. "Thank you, but no. Smoky and Shade have already offered and I've accepted. Dragons horde treasure beyond even ancient vamps. They want to do this and I'd like to let them." It was, I thought, the most tactful way around saying, *"Thanks but I don't want you having a stake in my bar."* Of course, Roman was smart enough to know what I was up to, but decorum had been observed and I knew him well enough to figure he'd accept my wishes.

He just laughed. "I know what you're pulling. Fine, then. Refuse my help. But if you need it, all you have to do is ask. I truly do not have a hidden agenda in helping you, you know. But Menolly, *we'll find out who did this*. I promise you all the help I can give to finding out who torched your bar. And when we do . . . they'd better pray to whatever gods they follow."

I wanted to tell him we had a pretty good idea of what was going on. Roman *did* know that I'd received a letter shortly before the fire, one from an attorney speaking for an anonymous client asking to buy me out. I'd ignored it.

A few days later, I'd received two threatening phone

calls, not directly aimed at my bar but hinting that I'd be better off dead, and that I would be sorry I hadn't listened to *"friendly"* advice. I got a half-dozen crank calls from hate groups every month and had chalked them up to that. The next thing I knew, the bar was on fire.

"We think we know who's responsible. I can't talk about it right now, because seriously—we have to walk cautiously on this one, Roman. I'll tell you as soon as I know for sure. But that letter I told you about is involved, as well as the crank calls I got after."

Roman nodded. "I promise to stay out of it until you ask for my help." His voice was soft, low and curled around me, inviting me in.

I leaned closer to him and he wrapped his arm around me, pressing his lips to mine. I leisurely returned the kiss, melting into his embrace. It was long and slow, without pressure. We both knew that tonight was a no-go and that I needed to head home, so we left it at that. But it stoked my fire, and once I reached home, I'd be dragging Nerissa down to our lair, to fuck her brains out.

Finally, I pulled away. "What's the other thing you wanted to ask me?"

He cocked his head, the frost of his eyes glittering. "It's about your daughter, Erin."

I'd turned exactly one person: Erin Mathews. Former owner of the Scarlet Harlot lingerie boutique, she'd been captured when my former sire came looking for me to finish the job he'd started. Erin was almost dead when we got to her, and I'd given her the option of letting me turn her into a vampire. Otherwise, she would have died. She'd chosen eternal life, and just like that, I'd birthed a middle-aged daughter. Erin was smart, and she was quickly adapting.

"What about her?" Erin had been working as secretary for Vampires Anonymous, a self-help club for newly minted vamps. Run by a friend—Wade Stevens, a vampire and former psychologist who had taken it upon himself to help the newly turned—the VA provided a place where the undead could bridge the gap with their living family and friends, and learn how to coexist without caving to their inner predators.

"I want to take her out of the VA. She's got the nature I'm looking for. I'd like to train her for my security department. She could rise quickly in the ranks." The tone of Roman's voice told me that he wasn't going to give up on this one.

I thought about the offer. Truthfully, Erin would probably love it. She wanted to be useful and she wasn't a woman who was happy sitting around. She'd hated the inactivity that Sassy had forced on her when I had left her with the socialite vamp. Sassy Branson had been a dear friend, but her inner predator had finally won out. I'd had to take her out—a promise I'd made when she was still in control of herself.

Erin loved the job she had now, but she'd told me she was itching for more to do. In the end, I decided she had too much talent and know-how to waste.

"I'll stop on the way home and offer her the opportunity. If she's up for it, no problem. Might do her a lot of good. If not, then you'll let her be."

He nodded. "Fair enough."

"Time for me to head out, then. My sisters will be waiting and we've got a lot to do. With the war in Elqaneve, we're running on nerves and caffeine—well, my sisters are. I'm just . . . running."

"All right, love, but the moment you feel comfortable telling me who you think torched your bar, I expect to hear a full report. I'll take on the world for you, you know that."

I frowned. Roman might take on the world, but he'd be biting off more than he could chew if he attempted to take on Lowestar and his cronies. That would be all Seattle needed—a corporate war between the daemons and the vampires.

I slugged back the last drops of blood and picked up my purse, but before I could slide out of the booth, Shikra glided up to the table. The owner of the Utopia was silent, like most vamps, and absolutely gorgeous. Her hair was full and thick, shoulder length, and a tawny wheat color that reminded me of my Nerissa. Her eyes were icy blue. She had been a vampire for only five years, if I remembered right, but she had adapted quickly. Wearing a PVC dress, with the zipper pulled down around her navel, she'd had implants before she died. Her breasts were gloriously round, but they looked fake as hell. I wondered how being a vampire affected having implants, but decided to keep my mouth shut for now.

"I trust the service was good? And your drinks?" She gave a little dip, curtseying to Roman and me. Which was smart, considering his status.

He glanced at me and I nodded. Since I was his consort, it was my place to deal with the niceties such as answering questions like this when we were out. In a sense, it was part of my job.

"You have a lovely club. Great service." I gave her a toothy smile.

"I wondered . . ." Shikra paused, obviously wanting to ask something but respecting protocol.

"Yes?" Again, I answered. It was also my job to field queries coming at Roman when we were out together unless his bodyguard intervened.

"I need to ask Lord Roman's advice, if I may. Something has come up and I don't quite know what to do. I thought about approaching the police, but something just . . . I'm afraid to."

She looked so worried that I motioned for her to sit down without consulting Roman to ask if he was willing to listen. But he gestured for her to join us.

"What seems to be the problem?" Roman leaned forward, his elbows resting on the table, his gaze locking hers. That was one thing that made him so popular—when he turned his attention to someone or something, he gave it total focus with an intensity that was frightening.

Shikra pulled out a letter and put it on the table. "I received this the other day. It was followed by two anonymous phone calls. I think there's a connection but I can't prove it. I'll let you read the letter first."

The minute I picked up the paper, I recognized the letterhead. From a law firm called Vistar-Tashdey Enterprises, it was an offer to buy the Utopia Club from Shikra. Strongly worded, it was almost a demand. There were no names listed, no signature other than that of the lawyer representing VT Enterprises and a phone number. Same as the letter I'd received.

On edge—the letter was as off-putting and self-important as the one I'd received had been—I held up the paper. "Can I have a copy of this? Do you have a copy machine on the premises?"

She took it. "Yes, I'll have one made. But as I said, the letter isn't the only problem. The phone calls are more frightening. Last night, and then about an hour ago, I received two calls, and both times someone threatened to torch my club. No reasoning, no blackmail demands. Just a gruff voice, making a death threat. I have no idea if the caller was male or female—the voice sounded disguised."

A shiver ran through me. "Roman . . ."

He seemed to be thinking along the same wavelength. "You're thinking there may be a connection?"

I nodded. "Could be." Turning back to Shikra, I asked, "As far as the letter, can you think of some reason anyone would want to buy your club? No offense, but . . . are you making a ton of money?"

Shikra shook her head. "That puzzles me, too. Oh, I'm getting by—business isn't bad. But it's not the best, either. There's no real reason to buy me out unless they want the land the building is on."

I thought for a moment. How could I not tell her about my experience? There had to be a link. But I had no clue what was going on, and until we knew, I was hesitant to mention that I'd received the same treatment.

"Be careful. I'm serious—I think this threat may be real. Keep an eye out, and make certain you post security at the doors. If you haven't got an alarm system, get one tomorrow."

"You don't think it's just a crank?"

"I wish I *did* think so." I paused, then shook my head. "Seriously, be cautious. Meanwhile, I want a copy of the letter, please. And by any chance, were you able to record the messages that came through?" It was a long shot, but I asked anyway.

As I thought, she hadn't.

"No, I took the calls when they came in, and I know it was the same person both times. Their words were muffled. I'm guessing whoever it was, was trying to disguise their voice. And both times the calls were short. I asked questions but they didn't answer."

"What did they say exactly?" Roman glanced around the club and I followed his gaze. The Utopia was unlike most vamp clubs, decked out in vivid crimson, green, gold, and black. The setup reminded me of a tropical lounge, with lush ferns and sprawling ivies spilling over the edge of built-in flower boxes. Booths, a muted crimson, were smooth and rounded, curving around dark walnut tables polished to a high sheen. The floor was a tiled linoleum, a black-and-white speckled pattern. There were no overwhelming drapes hanging low, like in some vamp clubs. No highly sexual statues, or macabre images. For the most part, the Utopia could have been any upscale and chic bar.

Shikra squinted. "Let me try to remember the exact words." After a moment, she shrugged. "He—or she, I have no clue why but I want to say it was a he . . . he said, *'Better count your hours, bloodsucker, because I'm going to send you and your fucking club up in flames.'* And then he paused. That's when I asked what the hell was going on. He hung up." She shivered, rubbing her arms. Vamps didn't feel the cold much, but I knew it wasn't a chill hitting her.

I closed my eyes. That almost mirrored to the exact wording what my caller had said. The only difference had been, *"Better count your hours, bloodsucker, because I'm going to take you and your fucking bar down so hard you'll never get up."*

That was all Shikra could remember. Roman told her to put a recorder on the club phone and see if she could capture the message if the freak called back, and then she left to print out a copy of the letter for me.

As we headed out, I glanced back at the Utopia. "I hope it's just somebody's bad idea of a practical joke." But as I stared at the neon sign, I kept seeing the flames engulfing the Wayfarer. "I hope to hell that's all it is."

Roman walked me to my car. I stood by the Jag, staring into the night. "I'll drop by Erin's and ask her about the job opportunity. I'll call or have her call you tomorrow night."

Roman drew me in for a quick kiss. His bodyguards were in the background, studiously ignoring us as his hands slipped over my body, cupping my butt. I moaned into his mouth, then pulled away.

"Night, doll," he whispered, ushering me into my car. He shut the door when I was in. As I drove off, he stood there, one hand raised, watching me go.

I stopped by Sassy Branson's old mansion—which was now the headquarters for both the Seattle Vampire Nexus, and Vampires Anonymous. Located on two acres, the estate was gorgeous, and the mansion spacious. I stopped at the gate to show my ID. When Sassy had been alive, there had been a simple intercom system, but back then, nobody outside the vampire community knew she was a vamp, and she hadn't been all that nervous. Now there was good reason to post armed guards around the perimeter, given the hate groups that were alive and thriving.

The guards told me that Erin was out for the evening— she was off to a movie with friends—so I left a message for her to call me when she got home, and I pulled out of the driveway.

I glanced at the clock. Ten P.M. It felt odd not to be down at the Wayfarer at this time of night.

I knew I shouldn't. I told myself not to, but I couldn't help it. I drove by the ruins of my bar and parked outside the burnt-out shell. After a moment, I got out of the car and picked my way through the rubble, making my way into

the hollow husk of the building. The sky had clouded over
and the scent of rain hung heavy. It was the perfect night
for walking in ruins.

As I stood on the threshold of what had been my bar, my
stomach lurched. The Wayfarer was more than a business
to me, more than my livelihood. It had given me a sense of
purpose. It had become a friend.

And now that friend was as dead as Chrysandra. I
started to turn away when I thought I saw something in the
corner. I spun around, ready to defend myself. There, in
the murky pile of sodden wood and plaster, hovered a faint
white light. I could swear a face stared at me from the mist,
but then it vanished as the lightning crashed overhead and
the rain pounded down in a steady stream.

I gave one last glance in the corner, but there was nothing there. Heading back to my car, I wondered if I'd really
seen anything. Was it a trick of the light? Something I
expected to see, given the circumstances? Or had it been
Chrysandra's spirit? Was she unable to rest even though
we'd done our best to free her spirit? Was she out wandering? Or maybe . . . maybe it was one of the others who had
died. Feeling numb again, and weary, I climbed back in my
Jag and headed for home.

The road out to Belles-Faire was slick, the water beading
across it as the steady rain became a downpour. My wipers
were going full steam and I was doing my best to see
between the streams of water racing down my windshield.
As I neared the turn that would take me to our house, a blur
emerged at top speed from one of the driveways.

Fuck! Another car! And it wasn't stopping!

I slammed on the brakes and the Jag began to spin. As I
drove into the skid, trying to regain control, the other car
loomed large and I realized it was headed straight for me.
Holy fuck, this was bad—*this was so bad*. I considered
jumping from the car—I could do it and live, but then my
Jag would lose all control whatsoever.

So I did what I could. Muscles and reflexes took over as
I attempted to gain control of the spinning car and steer it

out of the path of the oncoming vehicle. The other car was in front of me now, skidding wildly across the wet asphalt. And then, everything blurred as my Jag spun into a crazy dance, directly into the other car's embrace.

The crash was surprisingly muffled, but then a loud shriek filled the air as metal slid along metal and my airbag deployed. It was like being hit with a sledgehammer.

As my Jag slowly rolled to a stop, I realized that I was still sitting there, still intact. Instinct took over—and shaking, I forced my hands to unbuckle my seat belt, then struggled to open the door. I half climbed, half fell out of my car, stumbling out of the way. I'd seen too many movies where the cars went up in flames, and while I thought that might be more fiction than fact, I wasn't taking any chances. Fire could destroy me.

After a pause, in which I struggled to make sense of what happened, I realized there were no flames. No explosion. I patted myself down. I was okay. Jarred but all right, I turned my attention to the other car as I pulled out my cell phone from my pocket and put in a call to 911.

The heel on my boot was broken, so I limped over and yanked open the driver door, which was a mangled mess. My strength allowed me to pry it loose, thank the gods, and with growing relief, I saw that the only passenger in the car seemed to be the driver—a youngish woman. But she looked unconscious, and I could only pray that she wasn't dead.

Chapter 2

I leaned in to feel for a pulse. The scent of blood hung lightly in the air and, right off, I could see the woman had sustained several cuts from broken glass, though none of them looked like they were bleeding out.

While the adrenaline rush of fear didn't work on me the same way it did for someone who was alive, the psychological aspects were still there and they set me on edge. My thirst rose at the scent of blood, but I pushed it down, burying it as I took her hand in mine and felt for the beat of her pulse.

There . . . yes, strong, if a little fast. The emergency dispatcher had said a unit would be here in minutes, and I tried to gauge whether she needed help before then. But at that moment, the woman jerked back as she opened her eyes and sucked in a deep breath.

"You're alive." She stared at me.

"Yeah, I lucked out. How are you? Can you move? The cops are on the way, along with fire department and an ambulance."

She frowned and began to shift, trying to get out from behind the steering wheel, which had been pushed toward her. "You've already called them then?"

I eased the seat back—luckily the controls still worked—and offered her my hand. "Yes, I figured I'd better. They'll be here in a few minutes. Are you hurt?"

She shook her head and, ignoring my hand, slid out of the SUV, easing past the skewed metal frame. I stood to the side as she struggled away from the twisted auto.

When she had fully stepped away from the car, I realized she was Fae. Which probably accounted for her being more shaken than hurt.

She eyed me up and down. "Well, *that* was exciting. You're *sure* you're all right?" Her jacket hung oddly on her and she didn't look terribly pulled together. The jeans and motorcycle boots beneath the soccer-mom camel coat didn't jive.

Slowly, I edged back. "I'm fine. Shaken, but okay."

"Good. Very good."

As I glanced at her, rain pounded down, illuminated by the streetlights on the side of the road, and I could have sworn that she was scowling. Oh yeah. Alarm bells, for sure. But then again, could the alarms be ringing because I was already having a horrible week?

"Maybe we should move away from the cars, just in case there's a gas leak." I wanted to ask her what happened—why she'd been screeching out of the driveway so fast. But all the insurance agencies warned aga̶i̶n̶s̶t̶ ̶s̶a̶y̶i̶n̶g̶ anything about the actual accident, and I do̶n̶'t̶ admit her fault.

She followed me, but stood in a call to Bowman's Towin looked like superficial dama passenger door looked dente It would take a complete ins̶p̶ kind of a mess I was looking different angle, my car woul̶d̶ have easily either gone u̶p̶ some piece of metal.

But the SUV . . . when she had glanced off my car, she'd spun and hit into the concrete retaining wall, which had caved in the driver's side of her vehicle.

"Seems we've had quite the little adventure." She sounded almost disappointed.

"Yeah. But I'd rather get my adventure from somewhere else." I gave her the once-over. Something wasn't tracking right. "I'm Menolly D'Artigo."

She nodded. "Eisha te Kana." After a pause, she added, "You sure you're okay?"

Why did she keep asking that? It wasn't like I could sustain any real internal injuries. "Yes, I'm fine."

"Good. You know, I have to be somewhere in a hurry. Let me give you my insurance information, and then, if I can still drive that hunk of metal, I'll be off." She headed back to her car.

I was about to protest—there was no way in hell that she could get the SUV going again, but paused, something nagging the back of my brain. Then it hit me—why wasn't she running up to her house? She'd pulled out of a driveway. So either she lived there, or had been visiting a friend. Either way, wouldn't she go up there to let someone know what had happened?

She was OW Fae for sure, her name told me that much. Back in Otherworld I was Menolly Rosabelle te Maria. But we were a long ways from home, and on this dark, rain-slicked road, Otherworld might as well be a million miles away.

As I said, back in Otherworld, I'm Menolly Rosabelle te Maria. The mother's first name is always the child's last name among our Fae kin. But when we came over here to this side, my sisters and I chose to use our mother's last name our surname, so here, I'm Menolly D'Artigo.

and I are half-human from our mother's blood. Fae on our father's side. Unfortunately, our we were small, and our father, Sephreh ob ing and presumed dead.

We work for the OIA—the Otherworld Intelligence Agency. At first we were ostensibly sent over Earthside due to our poor performance evaluations. In reality, Camille's supervisor—Lathe—was out for retaliation since she wouldn't blow him. He bided his time, plotting his revenge, until he was finally able to get rid of her—and us. However, sometimes there's a silver lining. After a couple years here, and all too many battles, we now run the Earthside division. I'm not sure whatever happened to Lathe, but I have a feeling he's dead. If we were lucky, maybe some pissed off agent killed him. Whatever the case, he was a prick. One better off out of the gene pool.

During the time Camille worked for him, we were with the YIA—the Y'Elestrial Intelligence Agency. Y'Elestrial being our home city-state. But then, when the OIA was formed and the portals ES opened, Lathe assigned her transfer. He finagled Delilah's and my transfers, too. We spent a year training on the cultures, habits, and other features of our mother's people.

So a little more about us. Camille is the oldest. She was born a witch, but thanks to her half-human heritage, her natural powers fritz out at all the wrong times. She's also a priestess of the Moon Mother, and she's married to three men: Smoky, a dragon; Morio, a youkai-kitsune who is teaching her death magic; and lastly, but not least, her third husband is Trillian, a Svartan—one of the dark and charming Fae. Camille studies with the Queen of Shadow and Night, out at the ES sovereign Fae nation.

Delilah is our middle sister. A t‍‍‌‌‌‌‌ ‌‌‌‌‌‌natural Were form is that of a go‍‌ hair with billowing pantaloon trolling her shifting in tabb human thing. But the Autum his Death Maidens and she to transform into a black p decreed that she will one proxy father by her lover a shadow dragon, half-Strad

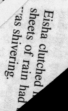

Eisha clutched sheets of rain had was shivering.

Wi
out be

Delilah had a twin. Our sister Arial died at birth—we never knew about her till after we moved over ES. Arial lives at Haseofon, the temple of the Death Maidens, emerging only in spirit leopard form. She drops by to help us on occasion, mostly during battles. Delilah was very naïve for a long time, but living Earthside has cured her of that and she's growing up strong and capable.

And then there's me, the youngest. Before I was turned into a vampire, I was a jian-tu, an acrobat and spy for the YIA. Hampered by my mixed-breed heritage, I lost control at a crucial moment and landed—literally—in the middle of a nest of vampires. Meaning I fell from my hidey-hole in the cavern roof. Dredge, the worst vamp in OW history, caught me. He tortured and raped me, then turned me. After that, he sent me home, a maddened, crazed creature, to destroy my family.

Luckily, Camille had her wits about her and stopped my attack. The YIA, embarrassed by their fuck-up—they'd sent me in without backup—decided to rehabilitate me rather than stake me. So here I am.

When we were sent Earthside, we thought we'd be pulling a long, leisurely sabbatical, exiled to an out-of-the-way pit stop where we couldn't fuck up. Little did we know that Shadow Wing, Demon Lord of the Subterranean Realms, was planning a coup on Earth and Otherworld.

He aims to raze both ES and OW to the ground and make them his private stomping grounds. And he's leading the war on two fronts. Telazhar, his necromancer general in Otherworld, is decimating the land as he leads his army of sorcerers in a war to rival the Scorching Wars of millennia ago. And over here, well . . . we're not sure what Shadow Wing's next step is. But I'm pretty sure we're going to find out before long.

her purse as she crossed to my side. The became a torrential downfall, and she

"Do you mind if I sit in your car for a moment? I need to call a friend."

Shrugging, I nodded. "Get in. It's cold and you're going to freeze your ass off while we wait for the cops to get here." I slid back into the driver's seat, pushing the airbag out of the way. She did the same on the passenger's side. I wasn't sure what to say next. I was already being sued once, and I didn't relish any more legal problems. And she really didn't seem all that friendly.

"So you're from Otherworld? Whereabouts?"

She blinked. "I guess you would recognize that I am. I've been over here for about eighteen months. I'm originally from Ceredream. I'm here studying comparative Earthside cultures."

A lot of budding anthropologists from OW came over to study ES cultures. It was a convenient way to take a long vacation to an exotic land and get educational credit for it.

The arrival of a police cruiser—from the FH-CSI, since I'd called them—saved me from any more small talk. I hurried out of the car, telling Eisha to stay where she was. No use both of us getting soaked through, and she would feel the cold more than I. The officer was Kane—one I recognized—and I ran down what had happened.

"I need to talk to the other driver next." Kane finished taking my statement. As he tucked away his notebook, the tow truck rolled up.

After pointing out Eisha's vehicle, we headed back to my car, but Eisha was nowhere in sight.

"Where is she?" he asked.

"She was right here a few minutes ago." I glanced around. She wasn't standing in the middle of the street, nor was she near her own car. In fact, there was no sign of her at all.

"Well, fuck. I don't know. She didn't seem hurt—where would she wander off to?" A thought struck me. "Maybe she went back to the house—she barreled out of that drive-way there."

I waited in my Jag, and Kane sent his partner up to see if she had returned to the dimly lit house at the top of the drive. A few minutes later, the officer was back. "Nobody there knows who you're talking about. They said they never had company tonight, and they don't know anyone by that name, nor anybody who owns an SUV like hers."

Confused, and more than a little suspicious, we hunted around the area for a while. Fifteen minutes later, we realized that she was nowhere in sight—she'd just vanished. Maybe she'd gone into the woods on the side of the road, but there was no sign of her whatsoever.

Kane finally shook his head. "I'll get a search party out here. Maybe she was hurt . . . but something tells me she's just vanished. Can you still drive your car?"

I tried the ignition and the Jag started up. "Yeah. I lucked out. I think most of my damage is superficial. And I'm not far from home so I'll just head there and have my sisters take it to the mechanic in the morning."

"I'll let you know if we find her. Meanwhile, call her insurance agent and file a claim, I suppose. From what you say, I'm writing it up that she was at fault. But be careful on the way home. We're in a storm cycle, I think, and it's supposed to rain like this for several days."

He motioned for the tow truck to haul Eisha's SUV off, as I fastened my seat belt. After a moment's hesitation, I found a knife in my glove compartment. I paused—could they even stuff the airbag back in? Would it ever work again or did they need to replace it? If I sliced through the bag, they'd have to reinstall it full. I frowned, staring at the material that was in the way of my pedals.

Fuck it. I didn't know enough about cars to make a good guess, so I finally just sawed off the material and dumped it into the backseat. As I pulled out onto the street, my car rattled and clunked, but I wasn't far from home and I made it safely.

Pulling into the driveway, I turned off the ignition and hoisted my purse over my shoulder. The three-story Victorian we called home loomed against the storm clouds, but it was a welcoming sight. A not-so-much haunted house, even though we were nearing Halloween and Samhain.

So much had changed in the past week . . . in the past few years . . . but this was my home. Here, I lived with my wife, my sisters, and their loves, and several of our friends. Come to think of it, I barely thought about life back in Otherworld anymore. I'd come to accept Seattle as home base, and I had the feeling that—given the chance to return to OW—it wouldn't be such an easy choice.

The past week had been anything but easy.

First, we'd been asked to help out on a case for a couple friends of mine. Tad and Albert, two vampires who worked at Microsoft on the night shift, were worried about Violet, their friend and coworker who had disappeared. We'd started the investigation thinking she'd just skipped town, but had all too quickly figured out that she'd been abducted by a sex slave operation run by Lowestar Radcliffe—a daemon. It was complicated, and involved a lot of hidden factors still, but the upshot was, Grandmother Coyote wanted the daemons stopped and we were in charge of doing so.

Before we could immerse ourselves in the case, my bar had burned down, and we'd been caught in the siege of Elqaneve. The former was heartrending, the latter—traumatic beyond any scope we'd yet experienced. Tens of thousands died as the sentient storm attacked the city, pretty much decimating it. And we'd been there for the throw down. I'd lucked out and been rescued before I could see what was going down in the city proper, but Delilah and Camille had been forced to make their way through the attacks, and the destruction they'd witnessed seemed to have scarred them both heavily.

The storm had wreaked havoc on the Elfin lands of Kelvashan, and now it was on the move to Svartalfheim. All we knew at this point was that the Svartan sorcerers and mages were readying themselves in an attempt to repel the annihilation headed their way.

While we had recovered Amber and Luke, and their spirit seals—along with a spare one—two of the spirit seals were still missing. Venus and Ben, two of the Keraastar Knights wielding them, had not been found. That's why Smoky and Trillian—Camille's other husbands—were in OW searching for them right now.

And our father's body still had not been recovered. He was missing, his soul statue back home had been shattered, and that pretty much spelled out that he was dead. All in all, the past week had been one big clusterfuck.

Nerissa was waiting up for me. She took one look at my face and jumped up from the table where she'd been eating cold fried chicken. Camille and Morio were nowhere to be seen, but Delilah was helping my wife polish off the left-over KFC. I didn't see the guys anywhere but that didn't mean they weren't around.

"Love, what the hell happened? You look shaken up." Nerissa was an Amazon of a woman. Aphrodite incarnate, she was five-ten, with a tawny mane that shook out wild and shaggy when she took it down from the chignon she usually wore. Curvy, she was voluptuous and ripe, and every time I saw her, all I could think was how wonderful it was that this woman was mine.

My lover, my wife, my companion. I played her body like a rock star's guitar—wild, passionate, and with a grip that wouldn't quit. And Nerissa gave as good as she got . . . she took me to heights no one else could. Roman, I could roughhouse with. With Nerissa, I soared.

I leaned into her arms, resting my head on her chest. "I had an accident."

"You what? Oh, my gods!" Nerissa pushed me back, staring at me. "Are you all right?" She immediately began to pat me down, looking for broken bones. Delilah took off out of the kitchen and I heard her calling for Camille and Morio. I snorted. That told me what those two had been up to. They never went to bed this early unless they were up for a little action.

"I'm all right. I was shaken, but not hurt. Unfortunately, I can't say the same for my Jag."

Vanzir headed outside to check on the car despite the fact that he had even less of a clue on how they worked than I did.

Nerissa shoved me toward the table and made me sit down. "What on earth happened?"

"Rain-slicked road. I skidded and went hydroplaning. The other driver was going too fast, too. But it was very odd . . . and I have no idea what to make of it all." I dropped into one of the chairs, leaning on the table with my elbows. "An OW Fae hit me. But . . . she vanished before the cops could talk to her."

"Whose fault was it?" Nerissa pulled a bottle of blood out of the refrigerator—one that Morio had enchanted, so it would taste like something other than type O negative. She popped it in the microwave for a moment.

I shook my head. "Hers. I was going under the speed limit and she pulled out from that driveway like a bat out of hell. I told the cops that, too. I'm not taking the heat for it. I tried to stop but skidded into her. If I hadn't hit her just right, my Jag would have been mincemeat. She was driving a big old SUV."

By that time, Camille and Morio had come running down the stairs, dressed in their robes. Camille was flushed and I had no doubt what they'd been up to. Delilah also had Shade in tow. As Nerissa handed me my warmed blood—which tasted like chicken soup—Vanzir popped back inside.

"The Jag looks like it hit the wrong side of a dubbatroll. I doubt if you're going to get out for under a couple grand on damages, but it's still drivable." He shrugged. "At least you were able to make it home."

I groaned. "Yeah. Would one of you take it to Jason's tomorrow, to see what he says?" I looked around. "Is Trillian still here?" Trillian had returned home through the portals, escorting Amber and Luke, two friends who had also been caught in the destruction of Elqaneve. Shadow

Wing would love to get his hands on them, since they both possessed spirit seals. Now that Queen Asteria was dead and Elqaneve in ruins, it was up to us to hide them and keep them safe.

"No. He went back to OW this evening. They need him there." Camille's eyes flickered, and her voice betrayed her worry. "Amber and Luke are sleeping. The spirit seals put high demands on their energy."

"Damn fine thing. You do realize that, whatever plans Queen Asteria had for the Keraastar Knights, they've gone the way of the buffalo? Unless Aeval or Titania knows what her agenda was, we have no clue what she was up to. The knights are bound to their spirit seals—they'll die if we try to separate them."

There was no good answer to that one.

"When are the dragons coming for them?" Delilah asked.

Smoky had contacted the Dragon Reaches, and his mother and the Wing Liege had agreed to hide the knights for us. They owed Camille big-time, and this fell directly into the help they'd promised to give her.

"Within a couple of days. They are preparing for them now." Camille turned as Hanna wandered into the room.

"I heard voices." She rubbed her eyes. She'd obviously been in bed. So I launched into recounting the evening's activities again. They needed to know about the Utopia, as well.

"I think we may have a serial arsonist targeting vampire bars. We're going to have to take action before anybody else gets hurt."

Hanna headed over toward the sink. "I don't know about these fires, but the Fae woman you crashed into? She's trouble. There has to be some reason she vanished. My guess is she was waiting for you. She was parked in the driveway of someone she didn't know, and pulled out at the very moment you passed by? Too much of a coincidence." As she put on the kettle, Hanna glanced over her shoulder. "I might as well bake a batch of cookies since you're all up. I made the dough earlier so all I have to do is fire up the oven."

I frowned. "Too much about the accident doesn't add up. At first, I thought she'd just been careless, but yeah. Too many questions. And as to her disappearing? There has to be a reason she didn't want to talk to the cops. She seemed unsettled when I told her I'd called them."

"I'd think it was insurance fraud, but you have to stick around to file a claim. Have you called her agency yet?"

"Fraud? Seems more up an FBH's alley than Fae." I pulled out my phone, along with the information Eisha had given me, and punched in the 24-hour emergency number. I didn't have to wait long—miracle of miracles.

The operator who came on the line took my information and asked me to hold, but when he returned, he sounded puzzled. "I'm sorry, Ms. D'Artigo, but we don't have a record of having anyone by that name as a client, or the SUV in question. I checked our records for the license plate to be certain. Are you sure you have the correct information?"

I knew I hadn't written anything down wrong. "Yeah, I'm sure. I guess she lied to me. Are you sure, though? You don't even have a lapsed policy under that name or license?"

Another moment and then, "No, I'm sorry. Nothing. I'm afraid I can't help you."

I hung up. "Great, the insurance information? A fraud. Want to bet she's using a fake name, too? That caps it. For some reason, she tried to run me down and when she didn't manage to get the results she wanted, she vanished. Which means . . ."

"She was probably trying to kill you. You said yourself that, had she been a fraction more on-target, your car would have been history. That could change the whole face of the game." Camille glared at the table. "So what about . . . could Lowestar be behind this attack, too? We know he's got to be the one behind burning down the Way-farer. So was he sending another message this time, or was he trying to kill you in the bar's fire, as well? Catch you in the blaze?"

"Maybe they were trying to kill me and this was a reprisal attack given I survived the fire. But if that's true, then Shikra is in danger. Because she got the exact same letter and phone calls I did. And she ignored the threats and refused to sell them her club. I told her to keep watch, to get security."

"Are you going to call Roman and tell him about tonight?" Nerissa leaned forward. "As his consort, don't you have to?"

"I suppose I should, but we're getting dangerously close to spilling the beans to him about Lowestar. And if he finds out what's really going on . . . a vampire as powerful as he is? Far worse than a testosterone-laden lover. He'd tear the Farantino Building down brick by brick and just make things worse."

"That may not be a bad idea, really." Camille glanced over at Hanna. "Chocolate chip?"

"Peanut butter chocolate chip." Hanna gave her a friendly grin as she slid the first batch into the oven.

I snorted. "I'm beginning to think we need a secretary to take care of all this crap. So we'll just add keeping an eye on the Utopia—at least on what's going down there—to our to-do list. Because chances are, Lowestar isn't going to take her refusal with good spirits."

Delilah sighed. "Speaking of our to-do list . . ."

"Please don't and say we did." Camille laughed, but there was a raw edge to her voice. We were all nerve-racked.

I cleared my throat. "You know, with all the chaos, I guess we should start having daily meetings to figure out where the hell we are in all of this. We can't afford to slip up on anything."

"Right." Morio motioned to Hanna. "Fuel us with tea and cookies. We're about to have a brainstorming session."

"More like a bull session," Camille grumbled. But she let out a long sigh. "Delilah, do you have our notes?"

Delilah jumped up. "I'll get them. Meanwhile, fill up my plate with cookies and pour me a glass of milk." She ran off into the living room, to retrieve her laptop.

"So where does this leave us?" Camille frowned at her cookie. It was piping hot and I could tell she was trying to decide how quickly she could dig into it without burning her mouth.

Delilah didn't exercise as much restraint. She took a huge bite and immediately began fanning her mouth. "Hot! Hot!"

I snorted. "If you weren't so impatient, you wouldn't burn yourself." I stared at the laptop's screen, frowning. "You know, we are having one hell of a time prying information out of the cracks about Lowestar Radcliffe. We know he's a daemon, we know he bought the Farantino Building, and we know he's been involved with the Farantino family for a couple of hundred years, it looks like. But it's not like we can just waltz in there and say, *Excuse me, would you have a moment to answer some of our questions? Oh—and by the way, fucking get your ass out of Seattle, please.*"

"So we need to go in under the radar." Camille handed Delilah a napkin and began eating her own cookie, which had cooled down enough now so that it didn't seem to leave a lasting impression.

"Right. And what's the best way to find out about an organization? From the inside." I glanced up at her.

Camille shook her head. "Oh no, not again! I was the guinea pig to ferret out Gulakah and I ended up locking heads with him in the Netherworld. I don't want to go through that again."

"I wasn't suggesting it be you." I frowned, looking over the list of facts we'd managed to accrue. "Violet used the Supernatural Matchups website, didn't she?"

Delilah nodded, wiping her mouth and taking another cookie. "Right."

"Then . . . suppose we create a fake persona? We go on there, see if we can get Lowestar's notice, and then we . . . well . . . when he wants to meet, or his crony—the one who looks like they nabbed Violet—we send someone in undercover. We can worry about who that will be later." The made sense to me. When you wanted to go fishing, y to use bait, and if you were after a particular kin you used the bait they liked best.

Delilah and Camille stared at me. At first, I thought they were entertaining the idea.

But then Camille sputtered. "That's fucking insane. He'd recognize us and no fucking way are we using any-body else for bait. And he'd know *you*, since we're pretty sure he tried to buy you out and then kill you."

Nerissa bit her lip. "I'll do it."

Horrified, I jumped up, hands on my hips. "Oh no you fucking *won't*. You're my wife and I won't put you in dan-ger like that." I was deadly serious. There was no way I was going to allow Nerissa to get near that goddamn place.

She let out a snort. "Vampire or not, you're not telling me what to do. I love you, but I want to contribute, and this, this I can do. All you're going to do is use my picture, right? And I might have to go meet somebody, in which case, you'd be following me—I know that without a doubt. I have the condo still, and nobody's living there right now. I can use that address so it won't lead them back here. I will use a fake name. Still going to argue with me?"

Everybody was staring at us. We didn't argue often, and when we did, it was usually in private. And it was usually Nerissa reading me the riot act for some stupid stunt I'd pulled or attitude I'd copped. Frankly, I was amazed the woman loved me enough to marry me.

I paused. How the hell was I going to deal with this? If I pushed, I knew Nerissa would push back. "What if you did this and they caught you? How would you cope with it? How do you think I'd be able to live with myself?"

"Remember, I was trained by Venus the Moon Child. I can withstand a lot more pain than you know."

Before he moved to Otherworld and took on the mantle of the Keraastar Knights, the wily shaman emeritus of the Rainier Puma Pride had put Nerissa through her paces in learning how to control pain and channel it through plea-sure, and how to heal with her sexuality. He'd also helped her develop her inner strength. When my wife set her mind to something, there was no stopping her.

Camille caught my eye and cleared her throat. "Why

don't we wait for a little bit and talk about it later? We don't have to decide anything tonight."

Sometimes she could actually be a good diplomat. Grateful, I nodded. "I'll agree to that. Nerissa?"

"Fine. But this isn't over."

I arched one eyebrow. "I never said it was." Leaning back in my chair, I shook my head. My cornrows clicked as the ivory beads threaded into them clinked lightly. I was the shortest one of the group—five-one if I was an inch, and I was petite. And my hair was burnished copper, unlike anybody in the family. We never had figured out where that recessive gene came from.

"I do appreciate you volunteering. I'm not saying you can't do the job right—I'm just frightened for you." I slaked my gaze over my wife. She would certainly catch Lowestar's eye, no doubt about it. And *that* was the problem.

Nerissa let out a loud sigh. "I wouldn't have offered if I hadn't meant it. I'm part of this family, too. I want to pull my weight like the rest of you. It's not like I'm human. I'm stronger, faster, and far more dangerous than any FBH. Ask Chase. He's thrilled to have me on the job."

Chase was our friend—a detective and leader of the Faerie-Human Crime Scene Investigation team, or the FH-CSI—who was currently living on our land with his newborn daughter.

"We'll talk again tomorrow night. If—and that's a big if—you do this, I want to be here when you create that profile. Speaking of FBHs, where *is* Chase tonight?" I had half expected to find him hanging out up here at the main house.

"He's at Iris's, learning how to be a father. I think he and Bruce are going to be doing a lot of bonding over their mutual experience in fatherhood." Delilah smiled softly. "I just wish Sharah could be here with him. I hope she's okay."

"Everyone back in Otherworld is in danger. Elqaneve is under siege from the goblins right now. Svartalfheim is gearing up for the sentient storm that destroyed the Elfin

City. I wonder . . . if King Vodox's defenses can't destroy it, where will sorcerers send it next?" Camille looked at me bleakly.

I knew where the next target would be, and so did she. And so did Delilah. We weren't kidding ourselves over that one. Nobody wanted to say it out loud. So I decided to be the one to call out the white elephant in the room.

"Y'Elestrial. Where else?"

As a hush fell through the room, a soft chiming sounded from the living room. The Whispering Mirror, summoning us. Which meant we had incoming news. I just hoped that whatever it was, it wasn't another emergency.

Chapter 3

❧❦❧

As we crowded around the mirror, Camille took her place in front of it. She was the one who understood it the most. I couldn't see my reflection, of course—that part about vampires is true. And anybody looking through from the other side wouldn't be able to see me, though they could hear me if I spoke.

We waited for the fog in the silver-framed mirror to clear. It was like having our own private Skype program hooked up to Otherworld, only the video portion was always on and we didn't need headphones and the mirror was the magical computer.

A moment later, Trenyth appeared. He was advisor to Queen Sharah—the new Elfin Queen. Until a few days ago, she had been a medic at the FH-CSI and Chase's very pregnant girlfriend.

Trenyth looked weary, beyond tired. I wondered how long he'd gone without sleep now.

He didn't waste any time on chitchat. "Girls, we found your father's body. I'm sorry. Sephreh was killed when a collapsing piece of wood . . . it . . . ." Here he paused, look-ing down at the table in front of him.

"Just . . . please tell us." Delilah's voice quavered and she bit her lip. "We need to know the truth."

I gave a sharp nod, even though Trenyth couldn't see me. "She's right. Tell us. No gory details, but the facts."

Trenyth started a bit. "I never get used to the fact that I can't see you through the mirror, Menolly." He sighed, and met Camille's eyes. She was our anchor and rock—every time there was bad news, it somehow found its way to her first, even when the rest of us were there in the room.

"Your father was impaled by a broken beam that fell from the ceiling. We found him beneath two cross beams that had held up some of the debris. We have his body. What do you want us to do?"

Camille looked over her shoulder at Delilah and me. "I'll make the arrangements." Her face was drawn but the fact that she needed to do this was apparent in her expression.

Delilah must have seen it, too. "We'll do whatever you need us to."

"What she said." I nodded toward Delilah. "Whatever you decide is fine with us."

Camille turned back to Trenyth. "Right now the war there is too dangerous for us to come get him. But if Smoky, Trillian, and Roz could bring his body back with them, we can have our ceremony here on Samhain. Then when it's safe, we will take him home to Otherworld and lay him to rest near Mother. Which reminds me, now that we know for sure that he's dead, we have to notify Aunt Rythwar."

"I have a spare messenger. I will send word to her." Tre-nyth's eyes were kind, and I wished to hell that his world hadn't been torn to shreds. Not only had he lost the love of his life—Queen Asteria—but he'd been forced to take on a new Queen who needed him more than anyone probably ever had in his life. Sharah was ill equipped to handle running a kingdom.

"Thank you." Camille shuddered lightly, then shook her head as if to clear her thoughts. "How goes the war, or should we even ask?"

"The storm is nearing Svartalfheim. King Vodox and his mages are waiting for it. We still don't know where the sorcerers who are controlling it are hiding, but they can't be that far away. Meanwhile, the goblin hordes—and they aren't just goblins, but trolls and Sawberry Fae and bogies and their ilk—they continue to enter Elqaneve thick and furious. As many as we mow down, still others take their place. But the legion of soldiers from Nebulveori are almost here and the dwarves are mighty fighters. They will help roust the enemy from the lands." At that, Trenyth actually smiled.

"What about the Cryptos and the others?"

"The Dahnsburg Unicorns are sending a contingent of their warriors—unicorns and ogres and all who answer to King Uppala-Dahns. King Vodox sent soldiers to help their lighter brethren even though they, themselves, are under siege. And you know that your own city-state, Y'Elestrial, immediately dispatched a legion of soldiers. They are fighting alongside our warriors."

"And the dark moon priestesses?" Camille looked uncomfortable. She'd only just recently found out some daunting news about her order.

"Derisa, the High Priestess, is sending them even as we speak. As far as the rest of Otherworld . . . they are waiting . . . and watching. Ceredream will still not take sides. Aladril is sequestered in debate over the matter now."

Delilah cleared her throat. "How's Sharah doing?"

Trenyth pressed his lips together. "As well as we can expect. The medications the healers have given her have dried up her milk, and her hormones are in a drastic flux as they return to normal." At Delilah's soft growl, he held up his hands. "If there had been another way, you know I would have taken it. But there wasn't . . . we needed Sharah to step up to the crown. She has been rallying our people— what there are left of us."

With that last statement, the finality of this mess hit home. The look on his face said it all. Kelvashan had been destroyed. The Elfin race was decimated. What had been a thriving culture now stood in smoking ruins, and the survivors were fighting for their lives.

"Can you bring the survivors—the women and children—over here?" Camille asked. "They'd be safe then."

"But would they? How long do you think Earthside has? If Telazhar continues to wreak his havoc across this land, you are not safe either. The storm Telazhar's sorcerers have conjured up can rip a mountain apart. Destroy a palace—you saw that firsthand, Camille. You know how deadly and devastating this creature is. I don't know how they created it, it truly is a construct of some sorts, but the storm has consciousness and will, and malevolent thought. If they can do that . . . what else can they do?"

At that moment, a familiar face appeared behind him. *Smoky!*

Camille let out a little cry. "My love!"

Smoky, her dragon husband, was six foot four, and his silver hair coiled down around his ankles. He was dressed in white, as always, and his piercing eyes were frosty and glimmered with the light of his heritage.

He looked harried, and tired, too. But as usual, the dragon was spotless. "Love, my sweet, I am so sorry about your father." He looked toward the rest of us. "You, too, Menolly and Delilah. If there's anything I can do, just ask. I'm here. We are family."

"Can you bring our father's body home to us?" Camille whispered. But we could all hear her plainly. All Fae—half-breed or not—had excellent hearing.

Smoky looked at Trenyth, who nodded. "Go ahead. One day won't make a difference. Not with the chaos that is rampaging through the land."

As Trenyth moved out of the way, Smoky leaned toward the mirror, staring directly at Camille. "We are still looking for Ben and Venus. So far, we've found no signs of them. We'll bring your father home, then return to continue the search."

Camille bit her lip. "Can you really spare the time to do this for us?"

"For you, I would spare the world."

And just like that, the big galoot of a dragon once again proved himself worthy of my sister's love. I liked Smoky, but he could be a handful and I had no clue how he managed to keep that tremendous ego under lock and key when dealing with Camille's other two husbands, but somehow, he did. And for that, I gave him props.

Trenyth retook the seat in front of the mirror. "Do not worry, girls. If they haven't been able to find Benjamin and Venus the Moon Child yet, another day will not matter. Perhaps foolish words, but in this turmoil, there has to be some measure of compassion. I know it's meager comfort, but you need your father's body with you."

Smoky nodded. "Trillian, Rozurial, and I will come home for the night and return here tomorrow. We'll be there soon. I can bring your father's body through the Ionyc Seas, and Roz can bring Trillian."

With that, the fog filled the mirror again.

"Well, that's that." I leaned back. "There is no doubt or hope left."

The whole thing was surreal. Even though our father's soul statue had been shattered, we still had held on to hope—ill-placed as it was—that perhaps it had been a mistake. That he had survived.

I had to admit that even I had clung to that thin thread, and I was by far the most prosaic and pessimistic of the three of us. Maybe . . . just maybe, we thought . . . something else had broken his soul statue besides his death. Maybe a rat or bird or cat had knocked it over. Now that hope was dashed.

Delilah wiped her eyes. "I didn't want to believe it, but . . . really . . . we all knew." With an inner strength that surprised me, she shook off her tears. "At least we know for sure, and now we can move on."

"I shall make another batch of cookies and also some sandwiches and soup and bread. The men are bound to be hungry and I doubt if they've had many a good meal the past day or so."

Hanna turned and marched back to the kitchen. A strong

woman, she had been through her own losses, and she'd helped Camille escape when Smoky's father kidnapped and tortured her. Her answer to sorrow was to fortify the mourners with good food, warm clothing, and a soft bed.

Vanzir frowned. "I'm not good at this, but I'm sorry." He shifted, his eyes whirling with a kaleidoscope of color. They never pinned down to just one—in fact, there was no word for the color of his eyes. It seemed to exist outside the usual spectrum, but still it was there, in the shifting haze that roiled through his eyes. Vanzir could never pass for human, that was sure, even though he took the form. And his natural weapons would give a hentai monster pause.

I gave him a half smile as Camille and Delilah wearily pushed to their feet. "It's okay. Don't sweat it."

Camille turned to Delilah and me. "I thought . . . I know it's not usual, but with the war and the fear that Y'Elestrial will be next, what do you think about cremating Father's body and keeping the ashes for when we can return them to the family crypt without worry?"

Even though she didn't say it, I knew she was thinking about Mother—and whether our house and land would be standing. Mother was laid to rest in the family shrine. What if the storm destroyed our home? What if our past went up in flames?

"I think that's a good idea," I said, forcing a smile. "We'll have an interment ceremony after the danger has been quelled."

"If they can stop it." Delilah turned a bleak look on me. "I'm not feeling very hopeful right now."

"No, but we can't let that stop us." I wasn't sure what to do next—grief has a way of freezing a person, and I could tell both Camille and Delilah were on the edge of a meltdown. While I'd managed to escape the destruction of Elqaneve without witnessing the worst of it, they'd been forced to journey through the carnage as it was happening and shell shock had set in.

There was a noise behind us, and then, as we turned around, Smoky appeared, a shrouded figure in his arms.

Rozurial appeared next, his arm around Trillian. They had come through the Ionyc Seas, silently, without so much as a whisper. As we stood, watching, Camille caught her breath and Delilah gasped. Me? I just stared. I had no breath to catch, no pulse to race . . . but still, a quiver in my heart told me that I hadn't fully been prepared for this.

Vanzir moved forward, pushed himself between us and the silent figure of our father. "Here, let's take him to the studio. We can . . . he can . . . we can use one of the bunks for the night until arrangements can be made."

"I want to see." Camille stepped forward. "I have to know—for myself."

"You don't want to see him, love. He's been dead for a couple of days, and while the conditions were dry and cool . . . I don't think you should witness the damage done. Remember him the way you last saw him." Smoky pressed his lips against her forehead. "Will you accept my word that it's him?"

She glanced at me. I nodded. There was no use in going through that—Smoky would never lie to us. At least not to her.

"Very well." She looked at the shrouded figure, and let out a choked cry. "Now that he's here, now . . . it's real."

Delilah wrapped her arms around Camille. "Let's get some tea." And for one of the first times in her life, except when she'd been attacked by Hyto, Camille's shoulders slumped and she let Delilah lead her away.

I turned back to Smoky and the guys. "Thank you for bringing Father home to us. I didn't have a good relationship with him, not after I was turned. But this . . . I never thought he'd go like this."

"Death is always unexpected, even when you know it's coming." Smoky lifted the body and Vanzir went to open the door for him. I watched them exit.

"So this is it." I stared at their backs as they disappeared.

Nerissa moved in and wrapped her arms around me, cradling me. "I love you, Menolly. Tell me what I can do. Tell me what you need." Her voice was gentle against my ears, and her lips tickled my skin.

I closed my eyes, relaxed into her embrace. "First, I have something to do. Then . . . I need to talk to Amber and Luke. I haven't really had a chance yet. And after . . ." I turned to her. "After, I want you. *Need* you."

She let go. She wasn't one of those clingy spouses who had to know everything I was thinking or doing. Lately we'd been on the scritchy side, but for the most part, I thought we understood each other.

"I've got some reading to catch up on. Just let me know when you're ready. I'm all yours." And with that promise, she vanished into the parlor and closed the door behind her.

I looked over at Roz and Trillian. Both men looked shaken and tired. "Has it been very bad?"

"Worse than you can imagine. Or maybe not. Delilah and Camille came through hell. As bad as the aftermath is, the storm must have been a fury beyond any I've ever dreamed of." Roz's usual good cheer had vanished, and he slumped down on the sofa. The incubus had seen far more than his share of death and dying over the centuries he had been alive, and still he looked shaken to the core.

"The dead are everywhere. The goblins are behind every tree, every bush. The smell of blood is so thick in some villages that it overpowers everything else . . ." His words drifted off, and he stared at his hands. "I thought it was bad when Dredge killed my family. But that was nothing compared to what we've witnessed."

Trillian clapped him on the shoulder. "Bad it is, and worse still, there's nothing we can do to help. The destruction is of such a magnitude that we give our food to the children we find sitting on the side of the road. They are everywhere. No place to go, no parents, no shoes or clean clothes or water. And no one to look out for them." His face was bleak, and for the first time, I began to see beneath the arrogant exterior. I knew there was more to him than met the eye—that had become clear over the past couple of years—but now . . . now it was visible.

"What . . . what can we do?" The thought of the devastation was enough to overwhelm anybody.

Trillian sighed. "Make damned sure Earthside is protected. The three of you and our ragtag army here, we're all that stands between the far worse carnage that would happen should Shadow Wing break through. Can you imagine the response if a horde of demons came trampling through? Opposing governments would assume it was their enemy, setting a new weapon to strike."

Morio joined the conversation. "Should that happen? Watch the nuclear bombs fly. And the resulting radiation would only strengthen the demons. All Shadow Wing would have to do is start the whole mess. The humans would do the rest and leave Earthside open to utter destruction and enslavement."

"He's right. What's going on in Otherworld?" Trillian said. "That will only be multifold should the Demon Lord make it through the portals." He brushed his hand over his eyes. "I'm going to the kitchen and check on my wife, if you'll excuse me."

As he left the room, I turned back to Roz, but the incubus was leaning back on the sofa, asleep. He must have been exhausted. I picked up a throw and gently covered him with it. None of the men had slept much—of that I was sure.

At that moment, Smoky and Vanzir returned.

I pointed to the kitchen. "Camille is in there. Trillian and Delilah are with her. And Roz is asleep. Let him rest, if you can."

Smoky gave me a gentle nod. "I'll go to her then."

Vanzir gave me a speculative look. "Do you need to be with them—your sisters?"

I shook my head. "I don't think I'd do much good right now. I'll be back in a few minutes." I stepped past him, then headed outside. I knew what I had to do, even though I didn't want to.

The rain was slashing down, stinging needles against my flesh. Vampire I might be, but I could still feel jabs and punctures and bruises. They may not hurt as much, in fact most of them bounced off, but I was aware of them.

Clouds boiled across the sky and I stared up at the racing

storm. We were in our rainy season, and it would last until June. The Seattle area managed about fifty-five to sixty cloud-free days a year, most of them in the summer. I relished the chill gloom—it seemed more appropriate than winters in more southern climes, where I'd still have to stay in my lair, asleep until the pull of sunset woke me. I loved the rain and wind that swept through, making the Northwest its semipermanent home.

As I approached the shed-cum-apartment, I stopped for a moment. I was better suited than either of my sisters for this, but still . . . I wasn't sure just how it would affect me. It had been only hours ago that I'd attended the funeral of a good friend. Now, I'd be standing vigil by another corpse, but this one . . . this one I had roots with.

After a moment, I summoned my courage and pushed through the door. There, neatly laid out on the sofa, was the shrouded figure of Sephreh ob Tanu, the man who had loved our mother, the man who had shared his genetic code with us. I knelt by the leather couch, pausing before I reached out and slowly pulled the shroud away.

It was Father, all right. Even through the pale, bruised skin . . . it was Father. I thought about lifting the cover all the way, seeing just what had happened to him, but then I decided to forgo the idea. I didn't need the gory details. I'd lived through my own death and torture. I didn't need to see what pain he'd been through when he died. I could afford him that much privacy.

As I watched his face, I realized I was searching for any sign of life—a flutter of breath, or a flicker of the eyelashes. But silence ruled, and Father remained still as the silence of my own body. Only for him, there would be no second chance, there would be no life after life, no living death. He had gone to our ancestors, and I had no doubt he stood arm in arm with Mother now.

The thought made me smile. He'd missed her so very much, and had never been quite right after her death. He'd become hardened, harsher—more demanding. Poor Camille had born the brunt of his expectations, but we'd all felt the withdrawal. A guardsman at heart, Sephreh's grief had turned him from stoic to rigid. But in the end, he'd given more than we ever thought possible, and he'd tried to make his peace with us.

"I don't know if I can ever forget the years you ignored me after I was turned," I found myself saying. "Or the way you treated Camille . . . she was just a little girl and you turned her into the household servant. You were only kind to Delilah, but even then you ignored her."

Pausing again, I thought about what I wanted to say to him. His spirit would most likely be around, and I was certain he could hear me. "But . . . despite all that . . . despite the way you treated Trillian, in the end, you made the effort to return to us. You were kind to my wife. You apologized to Camille. You apologized to Trillian. And in the end of things . . . I believe that you meant what you said. I believe you were sorry."

Falling silent, I realized I was almost done. Short and sweet, that was my style. "So I'm letting it all go. I'm letting you off the hook. And I hope you're with Mother now, in the Land of the Silver Falls. I hope you're happy . . . because I don't want you to be lonely anymore. You loved Mother with a passion I don't know if I can ever feel . . . but I'm trying. I'm trying to open up, to let my wife in, to love her as much as you loved Mother. So . . . thanks . . . thank you for the lesson. If nothing else, you taught me that such a love can exist. You taught me to hope."

With that, I'd said all I had to say. I gently leaned down, kissed the silent forehead, and whispered. "Good-bye, Father. We'll never forget you."

As I entered the kitchen and washed my hands, Hanna looked at me. The room was empty and her eyes were suspiciously red.

"Your sisters, they have gone into the living room. Would you like a goblet of warm blood?" She folded the hand towel and placed it on the counter, which was spotless. Both Hanna and Iris were meticulous about cleanliness.

I shook my head. "Thanks, Hanna, but no. I'm not thirsty."

"You went to say good-bye, did you not?" Her English was improving. The Northlander was learning the ways and customs here, and she seemed content, though she'd taken one hell of a journey to get here.

I glanced at the kitchen door, lowering my voice. "Yes, but please don't tell Camille or Delilah. They couldn't handle it. They need to remember him alive, loving them. Not cold and ready to go in the ground. I've been there before, Hanna. I've been dead. And I went home to kill my family. Camille and Delilah saw me the night I died. They don't need to see Father dead. You know?"

She paused for a moment, then gave me a gentle smile. "I understand. I truly do. You would not have wanted to see Camille when she returned from Hyto's lair. I had to tend her, keep her alive so he could abuse her again. I washed the blood off her thighs, I washed the vomit out of her mouth."

I stared at her, feeling like she was punishing me for some reason. "What are you getting at, Hanna?"

She tilted her head to the side. "Nothing, except you . . . you underestimate Camille and Delilah. You act as though you are the only one who has seen trauma enough to handle the harshness of life. You do them a disservice. You insult them."

Normally, when someone talked to me like that, I got mad and wanted to beat the crap out of them. But Hanna's clear gaze challenged me. I worried my lip. Reality was? She was right. But I seldom found anybody willing to read me the riot act. Most everyone was too afraid. Nerissa could stare me down—and Camille, at times. But very few had doused me with ice water and walked away unscathed.

If I breathed, I would have taken in a long breath and let it out slowly. Instead, I counted to four . . . to five . . . to ten. Then, when she still didn't move, I blinked and looked down at my feet.

"You may be on to something with that. But what am I supposed to do? Let them go look at his body? Trust me, I didn't even pull the shroud away that much, just enough to see his face and it was bruised and battered and scarred."

She shrugged. "You do what you feel is right. But make sure you do it out of compassion, and not an assumption. I am a mother, remember this. And you girls, you are still young. Still growing. Still in need of guidance at times, whether or not you choose to believe it. Iris, she is busy with her own kinderkins now, she cannot keep track of you the way she did. But I . . . my own daughters are scattered from me. I hope they live. My son, he is dead and you know that I killed him to save him. Let me take a moment, now and then, to remind you of what you might be overlooking. Would you do this for me?"

She was so sincere, so brutally honest, that I could do nothing more than nod. Speechless, I forced a smile to my lips, and then headed toward my lair.

"I'm going to talk to Amber and Luke before the night is over." At the door, I turned around. "Hanna . . . thanks. Thanks for being a voice of conscience."

"Conscience?" Hanna shook her head. "No. I have no conscience. If I did, would my son be dead now?"

"I think he would. Because you saved him from a life of captivity and madness. You gave him his freedom. Some of us . . . we didn't get that choice and now we live with the consequences." And with that, I vanished through the bookcase that hid the steel door leading to my lair.

Luke and Amber were sitting on the bed, playing a game of cards. Luke had been my bartender before Derrick took over, before his sister Amber had shown up wearing one of the spirit seals. Now they were both Keraastar Knights, sworn to protect the seals they wore, magically bound to them with an invisible chain that only death could sever.

I hadn't seen Luke for months, and now, as I gazed into his eyes, I realized he had changed. His eyes were stark, a deep brown against the wheat-colored hair that hung loose. He'd always worn it in a ponytail when he worked for me, but now it was loose, mid-back, and brushed to a silky sheen. The scar that had marred his cheek was almost gone—as if something had rejuvenated him, and I was pulled to him in a way I'd never before felt. Amber, his sister, had gone from pretty and pregnant, to seductive and voluptuous. Her child, a little girl, was playing with a doll on the floor. Together, she and her brother radiated a power that felt magnified to the tenth degree. Around their necks, the spirit seals glowed against their hearts.

What Shadow Wing wouldn't give to get hold of them. A sudden fear gripped me, and I wished the dragons had already come. They were due to show up and escort the pair to safety the day after tomorrow, but as we'd seen in the past, so much could happen in so little time.

"Menolly . . ." Luke stood, a smile grazing his face. He looked tired and so did Amber. Tired, intense, and far older than the last time we'd spoken.

"Luke, it's so good to see you. Amber, you, too. I see you had your little one." I smiled down at the girl, who was barely toddling around at this point.

"Her name is Jolina. That was our mother's name." Amber smiled, baring her teeth. She and Luke were were-wolves. Amber had escaped from a patriarchal pack that had abused her. Luke had been thrown out years earlier for disobeying their rules.

"Hi, Jolina." I knelt down to look at the girl. She was tiny, as were all babies her size, but she gazed up at me, and the flash in her eyes told me that she was older than she seemed. "She seems . . . very . . . aware."

Amber shrugged. "I wore the spirit seal throughout my pregnancy. By then it was already changing my nature. We don't know how the magic will affect Jolina yet, but yes, she's precocious. That much we can tell."

Standing again, I moved to a chair near the bed and sat, crossing my legs. "The Wayfarer burned down Monday night. Chrysandra died in the fire."

At that, Luke seemed to startle out of his silence. "No! I'm so sorry. Smoke inhalation or burns?"

Neither, to be truthful, although the extent of her injuries would have killed her anyway. But Luke didn't need to know that I'd been the one to give her release from the pain, so I lied.

"She died from her burns. We buried her early this evening." After a moment, I added, "I was there. In Elqaneve, when the storm came through. I managed to get out without seeing much of the damage, but Delilah and Camille were caught in the thick of things."

Both of them stared at me, unspeaking, and I realized that there would be no catching up. No discussion of how the spirit seals had changed them, of what Asteria had been planning for them and the Keraastar Knights. We needed to know, but it wouldn't be Amber and Luke telling me. They were so far removed from the lives they had led here that they might as well be speaking a different language.

I was going to have to say good-bye, to let go of the people they'd been. I was going to have to move Luke and Amber into my past, and accept that they were now fully Keraastar Knights—along with whatever that entailed.

Standing, I motioned for them to follow me. "It's getting near dawn and we've all been up far too long. I need my lair but you will be safe upstairs. Vanzir will watch over you. And the guards are thick on our land."

Amber lifted up Jolina and started up the stairs, but Luke paused to turn back to me.

"I never thanked you for all your friendship and kindness, Menolly. I can see it in your eyes—you think I've changed. Well, that's true, but I have never forgotten what my time at the Wayfarer was like. You had an effect on my life." With a slight laugh, he touched the spirit seal. "Rather obvious, yes. But seriously—I'm a better werewolf for having met you. I'll never forget you." And with that, he headed up the stairs.

I decided to let them go without me. I wasn't part of their lives anymore. A few moments later, Nerissa came downstairs. She took one look at my face and opened her arms. I had thought I wanted sex, but when she wrapped me tight, I laid my head against her bountiful chest and began to cry. As my tears stained her sweater, she moved me over to the bed, and we curled up together, and I wept for the losses in my life. Only I wasn't even sure what some of those losses were.

Chapter 4

〰️

Come dawn, I slept without dreaming—a blessing considering who I was and the baggage I carried. By the time I woke up, at sunset, Nerissa had long been up and was almost done with her day. Our opposite sleep schedules interfered with our lives at times, but we made it work. We had from sundown till late night together, and on weekends, she'd stay up late with me—till two or three in the morning. Weres didn't need as much sleep as FBHs, so she was good with a few hours.

Last night, after I'd cried myself out, we'd watched an old movie—*Mildred Pierce*—and then she'd snuggled down to sleep while I spent the rest of the night reading. The house was quiet during the late-night hours, and I relished my time to myself. I was in the middle of a biography of Rasputin, and the reading was slow and dense, but interesting.

Come sunrise, I'd curled up next to my wife and fallen asleep. We were safe enough in the same bed as long as she was awake and out of reach by the first moments I woke at night.

As I took a quick shower, then slipped into jeans and a turtleneck, I heard the phone ring upstairs. Even through the steel door, my hearing was so sensitive that I could hear the doorbell, the phone, loud conversations. There was a flurry of words that I couldn't quite make out. The steel door we'd installed muffled sound better than the old wooden one. But by that time, I was at the top of the stairs and could hear Camille. She sounded surprised. I sauntered out into the kitchen to find her staring at the phone in her hand, her head cocked to the side.

"You look puzzled."

"Yeah, well, that was cousin Daniel." She turned around, the quizzical look still present. "He wants to get together for dinner. He basically invited himself over tomorrow night."

That was a shocker. First, the very fact that our blood cousins actually wanted to hang out surprised me. Second, I'd expected to hear from Hester Lou first. She had dropped us an e-mail after she left the restaurant the other night to reassure us that she was thrilled we'd met and that she wanted to pursue a familial relationship. That fact that she had a wife, too, had created an instant bond between us. But Daniel? He'd seemed standoffish and taciturn, and not at all the sort who would suddenly go all touchy-feely over us.

"Well, then. I suppose we should all be here." I raised one eyebrow.

"I know—odd, isn't it?" Camille moved to the counter, where she poured herself a cup of risha-berry tea. "I guess we'll just have to wait to see what he wants, but I have the feeling that he's got something up his sleeve. I know the man is hiding something, though I don't get any negative feelings off of him."

"That's good, at least."

"I have something to tell you—" Camille started to say, but the phone rang again, interrupting her.

I was closest to it so I picked up. "Hello?"

"Menolly? Chase here." He sounded harried.

I glanced at the clock. Five P.M. "I take it you're still at work?"

"Yeah, love working Saturdays, you know. Anyway, we have problems."

The words we so did not enjoy hearing. "What's up and what do you need us to do?" I said it half-jokingly, but he didn't banter back.

Instead, his voice was low and solemn. "I'm serious. We have a situation here and we need you girls. Seriously, come *now* and bring all the reinforcements you can. We . . . *this is bad.*"

Fuck. More words that I didn't want to hear. "Our backup is depleted. I think Smoky, Roz, and Trillian went back to Otherworld—" Here, I glanced at Camille, who nodded. "We'll be there as soon as we can. What's shaking, and where do we meet you?"

"The Utopia Club. It's burning, and we have people trapped inside."

"Motherfucking son of a bitch! Shikra—did Shikra make it out?" The realization that she might be so much dust right now hit home and I flashed back to Chrysandra, lying blackened on the hospital bed. With vampires, though, there would be no slow death. Fire was one of the few things that could actually destroy us, and we burned bright and crisp and clear, wisping into a handful of ashes in seconds.

"She's safe, yes. But the club was torched. That much we are fairly sure of, and the firemen seem to be making headway with the flames. But there's something else going on in that fire. Shikra told Yugi that there was some spiritual activity going on there this evening—it started in the afternoon while she was still asleep. But her Supe bouncers and a couple of cleaning ladies had several nasty experiences. I'm wondering . . . is there such a thing as an arsonist ghost?"

He ran out of steam, his words stopping like a train that had suddenly put on the brakes. Chase didn't usually talk that fast, and I realized he was nervous.

"We'll be there ASAP. You want me to call Iris and tell her you're probably going to be late tonight?"

The sound of relief swept through his voice. "Thanks. Tell her to give Astrid a kiss for me, would you?" He sounded lonely, and I realized just how devoted a father he was going to be.

"Will do. Now hang up, and we'll be there as soon as we can." As I replaced the receiver, I whirled around. "The Utopia is burning. And signs of ghostly activity have been seen there this afternoon. That doesn't mean there's a connection, but we can't know that till we're actually there. Who do we have on hand?"

Camille had paled, her skin a stark white next to the black of her corset. "Delilah and Shade are upstairs—she took your Jag to Jason's. He checked it out and said that for now, it will run okay. He's swamped so bring it in next week. It's out in the yard, but why don't you ride with us? Vanzir is out in the studio with Father's body, and Shamas is still at work. Morio's in town and Nerissa isn't home yet."

"We're down, bad. We can't leave the house unguarded. Vanzir has to stay here. Even with Hanna to watch after Maggie, we can't chance Iris being alone at her house. Bruce is still at work, too." I didn't like this. For a while it felt as if we had too many people in the house, and now we didn't have enough.

"I have an idea. I don't like it but I'm willing to deal with him." Camille sneered slightly and I knew immediately who she was talking about.

"You'll be willing to work with Bran?"

"I don't think I have a choice, do I?" She headed toward the kitchen door. "You get Delilah and Shade, and tell Vanzir to watch the house with Hanna. I'll go get . . . Bran." And she was out the door, not even stopping to grab a jacket.

I dashed up the stairs. Camille detested Bran. He was the son of the Black Unicorn and Raven Mother, and my sister had taken an instant dislike to the man. Neither Elemental Lord—greater or lesser—nor truly Fae, Bran stood between worlds, much like the Elder Fae. It didn't help that Camille had killed his father, even though it had been her destiny and the Black Unicorn's choosing. Even after the

Black Unicorn was reborn, it seemed that Bran nurtured a grudge. Or maybe it was something else.

I'd caught him staring at Camille more than once over the past few days, and the look on his face unsettled me. If Smoky had been here to notice the look, he would have backhanded the man into the Ionyc Seas. It wasn't desire— not fully—but a desire to possess and tear down. And I was pretty sure Camille knew about it, though she kept her mouth shut.

She walked on slippery ground with Bran. He was leader of the Earthside Fae militia now, and he was the son of Immortals. You didn't mess with beings of that magnitude, not if you wanted to live.

Shade and Delilah were in Kitten's playroom, where her kitty condo and bed and toys were. A sofa stretched under a window so she could curl up on the back when we had the rare sunbeams creeping through the windows. Now, she was racing around like a maniac, all four paws skidding across the polished floor. Shade was curled up in a recliner, reading, trying to ignore Delilah's taunting him. I stood at the door for a moment, watching as she raced by and leaped in the air, grabbing the toe of his boot, swinging on it before dropping back to the floor and taking off in the opposite direction.

Wishing I could let them be and not intrude, I cleared my throat.

Shade looked up, and at my expression, he barked out a stiff, "Delilah. We need you."

She swiveled to look at me, and for a moment, a fleeting look of resignation passed through her eyes, but then, she padded over to the sofa, and a moment later, a shimmer in the air proceeded her transformation. Within another minute, she was standing in front of me, dressed in her pajamas.

"I'm afraid you need to get dressed, stat. Chase called. There's an emergency." I turned to go, then paused. "Don't wear anything too flammable. The Utopia's on fire, and while they're putting out the flames now, I have a feeling we're going to be sifting through the ruins looking for ghosts."

"Ghosts?" Her face fell. "What the fuck are ghosts doing in a vampire club?"

"I don't know. That's what we're going to find out. But there were reports of heavy magical activity there this afternoon. So get a move on, Kitten, and meet us downstairs." I turned to leave, but Shade moved to my side, laying a gentle hand on my shoulder. He was so quick that I didn't even see the blur. Dragons—especially shadow dragons—were good at that.

"Are you girls able to focus tonight, given what has happened?" He gazed down at me, his rugged jaw set firmly in a faint smile. A craggy scar marred one side of his face, but it only gave him a tougher, darker look, a dark line against the glowing coffee of his skin.

I held his gaze. "Why ask me? Why not ask Delilah? I'm the one who . . ." But I couldn't finish it. I couldn't finish the sentence. My throat seized up and the words would not come.

"Because Delilah and Camille, they grieve openly. You hide your sorrow, you hide your pain like the wounded animal you once were. I know you open up around Nerissa, but your sisters need to know that Sephreh's death was more than a blip in the road to you. If you don't show them this side of yourself, Menolly, you'll drive them away. Perhaps not now, perhaps not tomorrow, but in the near future, when the shock has worn away, they'll look at you and only see the tough exterior that hides the loss you feel."

My first reaction was that I wanted to hit him, to smack him back. The words *How dare you say this to me?* formed on my lips, but I left them unsaid. Because truth was, if I said anything at all, the sorrow I'd cried out last night would return. And right now, I couldn't afford to feel the pain.

"Yeah, well . . . right now I'm afraid I don't have that luxury. But Shade . . ." I paused, not sure of how much to say.

"Feel free. Tell me off, tell me what you think of my advice. I can take it." His eyes flashed and only a deep warmth, a dark compassion, rested there.

I worried my lip for a moment. "I know you mean well.

But right now, there's no time for this. I won't ignore what you said, though. That's the best I can promise for now."

With a nod, he moved back. Delilah entered the room then, pulling her sweater over her head. She glanced at him, then at me, then at Shade again.

"Something going on I should know about? A spat?" The look in her eyes was darker than I'd seen before, not jealous but . . . cautious.

Wondering where that was coming from, I shook my head. "Not at all. Shade was just expressing concern over my bar. And I thanked him but reassured him, I have things under control." I held his gaze a moment longer, challenging him to contradict me. But he just turned away to grab his brown leather calf-length duster, and then followed me out the door, Delilah on his heels.

Downstairs, Camille was waiting, Bran by her side. Neither looked happy about it, but they were there, Bran with his usual smirk that made me want to rub his face into the ground.

"We're ready?" was all she said.

I nodded. "Let's head out. You talked to Vanzir?"

"He's keeping watch here with Hanna. And I called Morio. He'll meet us at the Utopia Club." She swept out the door. "Bran, you can ride with Delilah and Shade—"

"I prefer to ride with you." His voice was soft, but firm, and I could tell there was no room for disagreement.

Camille rankled, but said nothing, merely headed toward her car. I followed, deciding to give my Jag a rest, and to hopefully prevent bloodshed.

"I'm going with you. I don't want to chance the Jag." I pushed past Bran. "I call shotgun."

Camille gave me a grateful look. Bran let out an exasperated laugh, but there was no humor behind it. He shrugged and climbed into the back of the Lexus. As I slid into the passenger seat, I glanced over my shoulder at him and gave him a wicked, fang-filled grin. Let him chew on that one for a while.

We took off, followed by Delilah and Shade in her Jeep.

I wanted to talk to Camille, strategize a bit, but Bran's presence put an unnatural strain on both of us and I found myself picking up her suspicion of the guy. He was gorgeous—pale as alabaster with long dark hair that he kept pulled back in a ponytail, and his eyes were shimmering pools that beckoned with a welcome that promised both passion and fear. He was built, but not rippling in the muscle department.

But the qualities that struck me the most were (a) his brilliant lips—he looked almost as though he were wearing lipstick, but it was a product of his breeding, and (b) the man oozed magnetism. Whether it was good or not, I wouldn't lay odds, but magnetism it was, stronger by far than any Fae glamour I'd ever been around.

As I watched him through the rearview mirror, I began to notice his fixation on Camille. He watched her intently, like a bird watching a shiny object. But it wasn't a leer. He didn't feel particularly lecherous, though I did sense a deep and vibrant passion below the surface that was probably better left untapped, given the circumstances. No, this was more . . . need. As if he was trying to quench his thirst by looking at her.

We were used to men going nuts over her boobs and curves—that was par for the course and it didn't bother her, nor did it bother Delilah or me. But this was something different and it gave me the creeps. I wondered if she'd noticed it, or if it had escaped her attention. But ten to one, this was what unsettled her around him and caused the sparks.

I decided to do a little prying. "So, Bran, are you engaged? Do you have a girl back home in Darkynwyrd?"

The look Camille shot me was priceless and I tried not to laugh. She gripped the steering wheel and I had the feeling I'd be in for it once we were alone, but for now, I wanted to see what kind of reaction I'd get.

Apparently, Bran didn't find the question engaging. He gave me a cool look. "No."

The clip of his words made me snarly. I was already a little wired from my discussion with Shade, but at least he meant well and wanted the best for us. Bran here was another matter. I was beginning to adopt Camille's dislike of the man.

"How about a guy?" *Let's just see the fur fly on that one*, I thought.

Bran leaned forward as far as the seat belt would allow. "I'm not into vampires, thank you for asking." I sputtered as he gave me a blasé look. "I assume you are interested, unless you have some other reason for being so nosy." Once again, the arrogant sneer punctuated his words.

I restrained myself from bolting over the seat.

Camille wasn't quite so diplomatic. "You're an asshole, you know that?" She flashed him a snide smile through the rearview mirror, but kept her eyes on the road. "But since we're stuck with each other for now, I suggest you keep your mouth shut and we'll keep out of your business. Menolly— no more questions."

Bran snorted. "You girls take the cake. My mother was right—barbaric and mannerless. Humans are pathetic, and you windwalkers are just as bad. What she wants with you escapes me. Why she would offer you a place in our wood— again, I have no clue."

I winced. The term *windwalker* was derogatory, all right, and meant half-breed back in Y'Elestrial. It certainly had never been used as a compliment. I forced a comment back down my throat and, shaking with anger, turned back around in my seat.

Camille kept her hands on the wheel, but her voice was so soft I almost didn't hear her at first. "You are staying in our house, eating our food. You're a guest of the Queen of Shadow and Night. I suggest you fucking keep to your manners because, dude, one more step over the line and I'll call Smoky home and ask him to beat your butt right back to Mama's doorstep."

I was still watching him through the rearview mirror, and so I saw the quiver of fear that ran over his face. So the little ass *was* afraid of something—big bad dragons made him nervous.

We spent the rest of the ride in silence, and it wasn't long until we pulled into the parking lot of the Utopia. The building was still on fire but most of the flames were quenched. Smoldering holes in the walls let the smoke billow out, and the scene through the windows was one of chaos and destruction. But it didn't look anywhere near as damaged as the Wayfarer had been. Somebody had caught the fire in time to prevent it from totaling the place.

Camille slammed out of the car, ignoring Bran, who slowly emerged behind her. I followed her, and as we strode across the parking lot, Shade and Delilah pulled up, hopping out and running over to join us.

Delilah glanced at me and mouthed, "Everybody still alive after that ride?"

I nodded. "Barely."

We found Chase near the entrance. He was talking to the fire marshal, a man we'd seen all too often as of late. As we approached, they finished up their talk. The marshal turned and, nodding to us, returned to his unit and began going over some sort of strategy with his men.

I glanced at the building. "So . . . what's the whole story?"

"I'm thinking ghosts. At least, that's what the maid told Shikra. Whatever happened, apparently things were moving around by themselves and a whirling misty form was seen. But it's hard to know for certain until we investigate. Who knows what we're dealing with?" He rubbed his chin. "This is arson, Menolly. And considering what happened to your bar . . . I'm thinking we have a serial arsonist on the loose."

I pressed my lips together. I *knew* we had a serial arsonist running loose, but I didn't know how much Shikra had actually told him. And I didn't want to spill any secrets she might have kept secret, like the letter. But I had the feeling I was going to have to, if only to keep other businesses on high alert.

Chase stared at me for a moment. "You know something."

"What could I possibly know?" I gave him a fangy grin.

"Yeah, right. Tell me another one. Okay, we'll play it your way."

"Just for now, Chase. We'll talk soon."

"So if you and your sisters could suss out the building when they've—" He stopped as the fire marshal approached.

He gave me a confused look, but then turned to Chase. "It's out, for all intents and purposes. They're just taking care of some of the embers. We got here in time to prevent any major structural damage, I think. Most of it's cosmetic. Will cost a bit to repair, but it's not like . . ." Pausing, he glanced at me.

I decided to save him the trouble. No use pussyfooting around, and it wasn't like I didn't know all too well what had gone down at my own bar. "The Utopia isn't fully destroyed, like my bar was."

"Right, ma'am. As to what caused the flames, well, we discovered something in one of the back rooms. Cloths still soaked in accelerant. The flames hadn't reached them yet. If they had, this whole building would have gone up like a bomb. Pretty clear this was arson. I'm now thinking that's what happened to the Wayfarer, only we didn't find the cloths because they burned up. I'll send someone over to your building, see if we can find traces of whatever this substance is."

Ten to one, they wouldn't. Because if Lowestar was behind this, he was smart enough to cover his butt. There was no way they were going to find the firebug who set this mess. Or mine either.

But all I said was, "Call in a tech from the FH-CSI, Chase. That may not be of Earthside design." I turned to the fire marshal. "So is it safe for us to go in and have a look around? I know it's still hot, but no roof going to collapse, or anything like that?"

He sighed. "Johnson, you think we need their input now?"

"Yeah, I think so." Chase gave him a dark look. "I don't think we're dealing with a simple arsonist. First, I'm convinced he's serial. Second . . . trust my judgment on this."

As the fire marshal shrugged and turned away, he said

over his shoulder, "Fine. Go in at your own risk. Try to avoid the hot spots that are still smoking. Don't make my men come rescue you." Sounding tired, he walked away.

"He's in a good mood." I stared at his retreating back.

"He's seen too many fires where somebody didn't make it out alive, Menolly. He's seen children burned to a crisp because their mothers were smoking in bed and fell asleep. He's seen his men devoured by the flames when they went in to rescue someone who had sparked the fire by a home-based Z-fen lab. He's seen houses go up like matchsticks thanks to the hoarders who refused to get help . . . too many deaths, too much destruction. Don't blame him for being weary. He's seen too much over the years. And I've been there, seen it all with him."

I glanced up at the detective. His jaw was set, and his dark eyes were glimmering. A year ago, he'd been given the Nectar of Life in order to save his ass, and it had—but it had given him a thousand years to look forward to, and to fill. And it had sparked off the latent powers that we'd faintly sensed before. Turned out, he had elf in his background—far distant elf.

A thought struck me. "Are you worried about Tristan? The elf who started your bloodline?" Tristan lived in Elqa-neve. No one had thought how this might affect Chase.

He caught my gaze, and for a moment, those wary shields dropped and I could see the naked concern on his face. "Yes, of course. I have hoped, ever since that visit, to find a time when we could sit and truly talk. He knows my heritage, my lineage, and perhaps can explain some of the things that have happened to me since I was first given the Nectar of Life."

"I sense a *but* . . ."

"But . . . my concern, my heart . . . is somewhere within that makeshift hiding place they're calling a palace, with the mother of my child. The woman I love."

I face-palmed. Of course, he was worried about Sharah. "I'm so stupid. Forgive me."

He shook his head. "Nothing to forgive. Too much going

on. But, I don't know what I'll do if something happens to Sharah. And yet—and yet—she's now the Queen. They separated us, and I don't know if she'll ever be able to see Astrid or me again. They took her from me, Menolly. They stole her away, and while I understand why I had to let her go, that doesn't make it hurt any less."

There was nothing I could say. So instead, I reached up on my tiptoes and did something I almost never did. I kissed him on the cheek, and stroked his hair.

"You keep hope, Chase. You keep that hope alive. My sisters—they kept the hope that I'd come out of my rage and fury the entire year I was being rehabilitated after Dredge got to me. They never gave up hope. I know this in my heart. You keep up hope for Sharah."

He blushed. "But . . . even if the war ends. She's Queen now. I can't move to Otherworld, can I? You told me once, I'd pale and fade there. And now that she's Queen, she can't very well abdicate the throne."

"Shush. Worry about that when it comes. For now, just know she loves you and misses you. And focus on giving Astrid all the love and joy she needs from both her mother and father. Okay?"

I wasn't going to take the lame route, I wasn't going to mouth platitudes like *everything will be fine* and *it will all work out* . . . but I could give him something to hold on to. And that something was his daughter. "Astrid needs you to be strong. She needs you to love her and give her hope that she'll be with her mother again. Right?"

Chase regarded me solemnly. "You're right. I have to focus on what I can do right now. Otherwise this will break me. It will interfere with me being the father Astrid needs, and it will interfere with my job."

"Good then. Keep that thought. You know Iris will do all she can to help you—and we all will. Now, let me go get Camille and Delilah and we'll see what we can find in the Utopia." As I turned away, Chase lightly put his hand on my arm.

"Menolly?"

"Yes?"

"Be careful. Just . . . don't get hurt in there. If there are ghosts . . ."

"If there are ghosts, we'll go in there and kick their fucking asses to hell and back." I winked at him, then strode over to where Camille and Delilah were watching the bustle as the firemen began to stow their gear.

Shade was standing nearby, keeping an eye on the general scene, and Bran was leaning against a lamppost, keeping an eye on Camille. *Wonderful.* He was going all stalker boy. When Smoky got back, we'd have to have the dragon take the Fae boy out back for a good ass-whipping.

"You guys ready? We're going in." I filled them in on what Chase and the fire marshal had told us. "Be careful. Camille, how are your shoes?" I glanced down at her feet. My sister had a predilection for stilettos and she'd often worn them fighting, but after a few days ago, in the race to escape from the fall of Elqaneve, she'd sworn off them for when we knew we were headed into a dangerous situation. Tonight, she'd put on her kitten-heel granny boots, and I saw that she was also dressed in her catsuit.

She noticed my appraisal. "Less chance of catching on fire without filmy skirts hanging near the floor." With a grin, she curtseyed, the jingling of her silver belt a light tinkle against the incessant rain that was pouring down around us.

I snorted. "Let's rock then."

"Before you go in, put these on." Yugi instructed several of the men to hand us hardhats equipped with built-in lights. They would not only protect our heads, but help us see. Roz had bought some of the same type of lights for us sometime back, but they were somewhere at home.

"Thanks, we left our gear at home."

"Just don't take any chances," the Swedish empath said. He'd been working with Chase since the inception of the FH-CSI, and as second in command, he took his job seriously. Yugi had helped us out more than once.

As we headed into the building, I automatically scanned the ceiling, looking for loose timbers, tiles, anything that might dent somebody's head. The hats would help put a stop to that, but we couldn't be too careful.

I went first, given that I was the least likely to be hurt. Shade followed after me, then Camille, Delilah, and lastly, Bran.

As I stepped through the broken-in door, the acrid stench of smoke and soot hung heavy in the air, and behind me, Camille and Delilah started coughing. The roof was still standing, yes, and the walls, but the inside of the club had been gutted to the point of being unrecognizable. The beautiful, vibrant décor was now clogged with soot and smoke and water, forming muddy streams along the floor, streaking the walls, and saturating what little furniture remaining that hadn't been destroyed. Most of the upholstered furnishings were gone, and the tables were charred and crisped. The booths were a disaster, and the bar had exploded as the liquor—there for sale to the FBHs and Supes who came along with the vamps—had gone up, one miniature fireball after another.

I stopped, flashing back to the Wayfarer. While I was grateful that the Utopia hadn't suffered quite the same fate— especially with the loss of life—a little part of me wondered why it had to be *my* bar that had burned to the ground.

Camille let out a soft murmur. "It's . . . there's something in here with us. I can feel it and I'm not even trying."

"She's right," Bran said, startling me. His voice was smooth, yet guttural, and it echoed through the shell of a room.

"What do you sense?" I hoped we could be forearmed. I was tired of being taken by surprise. But before they could say a word, a movement caught my eye and I turned. Out from the walls, and I do mean out from the walls—stepping directly through the solid drywall as if it were mere illusion—came five figures. They were bipedal, female by the look of their breasts, and they were composed of living flame. Burning brightly, with tongues of flames crackling off them, they looked like some CGI animated creatures, orange and yellow and all shades comprising fire.

As we stood there, staring at them, they moved toward us. Then one raised her hand, and a ball of fire lit up the air as she sent the orb heading in our direction.

"Holy fuck!" Camille yelled as she dove to the right. Delilah dropped to the floor. I wasn't sure what Bran and Shade were up to because, before I realized what I was doing, I raced forward toward the woman, and the next thing I knew, I had knocked her to the ground, trying to get hold of her.

Her skin burned my fingers, and I realized she truly was living flame. And that was when it dawned on me that I was in serious trouble. I tried to scramble away, but she caught hold of my wrist, and as my skin began to ignite, I realized I was about to die the final death.

Chapter 5

"Menolly!" Delilah's scream cut through the night.

Before she could say anything else, Shade shot past her, and the next thing I knew, I was in some dark, veiled space. Shade held me tight against him. I couldn't speak, I couldn't think—it had all happened so fast. And then I realized we weren't in the room with the fire creatures. And the flames on my arm were gone. Before I could wrap my head around this little fact, everything shifted again and we were back with the others, but in a different spot from where I'd been when he first grabbed me.

There wasn't time to figure out what had happened. Instead, I leapt up, looking around to assess the situation.

Delilah had backed away, and Camille was shooting some sort of spell at the fire beings, who were still lobbing fireballs. Bran had moved around to the side, but even he looked confused, his sword at the ready. He was smart enough to know, as was Delilah, that physically engaging these creatures wasn't going to do much good beyond getting a nasty third-degree burn.

Camille shouted in frustration. "We need Smoky! Or . . .
Iris." Her energy bolts were disrupting their progress but
not stopping them. In fact, I had the nasty suspicion that the
only reason they paused as she tossed bolt after bolt toward
them, was to quite possibly absorb the energy into their own
power.

"We can't ask Iris—" Delilah started to say but then
stopped.

"We have no choice. We have to have someone with her
power because whatever these creatures are, we don't seem
to have the wherewithal to fight them."

"Water! The fire hoses!" I didn't know if it would work
or not, but I raced back outside and frantically motioned to
Chase. "We need fire hoses, at full force. *Now!*"

Chase barked out an order, and three of the firemen who
were still stowing their gear pulled the hoses out again and,
within sixty seconds flat, had coupled them back up and
were following me.

By now, Camille and the others were backing away. The
figures were still coming. In their wake, their bodies had
started up the fires again as they passed through the still
smoldering ruins. I shouted for everyone to get out of the
way and we backed to the sides as the fireman pushed
through into the building again.

As the fire creatures came through, two abreast, then
two more, then one in the rear, I motioned to the firemen
and they let loose with the hoses. The water struck them full
force, and at first, they wavered. I thought they were going
to be swept off their feet, but somehow, the fiery women
managed to keep upright. Slowly, they began to make headway against the onslaught of pressure.

Fuck. I'd hoped maybe we could put out their flames. I
turned to Camille and Delilah, who were watching the pro-
gression of our opponents.

"What the hell now?" Delilah shook her head. "Can you
call Smoky?"

"I can send out a sense of distress but it would take too
long. No, we need Iris, and we need her now. She's the only

one who can work ice magic besides Smoky. And I think ice magic is the only thing that will counter flame." Camille grimaced, but the look she gave me told me she, too, knew it was our only option.

"Can she do this? So soon after having her babies?" Delilah sounded like she was choking on a hairball.

"She'll have to. Because if those things get loose in the street, do you have any clue of what damage they could do?" I turned to Shade. "You can't bring her via the Ionyc Seas, can you? Not with her nursing and being alive?"

Shade could easily carry the dead—including the undead like me—through the Ionyc Seas. They were vast currents of energy, oceans that connected all planes. But because he was from the Netherworld, he wasn't easily able to safely ferry the living. They usually ended up sick.

"No, I can't. And neither can Vanzir. But I'll have him get her here ASAP." And with that, the half–shadow dragon vanished.

Meanwhile, we had to somehow corral these creatures until she could get here. They'd be out of the building in minutes. I turned to the others, feeling unusually helpless. At that point, Bran sauntered forward.

"I know what they are," he said, leaning against the nearest car. "I also know that without a sorcerer or witch who can work ice magic, you're sunk."

I wanted to smack him and ask him why he hadn't spoken up earlier, but then again, we'd all been beating a retreat. "What are they?"

"Fyrun Fae. The Fiery Ones. They usually stick to warmer climes, near volcanoes mostly, but they also can enter through bonfires, house fires, or . . ." He motioned to the Utopia. "Through fires like that one. And ten to one, they were summoned via rune work planted on the walls before the arsonist torched the building. Probably an added little bonus in terms of causing confusion. Fire bugs tend to be more than a little anarchistic."

It was one of the longest speeches I'd heard out of him, and even with that smirk on his face, the concern was evident in his eyes. He knew we were dealing with someone dangerous, and perhaps over the edge toward the loony bin.

"Daemons. Can daemons summon Fyrun Fae?"

He nodded. "Some can."

"Ten to one they were in the Wayfarer, too." I wondered just how we could find out if I was right, but then pushed the thought aside. Right now we needed to take care of our present unwelcome guests before I went hunting through the ruins of my bar.

Shade reappeared then. "Iris is on her way. Bruce's driver is bringing her. I didn't want to leave the house unguarded, so Vanzir is still there."

"Fall back! Fall back!" The firemen stumbled back out of the building, running to the sides.

They were still carrying the hoses, but in another moment, a rumble echoed into a freight train as there was an explosion by the entrance of the building. Flaming shrapnel—wood and debris—went flying as everyone dove for the nearest cover.

Where the doors had been, there now existed a large hole. Stepping through the soot-filled and burning maw of the club, came the Fyrun Fae. They paused as soon as they exited the Utopia, looking around the parking lot as if they were pinpointing their next target. It felt a lot like watching a pack of hyenas scanning the horizon for food-on-the-hoof.

Delilah scrambled over to my side, and Camille followed her. "What are they looking for? Do they eat people?"

"Probably after they roast us," Camille grumbled.

Bran slowly stood from where he'd crouched behind a car and sauntered over to stand between us. He slipped his hands in his pockets and stared at the Fae.

"Eat people? No. No, they do not. Kill people? Yes. But what they're looking for now is more food."

"If they don't eat people, what do they eat? Steak?" Delilah's gaze was fastened on the Fyrun Fae as if she could stop them via wishful thinking.

"Think about it." Bran sounded a little exasperated. "If you were made of fire, what would you eat?"

"Oh crap. Wood. Trees. Grass . . . anything that burns."
I pushed past them and ran over to Chase. "We have to move anything combustible out of their way. Including all the cars. *Gasoline? Fyrun Fae?* Bad combination!"

Chase motioned for the other firemen to join us and we formed a semicircle around the Fyrun Fae. As we slowly backed away, we began to toss aside any debris that might be flammable. Three of the cops started to break into all the cars in the nearby area, hotwiring them and driving them to the other end of the parking lot. As we cleared the path in front of them, the fiery women spread out, their heads swiveling slowly as they searched for fuel.

I shouted at Bran. "Hey, *Unicorn Boy*, how long can they last without refilling their flames once they're out of the portal and in our world?"

He didn't even look my way. "Long enough to cause havoc. And when they finally get tired of our game here, you can bet they're going to be speeding up and then we'll see how long it takes them to break through our lines, considering they can firebomb us and crisp us to toast. How do you like that for an answer, *Bloody Mary*?"

The women glowed, like sunlight captured within the framework of a body. While we could see vague impressions of their faces, mostly they were encapsulated flame, living pillars of fire. They were so alien I knew we could never reason with them, and yet they were not Elementals. They were a Fae so far from our own natures that I couldn't see how we could ever even hope to communicate.

I darted to the side, grabbing a pile of loose boards that had once been a signboard. I tossed them as far away as I could. We'd do it again, once we reached where they landed.

Camille was scrambling to rip out a bush that was in a narrow island of grass. There was nothing we could do about the lawn itself—or was there?

Shade motioned for Camille to move aside. He knelt down, examining the grass. With a single glance at Delilah and me, he lightly placed his hand on the blades and closed his eyes. A flare of lightning moved over him, then down his arm—the purple crackle of his magic working deep and dark as it spread through the ground. A moment later, the grass began to wilt and vanish in a whiff of dust. Within another moment, only barren dirt remained, and the bush had also vanished, so much ash in the wind.

As we stared—we'd never seen that particular aspect of his magic before—a car screeched into the parking lot behind us. It was the limo, and the driver ran around to yank open the door and help Iris out. She looked tired, and harried, dressed in a warm winter gown the color of deep twilight, with silver stars embroidered on it. Her hair was braided up on her head, and she carried her silver wand with the Aqualine crystal on it. The tattoos on her face were glowing under the night sky, and their filigree gave her a haunted, ancient look even against her smooth, plump skin. We hurried over to her, ready to explain, but she pushed past us before we could say a word, staring at the Fyrun Fae.

"I haven't seen one of these in such a very long time. They are related to Loki, you know. And to the fire giants. They come from the land of flame, and they feed on everything that will burn." Her voice was soft. "They are volatile, like all fire-bound creatures. No sudden movements, please. I am bound to the ice, snow, and mist. They will sense me soon enough and it will be war."

"Are you sure you want to do this? We can find another way . . ." Delilah knelt down by Iris's side. "Little Mama, we're not going to let you hurt yourself."

Iris straightened her shoulders. "Kitten, step aside. Tonight, I am not Iris the mother, or Iris the house sprite. Tonight, I wear the cloak of Iris, Priestess of Undutar. These creatures, you see, they are my sworn enemies. While the balance is necessary, fire and ice will forever be bound and forever be fighting."

"What do you need us to do?" I motioned for Delilah to obey. Reluctantly, my sister moved away.

Iris assessed the situation. "I can take them, but not all at once. You must distract at least three of them. Two at a time, my magic can handle." She paused, looking thoughtful. "Whatever happens, I must not touch them directly. It would be . . . very bad."

"We won't let you get burnt," Camille said.

"No, that's not the issue." She shook her head slowly. "The problem is this: They come from the realm of fire. I am bound to the realm of ice. When both elements are brought together on a mundane level here—such as plunging a sword from the forge into the snow—we work together. But the Fyrun Fae and I are all deeply connected to our primary elements and realms. They, through their very nature. Me, through my goddess. If we touch . . . well, let's say this whole city block might be leveled."

Crap. That wasn't what we needed to hear. "Um, should we evacuate?"

She shook her head. "No, there is no time. They are hunting now, and if they do not feed soon, they'll grow restless. The last thing you want are rogue Fyrun Fae running around. Bran—you know enough to be able to help me." She turned to the son of the Black Unicorn and Raven Mother. "I require your help."

To our surprise, he snapped to attention, saluting her. "Priestess, I am yours to command."

"I want you to take Camille—don't argue, either one of you—and . . ." Iris stopped as Morio came running up.

"I'm so sorry I couldn't get here before now. What's . . ." His voice drifted off as he took in the situation. "Fucking hell. What do you need?"

Iris cocked her head. "Even better. Morio, I need you to strengthen Camille's Moon Magic. Camille, I need you to call down the storm in a way you've never called it before. We need a gusher. It won't snuff out their fire, but it *will* make it harder for them to navigate. Morio, feed her as much energy as you can. Bran? You and Menolly go tempt two of the Fae with wood or whatever you can scrounge up. Use it like a carrot to keep them occupied. Delilah, you and Shade do the same to two of the others. I'll take care of the one in the middle first. Go. Now."

And with that, she ordered us into position. Bran and I

gathered up armfuls of wood, as did Delilah and Shade, and we spread out, each targeting two of the Fae. If Iris could work on one at a time, it would be safer.

Camille knelt down on the pavement in front of Morio, facing the sky, arms out and head thrown back. He placed his arms on her shoulders and the thick thread of magic that bound them began to weave its way through the night. Like a snake, sinuous and ancient, it coiled around them, the serpent of power, the raw force of the night and of the Moon Mother. Camille needed to make this work, to not have it backfire, because with the Fyrun Fae running around, gods knew what a backlash spell might do.

She began whispering some chant as the energy rode down through Morio, jumping her shoulders, infusing her with the essence and life of the Moon Mother. They worked their powers together, blending them like fine scotch.

As the winds picked up, the sky began to boil and clouds danced in a frenzied swirl. With a crack, lightning split through the night, thunder echoing in its wake. A hail of bullets hit us—rain pounding so hard, so thick and fast, that the wind drove it sideways like stinging pellets. Harsh and wild, it slashed against us, blades of water, and the clouds blotted out any sign of stars or moon that might be peeking through. The only light we had was from the dim streetlamps.

The Fyrun Fae looked confused. They paused, staring up into the sky as if to ascertain from where their attacker was coming. Bran and I moved into position, taunting two of them with long pieces of wood. One raised her finger, pointing at us, and it looked almost as though she was sniffing the air. The other followed her gesture and they began to head our way. On the other side of the Utopia, Delilah and Shade were doing the same.

I glanced over to Iris. She stood there alone, having waved Chase out of the way. Worried, I wanted to run to her, but then I saw it clearly—the outline of energy that surrounded her. Her aura radiated pale blue streaks, infused with the purples and pinks that shadowed glaciers under the aurora-filled sky.

She held up her wand, pointing it at one of the creatures, and in a voice as faint and chiming as bells on the wind, she sang out some incantation in Finnish. I couldn't understand what it meant, but I could feel the intent.

Within a split second, the Fyrun noticed her and began to run toward her, the slow cautious pace abandoned in a fierce sprint. But Iris pointed her wand and a pale beam of snow and frost burst forth, shooting like a hail of ice pellets, a veil of mist. As it hit the Fyrun woman, we heard a loud sizzle, then a shriek, and like a blow dryer dropped in the bathtub, the creature began to spark, convulsing as the frost laceworked its way over her like a spiderweb. A moment later, the flames flared through the webbing of frost, then exploded. The sparks flickered brightly, then vanished into the night.

I didn't have time to understand what Iris had managed to do, but the Fyrun Fae had noticed what was going on and they were headed toward her in a fury. Delilah's two were also turning, ready to aim themselves at our house sprite.

"Fuck, we have to keep them from overwhelming her!" I stared toward one of them but Bran pushed me back.

"Fire can ignite you like dry tinder. Toss that piece of wood to the side. They'll have to go after it, and it won't offer much in the way of fuel." He headed toward the one he'd been taunting.

I raced alongside the Fyrun, finally managing to catch her attention by waving the slatted wood almost within her reach. A moment later, she turned, gazing at me calmly. I tossed the wood, hard, a few yards away. If I threw it too far, she might ignore it.

After a moment's hesitation, she headed toward the wood, her hunger palpable in the night. As she ignited the broken sign, I turned back to see that Bran had managed to get the attention of his opponent. She, too, was beginning to feed. The rain helped us, soaking the wood so that it made it harder to catch flame, and so it was taking them longer to ignite and devour it.

Delilah had lost control of her Fyrun, but Shade had

managed to distract his. Iris moved in quickly, aiming her wand at the approaching woman. Another burst of frost, and another flameout as fire and ice met. And then a third, and by that time, the two we'd engaged were barreling down on her. With one last push of effort—Iris looked exhausted—she managed to net both of them at the same time, and with a huge flash, they vanished to wherever it was she sent them.

Iris stared at the empty parking lot, then slowly began to collapse to the ground. Shade caught her up in his arms and we gathered round her. Camille and Morio broke their trance, but the massive rain storm continued.

"Iris, bless you. Are you all right?" Delilah fussed over her, brushing a few stray bangs out of her eyes.

Iris flashed us a weary smile. "I'm all right, yes. Tired? Definitely. Exhausted and needing my bed, I think. But they are gone and they will not return. However, we must find the runes that allowed them entrance and put a stop to them or they can be used again."

"What should we be looking for?"

"It will look similar to a Demon Gate. And will most likely be where the fire originated. That would burn the brightest and hottest. When you find them, come get me and I will take care of them. I am the only one here who can destroy them."

As we hesitantly reentered the building, Chase came with us. We left Morio and Bran outside with Iris to protect her. We worked our way through the darkened, soggy remains of the club, and I tried not to think about the Wayfarer and the people who had died under my watch. This one was going to haunt me for a long time. I knew it wasn't my fault, but knowing something didn't always translate into feelings. Emotions didn't play by society's rules, nor did they pay much attention to logic. But now, I knew that we had to look for signs that more of the Fyrun Fae had been loosed in my bar's fire. And if so, were they still running around Seattle?

Camille sent out feelers, trying to home in on where the

magic that had summoned the Fyrun Fae might be based. And then she paused, as if listening.

"I think I have it. I hear it . . ." She began to hurry, stumbling over fallen timbers and piles of ash and charcoal. The scent of soot was so thick that she and Delilah were both coughing, but rain was now pouring in through a couple smallish holes on the ceiling and that only added to the confusion. Thank the gods for the lights on our helmets or we'd all have ended up with broken legs.

We passed through a hallway, then into one of the back rooms, following Camille as she sped up. "Here, this way— it's there, and we have to hurry because whatever it is, it's still activated."

Chase reached out to grab her elbow when she stumbled. "Don't hurt yourself. We're headed right to the point of origin. We know it broke out back here because a couple of the waitresses who were checking the supply closet noticed the flames when they began. But the fire was so strong, they couldn't put them out with the fire extinguisher, so they evacuated the building and called the fire department."

As I looked around at the mess, a shiver ran down my back. There but for the grace of the gods . . .

"I'm just grateful everyone got out alive." I set my lips, thinking that it was going to cost Shikra a pretty penny to rebuild. Luckily, she was a vampire and had probably accumulated a good savings by now. That was one advantage to being able to charm almost anyone you chose to. She could have a billionaire boyfriend without too much of a stretch. At least long enough to get her hands on his bank account.

"I guess we aren't dealing with ghosts after all." Delilah let out a small sigh of relief.

I echoed her sentiments. Given all that we'd faced, we were getting very tired of spirits and hauntings.

Camille stopped by a storage closet—or what had been a storage closet. It was now a burned-out shell.

"Here. What we're looking for is in here. Go get Iris." As she leaned in, shining her light on the walls, Shade took off for the door.

Etched against one of the timbers that was still standing were brilliant runes, the color of flame, the color of white-hot fire. Mesmerizing, they lined the wood, difficult to look at and yet more difficult to look away from.

Camille reached toward them, then stopped. "Daemons. These are not demonic, but they are akin to it—it has to be daemon in origin." Daemons were akin to demons, but usually less chaotic and more organized. They had different natures, that much was for sure, though neither of them tended to be very pleasant to deal with.

Delilah let out a sigh. "Lowestar? He's the daemon at the top of our list right now."

"Probably. I do know that I am reluctant to touch them." Camille backed away. "Something tells me that touching those runes would be very, very bad. Any other thoughts on the matter?"

Shade returned, holding Iris well above the floor.

She examined the runes. "This is it. These activate the portal to the realm of the Fyrun Fae. It's intimately connected with the Elemental plane of Fire, but a step to the side, you might say. And you're right, if any of you touched these, it would suck you in and you'd be so much toast."

With a glance at Shade, she added, "Put me down. I need to be on firm footing to do what I'm about to do. And the rest of you back away. No telling what will happen when I blast those suckers."

"Be careful, Iris." Chase knelt down. "Please, be careful. Bruce and the babies need you. *Astrid and I need you.*"

She gave him a tight-lipped smile and patted his cheek. "I am made of tougher stuff than you may believe, dear detective." And then she motioned for him to move away.

We backed off, watching. Camille and Delilah were breathing tightly, I could hear the shallow intake, see the tight rise and fall of their breasts as they tensed, waiting for Iris to act. If I was a breather, I'd be right there with them. As it was, I poised myself to move, whether it be to throw myself on Iris to protect her, or run like hell if everything blew.

She stepped back, tested her footing against the debris on the floor, then aimed her wand at the runes. She closed her eyes, lowered her head, and began whispering a conjuration, a combination of song and chant. Her voice was clear and light, and though I didn't understand the words, the force behind them was sovereign.

A stream of frost came from the wand, narrowly focused, and she trained it on the center rune, which was a little bigger than the rest. As frost met fire, the runes began to fill in with ice, and a crackling static rattled the air. A low rumble began to shake the hall as the frost worked its way through each rune, freezing them into stillness, quenching the fire within.

The rumble became a quake beneath our feet, yet still Iris stood steady. When she reached the top rune, a gust of flame burst out from it, shooting over her head. If she hadn't been so short, it would have hit her in the face, but as it was, all it did was shower her with sparks, which sizzled into vapor before they reached her hair.

And then, as the last rune completely filled in, all the runes blazed bright bluish-white, the shimmering blue of ice in winter, and they exploded, shattering into a thousand shards, which flew every which way.

Iris shouted, but when I would have run to her, she held out her hand. A moment later, the fragments of ice fell to the ground as a cloud of mist rose. They began to melt. The wall where the runes had been inscribed was gutted, as if it had burned right through to the core. But no sparks remained, no sign of the magical flames that had caused the gaping rectangle of a hole. Instead, the drywall and wood surrounding it looked saturated, as if a surge of water had thundered through.

When the air cleared from mist and smoke, Camille was already by Iris's side. Delilah and I joined her, anxious.

"Are you all right—do you need help?"

"Did you get hurt?"

I swept Iris up in my arms. "You look exhausted."

And she did. Her face showed the strain of the magic,

and she leaned against me, her arms nestled against my chest, her head on my shoulder. I could feel her weariness, and the electricity that still charged around her body. A faint scent of ozone lingered around her like a perfume—like the smell before a snowstorm. As I shifted my grasp to hold her better, she let out a long, slow sigh.

"I don't think I can stay awake much longer." Iris gazed into my eyes. She wasn't afraid of me. I knew she respected me, and she never seemed repelled by my nature, nor did she show outright fear. "I'm so tired, and my breasts ache. My babies will want their feeding, and so will Astrid."

I nodded for the others to move as I carried her out of the building, cautious so as not to jolt her. At the limousine, I slid her into the backseat. "Take Mistress Iris home, please. And make certain she has help getting to the house. She'll need a long rest tonight, and food. Tell Master Bruce that . . . tell him we couldn't have saved the day without her. That she saved our asses."

With a grin, the chauffer tipped his hat, made sure she was belted in, and then pulled into the silent night, ferrying our friend home.

I turned back to the others, who had joined me. "So we have a daemonic gate into the realm of the Fyrun Fae. I wonder if there was one in the Wayfarer. And if so, is it still there?"

"We'll look. But for all we know, if there was, it might have been rigged to recall them after a certain time." Shade stared at the parking lot. "Lowestar Radcliffe's prints are all over this."

"There are other daemons around, but Trytian knows that if we found out he was doing something like this, we'd crush his balls." Camille leaned her ass on the back of the Lexus, looking exhausted. "And given Lowestar is attempting a coup on Seattle Supe-owned businesses, and that he's attempting to open a gate to Suvika, the demigod of vice and finance, yeah, I think we're on the right track."

My stomach lurched. Lowestar was not only a white slaver, but also a murderer. In my gut, I knew that he was the one who had ordered the arsonist to torch the Wayfarer. And that meant he was responsible for Chrysandra's death, and the deaths of the other patrons who had lost their lives in my bar.

I wrapped my arms around myself. Though the chill didn't bother me, I felt empty and cold and angry. And I wanted revenge. For me, and for all of Radcliffe's victims.

Chapter 6

By the time we got home, we were all done in. Bran split off, heading out to the studio where he was staying for the time being. Relieved that he decided not to join us, we trailed through the door and straight into the kitchen.

As I glanced around at the cheery domestic warmth that welcomed us home, it occurred to me that Camille had been about to tell me something when the call from Chase came in.

"What was it you wanted to say before we headed out?"

Camille dropped into a chair. "Oh, yeah. That." She looked exhausted. "I made arrangements today for Father's body. The Summerland Mortuary picked him up. They're an Earthside Fae-run business. They will understand the care we need for him. They're going to cremate him, and we'll hold a service here until we can take him back to the shrine to rest next to Mother."

"I think . . . I think he's by her side already. All we have left is his shell. She's waiting for us, you know. I saw her when Dredge killed me. She tried to help me, but when he turned me, she couldn't hold on." I'd never mentioned the fact that Mother had been waiting for me, with open arms, when I was killed. Camille knew from going through the ritual with me, where I'd cut Dredge off, but we'd never really talked about it.

Kitten made a small sound as she leaned against the counter. "I didn't know that. I wish you would have told me earlier."

I smiled up at her, feeling a hell of a lot older than I had a few years ago when we first came Earthside. "I wish I had, too, Kitten."

"Enough long faces. I know these days have been hard on you, but you must breathe, let the tension go." Hanna was busy as ever, and the room smelled like hot chicken soup and biscuits. "I thought you girls might like a bite to eat after all the fighting. You all look too pale." She frowned. "Before you get too comfortable, everybody get to washing up while I dish up the food."

"She's right, but someone should check on Iris."

"Vanzir has gone down to see her." Hanna dusted her hands on a dishtowel. "He wanted to make certain she was all right when the driver brought her home."

Speak of the devil, the kitchen door opened and Vanzir entered. He gave us the once-over. "Damn, you all look nasty. Iris told me all about it."

"How is she?" Kitten wearily bit into a roll, crumbs trailing down her chin.

"She's okay. Exhausted. Her mother-in-law was harping in her ear about running off and leaving the twins, but Bruce was seeing to her when I left. I don't think tonight hurt her, but she's going to need a good resting up. If I were you, I'd ask Smoky to get his ass back here in case you need any more ice magic."

"Right. I suppose we have no choice. I'm done in. Let's go wash up, have a bite to eat, and just . . . spend some time breathing." Camille motioned to Morio. "We'll use our bath. Meet you back here in ten minutes."

Shade and Delilah headed up to their room, and I used

Hanna's bath, washing my hands and face. A glance at the clock told me it was barely seven thirty. I'd risen at four thirty, as soon as the sun set, and the ordeal with the Fyrun Fae had taken us around two and a half hours. As I headed back to the kitchen, Nerissa arrived home. She looked wiped, too.

I wrapped my arms around her. "I missed you."

She kissed me, long and slow, her tongue playing over mine as a hazy wash of desire raced through me. I melted into her kiss, once again thanking my lucky stars I'd found her.

"You smell like you just came from a bonfire. Dancing around one out back?" She laughed lightly, but I shook my head and the smile died on her face. "What happened? Another fire?"

"Yeah. I guess you didn't hear? The Utopia went up in flames. Luckily, they managed to save it, and we fought off several Fyrun Fae, though we had to bring Iris in to help. She's exhausted, but we needed her ice magic, and since Smoky's not here, we had to ask her to join us."

Nerissa paled. "I had no clue. I stopped off to do some shopping on the way home. Is everyone okay? Did anyone . . ."

I shook my head. "No, no casualties this time, thank the gods. The club suffered heavy damage but it was all superficial. We ended up fighting some Fyrun Fae, though, and had to call in Iris to take care of them. She destroyed the gate through which they were coming. But she wore herself out big-time."

A sound in the living room alerted us. The Whispering Mirror. Again. Since Camille was still upstairs, I went to answer it. As the fog cleared, I spoke to let Trenyth know I was there.

"It's me, Menolly. What's up?" Every time the mirror chimed now, we feared the news, because it kept getting darker and darker.

Trenyth motioned to the side and a rustling told me someone was there. A few seconds later, Aunt Rythwar appeared. Taller than Delilah, she was statuesque and regal, with hair as dark as Father's and Camille's, and eyes that were a brilliant blue. She was wearing a pair of trousers—which I'd never seen her in before, and a tunic. A dagger was strapped to her thigh, and she had a bow slung over her shoulder. *This* was a new side of Aunt Rythwar, for sure.

Her brow creasing, she cocked her head. "Menolly? I see Nerissa there in the background."

"Yes, it's me. The others are washing up." Even as I spoke, a noise on the stairs alerted me to Camille and Delilah coming down. Shade and Morio followed them. "Just a minute."

I called out, "In the living room! Aunt Rythwar is in the mirror!"

As they crowded in, I gave up my seat to Camille. She was keeper of the Whispering Mirror, and I was all too aware of how disconcerting it could be to talk to someone you couldn't see.

"My girls . . . I'm so sorry." Her own face was a mask, neutral. Full-blooded Fae could be incredibly volatile, and they could also be incredibly stoic. Right now, Rythwar in no way looked like she'd just lost her dearest brother.

"We cremated Father's body today. We'll bring him back to Otherworld when it's safe enough. I hope you don't mind. We're going to hold a brief ceremony over here on Samhain, but we'll wait till we can bring him home for full rites." Camille let out a long breath.

Our aunt nodded. "I think that's best. Meanwhile, I wanted to let you girls know that I'm moving into your father's house—well, now it's yours. But I've decided we can't afford to leave it unguarded. So I'm taking some of my household guards and going to stay there."

"Is that why you're dressed like that?" I couldn't help but ask. Aunt Rythwar had never worn anything but the most extravagant of outfits, and now she looked ready for a jaunt through the forest.

"There is too much danger to go about in fancy robes and gowns. I was trained in combat early—all of those who sit in the Court are. I still practice my skills and work with my trainer every month. I can handle myself. At least, I am not a burden to any who travel with me." She winked in the direction of my voice. "I love you all, and wish you could come home, but Y'Eírialiastar is not a safe place to be. I heard about your escape from the palace. Your father would be so proud of you."

I swallowed hard, choking back my tears. Camille and Delilah were trying to do the same; I could see it in their shoulders, in their faces. It was going to be rough for the next few months; that was obvious. We didn't have the luxury to really let go and grieve.

"Auntie, please, be careful." Delilah leaned toward the screen. "We can't lose you, too."

"I'll do my best, and I'm taking guards with me. Tell my foster son Shamas I love him and miss him. And girls . . . be safe. Be careful. And I'll see you as soon as we can meet." She moved away from the mirror and Trenyth returned.

"I have more news." He looked somber. "Smoky and Trillian found Venus the Moon Child. They will be returning home in a short while."

There was more. There had to be, or he wouldn't look so solemn.

"What's going on, Trenyth? Was Venus dead when they found him? Or—Roz? He's not hurt, is he?" I leaned over Camille's shoulder, even though he couldn't see me.

"No, both Rozurial and Venus are alive. Venus has his spirit seal. But your men found Benjamin's body. The seal was missing. We don't know where it went or who has it."

Camille let out a soft murmur. "Not Ben. He was such a nice young man. And for so long, he thought he was crazy."

"I'm sorry, I know you neither wanted nor needed this news. But you must know the truth of where we stand. As of now, we have no idea who possesses that seal. It could be Telazhar, it could be some random creature. All we know is that Benjamin was murdered, and whoever did it wanted to make sure he stayed dead." He grimaced. "I will spare you the details. If you want to know, ask your men. They will be home within the hour."

He leaned back in his chair. "I think, girls, that we have to settle in and accept this is going to be a long road to haul. We aren't going to win this one overnight. Telazhar has seen to that. We are witnessing the dawn of a new age in Otherworld. Or perhaps, the reemergence of an old one—one we hoped never to repeat. Whatever the case, cinch yourselves in for a rough ride."

"To quote an Earthside movie, *Fasten your seat belts. It's going to be a bumpy night.*" Delilah chewed on her bottom lip. "All we can do is our best. Meanwhile, the world will keep turning."

"That about sums it up," I muttered. "We're a cheerful little group here, aren't we? But seriously, is there anything else we can do that we're not doing?"

Trenyth slowly shook his head. "No. Just protect the Keraastar Knights and the four spirit seals we have in our possession. And find that last spirit seal remaining Earthside if you can. Meanwhile, we will search here for the one that belonged to Benjamin. We know that Shadow Wing possesses at least three. We cannot allow him to gain control of any more, or all is lost."

And with that, he saluted us, and the mirror faded to mist again. Camille covered it with the black cloth that protected it and sat back, staring at the wall.

"Things are so fucked. Things are beyond fucked. I'd ask where we go from here, but there is no *where*. We just . . . maneuver through this mire one step at a time, and hope to hell we are still on the right path." She sighed as Hanna entered the room.

"Time for food. You can worry later." Her voice was as stern as Iris's and we all jumped to attention.

As we filed into the kitchen, Nerissa spoke up. "While we eat dinner, why don't we revisit my idea of creating a profile on Supe Matchups?"

Too tired to fight anymore, I gave in. "Fine. But I don't

like it. Two rules, though: You run all e-mails past us. And
you don't agree to anything without our permission."

Nerissa stuck her tongue out at me, but nodded. "Oh, all
right."

Delilah fetched her bag and pulled out her laptop. As we
gathered around the table, she fired up the computer and
set it to the side of her plate. Thanks to the huge wooden
table that Smoky had bought, we were able to seat a veritable army in the kitchen. And after they built Iris and
Bruce's house, the men had finished the addition to our
dining area, which gave us plenty of room.

As Hanna served the food, Delilah pulled up the website, then slid the computer in front of Nerissa, who pored
over the information.

"I still don't like this." I sat back, grumbling. "But if
we're going to do this, let's do this right. Do we have a clue
as to what they're looking for?"

Camille frowned. "Violet was into bondage and domi-
nation. She was looking for multiple playmates. She wasn't
into pain, but that wouldn't matter to the sex slave industry.
They don't care what their victims want or don't want."

She looked Nerissa up and down. "You should change
clothes, though, if we're going to shoot a video and put
it up. Show off those amazing boobs of yours." She wiggled
her eyebrows at my wife. "How about a kiss, sweetheart?"
Her attempt at a Humphrey Bogart impression fell as flat as
the cake I'd attempted to make for Nerissa's birthday.

I cracked up. "Oh please, if the two of you ever ended up
trying to kiss, you couldn't even reach each other. Between
the two of you, the cleavage factor would keep you at arm's
length." Shaking my head, I turned to Nerissa. "She's right,
though. You should probably put on something skanky. Or
sexy. Whichever you choose."

Nerissa headed toward my lair. "Will do, but if anybody
touches my dinner, they're dead meat."

By the time she returned, everyone had been served.
Chicken soup and biscuits and a hearty bowl of fruit salad
were on the menu for the others. For me, Morio had enchanted

a bottle of blood to taste like soup. Heated, it did my spirits more good than just about anything else could tonight.

Ever since he'd volunteered to give me some sense of my old life back through food-flavored blood, I hadn't felt quite so much the outsider. I realized I'd never fully told him how much this meant to me. I'd have to remedy that. Maybe a present, or maybe just a quiet word when we had a moment.

Nerissa returned to the kitchen, wearing an off-the-shoulder cream top that gave full vantage to her ample bosom, and a high-waisted pink miniskirt with ruffles that grazed her mid-thighs. I set down the bottle of blood, the fire rising as I stared at her. I wanted to drag her down to the floor and fuck her brains out right here. I let out a low growl.

She picked up on it; her eyes met mine. "Tonight," she mouthed, and I nodded. It had been several days—too long for us, but what with all the crap going down, sex wasn't exactly high on the priority list.

As she passed by, resting a hand on my shoulder, I grabbed her fingers and brought them to my lips, turning them so I could kiss her palm. Then I let go, and she settled in front of the laptop.

"What should I say? I guess I use the webcam to make a video?" She licked her lips to moisten them, then glanced over at me. "I really don't flirt. Well, I haven't much since I met you."

As the others dove into their food, I took notes.

Delilah and Camille threw out possible lines. Some of them Vanzir and Morio nixed on account of "a guy wouldn't respond to that," but finally, we had a short, sexy script and Nerissa fluffed up her hair, adjusted her off-the-shoulder top to reveal as much as she could without showing her boobs in toto, and she stood back so the webcam could catch her entire outfit and recorded the canned dating video. After that, she created an account under the name of "Puma Girl" and filled out the forms, uploaded the video, and that was that.

"Now we just wait for them to take the bait." She sat back, frowning. "I just hope they do."

"I think . . . whoever Lowestar chooses to replace Hanson will want to make a name for himself. He will probably be trolling the new members for any likely subjects." Delilah frowned. "That's what I'd do."

Nerissa bit into a biscuit. "I have e-mail on my phone, of course, so I'll add the account I created to use for the profile. I didn't want them checking into my personal account. I tried to leave as little of a trail as possible that they might be able to track back here. Can't help if they figure out that I'm not just renting my condo. But I doubt they'll check on who owns the place. And I've been seen with you guys, but I'm not that high profile."

My wife had just bought a condo when we decided to get married. She rented it out now, but it had stood empty for the past month after the last renter had to abruptly vacate for a new job.

"With a little luck . . ." Camille let out a sigh. "And we need a little luck right now."

As they ate, and I drank my bottle of blood, there was a noise in the living room. I was closest so I ran in to find out what was going on. As I entered the room, I saw Smoky and Venus standing there. Roz showed up a moment later, his arm around Trillian.

For a long time, Roz had been unsure about ferrying people through the Ionyc Seas, but after a little practice on me—I was already dead and he couldn't do much to hurt me—he'd discovered that he could take a passenger with him. One at a time, but he could do it. That little discovery had made life easier over the past months.

Delilah, who was right behind me, gave out a little squeal. The others followed behind her.

"Venus!" She ran to the old shaman. He looked older than the average Were, which meant he was incredibly old, but his hair still streamed golden down his back, and his eyes were the same color as Nerissa's—a brilliant topaz. He was handsome, sturdy, and solid.

As he stepped forward, it seemed odd to see him without a limp, but then I remembered. The spirit seal he had carried in his leg for so many years had caused that limp. Now the fire opal was hanging around his neck, sparkling in a way that was almost frightening. It seemed a part of him—and he a part of it.

Venus the Moon Child had been the shaman for the Rainier Puma Pride, until he'd been conscripted by Queen Asteria for the Keraastar Knights. I wondered how the grizzled and crude puma had fared among the regal elves. Chances were, he could strike any one of them down without a problem. The man wasn't just a Were; he was magic incarnate.

He held out his arm and pulled Delilah to him, kissing her on the cheek. With his other arm, he motioned for Nerissa to join him and he squeezed her to his chest, kissing her soundly on the lips. He had taught my wife how to handle pain, how to translate it into pleasure and use it as a healing force. And he'd taught her well.

Camille let out a shout and ran over to Trillian and Smoky. The dragon caught her up, whirling her around, kissing her soundly as he set her back on the ground, for Trillian to take his turn.

I turned to Hanna. "Can you fetch Amber and Luke? They'll want to say hello to Venus."

She nodded and took off for the parlor as Venus motioned for room.

"Let an old man have a chair, would you?" His eyes sparkled, though. As ancient as he might be, he was far from old.

As he dropped into the rocker, Venus gave us a long look before leaning his head against the back of the chair and closing his eyes. It was then that I could see the weariness below the surface that seemed to ooze out of his pores. Smoky and Trillian looked beat, too. So did Roz.

"Trillian, Smoky—why don't you two go shower and change? Roz, use Delilah's bathroom." Camille motioned to Vanzir. "Meanwhile, somebody fix a plate for Venus. Soup and biscuits . . . whatever we have. Unless you'd like to wash up first, too."

As Vanzir vanished toward the kitchen, Venus shook his head. "I took a shower at the Elfin camp this morning. I'll bathe after eating. I know you have many questions for me and I'll do my best to answer."

At that moment, Luke and Amber entered the room. They greeted Venus in an odd dialect, one I knew I'd heard before but wasn't conversant with.

But Camille touched her nose. "You speak in Melo-sealfôr?"

Venus nodded. "Queen Asteria ran us through an intensive course. It's a rare dialect, and not many goblins or other miscreants would speak the tongue."

She nodded. "It's said that if the language falls from the tongue of an enemy, it will burn their lips with every word. Most of the powerful Cryptos—the ones who are of relatively good nature, that is—know it. And all of the Moon Mother's witches and priestesses are schooled in it."

Luke and Amber sat on the sofa. Luke looked a little more comfortable, but Amber still seemed disconnected. My heart hurt to think how good a friend Luke had been to me, and how strained things were now.

Venus seemed to pick up on my thoughts. "The seals, they change the wearer, Menolly. I've carried mine since I was first initiated as the shaman for the Pride. It changed who I was long, long ago. You have only ever known me this way. I was vastly different before I underwent the ritual that implanted it into my leg. This pair—this brother and sister—they are young still, in the way of the werewolves. The seals will work on them for many years and alter them. It is the nature of the artifact. Don't feel bad. This is the way of the world, girl."

His smile was genuine, if stern. I nodded, holding his gaze. He was a handsome man, that was for sure, in a seasoned, wounded way. I could understand how Nerissa had been drawn to him.

Camille let out a slow breath. "Can you tell us what Queen Asteria was planning to do with the Keraastar Knights? And if those plans are still viable?"

A crafty grin spread across Venus's face and he let out a low laugh. "Oh, my fair girl, yes I know what she was doing. And I can, and will, let you in on her plans. As for the question of whether they are still viable . . . that I do not know. The seal Tom had, and Benjamin—if they can be recovered, we can bind them fresh to others who fit the energy signature. The spare one that Luke carries? We were seeking a match for it when the storm hit."

"So what were you guys doing over there? What were Queen Asteria's plans for you?"

The silence hung heavy. Venus stared at me, then his gaze moved to Delilah and finally to Camille. It seemed like he was debating whether to answer us—or rather—*how* to answer us.

"Should we tell them?" Amber spoke up. She didn't seem nervous, but rather reticent, and I thought I could detect an edge of resentment in her words.

"*Of course* they must know, especially now. We are not autonomous, Amber. The Keraastar Knights were never meant to be. At best, we are pawns in the hands of destiny, and you would do well to remember that. And now, with the star who guided our destiny sadly under a mound of dirt, we must seek out another to lead us. We were never meant to rule ourselves." Venus let out a long breath as Vanzir brought him a mug of soup and a plate of biscuits sopping with butter and honey.

Venus eagerly slurped the soup, and we waited patiently. Meanwhile, Smoky and Trillian returned from washing up, and Roz trailed in after them.

"Queen Asteria had stumbled over an ancient text—did she tell you? The Maharata-Verdi?"

This was a new one. We shook our heads. "No, go on. What is it?"

"A scroll from when the spirit seal was first created and broken into nine pieces. It comes from the great Fae Lords. They wrote it down . . . it is both a prophecy and an incantation. They predicted that one day, a force of nine knights would carry the spirit seals forth . . . that they would lead an army of magical warriors against a 'great horde' who was set to bring the worlds crashing in on each other again."

"The Keraastar Knights," Delilah said, staring at him.

Venus nodded. "Yes. The scroll directed that the knights were to be called the Keraastar Knights because of the central stone their Queen wore—the Keraastar diamond. When all nine knights come together, with the nine seals, and their Queen at their helm, it will create a shield that would repel Demonkin and hold the worlds apart. Because the Maharata-Verdi claims that if the portals implode, the worlds will crash together in a cataclysm that will destroy much of both. Not so much like a nuclear bomb, but it will have far-reaching impact on the future of both OW and ES, and release a fuckton of magical chaos."

With that, Venus fell silent.

We stared at him. He'd pretty much dropped a bombshell on us.

"Okay, do you have the Maharata-Verdi?" It wasn't that I'd ever doubt him, but had Queen Asteria truly possessed this document? She wasn't the lying kind but we'd been taken in before.

Venus glanced at Luke and Amber, then slowly reached into the bag he had kept by his side and brought out a small leather tube. He opened it and withdrew a crackling scroll. The antiquity of the paper oozed off it, and at first I wondered how it had lasted so long, but when Camille whispered, *"Magic . . . ,"* I knew that it was enchanted.

As the old shaman spread out the vellum on the coffee table, the energy rolled off it so thick that even I could feel it. Camille and Morio knelt down by it, almost reverently. The writing on it looked old—very old.

Camille pored over it. "A very ancient version of Melosealfôr, it looks like. I can pick out part of a word here or there but nothing substantial." She ran her hand over it, then stood up. "Venus is right, this is ancient beyond counting. I'd say it was created before they made the spirit seal— before the Great Divide."

Morio nodded. "There's magic in this scroll that even the Scorching Wars couldn't rival. You said that there's an incantation in it?"

"Queen Asteria could read this . . . and she herself performed the incantations. It binds the spirit seal firmly to the bearer on a soul level, but there has to be a match there— you cannot be bound to the spirit seal if you don't resonate to it on an energetic level." Venus took a big bite of a biscuit slathered with honey and butter. "In essence, this scroll creates the Keraastar Knights."

The room fell silent. I stared at the ancient scroll. "You mentioned the Queen bearing the Keraastar diamond. Did Queen Asteria have that?"

He frowned, then shook his head. "No, but the scroll has a twin, and that twin bears the location of the diamond. And . . . I know the location of the twin scroll. Queen Asteria entrusted it to me. Why, I don't know, but she had her reasons and told me one day I'd find out."

"But if *she's* dead, then what good would the diamond do?" Delilah frowned, a confused look on her face.

Venus took her hand. "Little Kitten, understand that the scroll predicts a Queen will wear the diamond . . . but not *which* Queen. Queen Asteria was not the one destined to finish the task. It was not for an Elfin Queen . . . but a *Fae* Queen. The great Fae Lords made the spirit seal to begin with. Asteria was not, at first, in favor of dividing the worlds. She came around, but it was the *Fae* race who forged the seals, it was the *Fae Lords* who rained terror down in the form of the wars that surrounded the Great Divide. *They* locked Aeval and Titania away. *They* drove the juggernaut that created Otherworld. So . . . my belief is that it will be a Fae Queen—an *Earthside Fae Queen*— who will wear and wield the Keraastar diamond, and she will finish rebuilding the Keraastar Knights and become their leader and champion."

Camille let out a long breath. "But who . . . Aeval? Titania?"

I slowly turned to her. "I pray it's not Morgaine. We would be in for so much trouble if she rose to that kind of power."

"We can't let her know about it. But if we keep it from her, that means we keep it from Aeval and Titania. I don't know how feasible that is." Camille frowned, pacing the room. "For now, though, as long as the dragons protect the knights, we should be okay. But Venus, you must not let the dragons know about the Keraastar diamond."

We all glanced at Smoky and Shade to see how they'd take that statement. But both of them nodded in agreement.

Smoky spoke up. "My wife speaks correctly. My people are avaricious. Especially the white dragons. My father's kin are among the worst of the lot, and they will stop at nothing to attain power and treasure. For now, when you return to the Dragon Reaches, keep silent. And you must hide this scroll."

Venus paled. "Where, though? It must be protected."

"Carter. Carter could protect it, couldn't he?" Vanzir stopped short as soon as the words left his mouth. "Never mind. No, you do not want a demon having that much information in his grasp. Not even a half-demon. I'm amazed you spoke of this in front of me, considering my nature."

"You are not out to destroy this world," Venus said.

"There is a place," I said, mulling over every word, trying to decide if what I was thinking was actually a good idea or not. "What about your barrow, Smoky? It's sealed off from the rest of the world more tightly than just about any place we know of."

Camille nodded. "Yes . . . of course! The barrow. There are spaces deep within the chasm there that we could hide the scroll in—no one would ever find it unless they first destroyed all of us, then decided to go mucking about in there." She turned to Smoky. "Can we hide it there, my love?"

A strand of his hair reached up to tickle her and then he nodded, his eyes gentle. "You may hide it in my barrow. But we'd best do it soon because once my mother and her helpers arrive to take Venus and the others back with them, they'll sense anything this old in the house. Shade, stay here. Menolly, you and Rozurial—bring the scroll. I will go with you to help you through the barriers. You can find a place to hide it that even I will not know about."

"You'd best go quickly." Shade cocked his head. "I sense a stirring on the wind. The dragons will be here soon."

"Then we go now, and will return as soon as we finish."

And with that, we scurried to gather our things, and to go hide the scroll.

Chapter 7

❦

Traveling through the Ionyc Seas wasn't always the most pleasant thing but it got the job done. And really, considering I was already dead and that it took one hell of a lot to knock me out of commission, the shifting waves of energy rolled over me like water on a duck's back. I closed my eyes and leaned close to Smoky as he sheltered me in his arm.

Dragons smelled different than humans or Fae. Their pulses ran differently, too. The steady beat of his heart was similar, but it echoed a different rhythm, deeper, like the ancient pulsing of drums in the darkness. I'd noticed it before. As Smoky stepped off the Ionyc Seas, it felt as though we were exiting from a womb, breaking through a psychic amniotic fluid sac. We stepped through, with a sucking sound, and were once again on solid land, in the physical world.

We were standing in front of his barrow, which was out near Mount Rainier. When Camille had first stumbled on the hillock and met the dragon who now claimed her heart, Smoky had been embroiled in a dispute over the ownership of the mound with Titania, the Queen of Light and Morning. But at that point, she had not regained her powers, and had been a pale drunken shadow of her true self. She had been arguing with Smoky over who owned the barrow, while living in a cave inside it.

Now there was no issue. Titania ruled with Aeval and Morgaine in their sovereign nation of Talamh Lonrach Oll, giving up all pretenses to owning Smoky's land.

Not far from the barrow, through the forest along a wooded trail, was a snug house where Smoky had offered refuge to Georgio Profeta, a man who believed he was Saint George. His childlike vision allowed him to see through the trappings and to know that Smoky was a dragon. For years he had sought to destroy the beast, dressed in his plastic chain mail, with a rubber sword. When his dementia grew too strong, Smoky hired a caretaker for him, and now Saint George and the dragon lived in a peaceful truce.

The barrow itself was a huge earthen mound that looked like a uniformly shaped—and good-sized—hill from the outside. To the outside world—and to us—it was lovely and pristine, a field that was incredibly beautiful. But beneath that glamour lay a charred and scorched area of the woodland. Smoky had done a number on it in his dragon shape, what with the let's-breathe-fire habit he had.

A door led into the barrow on one side, but I knew that farther along the mound was the entrance to a cave. Camille and Morio had explored in there when they went searching for Tom Lane—or rather, Tam Lin. Yes, *that* Tam Lin, from the songs and stories. Tom, as he had been known to us, was Titania's foggy-headed lover from eons past, before he had become one of the Keraastar Knights, and now—sadly—a victim of Telazhar and the sorcerers.

Roz jumped off the Ionyc Seas and blinked, steadying himself. The more we all traveled through the vast channels of energy, the more we adapted to the nuances and sluggish pull of the currents.

After a few minutes to situate ourselves, Smoky led us through his magical charms to enter the barrow. If we'd tried to breach the wards without him, we would have died in any number of horrible ways. Dragons were protective, and territorial, and they had exquisitely painful methods of preventing anybody from fucking with their stuff. Even so, as we crossed the threshold, a crackle of electricity sparked around us, and if we'd been unwelcome visitors, we would have been turned into crispy critters.

The outside might be rustic, but inside, Smoky's barrow was a bizarre mix of stone and chasm and old world charm. The living room was laid out on tiled floor, and the walls were the stone of a deep cavern. The barrow on the outside was far smaller than the world into which we had stepped. Barrow mounds were magical; the entrances were portals into another dimension. So on the outside, the mound could be a small hillock, but once inside, the world grew larger.

As we entered the living area, the smell of cigar smoke and old leather surrounded us. Smoky was still allowed to smoke in his own barrow, provided Camille wasn't coming out here for a while. Smoke bothered Delilah and Camille a lot—especially cigarette and cigar smoke. It had bothered me when I was still alive but no longer presented a problem. That didn't mean I *liked* the smell, but it didn't make me choke now.

The brown sofa and chair were old, luxurious—the leather buttery and supple. Heavy walnut tables buttressed the ends of the sofa, and a matching bookshelf spanned one cavern wall, filled with leather-bound books and scrolls. The tiled floor ended at what would have been the back wall, but the cavern opened up into a chasm at that point. A staircase led down into the pitch dark of the cavern below. Mists boiled from the bottom, and the sound of a stream echoed out from deep in the rocky ravine.

On either side of the living area, two doors led into what I knew were a bedchamber and bath, and Smoky's kitchen. Eye catchers shimmered around the ceiling—Smoky had managed to snag them from Otherworld, or perhaps when Titania had lived in the caves connected to the barrow, she had enchanted them. Whatever the case, their illumination brought a soft, gentle glow to the cavern, and even though it was underground, even though it boasted dark depths that led to unknown haunts, there was a sense of comfort here, and safety. Smoky had definitely imprinted his presence on this place.

I was carrying the scroll. One of the reasons we'd left Venus at home was that, if he didn't know where the scroll was hidden, he couldn't leak the information in case he was caught. Because while we still weren't sure of how important the Keraastar Knights were to the future, we didn't dare chance losing the powers inherent in the parchment.

Smoky led us to the back edge of the living area. There, below, was the deep chasm into which he dove when he shifted into his dragon form in the barrow. I wasn't sure how he got from there to the outside, but it was none of my business and I had never asked.

A narrow set of stairs led down on one side, steep and with no railing. They descended into the darkness, treacherous and foreboding. I wondered just how many feet had traversed the stones, how many people had attempted to venture into the gaping fracture that split the cavern.

Smoky stood up top. He paused for a moment. "I shouldn't be witness to where the two of you hide the scroll. That way, the Wing Liege cannot command me to hand over information I do not have. While I doubt that my people would have any desire to administer the Keraastar Knights, it is best we take no chances. If you need me, call, and I will help you out, but unless it's an emergency, probably best that I don't know where you're going."

I glanced at Roz. It made sense. "I guess we'd better get a move on. I don't want to miss saying good-bye to Luke and Amber before the dragons take them away."

"Not to mention, it would be a really *good* idea if I were there when they arrive." Smoky gave me a twinkling smile, but there was a worried sense lurking behind those frosty eyes.

"Right." I motioned to Roz and headed toward the steps. "How will we be able to see in the darkness?"

"Here . . ." Smoky paused, holding out a silver lantern. He let out a low whistle and two of the eye catchers broke free from their place where they hovered near the ceiling and slowly floated into the metal cage. He shut the door on it, then handed it to me. "Take this with you—they will light the way."

"Thanks. Now all I need is a stick to test the steps."

Again Smoky came to the rescue and provided me with a staff. It was old, smooth from many centuries of handling, and the wood felt sturdy but not heavy. A tingle ran through my palm as I wrapped my hand around the hilt of it, and I knew there was magic within the staff, though there was no way I could know what kind it was.

"What is the wood?"

Smoky gave me a gentle nod. "Apple."

Heading over to the edge of the chasm, I was grateful that I wasn't acrophobic. Camille was to a degree, and it had caused some problems over the years.

I handed the lantern to Roz. "You take this. I'll use the staff and go on ahead." Making certain the scroll was firmly tucked in the bag I'd slung over my shoulder and neck, I stood on the top step. The scroll couldn't fall out of my grasp this way. The Velcro keeping the flap closed was firmly shut. Unless I toppled over the edge, we wouldn't lose the scroll on the way down.

"We're ready."

Roz took the lantern, and without another word, we headed down into the depths.

I leaned close to the wall as I began tapping the stairs in front of me. They were narrow and steep, at the most twenty inches wide by ten inches deep, by twelve inches high. In other words, they were hell on earth to get down and left us clinging to the wall.

If I took a fall, I could recover, unless I landed on something sharp and pointy in just the right place. Roz *might* have time to shift into the astral—incubi had their own modes of travel and Roz could vanish into the Ionyc Seas if need be. But still, if he didn't manage to shift fast enough, he could die from a fall like that. And given the sound of the stream and the mist below, I wouldn't count on a smooth landing. So both of us pressed against the stone wall to our left, out of which the steps had been carved.

Holding the staff in my right hand, I tapped each step as I went, testing for broken stone, for cracks that might crumble the step beneath our feet. Mount Rainier—which we were very near—was an andesitic volcano, and the rock out here was deep gray, with inclusions of quartz and feldspar. While the stone was extremely hard, earthquakes were frequent because of the volcanic nature of the area, and could easily fracture it.

The walls of the cavern were rough, carved out by whatever ancient hands had built the steps, and the eye catchers softly illuminated a small swath of the rock wall to our left, and about ten feet of the stairs that descended in front of us. From what Smoky had told us, the bottom of the chasm lay some five hundred or so feet below. We could hear the sound of the water rushing even from here. There was an underground river—small, but a river nonetheless— flowing along the bottom of the ravine.

Hoping there were no viro-mortis slimes along the rock, I kept my left hand and shoulder firmly pressed against the stone. It was cool, and as we worked our way into the depths, the smell of damp moss and mildew grew stronger. A gust of air brushed past, though I had no clue where it was coming from. It swept up and out of the ravine to rattle by, a hollow husk of a voice susurrating in my ear. I tried not to think about ghosts or spirits, and focused on what I was doing.

Down we edged, down another step, another five, another fifteen. Neither Roz nor I tired quickly, but the going was slow, and while I was more light-footed and sure than he was, the task was daunting. After about forty-five minutes, a ledge came into view. It was narrow, but from what I could tell, the stone outcropping led into a cavern. I tapped it with the staff and a few pebbles gave way, falling into the chasm with a loud trickling sound, but the ledge itself seemed sturdy enough.

Cautiously, I set one foot on the stone and waited. One beat. Two beats. Nothing happened. I slowly edged the rest of the way onto the ledge. Again, it seemed safe. Staring at the opening, I debated the wisdom of going in blind. Roz had the eye catcher lantern and I leaned back to where he was waiting for my go-ahead.

"Give me the lantern. Then let me step into the cave to see what's in there before you come onto the ledge. I think it will hold both of us at the same time, but I'd rather not chance it." As he lowered the lantern to me, I reached up and managed to catch hold of it. Retreating to the wide entrance of the cavern, I slipped inside.

The tunnel mouth was as wide as the ledge, and I paused inside to let my eyes adjust. The soft glow of the eye catchers illuminated the area around me, and I could see that the cave was shallow, only about seven feet deep. The walls and ceiling glistened with some sparkling material that seemed to hang down like wisps of thread, gently moving in the soft breeze that channeled into the chamber. As I crept closer to one wall, I realized the sparkling strands were glowworms, bioluminescent and beautiful.

Cautious not to disturb them—they weren't dangerous as far as I knew, but now wasn't the time to find out—I scoped out the floor. Empty, for the most part. Scattered stones and pebbles. No real danger, and no good place here to hide the scroll. It would mean clearing out the glowworms to look for a nook, and I didn't feel like doing that.

I emerged from the cave and looked up at Roz, handing the lantern back to him. "Nothing to worry about, but not what we're looking for either. It's down we go. Let me get off this ledge before you cross it."

"Not a problem," he said, waiting as I descended to the stairs on the other side of the outcropping before following me.

Another ten minutes, another twenty . . . The sound of

water grew steadily louder as we closed the distance between us and the bottom of the ravine. And then, almost ninety minutes since we'd started the journey down, we were near the bottom.

The cavern itself was immense. I couldn't tell how far across it went, but the river rushing through it was a good seventy or eighty yards across. The water churned along, white caps covering the surface as it thundered through the cave. I wasn't sure where the source for this river was, or if it was purely an underground waterway coming from deep within the glacial walls of Mount Rainier, but whatever its name might be—if indeed it had one—the river's currents were strong and I wasn't sure I'd want to try to cross it.

As I stepped off the staircase, onto the rocky shore, Roz joined me, and we stood in silence, watching the roar of the waves pass us by. After a few minutes, I shook my head. The water had a mesmerizing effect that made it difficult to look away.

"Let's scout around the back wall. Maybe we can find a good niche in which to hide the scroll where we won't lose track of it." I motioned to the wall of the cavern that rose up. The staircase switched back and forth on its way back to the top.

"I brought a magical *trace*." Roz said.

I stared at him. "You're brilliant, why didn't I think of that?"

"Because I'm the gadget guy?" He laughed. "Seriously, no matter what sign we paint near it, no matter what landmark we erect, chances are a quake or some odd creature coming through will disrupt it and we won't be able to find the scroll again. But if we keep a magical trace on it, we can follow it through rubble and stone."

I grinned at him. "Good thinking. You're worth something after all."

He snorted. "Yeah, yeah. I know. I'm a lazy bag of bones." But he knew I was kidding.

We hunted along the wall for another ten minutes until I spotted a tunnel, about four feet off the ground. It was rough, about five feet high, and I hoisted myself up into it, reaching down for the lantern. As I inched my way forward, I realized there were dozens of catacomb-like holes in the wall here. The tunnel itself was only about four feet deep, and again—no creatures, no scary dangers in here. But the scroll would fit perfectly in one of the latticework holes.

Leaning out of the passage, I motioned to Roz. "Found the place. How do we work the magical trace on the scroll?"

He opened his duster—or should I say the walking arsenal he carried. His coat contained more weapons than a gun shop contained guns. He dug through the pockets. After a moment, he pulled out a small charm. I pulled out the tube containing the scroll and the charm fit neatly inside. After making sure it was carefully closed, I slid the tube inside a plastic bag and sealed it. No use chancing water getting in to ruin it, and we had no idea if—or how much—the river ever flooded.

Rozurial held out an amulet and closed his eyes. "Yep, the trace is working. Go ahead and hide it and we'll check again."

I carried the scroll back inside the passage and slid it into one of the latticed holes, then returned to the shore of the river. We walked downstream about twenty yards and Rozurial tried the trace again.

"Works like a charm." Laughing at his own joke, he tucked the amulet around his neck—it was on a leather thong—and slid it beneath his shirt. "I guess we're done here."

"As much as we can be." I stared up at the stairwell. "I really don't want to climb all the way back up. Would you mind if I turned into a bat and flew up?"

Roz laughed. "I'll do you one better. I can carry you through the Ionyc Seas to the top, now that I've seen it. I couldn't carry us down because I wasn't sure where the hell we were going, and stepping off the Sea could have landed us in the wrong place, as in *plunging us to our death* wrong place. But now that I know my target, we can journey up the easy way."

He opened his arms and I stepped into his embrace. As the world faded away, he swept us into the swirling sea of energy that connected all the realms. The Ionyc Seas kept the planes of existence separate and from running into each other, which would not have a been a good thing. Come to think of it, the Ionyc Seas were like natural portals.

The journey was short and we stepped out of the mists into Smoky's living room, about three feet from the drop-off. I took an involuntary step back—the sudden swirl of the ravine into which we had plunged seemed all too terrify-ingly deep. The plus side was that Roz had been down there now. And if we had to go again, he could shift through the Ionyc Seas to get there. I was pretty sure Smoky could, too, for that matter. I had no doubt he had been to the bottom, and that he knew every nook and cranny of the cavern. Dragons weren't stupid, and he wouldn't have allowed any surprise denizens to have access to his barrow.

Smoky was sitting there, reading a book. He glanced up at us, then carefully marked his place with a silver cord and closed the volume, setting it back on the coffee table.

"You are done?" He stood, towering over me—the dragon was six-four and his hair was longer than I was tall.

I nodded. "We are. And there's a magical trace on the scroll. Roz thought to bring one."

Smoky cocked his head. He had a natural antipathy toward the incubus, but they worked well together when needed. It was a stupid rivalry, brought on by one indiscre-tion Roz had made with Camille—involving his hand on her butt—and it had led to a thrashing the incubus would likely never forget, but the two were good-natured in their threats now.

"Well, nice to know there are other thoughts rolling around in his brain beyond getting laid." Smoky snorted, and then motioned to the door. "We need to leave. I do not want to miss my kin and it's been two hours since we arrived here. I will not mess with the barrow time just to buy back one hundred and twenty minutes."

I stopped, staring at him. "What do you mean?"

"You know time in barrows runs differently than time on the outside, if we choose to make it so. But doing so can produce severe ramifications, as well as causing discontinuity issues."

"I thought only Fae barrow mounds worked like that." I was confused now. I'd never heard any stories of dragons being able to mess with time.

But the galoot gave me a smirk. "What kind of mound do you think this originally was?"

Incredulous now, I rested my hands on my hips. "You aren't serious? Then Titania was telling the truth and this was her barrow and you ousted her from it?" Somehow, this didn't come as a great surprise, but still . . .

Smoky stared at the ceiling. "The woman was deep in her cups. She wasn't taking care of it, and it was the perfect space for me to both live in and also change into my dragon form." Then, a little more belligerently, he added, "I am not defending my actions to you, woman. You may be my sister-in-law, but I answer to no one."

"Except Camille." I couldn't help it, I was feeling my usual smart-ass self. "Right, Roz?"

But the incubus was smart. He shook his head, holding up his hands. "I'm staying out of this one. So not going there!"

"Smart move." Grumbling, Smoky motioned for us to head outside. Once we were through the wards, Smoky set them up again—with a wave of the hand and a tangible feel of some sort of magic wafting off him—and then he turned back to us. "Come. Time to fly."

As he enfolded me in his arms, Roz vanished. And then Smoky stepped into the Ionyc Seas, carrying me with him, and we headed home.

We appeared on the porch. Smoky released me and stiffened. "They're here."

"The dragons?" I glanced at him and he nodded. As I reached for the door, he stepped in front of me.

"Let me go in first. Just . . . in case." His warning look

was enough. Dragons were volatile creatures, and even though Shade was there to try to smooth the waters should anything happen, the chance that one half-dragon could hold against several full-bloods was small.

I stepped back to allow Smoky to enter first. Roz swung in behind him, and I came last. There were voices coming from the living room—loud, and for a moment I thought there was an argument going on. But as we entered the room, I saw that Shade was in the corner, laughing his ass off, and next to him, sitting on a footstool, was a woman with skin the same color as his—coffee and cream.

His sister. *Lash*—this had to be Lash. Her eyes were brilliant topaz and she had hair the color of spun caramel. Clinging to her ample curves, a silky gown the color of ivy, with orange flames licking the hem, showed off her rippling muscles. Not many people could work the color orange, but it was obvious that this woman could make just about anything look good.

Shade stood as we came into the room. I glanced around. Camille was nowhere to be seen, but Delilah was sitting primly on the sofa and she looked like the cat who had been *caught* by the canary. And what the hell . . . Delilah was wearing . . . a dress? Delilah never wore dresses except for rituals. And frankly, though she looked good in them, with her personality, they always seemed off. Our Kitten just wasn't a gurly gurl in any shape or form of the word.

She was wearing a slightly-above-the-knee-length olive green sheath, belted with a brown leather band, and she had on flats—loafers. But with the spiky hair and the deer-in-the-headlights expression on her face, she looked like some demented Bambi. Her hands were firmly folded in her lap, and she had a smile plastered on her face.

I glanced over at Shade. He seemed intent on talking to his sister, and I had the feeling he had no clue how terrified Delilah was. I slid over to her side and sat down, prying one of her hands out of her lap and holding it firmly in my own. As she caught her breath, the tension transmitting through her body like a radio beacon.

"Hey, aren't you going to introduce us?" I glanced over my shoulder, nodding at Lash.

She cleared her throat. "Yeah . . . I'm sorry—I . . ."

Smoky suddenly appeared by my side. He reached across and took Delilah's hand, pulling her to her feet. He gave her a courtly bow. "Sister, you look lovely today." Then he turned to Shade and Lash. "Perhaps you will introduce me to your future sister-in-law?"

Lash took in Smoky, her eyes growing wide. And then I understood. Smoky was the son of an influential and powerful dragon. He was half-silver, and that put him at the top of the food chain in the Dragon Reaches. He was also full-blood dragon, and Lash and Shade were only half.

Lash slowly stood. Shade stood beside her. Delilah, holding Smoky's arm, led the way to their corner where they were having their reunion. Lash gave her a look that I couldn't quite read—it wasn't scornful, but it *was* aloof, and a little too haughty for my tastes. But with another look at Smoky, she tentatively smiled.

Delilah cleared her throat. "Smoky, may I introduce Lash—Shade's sister? Lash, this is Smoky, one of my sister Camille's husbands."

"Her only *dragon* husband," Smoky interjected with a smile. "Charmed to meet you." He gave Lash a long nod, polite, but did not offer his hand. Hmm. He was up to a power play. By putting his support behind Delilah, he was giving her a one-up on Lash. Which would give her standing in the dragon realm.

Lash blinked. "You are Delilah's *brother-in-law*?"

Smoky's expression took on a somber look. "Most happily, I might add. You are lucky to be gaining such a brave and talented woman as part of your family. I consider myself fortunate to be aligned with the D'Artigo household."

He was laying it on a little thick, but then again, in the realm of the dragons, formality counted and sparring via words and lineage was commonplace. As he gazed into Lash's eyes, she shuddered, then forced a smile to her face as she turned to Delilah.

"We are lucky, I'm sure, and I'm grateful to be gaining a sister." She glanced over at me and Delilah pounced, quickly picking up on the interplay that had passed beneath the surface.

"Lash, may I present my other sister—Menolly."

I gave Lash a nod, not bothering to offer my hand. I had no use for head games and lineage snobs—we'd had enough of that shoved down our throats when we lived in Otherworld. But I gave her a fangy smile.

"You're a vampire." It was a statement, neither disdainful nor approving. She cocked her head; the topaz irises of her eyes were glowing, encircled with a purple ring. "You exist more within our world than most of the mortals we have met."

"That's right. You and Shade come from the Netherworld. You live in a land of spirits and ghosts." I had known this, but I suddenly understood the connection she was making. I was dead—well, one of the undead, if you wanted to be technical about it—and that made me more understandable to her. "You do know that Delilah is a Death Maiden?"

Delilah gave me an odd look, but Lash let out a soft sound and turned to her brother. "You did not tell me that your fiancée is marked by the Autumn Lord. I should have sensed her connection." She stepped forward, brushing Delilah's bangs back from her forehead. "The mark—you do bear it. And your arms . . ."

Delilah held out her arms. The orange and black leaves and vines winding up her forearms had grown vivid over the past couple weeks. She straightened, and for the first time since we'd returned home, she seemed like herself again.

She tipped her head up to look at Lash—the half-dragon, half-Stradolan woman was a good six-five, and with a soft sigh, her shoulders relaxed. "I belong to the Autumn Lord, yes. He is the one who picked Shade for me."

"And it is a match meant to be." Shade wrapped his arm around Delilah's shoulder. He glanced at her, a soft light in his eyes. "You are nervous, aren't you, my love?"

She shrugged. "What can I say? You bring your sister

here, you ask me to dress up when I never dress up . . . I know I'm being scrutinized as to whether I'm worthy to be your wife."

Lash frowned. "My brother asked you to dress up for me? You do not normally wear . . . this sort of wear?"

Delilah snorted. "Are you kidding? I'm more comfortable in jeans and a tank top, but I love your brother and wanted to make a good impression on you for his sake."

Whirling around, Lash faced Shade. "How could you ask her to be other than she is? Men, you are all alike." She motioned to Delilah. "Go, change into whatever is comfortable. My brother is as dense as most of his gender. And yes, you are right, I was sent here to observe you for my family but . . . I have a change of heart. I want to get to know you—not just carry tales home. And if you have the support of Iampaatar's family . . . then I offer you my support."

Smoky chuckled. "As you should. Camille and her sisters . . . well . . . you will learn."

As Delilah excused herself and ran off upstairs, Camille entered the room. She yawned and I realized that she was looking a little tired. We'd all been under a fuckton of strain over the past couple of weeks, and with Father's death, the stress had just exacerbated.

She leaned into Smoky's embrace as he introduced her to Lash, who gave her a surprisingly docile nod.

"Tired, love?" Smoky leaned down to kiss her head, a tendril of his hair reaching up to stroke her arm.

"Yes . . . but the evening is far from over." Camille let Smoky sweep her up into his arms as he carried her over to the rocking chair, where he sat, placing her firmly on his lap.

Shade motioned for Lash to join him on the sofa. Vanzir and Roz were heading out of the room when a noise from the corner alerted us. Within seconds, a blur shifted in the air, and then a woman and two men appeared. Tall and brilliant, sparkling with power, the woman gave us a gracious smile.

Smoky and Camille jumped to their feet.

"Mother!" Smoky moved forward, dropping to one knee as he pressed her hand to his lips.

"Iampaatar . . . Camille . . . we are here to retrieve your . . . parcels and to bring you a message from the Lords of the Realm. The dragons are discussing joining your war efforts in Otherworld. I have brought the Wing Liege and one of my private guards with me tonight. We have much to discuss."

And with that, Vishana, Smoky's mother, strode over to the recliner and settled back, crossing her legs on the raised footrest, as Lash sank to her knees, her eyes fastened on the silver dragon as a look of awe swept over her face.

Oh yes, this was about to get interesting.

Chapter 8

❦

Vishana was a striking woman—well, *all* dragons were striking when in their human form. But that was simply an illusion. The dragon behind the human form seeped through. Seven feet tall in human form, Vishana was pale to the point of being an ice sheet in the frozen north. Her eyes were the color of gunmetal, and her hair flowed down past her ass, silver with a sheen of blue sparkling through. Her tresses—like Smoky's—writhed on their own, shifting as if with her moods. She was wearing a long white dress, elegant with silver embroidery, and a cloak as blue as the early dawn.

As Smoky's mother settled back into the recliner, Lash looked up from her position on the floor. Vishana gazed down at her.

"We don't often meet our shadowy kin, be they half- or full-blood. I knew that one of Camille's sisters was engaged to half-blood black dragon. I assume you"—here she nodded at Shade—"are the gentleman in question?"

Shade laughed. "If *gentleman* be the correct word to

describe me." He gave her a short, but respectful, bow. "Lady Vishana, be welcome. May I present my sister, Lash? She is visiting with us for a while. She came—"

"I assume she came to get to know her future sister-in-law? For if I were your mother, I would send in a spy to scope out who was going to be marrying my son." She flashed a brilliant grin at both dragons. "In fact, I did this, although Iampaatar did not know."

Smoky started to protest but Vishana held up her hand. "Quiet. It is long past and you do not need to know all my secrets." She turned to Lash. "As for you, girl. Stand. I am not the Empress, and while I am above your station, I am not one who demands supplication."

And with those words, I began to get a clearer picture of the hierarchy of the dragon world. Camille didn't talk much about it, and Smoky seldom mentioned his home, not surprising given what his father had done to Camille. But Vishana, she was elegance embodied in form, and now I saw that while she definitely was dragon through and through, she was also gracious.

Lash stood, smoothing the front of her gown. She hesitantly raised her head to look at Vishana. "Thank you."

"Are you clutchmates with your brother?"

Lash shook her head. "No, I was in the second clutch. We are part Stradolan, so the clutches were small."

Vishana nodded. "The shadow walkers are the only species who can interbreed with black dragons, so yes, I know of your other heritage. Which side holds more sway with you?"

Delilah shifted, and her gaze latched on to the interaction. I realized that she knew very little about her lover's heritage. Dragons were cagey, even with their mates. Had she known anything we were hearing now, Camille and I would have already been privy to the information.

Lash swallowed, glancing at Shade. He nodded for her to answer.

"Unlike my brother, who followed more in the footsteps of our mother, I identify with the shadow walker part of myself. I work with my father. I've trained with him since I was little."

Delilah glanced at Shade, then interrupted. "What does your father do?"

Lash tilted her head. "Hasn't my brother told you? Our father is a judge. He sits on the Jury of the Damned."

Camille and Delilah stared at her. I was right there with them.

"What the fuck does *that* mean?" Camille's voice cut through the silence with a resounding trill.

"I'd like to know that myself." Delilah stood and moved toward Shade. "You've never told me anything about your family."

"Dragons are tight-lipped, my dear werecat." Vishana leaned forward, leisurely resting her elbow on the arm of the recliner, and her chin on her hand. "I doubt if Iampaatar has told Camille as much as he perhaps should have."

Lash looked crestfallen. "I didn't realize . . ."

"This is not a problem." Shade let out a sigh. "The only reason I haven't said anything, Lash, is that I hate what Father does. You know this."

Lash let out an exasperated sigh. "This again? Are you going to forever carry a grudge against him because of what he chooses to do?"

"What he does is what he *is*." Shade's normally tranquil expression took a leap south and he turned away. "Delilah, I think we have rounds to make on the property. Lady Vishana, Honorable Wing Liege, please grant me leave?"

Vishana stared at him thoughtfully, then nodded. "You are excused."

Shade practically dragged Delilah out of the room. Lash watched them go, then turned back to us, flustered.

"I apologize. I didn't mean to air any family laundry."

"What's the Jury of the Damned?" I got tired of standing and took a seat on one of the ottomans, crossing my legs.

"Why don't you enlighten the girls?" Vishana looked as though she might be enjoying this little tiff. I wondered about her for a moment. But then again—she was dragon and that right there was explanation enough.

Lash looked like she wished she'd never opened up this can of worms, but it was too late to put the lid back on.

"The Jury of the Damned is a court in the Netherworld, where the restless spirits are judged and dealt with. The angry ghosts are taken to the Ocean of Anger and linked to it in ritual. This keeps their residual anger from spilling over into the rest of the Netherworld. The mourning ghosts are assigned a wailing spot. And so forth. Father sits on the jury as the lead Elder." She shifted uncomfortably.

"Do the spirits have to obey the Jury?" I had a feeling she wasn't being totally up front with us.

Lash rubbed her hand on the back of the chair. "Yes."

"What happens if they don't?" Camille asked.

"Yes, why don't you tell us what your father is known for?" Vishana's eyes flashed and the cat-chasing-the-mouse came out, full force.

"You already know?" Lash jerked her head up, fear clouding her eyes.

"Oh, most certainly I do. And trust me, it suits your brother's reputation in the Dragon Reaches that he removes himself from the office. His connection with the Autumn Lord is acceptable but . . ."

Okay, *that* sounded like a threat. And if Smoky's mother was threatening Shade's sister, I wanted to know the reason for it.

After a long, awkward pause, Lash let out a long sigh. "Our father is known as the Enforcer. He punishes the ghosts who do not obey. I work for him—I'm learning to do what he does."

Vanzir, who had been silently watching the scene, stepped forward. "You have the gift, don't you? You can unleash pain on noncorporeal entities?"

Lash covered her face. "I inherited it. Shade did, too, but he chose to walk away from the family when Father wanted him to follow in his footsteps. Stradolans are able to wreak havoc on the spirit world—to administer pain, to trap and contain spirits. As I said, I took after my father and inherited his nature, while Shade followed in Mother's footsteps."

"So you punish the spirits who disobey." Vishana stood then, rearing up to her full height. "You trap them, then torture them until they submit."

The way she put it made Lash and her father sound like monsters. And I wasn't sure they weren't—but we knew nothing of the politics among the dead, and the Netherworld was as alien as the moon. I tried to reserve my judgment.

"Yes. Yes, we do. It is the way. It is the nature of the Netherworld. My father is honored for his talent and I *choose* to follow his path." Lash stared at the silver dragon defiantly, but her bottom lip still trembled.

"Then own it, girl. Own it and stand behind it. As distasteful as I find the idea, claim it and be proud of what you do. If you apologize for it or attempt to conceal it, you will only arouse suspicion." And as abruptly as she'd focused in on Lash, Vishana dismissed her with a wave of the hand. "Camille, where are the Knights?"

Camille cleared her throat, looking as startled as everyone else.

Smoky sprang into action. "Menolly, will you please bring Luke, Amber, and Venus here? Bring all their clothes, too."

Relieved to be dismissed and given the chance to get out of what was an all-too-tense situation, I headed toward my lair. So Shade's father was a torturer. Or rather . . . well . . . what *would* you call him? Shaking the whole mess from my mind for the time being, I scurried down the steps. Amber, Luke, and Venus were talking, and I motioned to them.

"The dragons are here. Bring all of your things with you." I felt rather sorry for them. They had all been transplanted from Earthside to Otherworld, having to learn a whole new style of living, and now they were on their way to the Dragon Reaches. Only the gods knew what would be facing them there.

"Listen to me," I said. "Dragons are presumptuous.

They're pompous, belligerent, arrogant, and obnoxious. One alone, hard enough to handle, even if you're on his good side. Get a bunch of them together? Walk softly. Be polite. And for the sake of the gods, don't make waves. Smoky's mother is taking you in, and we rely on her good-will. Don't fuck it up. Got it? Oh, and be careful."

Venus laughed. He sauntered over to me. The werepuma clapped me on the back. "Oh, Menolly. Don't give us a second thought. We will survive and pull through this. And before long, my guess is that a new Queen will command us. And I have my suspicions as to who it will be."

"Care to enlighten me?" I flashed him a crooked smile.

"Not at the moment, sweet-fangs. Not at the moment."

And then, after an awkward good-bye to Amber and Luke, Amber gathered up her daughter, Jolina, and we headed upstairs.

The Wing Liege was standing at attention, straight shouldered, with knee-length hair the same color as Vishana's. His eyes were the color of steel. He was dressed in a long, shimmering tunic the color of clouds against the water. A knotwork pattern bordered the hem, black lines weaving in on themselves along the edge of the material. Beneath the tunic, which was belted with a black leather belt and a silver buckle, he wore a pair of black pants and black leather boots. At his waist, a scabbard, worked in white leather, held what appeared to be a hefty short sword.

He crossed his arms across his chest as he stared at Luke and the others. "You will accompany us to the Dragon Reaches. Lady Vishana has agreed to house you in her apartments but this must be done quietly and no one else in the Dragon Realms must know. If word were to reach certain ears, there might be trouble. You will obey our commands, and you will make no decisions without consulting either Lady Vishana or myself." He darted a glance at Venus. "That goes for you, too, you wily old shaman."

Venus winked at him. "Understood."

Vishana turned to Lash. "I give you an order. What you have just witnessed and heard here tonight, you will seal in silence. Never to speak of it. Do you understand me?" The threat was implied.

Lash nodded. "I do, Lady. I'm not even sure what I *have* seen."

Camille stepped forward, curtseying to her mother-in-law. "Lady Vishana, I have a favor to ask of you."

Vishana smiled, and her hair trailed out to touch Camille's hand. "Yes, my dear? What do you need?"

Camille turned to me, then hung her head. "The war in Otherworld. Our friends are being slaughtered. Our father was killed. Can you help?"

The dragon's smile slipped away and she let out a soft murmur. "I am truly sorrowed to hear this. Your family is our family. And we owe you much in return for what my former husband put you through. The Wing Liege and I will take this up in Council. I promise you, we will give it our full attention. Meanwhile . . ." She turned to Smoky. "There is another dragon in the area. You should be aware of this."

At Smoky's quizzical look, the Wing Liege chuckled. "She is a Blue . . . and should you meet her, be aware she is soil-bound for now—a punishment I've enacted on her. Keep your eyes open, in case you are to meet her. She goes by the name of Shimmer."

"Is she dangerous?" Smoky frowned.

"No, but foolish at times. And headstrong. She is working off a debt, let us say." And with that, he clicked his heels and nodded.

Vishana motioned to the guard. "Take the male Were. I will carry the woman and girl. Liege, if you would—the Shaman." As the dragons moved into position, Amber, Luke, and Venus cautiously approached them. Vishana gently wrapped her hair around Amber and Jolina. The Wing Liege did the same to Venus, and the guard to Luke. Vishana raised one hand, palm facing out.

"Until next we meet. My son, take care of your family. Camille, take care of my son. Lash—do not be so quick to judge those not of your kind." And then, in a flicker of light, the dragons shimmered slowly, growing brighter and brighter, and then—like lights being extinguished by the flick of a switch—vanished.

The room seemed empty. Lash had faded to the far wall, and now she eyed me cautiously. I could see the concern and—to some degree—ready hostility in her face.

While the others broke out in discussion, I segued my way over to her and leaned against the wall. "You seemed a little overwhelmed. I must admit, I don't know much about the dragon hierarchy, but Vishana and the Wing Liege could intimidate anyone."

Lash let out a snort. "That's an understatement. Even in the Netherworld, the Silver Dragons hold sway over those of us with dragon blood. And in the Southlands, in the Dragon Reaches of fire and heat, the red and golden dragons still bow to the silvers. They are the imperial dragons, the most powerful. It has always been so, and so it will always be. It is *tradition*."

Her voice fell on the last word softly, and by the soft glow in her eyes, I realized that Lash was dedicated to tradition and routine. She would accept her place and bow to Vishana because, in her mind, it was the correct thing to do.

"My sister loves Shade, you know. Passionately, fervently . . . with all her heart. She is dedicated to him, and he is to her. I hope you can accept this, because the Autumn Lord has brought them together and I doubt if anybody—sister or not—can separate them." I wasn't much for subtlety, but I had to make certain that Delilah was safe.

But Lash just reached out and laid light fingers on my arm. "No fears. I will not harm her. I admit, when I arrived today, it was with the mind that their union was wrong and should be severed, but I would never have hurt your sister in order to come between them. And after seeing my brother with her, it's obvious that he's dedicated to her, that he will uphold his duty."

I frowned. It was *obvious* to me that Shade *loved* Delilah. She wasn't just a duty call. But whatever the case, it was enough that Lash was willing to let it be. She didn't have to like Delilah; she just had to avoid hurting her.

"So what are your plans? Are you staying for a while?" I was trying to find some common ground, to make her comfortable so that she'd be more comfortable with Delilah.

But she surprised me. She let out a sigh and straightened her back. "I suppose I'm going home. You seem to be at rough ends right now, and I think my presence here will just make things more tense than they need to be. I don't want to upset my brother, or Delilah, so I will leave in the morning."

"I don't want you to feel unwelcome." Where was Camille? She was so much better at playing hostess than I was. I glanced around and saw that she'd slipped out of the room, so I was going to have to field this one myself.

Lash smiled, though, and shook her head. "Quite the contrary. I don't feel like you're trying to shut me out. I did sense your not-so-subtle threat about not harming your sister, but that—too—I understand. No, I really do think that you need all your focus right now. I don't pretend to understand everything that's going on, but I gave Lady Vishana my word. I will never mention anything I've seen here to anybody. I'll go home and tell my mother that Delilah is an appropriate match for Shade, and then I'll get back to my work."

She paused, eyeing me carefully. "You do know I'm proud of the work I do? And that I feel my brother is selling our father short? We all have our places in life, and Father was chosen for his post because of his abilities. You are not one to judge his actions so quickly, I think."

I shrugged. "What can I say? Look at what I am—what I became? My father taught us to hate vampires. *He* hated vampires. Then, I fell into a nest of them—literally—and here I am. I had to learn how to cope with being what I am. I've had to unlearn a lifetime of hatred or I'd be walking into the sun. I don't have to kill to feed, to survive, but the truth is, I choose to. Oh, I choose my victims carefully, unless we're in the middle of a battle—and that's war. But I kill, and feed on others."

A little smile crept across her face. "What about when there's no one *suitable* around?"

That was a good question, with no really adequate

answer. "When I feed, I take into consideration who they are—what they are like. Sometimes it's easy. Some freak who I catch trying to rape a woman, or pimp out kids? No sympathy. I take them out and am happy to do so. But when I have to feed on someone who doesn't deserve what I do to them, I try to make it pleasant. Then, I wipe their memory and tell them to go home and rest and have a steak and anything else I can think of to ensure I do no permanent harm."

As I finished speaking, my phone rang. Eager to extract myself from the increasingly uncomfortable conversation, I gave Lash a polite nod. "Excuse me, I have to answer that."

I punched the Talk button to find my wife on the line. "Where the hell are you? I thought you were in the kitchen."

She laughed, her voice throaty and rich. "I'm downstairs, waiting for you. Make some excuse and come down here now."

The soft suggestion ran through me like a blazing fire. "I'll be there in a minute. Don't start without me." As I hung up, I glanced at the clock. It was well past midnight by now, and I was ready for a break. I flashed Lash a wave, then shoved Trillian in her direction.

Whispering so she wouldn't hear, I told him, "Entertain her till Camille gets back. I have things to do."

"Yeah, I overheard your phone conversation. You have to go *do* your wife?" But he was grinning and nodded me off, heading over in Lash's direction.

Trillian was a handsome man. His skin gleamed, obsidian smooth, and his mid-back hair was caught back in a ponytail, silver softly shimmering with cerulean accents. He could be an arrogant bastard at times, but he backed it up with action. And . . . really . . . he was a good guy. I'd grown to appreciate the Svartan over the past couple of years.

As I headed into the kitchen, toward the door to my lair, it hit me that right now, Trillian's home, city of Svartalfheim, was awaiting siege from the sentient storm. None of us—except probably Camille—had even bothered to ask him how he felt, or if he had family or friends he was worried about. The Dark and Charming Fae—actually an offshoot of the elves—didn't have the best reputation, but truth was, they'd sent help to Elqaneve. And when Shadow Wing threatened to force them under his rule, they had packed up the entire city and their sorcerers transported every building, every person, to Otherworld.

I had no clue how much the effort had cost them. That kind of magic took an enormous toll, and it had to have hit the mages hard. Unless they had somehow sourced their power off some object, or opened a door to one of the Elemental planes. That was a possibility.

With that in mind, I turned back to the living room, peeking around the corner, but Trillian was already engaged in talking to Lash. Ah well, I'd save my thoughts for later. Nerissa was waiting for me, and I didn't want to disappoint her.

As I slipped through the door and clattered down the stairs, I could already sense her waiting. Over the past months, since we'd been married, Nerissa and I had developed a bond that went beyond words. I could feel her needs, and she seemed to sense mine. I wasn't sure if this was normal for lovers, having never really had much of a love life before I was turned—and none to speak of afterward until I met Nerissa—but whatever it was, I didn't question it. I just accepted the connection.

My lair was set up like a studio apartment. Here I could ride out the night in safety. For the first couple of years nobody except my sisters, Iris, and I had known where the entrance was. But as our family grew, keeping it hidden became too much of a hassle, so we'd traded in the wooden door behind the bookcase in the kitchen for a steel one that could lock from the inside. Now it might be easier to find me, but it would be harder to get to me.

The stairway led down half a flight, then turned back on itself for another half flight, opening into a hall. To the right was the ventilation shaft through which I could come if I was too filthy to walk through the house. Directly ahead was my bath. The bath was done in pale sage, with white tiles. While I didn't need a toilet, anybody staying with me might, and I definitely needed the walk-in shower to hose off after fights, or if feeding had gotten messy.

To the left, the short hall opened into a living area with Nerissa's desk, a filing cabinet she needed for work, and bookshelves. The layout was a lopsided U, with the hallway wall dividing the bath and living area on one side, from the bedroom on the other. The "bottom" of the U contained love seat and chair in a dark hunter green and, opposite the sleeping area, a floor-to-ceiling wardrobe. The wardrobe had a full-length mirror on the door. It wasn't for me, since I couldn't see my reflection, but for Nerissa.

My bedroom—or rather, ours, now that Nerissa was living with me—contained a king-sized bed, two night-stands, a rocking chair, and a TV/DVD player. We'd had cable run though, so now the TV actually worked, though I wasn't much of a television buff. But Nerissa liked it and she didn't always want to watch the trash TV that Delilah so loved.

I rounded the corner into the bedroom, where I stopped short. There she was. My wife. Waiting on the bed, in a pink baby-doll. She was curled up beneath the comforter—my green toile had been switched out for a gold-and-black spread, and though I'd been fond of my choice, Nerissa's tastes had grown on me. They were luxurious, and opulent, and now that we were together, they didn't seem self-indulgent. I would have felt like a stereotype if I'd turned my bedroom into a passionate love nest while alone, but now it felt natural.

Nerissa languidly draped herself over the mound of pillows, thrusting her breasts in the air. I could see the warm glow of her skin through the sheer nightgown, the rose-brown nipples jutting against the silken cloth. She stretched out those long legs, which seemed to travel on forever, and slightly spread her thighs so I could see the thatch of tawny, well-trimmed curls between them. Her bush was as silken as the hair on her head, which now tumbled over her shoulders, free from the ever-present librarian's chignon.

Her hips were ample, her waist smooth and firm, and

her boobs could rival Camille's. All in all, my Amazon werepuma goddess was one big sex kitten. She let out a throaty laugh and crooked her finger at me, motioning me over to the bed.

I moaned softly, desire rising to flare in my heart. I wanted her, wanted to sink my lips into her pussy, to kiss every inch of those long legs, to lick and suck her breasts, to slip on a strap-on and go at her.

She rose up then, turning to kneel on the bed. Her skin glimmered under the light, and I stood, still as night, unable to take my eyes off her.

"Strip." She pointed to my jeans. "Get your ass over here into bed." As she cocked her head to the side, I was mesmerized by the sight of her ruby lips working their way around every word.

Slowly, I reached down and unbuckled my jeans, pulling the belt slowly through the loops to drop it on the floor. Then, just as slowly, I slid my jeans down over my hips and kicked them off. As usual, I was going commando, and I reached down to gently stroke the mound between my legs. Dredge had shaved me, carved his name into me, and the scars were still there, but now I didn't notice them; they were simply the topography of my body. I stroked my fingers across my mound, waiting as Nerissa leaned forward on her hands and knees.

She wriggled, kittenish, cocking her head to one side as a wicked grin slid across her face. Then, as I stepped toward the bed, the smile slid away and her eyes took on a golden glow as she whispered, "I want you. You know how much I want you. Please, tell me you know how much I love you."

I shuddered, her words hitting deep in my core. I'd never expected to feel this way—never in the world thought I'd find someone who made what life I had so very important. After Dredge, I'd given up hope. Then came Nerissa. And like water to a dying man, she had quenched the flaming thirst I hadn't even realized was there. She was my everything. My all. Even though I loved to play with Roman, I'd kill a dozen of him just to keep my bronze goddess happy.

With a low growl, she reached out, grabbed my wrist, and yanked me to the bed. She had me down, her lips covering my neck, my chest, seeking out my nipples. As I spread my legs, she reached down and her fingers lightly trailed over my pussy, lingering along my clit, as the fire began to build.

I wrapped my arms around her, forcing my fangs to stay retracted. And then, I was exploring, my own fingers playing a melody with her body, cupping her breasts—pendulous and ripe. I squeezed, lightly at first, but then she pushed herself up, kneeling over me.

"Don't play nice. I want it rough." Her eyes were on fire. "I want it dark and delicious and deadly."

"You know I can't drink you—you know I won't." I shook my head, unwilling to subject her to my dangers.

She laughed. "There are other ways. Your glamour—you can use it without drinking from me."

I understood then. I knew what she wanted. My lover was more like Camille than anybody knew, although Camille and Nerissa had talked about their needs before.

Unleashing my glamour, from both my Fae and vampiric natures, I focused on her. I willed her to hunger for me, to ache for me, to beg for me. And she growled again, low and throaty, and I knew her inner puma was on the prowl.

"Fuck me. Fuck me, please, fuck me. Eat me out, take me down, make me crawl for you." Nerissa was panting now, clutching the sheets between her fingers. I pushed her away and rose up to my knees. She groveled in front of me, her butt in the air, her forehead on the bed.

I reached out and smacked her ass—hard—and she let out a sharp cry.

"You want this, baby?"

She whimpered.

"You need to get out of your head?"

With a nod, she let out a choked cry. "I had to help a werewolf today whose partner had been raped and murdered. I went with her to identify the body, then counseled her. I saw the look on her face, in her eyes. I need to get out of my head, out of my thoughts."

"Too bad Venus is gone." Venus the Moon Child had guided her through learning both how to heal through sex, as well as how to release pain through it.

"You know what to do. You understand." Nerissa gazed up at me, her eyes teary. "Please . . ."

I nodded. I knew. I understood all too well. Sex for us was always loving, but it also mirrored our natures—feral and wild. I jumped off the bed and opened the drawer to my nightstand, withdrawing the black satin cord. Nerissa gave me a mute, grateful look, and I motioned to her hands.

"Wrists together."

She presented her arms. I tied one end of the long cord around her left wrist, then the other end around her right wrist. She let out a soft sigh, almost of relief. As I looped the middle of the long cord around the hook that was screwed into the wall over our bed, forcing her to lie on her back with her arms taut but not to the point of pain, she began to cry, gentle tears, but she was smiling through them.

Just as silently, I removed a blindfold from the drawer and slid it over her eyes. Then, fetching the spreader bar from beneath the bed, I buckled the cuffs around her ankles, forcing her knees into a bent position, taking care not to cause her muscles to pull.

After she was trussed up, I laid a thick dildo to one side, then stood by the bed, just watching her. Her tawny hair spread over her shoulders in a mass of waves and her lips were bubblegum pink and glossy. The blindfold and bound legs and arms gave her a vulnerable, dewy look.

I leaned down, tracing my index finger along the outline of her lips. Nerissa moaned and her tongue flicked out to touch the tip of my finger. I slid my finger inside her mouth as her lips clenched around it, sucking against my pale skin. My hunger flaring, I pulled it out, abruptly, and pressed my lips against hers, kissing her deep, probing her mouth with my tongue, barely giving her the room to breathe as the kiss went on and on, and I melted into her need.

Nerissa moaned, and a soft *"Please, oh please ..."* escaped from her lips.

I swung on the bed, carefully crawling between her legs. As I lowered my lips to her clit, my tongue circling softly around the bud, Nerissa let out a sharp cry and I felt the trembling in her thighs as she began to climb. I sucked harder, sliding two fingers inside her pussy, gently fingering her, then thrusting harder. She bucked beneath me, but I wouldn't let her go, wouldn't let her rest. Her juices smearing against my face, I abruptly pulled away.

"What do you want?" My voice was harsh, stern.

"I want you to fuck me. Make me come."

"Ask nicely." Again, the command.

And my beautiful Nerissa burst into sobs, the tears trailing down from behind the blindfold. "Please, please make me come. Please fuck me, please . . . I need you. I need *it*."

At that moment, I yanked off her blindfold with one hand, and grabbed the dildo. "I want to see your face. I want to watch your eyes."

She turned her gaze to me as I slid the dildo inside her slit. She was slick, she was wet, and as I fucked her hard, she began to writhe, crying out. Laying my head on her breast, I suckled hard, and then—leaving the dildo inserted deep within her—I lowered my lips to her clit once again. As my tongue met her sex, Nerissa buckled hard, stiffened, and then as a series of shudders rippled through her muscles, she cried out—sharp and harsh and almost in anguish. The cry stopped abruptly, followed by a sudden burst of laughter that went on and on, deep and rich and filled with freedom.

I glanced up, following the line of her body, watching the mingling of relief and joy and passion flicker across her face. A moment later, and she came to rest. I rolled up to a sitting position, slowly unlocking her from the spreader bar. She was breathing hard in the way that I knew meant she'd gone deep, yanked out the pain and worry and whatever thoughts lurked within that made her want to flee from her own mind. As I untied her wrists, she pulled me close, her lips closing in on mine. A moment later, and I was on my back, as she smiled, her puma showing through her eyes.

"I can't imagine being without you." And then, her fingers lowered to my body, and she led me into my own dance of dangers. As the night passed, the world outside faded, and there was only the two of us, together, and the passion between us.

Chapter 9

By the time Nerissa and I were done, everyone upstairs had calmed down and gone to bed. Nerissa had immediately fallen asleep, resting soundly, and I didn't want to wake her, so I decided to go outside for a walk. The night was blustery, but a little rain and weather wouldn't bother me. It had been a while since I'd had the chance to walk the land. I was becoming more of a city girl than anything else, but tonight, the creaking of the trees beckoned to me, and the stinging rain that pelted along my cheek enticed rather than warded me off.

I shrugged into a jacket—no use getting my shirt soaked—and quietly slipped out the back door, into the yard. From the bottom of the porch steps, I could see the outline of Iris's house, a light was burning in one of the upstairs rooms, and my guess was that one of the babies, or maybe all of them, was awake and demanding food. The thought of children seemed so alien. I didn't know how anybody could be brave enough to tackle the job—it was so overwhelming and all-consuming from what I'd seen.

Nerissa had never mentioned wanting kids, but I suddenly wondered . . . how did she feel about the subject? Would I be depriving her of having them? Relationships were complicated enough, especially with me a vampire. Then again, she was a grown woman. Surely, she'd thought it through. Pushing the thought out of my mind—we had enough to worry about right now without adding that to the list—I decided to cross that bridge later and turned my focus to what remained of the gardens.

Almost everything outside had been harvested except for some of the winter root vegetables. The guys had built an addition on to Iris's house—a greenhouse. So now we'd have herbs and tomatoes and lettuce and a few other goodies all year round. Smoky had also filled both freezers that were in the shed with a couple of deer, a cow, and at least two pigs. I wasn't sure where the animals had come from, but knowing Smoky, he'd caught them while in dragon form. I *did* know that the guys had butchered and dressed the animals themselves.

As I was wandering along, thinking about going down to Birchwater Pond, I saw a figure up ahead, sitting on one of the benches we'd strewn along the walkways on our land. It was cousin Shamas.

Shamas's mother—Olanda, our aunt—had died some months back. He'd landed over here, Earthside, when there was a price on his head, and had gone to work for Chase. Not all that long ago, we'd discovered that he'd studied sorcery back in OW, and that he'd fucked things up royally in an attempt to pull himself back from the darker elements he'd been connected with. It had almost gotten him killed. The news had set Camille at odds with him, something I knew broke his heart.

"Shamas, what are you doing out here? You'll get soaked through." I gingerly sat on the edge of the bench. Water didn't bother me, but that didn't mean I wanted my butt wet.

He let out a slow sigh, the air whistling between his teeth to match the gusting winds whistling through the treetops.

"Doing some serious thinking. I'm sorry about your

father. Everything has been so crazy the past few days, I don't think I got a chance to tell you that." He was the spitting image of Camille, and as I gazed at him, I thought that Sephreh had looked like this when he was younger.

"That's all right. We've all been under the gun." I had the feeling something was bothering him—something big. "So what are you thinking about?"

He ducked his head, the rain streaking down his face. "Camille. She could have died over in Otherworld. Delilah, too. You *all* could have. The three of you are so brave. You tread into these situations never knowing what you're going to find, and you face death on a regular basis."

I wasn't sure where this was going, but it sounded like a pity party to me. "We aren't that brave. We just believe in what we are doing. We don't have much of a choice, you know. Either we do it, or it goes undone." I didn't want to be cross with him, but I had the feeling that if I didn't shake him out of whatever funk he was in, he'd be useless to Chase and to us. It wasn't that depression was such a bad thing, but we needed Shamas to be at the top of his game.

"See, that's the thing. I've never really believed in anything. I've never had a cause I cared about. I'm a selfish bastard when you get down to the core. But I've made a decision." He straightened his shoulders. "With the war going on back in OW, the elves and the Svartans need help. I'm going home to enlist in their army. I'm a damned good sorcerer. They can use me against Telazhar."

Okay. So I hadn't expected that—not in the least. I wasn't sure what to say. On the one hand, we could use him right here. On the other, as long as he was around Camille, he was going to pine for her and that could end up with him in a world of hurt. Unless we were all reading the situation wrong.

I cleared my throat and turned to him. "Tell me the truth, Shamas. Are you still in love with Camille? I won't say a word."

He regarded me quietly for a moment. Then in a hushed voice, he answered. "I've never stopped loving her. Even when the Court forced me to abandon her, I never could shake her. She and I . . . we were a lot alike. We had a connection that we never talked about, but it was there. We had so much in common, but between my envy over her magical abilities, and the nobility pushing me to marry within my own caste . . ." Shrugging, he held up his hands in a helpless gesture. "I was too weak-willed to fight them."

"You know that it can never happen, right? You lost her when you turned your back on her. You lost her again when she found out you'd gone over to the enemy to study sorcery . . . when you were involved in a plot to attack the Moon Mother's grove. And don't even start about how you backed out and warned them. That was a *good thing*, but that you let yourself get mixed up in that mess in the first place . . . I doubt if she can ever truly let it go."

He pressed his lips together and I recognized the stubborn gesture from both Camille and Father. Yes, Shamas was family, all right.

"And . . . she is happy. She has three husbands and I doubt if they'd welcome a fourth." I hesitated to remind him of that fact. For one thing, I really had no clue as to how Smoky, Morio, and Trillian would feel about Shamas horning in. I could place a good bet, but I wasn't positive. But I also knew how betrayed Camille had felt and I wasn't going to ever chance that happening again.

"You're right, of course. And hanging on here, even though I try to help, it's not good for me to watch her with them. Her pity is worse than her anger." He inhaled deeply, his chest rising, then let out a sharp, strong breath. "My mind's made up. I'm going home to Otherworld, and I'm going to offer my services to King Vodox. I'm sure he'll take me on."

"My guess is that if Lethesanar herself were still in office, she'd take you back into the fold. Be careful over there, though. She still walks free somewhere, and she has a long memory." I reached out, took his hand.

"I will. You haven't seen the last of me yet." He stood, kissing the top of my hand gently. "Thank you, Menolly.

I've been wrestling with this for some time. You helped me see what I needed to see. There is no home here for me. At least not right now."

Feeling both vaguely guilty and unsure I'd done the right thing, I squeezed his fingers, then let go. "When will you leave?"

"I hate to leave Chase on such short notice, but he really doesn't need me that much. I'll go now, before I change my mind. Please, tell the others for me. I don't want any protracted good-byes or scenes. And . . . if I were to see Camille again . . . I'd probably change my mind." And with that, he turned and headed back to the shed we'd converted into a studio for Roz, Vanzir, and Shamas.

I watched him go, thinking maybe I should call him back. Maybe I should stop him. But I kept my mouth shut, and ten minutes later, I watched as he silently emerged from the studio again, a knapsack over his back, and headed down the driveway. He'd be heading to Grandmother Coyote's portal . . . and then home.

As Shamas vanished from sight, I realized that I was thoroughly soaked. I didn't feel the chill as badly as nonvamps, but it wasn't pleasant either. And the walk had brought me very little in the way of peace of mind.

I turned back to the house, and when I got inside and locked the door, I stripped off my wet clothes and shimmied into a pair of PJs I kept in the laundry room. I had no intention of disrupting Nerissa's sleep until I had to be in bed and safely away from sunrise. As I padded into the living room, I saw Delilah sitting there, watching TV with the sound turned down low. She flashed me a pale grin and patted the cushion next to her.

"Kitten, what are you doing up?" I headed over to her side and situated myself next to her on the sofa. She was in her Hello Kitty nightshirt, with an afghan wrapped around her legs.

"I couldn't sleep. Lash told me she's going home in the morning. That she's not going to interfere with my relationship with Shade. She said she had a long talk with you.

Thanks . . . I was afraid she might try to break us up." She was clutching a bowl of Cheetos, staring at the TV.

I glanced at the set. She was watching *The House on Haunted Hill*. Vincent Price was looming in the foreground, and the music was cueing up for an ominous scene. I leaned against Delilah's arm, wrapping my own through the crook of her elbow.

"Lash won't bother you." I paused, then added, "Speaking of talks . . . I just saw Shamas outside. He left for Otherworld tonight, Kitten. He's going to enlist in King Vodox's army of sorcerers to try and stop the storm."

She stopped, her hand midair, still clutching a handful of the orange cheese puffs. "Wow. I didn't expect to hear *that*."

Stuffing the snacks in her mouth, she tried to say something else but just showered the afghan with a sputter of crumbs. I snorted and handed her the glass of milk that was on the coffee table and she took a long sip, clearing her throat.

After she'd wiped her mouth, she muted the sound on the TV. "So what do you think Camille will say about him leaving?"

"I don't think she feels the same way he does. I finally got him to admit that he's never stopped loving her, and to be honest? I think maybe it's a good thing he's going away. I doubt if he'll ever shake his infatuation with her, but maybe if he's not around her all the time, he can move on."

"There's one little problem with that." Delilah frowned, shaking the crumbs off the blanket. "Suppose he goes over there and gets himself killed? You know how dangerous it is there. How is Camille going to feel then? If she even so much as suspects that he went there to get away from her, she'll blame herself."

It hit me that, at times, Kitten was much more astute than I was. Both of my sisters were. I didn't see the world in the nuances they did, and for me, life seemed like it should be more straightforward than it really was.

"Fuck. I hadn't thought of that. I guess then we have to stress that he went home because he wanted to help in the war efforts. Leave her all the way out of this one. Tell her that . . . well . . . tell her the truth. He told me he felt like he needed a cause to work for—to believe in." While that wasn't quite the truth, it would do for now and it was close enough to what he'd said that I didn't really feel like I was lying.

Delilah nodded. "Makes sense to me. I know he's been basically just putting in time with Chase. I don't know if he really liked the job or not."

"Okay then, we tell Camille that Shamas felt like his talents could better be utilized back in Otherworld, so he went home to help."

With that, Delilah turned up the sound again and I sat beside her in comfortable silence, snuggling a little, as we watched Vincent Price and the forces of the dark. As the movie droned on, Delilah fell asleep and I covered her with her afghan and turned off the television. It was still an hour or so till dawn, but I decided to go curl up next to Nerissa and rest my eyes. I wouldn't be able to sleep until dawn, but as I crawled into bed and felt her gentle pulse next to me, and the warmth of her body, I was able to drift in the comfort of being next to the person I loved most in the world.

The next evening, I awoke to find that Nerissa had left me a little love note on the pillow when she'd headed out for work. I kissed it, then tucked it away in my memento box, and headed upstairs. As I entered the kitchen, the first thing that hit me was that tomorrow night was Samhain Eve—October thirty-first. The second thing that nearly hit me was Hanna.

She was bustling from the fridge to the counter, her arms full of vegetables. A thick pack of steaks sat on the other side of the stove, and I could see Trillian on the back porch. He had fired up the grill and by the *Kiss the Cook* apron he was wearing, it was my guess he'd been dubbed the grill master for the evening. As he watched over the crackling flames, Bruce was sitting on the counter next to him, and they were talking.

Then I remembered: Our cousin Daniel was coming over for dinner. I glanced at the clock. He was due here around six, and it was a little past five now, so we had an hour.

"Excuse me," Vanzir darted in front of me, a basket on his arm. It was filled with fresh herbs from Iris's greenhouse. Camille was chasing after him, waving a trowel.

"You give those back! I was going to bundle them up to hang dry!"

"Only when you say please! I helped you harvest the damned things and then you turned around and squirted me with the plant mister." Vanzir held the basket over her head, just out of her reach.

At that moment, Smoky swooped in from behind him and plucked the basket away. He gave Vanzir a guarded look. "Don't trifle with my wife."

Vanzir snorted. "A little late—we trifled some time ago, but I don't intend to do so again. Now teach your wife some manners and maybe I won't go swiping her herbs." But he was laughing, and—after a tense moment—Smoky let out a chuckle and handed the basket back to the demon.

"Very well. Camille, say thank you to the demon for his help."

Camille glowered at him. "Big lizard. Okay, okay . . . thank you and I'm sorry I squirted you with the mister. It just seemed the thing to do at the moment."

The phone rang, interrupting the chaos, and since I was the closest, I answered. A male voice I didn't recognize came on the line, but I knew his name when he introduced himself.

"This is Tanne Baum. Am I talking to Delilah or Camille?"

It was Violet's boyfriend. He was from the Black Forest Woodland Fae in Germany, and according to what Camille and Delilah told me, he had some sort of bond with Violet that allowed him to know she was still alive.

"Hi, and no. I'm Menolly, their sister. What can I do for you?"

A pause. Then, "I have some news on Violet—I performed the ritual I told your sisters I was going to do. I don't know exactly where she is, but I did come up with some information that might help find her. Can you meet me tonight?"

I glanced at the clock. Dinner with Daniel would probably take a couple of hours, at least. "It will have to be later tonight. Ten P.M. okay for you?"

He paused, then, with a resigned sigh, acceded. "Yes, if we have to wait till then, that will work. I suppose she's been missing so long now that another couple of hours isn't going to hurt anything. Where shall we meet?"

I frowned. "What about the Starbucks on Blackthorn Street? It's on the corner, cross street Wales Avenue. They're open half the night." Also, the coffee shop was on the outskirt of Belles-Faire, which meant a shorter drive for us.

Tanne grunted and I heard the scribbling of pencil on paper. "I've got it noted down. I'll see you at ten. And, Menolly, thank you. And your sisters." And with that, he hung up.

"Who was that?" Camille had her basket of herbs and was sitting at the table, tying them up in bundles to hang from the ceiling out on the back porch.

"Tanne Baum. We're meeting him at ten tonight, at the Blackthorn Starbucks. He thinks he has a lead on Violet—said something about a ritual he told you he was going to do?"

"Oh thank gods." Delilah stopped in the middle of frosting cupcakes. She set the piping bag down and turned. "I hope he's right. This whole mess with Lowestar Radcliffe and Violet has gotten shoved to the side by everything else that's been happening, and I keep thinking, where is she? Is she all right? What must she be thinking now?"

"Well, we'll meet him after we talk to Daniel and see what he has to say. Meanwhile, what can I do?" I jumped up, eager to be busy, but the phone rang again. This time it was my cell phone, and it was Nerissa.

"Sweetheart, I'm so sorry but I'm going to have to work late tonight. Chase is, too, but he's already called Iris to tell her. So don't wait dinner for either of us. We have a rather sticky situation here—nothing you guys need to know about, but it's not very much fun. And Chase needs me here to smooth the path over between a disgruntled FBH family and their all-too-volatile OW houseguest. A few broken bones involved, and some very hurt feelings and threats of lawsuits and further assaults."

"That's going to take all evening? Sounds like an easy situation to me." Of course, compared to the crap we'd been through, anything less sounded easy.

"Well, there are extenuating circumstances. Father of the household has a daughter who is seventeen and pregnant from the very handsome, very charming young man from Otherworld. The two obviously are down with each other, but Daddy is threatening to slap him with a statutory rape charge. That's what started the argument." Nerissa sounded put out and I did not blame her. That sort of crap was a ridiculous waste of the authorities' time.

"Oh, for fuck's sake. That's . . . yeah. I can see. Tread lightly and try not to break any skulls, though if you need some help, I'll come down there and shake some sense into the pair of them. What about the girl?" I had a feeling she wasn't playing any sort of victim in this case.

"She's enjoying it. I think it tickles her to see Daddy and Lover Boy fighting it out. I have a feeling the little princess doesn't get much attention otherwise." Nerissa's laugh was derogatory, and yet I also sensed a hint of sadness there. "So yeah, don't count on us for dinner. We'll grab something here. I'll call before I'm headed home."

I punched the End Talk button and slid the phone in the holster hanging off one of my belt loops. My jeans were too tight for me to put anything in the pockets. As I once again turned my attention to the bustle of the kitchen, I thought about mentioning Shamas's departure but it wasn't really the time for that. Camille would have to know by tomorrow, but I didn't want to throw off the rest of the evening. I could tell her afterward—on the way to meet Tanne Baum.

I tried to find a way to help out with the rest of dinner, but there just wasn't room. Too many cooks, and all that. So I meandered into the living room. The first thing I saw was Delilah's laptop, sitting open. And then I noticed a file folder next to it, open. I could tell it had come from Carter's because he used specially colored folders, and a special archival brand, and this was no ordinary cream-colored file.

As I sat down, nosy, and flipped through the articles in the folder, I realized they were about the Farantino Building. That's right! Camille had said Carter gave them a folder on the building, but then with the disaster in Elqaneve, everything had slid by the wayside. Apparently somebody had decided to dig it out today.

There wasn't much in the file—a few clips out of the *Seattle Post's* business section. A couple from the *Seattle Tattler's* social section—the damned rag was going strong fifty years back, long before the Fae and Supes were out of the closet. Then, there were Carter's notes. Indications of unusual spiritual activity, in his spidery, very clear, handwriting. The dates went back to around 1914 . . . a few years after the building was erected. All in all, there had been some hints of daemonic activity since near the beginning, but it was strung out enough to where, unless someone was specifically keeping an eye on the building, it wouldn't have been all that noticeable.

So . . . let's see.

Fact number one. Lowestar was attempting to wake a sleeping demigod. Which meant that Suvika—the demigod in question—had to be sleeping *somewhere*.

Hmm . . . it occurred to me that we hadn't looked into him much yet. We hadn't had the time. I frowned. Maybe there was some information online, though I rather doubted it. He was obscure, and all we knew about him was that he was one of the triple lords of debauchery and vice. What pantheon or mythos he hailed from, I wasn't sure. At first, with his name, I'd thought maybe Hindu or Asian, but that felt off to some degree.

I pulled up a new browser and typed "Suvika" into Howl, a new search engine that was aimed at Supes and dealt first and foremost with magical information. A few seconds later, a handful of links came up. I scanned through them. Most looked like reference material.

Clicking on the first one took me to a brief, four-line entry in the MythicaPedia. Nothing there we didn't already know. I clicked back to the listings and tried the second. Again, a brief mention, only this time whoever had Tumblr'd the information had included a painting that was supposedly of the three lords of vice. The drawing looked almost Japanese in origin, but I had the feeling it wasn't. A third link led to nowhere, and a fourth. But on the fifth, I realized I'd stumbled onto something.

It was a personal entry in a magical blog that an FBH pagan had written. I glanced at the profile of the blogger, but it was only a magical name—and no information on where the writer was actually from or who he really was. But TheoLogos, the blogger, had apparently discovered mention of the demigod somewhere.

I cast a Circle of Summoning and used the root powder my grandmother taught me how to make. I was determined to bring Suvika here, to my life, even though the old texts say he is sleeping in his tomb. The conjuration worked, all right, but it wasn't the demigod who showed up. Instead a handsome man, tanned with a glow that seemed to emanate through his clothing, appeared. He was in modern wear—and I would have mistaken him for a human if I passed him on the street.

When I asked him who he was, he would not say. He only laughed and told me I was foolish and lucky— foolish because I had no idea what I had asked for, and lucky, because my demands were not granted. And then, he told me that should Suvika wake for the wrong person, he would rain down mayhem and anguish on the summoner, and his freedom would be complete.

If not controlled by the proper channel, Suvika would be all too willing to rampage through the city and take whatever—and whoever—he wanted. And then, with a pale flash of light, the demon—I believe it was a demon,

*though he might as well be a guardian angel—vanished. I
decided to abandon my quest to waken Suvika and con-
centrate on invoking someone more compliant.*

Here, the entry ended, and I quickly scanned the entries
before and after, but there were no further mentions of
Suvika. Only haphazard ramblings of a wannabe magician
who had gotten cocky, dove in over his head, and then had
gotten very, very lucky. But who had he summoned? Obviously a creature from the Subterranean Realms.

I jotted down a few notes and bookmarked the site, then
checked out the remaining links. The first three added
nothing we didn't already know, but the fourth was from a
university site. Frowning—usually universities kept their
online records to academic papers and the like—I scanned
the page, trying to figure out what I was reading. The page
looked like an image rather than text, and then it hit me. I
was reading what appeared to be an old—perhaps
ancient—book or scroll that had been scanned into the university's databanks. And there, in a few concise sentences
below a line of runes, was the entry I was looking for.

*Suvika will waken from his tomb deep in the ethers. Born of
a goddess and a daemon, when he rises, gold and silver will
fly to his beck and call. Suvika will lay claim to all women
he finds suitable for his use, and their screams will echo
against the chamber walls. His carnal lust is equal in
nature only to his lust for coin. And then, when his thirst for
both is sated, he will waken his brothers, Viatu and Levvial,
and they will use the greed of men to control the world. As
was in the days of Atlantea, and then again in Rome, so
shall be the new regime until once again, their enemies
rock them back to sleep until the next turn of the cycle.*

Okay then, that was promising. *Not.* I didn't much like
the sound of any of that, and I had no doubt that if Lowestar Radcliffe was able to wake up this demigod, we'd all
be in for a world of hurt.

Using the URL, I followed the path back to see if there was any information about what it was I was looking at. The trail led me to an entry about an archaeological find deep in a group of caverns in Mongolia. Among the antiquities discovered there were a group of scrolls, one of which I'd been reading. They had all been scanned in, but only some of them translated—hence I'd lucked out by finding that one in particular. Who knew what the others held? But by what I could piece together, it appeared that Suvika had originated as either a Mongolian or a Finnish deity—the former seemed more likely.

Considering the power-crazed lust the Khans had possessed, it didn't seem surprising to find Suvika attached to that culture. Feeling like we had a little more of a handle on things, I finished my notes as the doorbell rang.

"I'll get it!" I headed to the front door. As I swung it open, a short, thin man with brilliant blue eyes was standing there. He was grace, fluid in motion, and his hair looked like he'd just crawled out of bed but it was a good messy. He was in his late forties, perhaps early fifties, but he looked trim and fit. Dressed in a pair of indigo wash jeans with a button-down silver shirt and a black blazer over the top, he was wearing sneakers—seemingly incongruous to his outfit, but when I took the entire picture in, he made it all work. Daniel had two bottles of what looked like very expensive wine under his arm. I nodded for him to enter and he silently slid past me.

Not sure if he'd remember me, I held out my hand to him. "Cousin Daniel? I'm—"

"Menolly. I remember." He handed me one of the bottles, then took my other hand briefly, pressing my fingers with a light, deft touch. Just as quickly, he let go and looked around. "Am I early?"

"Not to worry—everybody's just in the kitchen getting ready for dinner. Come on in and meet the gang." I wasn't sure just how he'd react when he realized he was talking to a dragon, a youkai, a demon, an incubus, and whoever else might be hanging around. But we might as well test him out and see how much he was able to stand.

As I escorted him into the kitchen, I put the bottle I was carrying on the table and he followed suit. Camille and Delilah gave delighted little waves. I grinned. Suddenly, it seemed so very cool to have our very own FBH cousin in the room with us.

"You know Camille and Delilah. But the rest—this is part of our extended family." I turned to Smoky, getting ready to introduce him.

But Daniel surprised us all. He interrupted with a flourish. "Smoky—I hear rumors you might be a dragon? And you"—he turned to Vanzir—"you are some sort of demon, I believe. And unless I miss my guess—Morio, is it? Camille's second husband and a youkai? And Trillian—her third? A Svartan, I gather. You are all lucky men."

As he went around, getting everybody's name *and* background right, including Hanna's, I stared at him, open-mouthed. How the hell did he know who everyone was? Something about his easy familiarity unsettled me. We needed to figure out just how our cousin was privy to all our secrets.

Chapter 10

∾⧉∾

"How the hell do you know who everybody is?" Camille beat me to it.

Daniel grinned. "I have my ways. Trust me, I know how to find out what I need to know. And I choose to never go into a situation without knowing everything I can about what it is I'm getting into." He pointed to the wine. "I hope you like it—I wasn't sure what to bring."

I noticed Vanzir slipping out of the room, after a guarded stare at Daniel. He saw me watching him and shrugged, arching one eyebrow, then vanished around the corner and I heard the door close behind him.

Absently picking up one of the bottles, I glanced at the label. *Château d'Yquem, 1944.* Fuck, this must be one hell of an expensive wine. I glanced up at Daniel. "This looks . . . I'm not familiar with Earthside wines—for one thing, I can't drink them. For another, even though I own a bar, I've never seen this brand."

Daniel smiled. "Only the best for my newfound cousins. I have a few bottles of that tucked away."

Replacing the bottle on the table, I gave him a tight smile. Something felt off here. I glanced at Camille, and she, too, had an odd look on her face.

Morio smoothly interjected himself between Daniel and me. "So why don't you come on into the living room? Camille, escort your cousin in while I bring some appetizers." And just like that, he maneuvered Camille over to Daniel's side and had them walking through the foyer. He caught my eye, nodding for me to wait.

As soon as the pair vanished, Trillian motioned me over to his side, where he was getting ready to take the steaks out to the grill.

"He's got some game going. I can feel it. Nothing demonic, nothing like that, but he's playing a line and I have no idea what it is. That wine he brought?" He pointed to the bottles. "I know that brand, believe it or not. And that year? Those bottles? Each easily costs around thirty-five hundred dollars."

I coughed and Delilah blinked and let out a soft "mew."

Smoky sidled up. "Not only that, but his outfit? Might look casual but that jacket is expensively made and well tailored."

"Right." Trillian nodded. "Your cousin has deep coffers and I'd like to know how he got them. If I remember right, he said he's a personal shopper? Newsflash: Personal shoppers don't make much money." And with that, he picked up the platter of steaks and vanished out to the porch.

I glanced at Delilah. "Okay, then. We find out what he does. Say, where did Vanzir disappear to? I saw him skulk out of here."

"Not sure. But you know, I don't think we want Daniel seeing the documents that are on the coffee table. I'm going to go gather them up." Delilah made a beeline for the living room but I was faster. She was right—we didn't need him nosing around in what we were doing.

But we needn't have worried. By the time we got there, Camille had managed to seat him well away from the sofa and the computer. I reached the living room seconds before

Delilah, but since she was better with tech than I was, I let her slide behind the computer. She quietly shut it down and gathered up the sheaf of papers, moving them to the corner desk, along with the laptop. I was watching Daniel. He knew something was up; he followed her with his eyes, his gaze landing on the computer, then darting away to once again pick up the thread of the conversation in which Camille was engaging him.

"So, Daniel, do you work out of your home?"

I recognized that tone of voice. Camille had unleashed her glamour. I glanced sharply at her and she flickered a smile to me. *She knew.* She knew something was up.

Startled, Daniel leaned away, his eyes flashing. A fraction of a second later, he relaxed and gave her a slightly dreamy smile. "You might say that. I don't have a storefront, if that's what you mean, though I do have a private office where my . . . clients can reach me." Another second and the wariness was back. He was fighting her charm, that was for sure.

"So have you and Hester Lou always lived around here?" I had my own glamour, and cousin or not, I poured it on thick. Time to throw him off the track.

Again, a look of brief confusion crossed his face, but he shrugged and relaxed even further. "We were both born in Shoreline. I served a stint with the ISA, then left and moved back here. Hester bought her coffee shop well over fifteen years ago and it's been going strong ever since. She caters to the lesbian crowd, and they have a lot of disposable income around here."

After being Earthside long enough, I would normally have bristled at the *lesbian crowd* reference, but he said it in such an offhand way that there was no way I could take offense. But the mention of the ISA—the International Security Alliance—was what *really* caught my attention.

The ISA was an international legal organization involving the United States, Canada, and Europa, focusing on international crime. There were rumors of secret military divisions that made the Special Forces look like kindergarten.

"What did you do in the ISA, Daniel?" I didn't expect

him to answer. That kind of information would most likely be classified under a need-to-know basis. And I was right.

"Sorry, Menolly, but that's NTK." He shook his head and his gaze cleared. Apparently, our glamour wasn't having the usual effect, and ten-to-one, he'd been trained against brainwashing and that was how come he kept phasing in and out.

With a nod, I sat back, unsure of what to say next. Really, we were attempting to interrogate him, which was rude considering he was a guest and our relative, but the truth was: We needed to know what was on the table. Just then, Vanzir entered the room. He looked a little flushed, as if he'd been rushing.

He sauntered over to Daniel, and held out his hand. "Dude, nice to meet you. So you know I'm a demon."

Daniel shrugged. "It has crossed my desk that you are, yes."

"Well, *my good man*, it's crossed my desk that you're a thief." That was Vanzir. Blunt and to the point.

Daniel jerked, his eyes narrowing. "Excuse me?"

"Personal shopper, my ass." Vanzir turned to Camille. "Seems your cousin here has been hiding a rather lucrative career from the police. Perhaps he'd care to come clean unless he wants the authorities to know that he's one of the most influential, talented cat burglars—for want of a better term—of all time."

Epic. Silence. Nobody seemed to know what to say, least of all, Daniel. He sat there, silent, a quixotic look on his face.

After a moment, Camille cleared her throat. "Daniel, is this true?"

He shrugged. "You might say that. I suppose now that the cat's out of the bag, we'd better talk about it. I was going to tell you anyway, when the time was right. Truth is, it occurred to me that forming an alliance with you might benefit the both of us."

An alliance with a thief. That was a new one, though we'd allied ourselves with far stranger people. And creatures.

"How about you tell us what gives first? *Then* we'll

decide what to do." We were back to a place where I was comfortable—leaning on people.

Daniel grinned. "Don't go all fang-gurl on me, Menolly. I'm not afraid of you. I respect you, don't get me wrong, but I've been up against worse than the likes of you over the years."

Curious now—the fact that he knew about everyone in the house combined with his lack of fear made me want to know more—I motioned for him to continue.

"Since your friend here decided to investigate me before I could break the news myself, and since I have a feeling there's no way I can get out of this house without coming clean, then here it is. Vanzir—it *is* Vanzir, correct?"

Vanzir nodded, nonplussed.

"Very well, then. Vanzir has somehow managed to find out my trade. I pose as a personal shopper, and in a way, that's the truth. I take commissions from many powerful and influential men and women around the world. And then, I do my best to fulfill their desires."

"Thief for hire." I couldn't help but smirk. It had such a ring to it.

He winked at me. "I prefer to think of myself as a *procurer of wondrous and rare commodities.* As I said, I belonged to the ISA for ten years, and what I did there, I will never tell anyone. Some memories you do your best to forget. After ten years, I quietly resigned, citing my health, and went about business for another five—cultivating contacts in the art circles, in the antiquities world, among jewelers. I'm blessed with a natural charisma, which against your Fae glamour seems a bit sparse and tacky, I'll admit. But trust me, I can charm my way into almost any social setting."

As he spoke, his voice took on a rhythmic cadence. After a few moments, I realized he wasn't bluffing when he said he had a natural charm. Daniel was gifted, and while he was an FBH to the core, he'd been blessed with the gift of oration.

"So what made you decide to turn thief?" Smoky cut him off, and while he had a smooth, silky voice himself, it was almost as though something big and huge had rammed itself through Daniel's story.

Daniel gave him a sideways glance. "I have expensive tastes. There aren't many ways a man can make money. Real money. Good money. The kind of money to keep me situated in the lifestyle I've chosen. And I prefer not to steal from those who can't afford it. I consider my *liberation* of these objects to be ... well ... let me just say— most of the items I procure for my clients are investments, more than beloved treasures. I sleep very well at night."

He sat back, waiting. I glanced at Delilah, who had cocked her head and was staring at Daniel with a bemused look. Camille's expression read differently. Hands on her hips, she leaned forward.

"Nice whitewash. But really, dude? Let's face it, you're a high-class thief, just like a call girl is a high-class prostitute. Only the hooker comes by her money honestly and provides a necessary service."

"My services are necessary—"

"Oh, please." She stuck out her tongue and made a *pfftting* sound that was reminiscent of Delilah and her hairballs. "Necessary for who? Will your clients die if they don't have that Monet?"

"No, but I might. Consider this: I might die if I don't make sure they have it. My clients are not prone to being disappointed. On the rare occasions I failed to procure what they wanted, I learned the hard way just how rough some of those high-and-mighty genteel moneyed types can be." He chuckled, then took off his jacket and pushed up his sleeve. The scars on his arm were nasty. Nasty enough to make even me wince, though it was hard to tell what had happened to him.

He pointed to a jagged scar. "That's where the bone came ripping through the flesh. After I told him I couldn't provide what he wanted, Tobi—well, let's just say my client—told his body guard to break my arm. His man did a wonderful job, I have to say. He shattered my arm as if it were a toothpick and, in his enthusiasm, managed to rip the jagged edge of the bone through the skin. Obviously, I lived, but it took two hundred stitches and six months in a cast and rehabilitation to regain full use of my arm. So I now pick and choose my clients wisely, and I *always* come through, regardless of what it costs me."

I stared at him. He was so nonchalant that it began to dawn on me just how strong our cousin was. He didn't flinch, didn't even wince when he was talking about his injury. And considering he had been a member of the ISA, my guess was that he'd been trained to withstand torture.

"You were part of one of their elite forces, weren't you?" Maybe we couldn't glamour him, but I could force the issue.

He contemplated me for a moment, and the jovial smile slipped away. Beneath it lay the cold, harsh gaze of a predator, and I had the feeling that Daniel could be as deadly as we were.

"Cream of the crop, Menolly. I was the cream of the crop, top of the line. They didn't want to let me go." He shifted in his seat. "Before you ask, the reason I left was twofold. I wanted out of the danger zone. And . . . there were things we were trained to do—things I've done—that I could no longer bear on my conscience. They still haunt me, and while I know I can never atone for some of them, I had the strength to walk away."

Camille shifted in her seat. "Did they object?"

He shrugged, still somber. "It was either let me go or kill me. And I had installed a few . . . shall we call them, safety nets. They knew—and they still know—that if there's any question about my death, dominos will fall and a great deal of information about their covert operations will be revealed to the public. I'm a bitter, dangerous enemy to have, girls. And my former commander knows just how deadly I can be."

A shift in the pit of my stomach made me nauseous, and that was a rare event. I slowly lowered myself into a chair. We'd let a viper into our midst. Daniel had managed to dig up a lot of information on us in a short amount of time. I wondered—did he know about the war? And would he use that to blackmail us?

As if reading my mind, he leaned forward. "For instance, I know what you are battling. Not by name, but I know you're keeping the demons of the world at bay. And I also know you don't want that information to get out. But fear not, I didn't come here to threaten you." His eyes flashed and the smile was back. "I think we can help each other."

"How so?" Delilah stood, folding her arms across her chest.

"I can get into any place you need me to. I don't care how carefully it's armed—at least with human traps—I can spring it. I can disarm security systems. I can disarm bombs. I'm *that* good. I can dig up the actual—not just the public—but the actual floor plans of any building in this city. And in most big cities. I have contacts who can procure anything you need to work with, illegal or not."

"Are you offering to work with us?" Morio asked. He cocked his head to the side, his soft, smooth hair trailing over his cheek.

"And if I am? Are you interested?"

Camille and Delilah looked at me. I nodded for them to follow me into the kitchen. Daniel just leaned back in his chair and began to whistle.

When we were near the table—which was almost ready for dinner—Camille turned to us. "I don't know what the fuck to think about this."

Delilah shook her head. "He's certainly unlike any other FBH we've worked with."

"Not quite." I took a seat, making certain not to disturb the place setting Hanna had set. "Wilbur. Wilbur's an FBH and he's ruthless and dangerous. Just more uncouth than our cousin."

"True that." Camille frowned, poking over the cookie plate and biting into a chocolate chip one. Hanna glared at her but said nothing. "So what do we do? He obviously knows about the demons; he knows about all of us. Who knows how much other information he's managed to dig up?"

I knew my suggestion was going to garner more than a questioning look but decided to speak up anyway. "Give him a chance."

Delilah snorted. "Say what?"

"We don't have much choice. I doubt if Daniel feels any family fidelity at this point—how can he? We barely know each other. And the International Security Alliance? Dangerous and deadly. I wouldn't put much past what he's been trained to do over the years. He's probably killed as many people as we have, and my guess is a number of them have been innocent. But we also have a good deal of info on him, and we could easily turn the tables if he double-crosses us."

"So what you're saying is that we're at a stalemate?" Delilah laughed. "Why doesn't that surprise me?"

"Because it's par for the course? I truly doubt that Hester Lou knows anything about her brother's background, so we have leverage there, too. I don't know how or where Vanzir got his info but I'm damned glad he did. I just wish we could have found out before Daniel showed up here." I tried to think out the potential disasters that could come out of this situation but there were just too many variables. "We are playing poker with a master, but we both have good hands. We need to find out what he expects to get out of this, though."

"Good point." Camille smoothed her skirt. "Let's get back in there. I'm going to trust your instincts on this. He seems more prone to answering you so why don't you take the reins on this. We also have to get dinner over with so that we can go meet Tanne Baum."

Hanna cleared her throat. "Ten minutes and then I start clearing the table if you aren't in here. I'm not keeping this food warm while you all sit in there and chatter."

"Yes'm." Delilah saluted her as we filed back into the living room.

I decided the time for formality was long gone. Walking up to Daniel, I planted myself in front of him, one booted foot resting on the arm of his chair as I crossed my arms and leaned down. He gave me a leisurely smile.

"First: What the fuck do you expect to get out of this? You've told us what you have to offer, but what do you think we can give you?"

He leaned back in the chair, stretching his legs so they rested between mine. I could sense a curious energy off him, but it wasn't sexual. It was more . . . *power plays*. There was his key. Cousin Daniel liked to play with power and he liked to run the show. Whatever he'd done through his life had left him with a love for control. And he was thoroughly enjoying this.

"What do I expect from you? Knowledge. Contacts. Potential clients. I'm not looking to chase treasure with you—from what I've learned about you, you're not concerned with such things." He glanced over at Smoky. "And I have no intention of ever trying to find your treasure hoards, if you have them. I know enough about dragons to know that would be a stupid move."

Smoky let out a low snarl, but remained where he was. "You are a wiser man than many, then. Camille's cousin or not, should you come sniffing around my premises in hopes of stealing a coin or two, I won't hesitate to teach you what it means to incur the wrath of a dragon."

I had to repress a bark of laughter at the look on Daniel's face. It was the first time the veneer had cracked, and while it was only for a second until he gathered himself and the easy smile returned to his face, the brief alarm I'd spied gave me an odd comfort. It meant that—resistant to our glamour or not, and special agent or not—he was vulnerable. While I knew he was human, I'd begun to wonder just what the hell we were up against with our cousin. FBH didn't always equate to easy pickings.

"I wouldn't think of it, Smoky. I never cross friends or loved ones, or relatives." And as he said those words, a ring of truth echoed through them that even I could feel. So Daniel had his own code of honor, as skewed as it might be.

Hanna popped her head around the corner. "Either you come to the table now, or no dinner." And with a stern look, she disappeared again.

"She means it." Camille stood, motioning for us to follow. "I don't want to test her on it."

As I backed away, Daniel rose smoothly to his feet. "I want you to know, I *am* happy to meet you—not just because you are who you are and because I think we can benefit each other, but because . . . what family I have, the family I choose to remain in contact with, mean a great deal to me. I value them and I protect them as best as I can. In case you're wondering, Hester knows nothing of my activities. I keep her protected from the truth. I have no doubt of her reaction, and I don't want her worrying herself. She's got enough troubles as it is without me adding to them."

I wasn't sure what it was, but despite the weirdness of what was going on, I found myself liking him. And one glance at Delilah and Camille's faces told me they felt the same. As we filed over to the dinner table, conversation turned toward other matters.

Delilah turned to him. "So no wife, husband, children . . . ?"

Daniel grinned. "I'm straight, and no. I never married, I never will marry, and I certainly never intend to have a pile of rugrats around. In my line of work, it would be dangerous to have ties of that nature. And I do best on my own. Sex, paid companionship, suits my needs. But relationships? Not my style."

"Are you ever lonely?" I took my usual place up near the ceiling—something about levitating above the table soothed me.

"I learned long ago that I'm geared for a solitary lifestyle. And with my training? It would have been a recipe for disaster to become emotionally involved with anyone. We were on constant missions, and if I were worrying about anyone at home, I would have put my unit mates in danger."

Daniel started to pull out a chair for Camille but Morio smoothly slid between them and led her to a chair between him and Smoky. Smoky pointed to Daniel, and then the chair next him, and Daniel obeyed. Shade sat on his other side, with Delilah beside him.

Hanna had piled the table high with salads and breads and fruit and cookies, and now she held the door for Trillian as he emerged from where he'd been grilling to slide an enormous platter of steaks on the table. They were sizzling, and—for the millionth time—I wished I could eat. Even though Morio had opened up a new door for me with the flavored blood, I was always aware of what I was drinking, and always too aware of how much I liked the feel of it in my body and my throat, of how it both satiated and stoked the hunger within.

As the others fell to their food, I watched Daniel. He had lightened up and was chatting about the house, and his mother and father, and my sisters were soaking it up. It was almost as if there were two Daniels—the one who had come in preening and hinting at blackmail should we refuse to help him, and the one here—jovial, friendly, and with a winning smile. It was hard to keep from taking the bait, hook, line, and sinker.

Were both Daniels simply aspects of a very complex man? Was one side of him a carefully cultivated fake? If so, which one was real? As the evening wore on, I was no closer to having even a clue as to the answers to those questions, and by the time he said good night—at nine thirty— I shut the door behind him, feeling oddly tired.

As I turned around, Camille was sliding into her coat and Delilah had zipped up her jacket. I stared at them for a moment, wondering where they were going, but then remembered we had to go meet Tanne Baum.

"Can we all take one car? I want to talk over tonight's visit on the way." I shrugged on a denim jacket, more out of habit than anything.

"I'll drive. I've got the most room." Camille held up her keys. "And yes, I think that's a very good idea."

"Are you sure you girls want to go alone?" Trillian was leaning out of the kitchen. He glanced over his shoulder and said something that sounded like, "I'm on it."

"You want to come with?" Camille motioned to the closet. "Grab your jacket then."

Trillian slipped on his calf-length black duster. "The stakes are too high to go it alone. There are too many games going on and we seem to be pawns in a number of them."

And with that, we headed out the door.

The road was slick with rain, the wind picking up tree branches and tossing them about like leaves. We were in for one hell of a storm, it seemed, and once again, my mind raced back to Elqaneve. But the storm there was sentient, alive in a monstrous way. The storms here had energy, they had some semblance of consciousness, Camille had told us, but nothing like what was going on back home.

As she navigated the standing water that was accumulating on the roadway, Camille finally said, "I heard back from the crematorium. Father's ashes will be ready to pick up tomorrow, in time for Samhain."

"What are we going to do about a Samhain ritual?" Delilah stared out the window, her voice shaky. "We can't just let it go by. We've lost too many people. We have to—"

"We have to honor them." I normally wasn't all too upset if we put off the holidays for a day or two, but this time, I knew what it would do to my sisters. And marking the deaths of our father, Queen Asteria, and Chrysandra would go a long ways to helping us move on and focus on what we needed to be doing.

Camille sighed. "We'll do something, even if it's simple. So . . . what did you think of Daniel? I never expected anything like the bomb he dropped on us. The dude is wacked, but I kind of like him. I don't have any sense that he's out to cross us—though that isn't a guarantee."

"No guarantee at all." Trillian glanced over at Camille, then in the backseat at Delilah and me. "I would walk softly for now, but there's no real way you can put that genie back in the bottle. But tread with caution. He could be a snake, and really, what do you know about him? I'm not sure where Vanzir found out his information, but he's proving himself more than worthwhile."

"I'd also like to know how he found out about Daniel." I frowned, leaning back against the seat. "This torques me off. Why didn't we think to check him out? We're slacking."

"No, we're not." Delilah rubbed her forehead, looking stressed. "Look what the hell we've been dealing with the past week or so. Just when would we have had time to check out Daniel?" Her voice began to rise and I could tell I had upset her. "During the time we were staring at Father's body? Or when we were running for cover from the storm? Or when Camille had to steal the moccasins off of a corpse to protect her feet from the broken stone that covered the ground? Just when would we have had the time to go digging into Daniel's past?"

I held up my hand. "Okay, okay . . . I get your point. But now that we know this much about him, we'd better find out whatever else we can about him. If he can dig up the info he did on us, there has to be a way we can pry into his past. I want to know if we can trust the guy."

"That reminds me." Delilah poked me in the arm. "You better tell Camille about Shamas, if you haven't already."

"What about Shamas?" Camille glanced at Kitten through the rearview mirror.

Another little tidbit that I wasn't looking forward to revealing. "Shamas went home to Otherworld this morning."

"What?" The car swerved as she pulled over to the shoulder and turned around to stare at me. "Why? For how long?"

I stared at the back of the seat, not meeting her eyes. "I don't know how long . . . he's gone to enlist in the army, to help Svartalfheim. He told me he wanted to make a difference. We talked shortly before dawn. I was out for a walk and found him near the trail. He asked me to tell you good-bye."

She said nothing for a moment, but then Trillian reached over and lightly stroked her arm. "He'll be all right, love."

"We don't know that." Her voice was tight. "We don't know that anything will ever be all right again. But what's done is done and there's nothing we can do to stop him. We can only hope and pray." And with that, she started up the car again. "We're almost to the Blackthorn Starbucks. Tanne Baum told you he might have a lead on Violet?"

I nodded, but then realized she couldn't see me in the mirror. "Yes. At least that's one potential piece of good news."

"Great Mother knows, we need all we can get of that." She stared ahead at the road. The windshield wipers beat a steady tattoo against the rain, swishing it off to the sides, as we swept through the darkened night.

I looked out the window. So much danger for all of us. So much worry. And we weren't even facing Shadow Wing yet. What would happen if—or when—he broke through the portals? We had four of the seals. Shadow Wing had three. Two were missing. If whoever had stolen Benjamin's was aligned with the Demon Lord, then we were evenly matched. Either way, it spelled trouble with a capital *T*. I settled myself back and tried to turn my thoughts to something less daunting. Because there wasn't a rat's ass of anything that we could do about it on this cold, dark night.

Chapter 11

The Blackthorn neighborhood of Belles-Faire wasn't exactly run-down, but it had a wild, thorny feel to it. The houses were hidden behind tangled vegetation, thick hedges, and overgrown ferns. They weren't dilapidated per se, just mysterious and hidden. The area had become a haven for both Fae and Supes. Truth was, most of the Supe Community—and the Fae—felt more comfortable around others of their kind. Which was why the spate of vampire apartments going up were so popular. Wade, the leader of Vampires Anonymous, lived in the Shrouded Grove Suites—a tower of condos specifically designed for vamps. And there were at least two more condo towers going up.

When it came down to it, there was still a great deal of segregation going on among Supes and FBHs . . . but then again, there was a great deal of self-segregation as well. It would be a long time before the races were intermingling in a comfortable fashion, but overall, I thought we were doing pretty well. Change didn't happen overnight, but what mattered was that people made the attempt.

The streetlights shaded the street with a yellowish light, which highlighted the rain as it slashed down. Swirls of smoke rose from brick chimneys as we drove down the street. The wind caught them up, whipping them round and round before being absorbed into the darkened night.

I loved this time of year. Autumn, with its burnished leaves and whistling winds and incessant rains. It was my time—and Camille's and Delilah's, too. The time of the vampire and the witch, of the werecat. It was the time of ghosts and spirits and our goblin menaces—all sorts of bogies in the night.

Camille made a left turn, easing into the parking lot in the Rosecross MiniMall. There was a supermarket here—a QFC—and Bartells, a drugstore. A pizza joint, a Pad Thai noodle place, a small bakery—Seattle Supe Cupcakes—a dry cleaners, a yoga studio, a satellite branch of the King County Library System, and—of course—Starbucks.

As we dashed out of the car and into the coffeehouse, trying to dodge the stinging drops that splattered hard and heavy against us, I glanced up at the sky. Once again, the roiling cloud cover made me think of Elqaneve. While I hadn't been out in the storm proper, Delilah and Camille had described it so vividly that I could all too easily imagine what it had been like. Hell on Otherworld.

Once inside, Camille glanced around, then headed toward a table near the restrooms. A pale, tall Fae sat there. His hair was the color of spun platinum, and his eyes frosty blue—almost mirroring my own.

He stood, clicking his heels and giving us a short bow. "Thank you for coming." His accent was thick—Germanic to a degree, but more exotic, with a hint of the ancient woods lingering in his voice.

Camille got herself one of her mega-lattes, and Kitten bought hot chocolate. Trillian opted for a cup of tea. As we gathered round the table, the Black Forest Fae sat back, toying with his coffee cup. His hair was a mop of unruly curls, cut short, but it was his eyes that entranced me. Alpine pools in the winter. That was what they reminded me of. Ancient and frosty and veiled. I wondered how old he was.

The Earthside Fae were from the same stock we were, but they had evolved in a different way. They'd had to live in a world filled with FBHs, and an evolving world of technology where they were long thought a myth. Now they were emerging into the light, along with the rest of the Supes, and I had a dread feeling that there would be a backlash as they tried to reclaim their lands and the humans fought back.

"Not to slide past niceties, but you said you've had a vision of Violet?" Camille leaned forward. "We want to save her—to find her. So give us what you have."

He toyed with a piece of lemon pound cake. "I was performing a ritual that . . . I told you we are bound through a ritual, did I not?"

Camille nodded. She motioned to Trillian. "This is Trillian, one of my husbands. He and I went through the Eleshinar ritual many years ago. It bound us together like that. And all my husbands and I are soul-bound. I understand what you are talking about."

Tanne studied the pair, then gave them a faint smile. "I can see the tattoos layered under your skin. I see the connections in your magical signatures. I have that gift. So yes, you know of what I speak. I was deep in a ritual to search for Violet's signature and I finally caught a trace of it. I followed it—sending my spirit out—and what I saw was a dark labyrinth of tunnels. Bricks and broken boards lining them and faded writing on signs."

I perked up. "That sounds a lot like Underground Seattle." We'd had a number of run-ins down there. The labyrinth of underground tunnels had been created during the great fire in Seattle, when the entire area that had gone up in flames was raised up. The storefronts and shops that had once stood aboveground now lurked below the city, a testament to a forgotten time. But over the years, creatures had built new tunnels, and forged homes in the old ones, and now there was a thriving but dangerous community that utilized the underground in all too many nefarious ways.

"I traced her energy through a coiling path, until I arrived at a brick wall that covered the walkway. There were two sconces to the side, and her signature stopped there. The sconces were all a pale glow. And as I watched, a man in a suit appeared."

"Human?" Camille took a long sip of her iced latte.

"I think so. His signature reads as human. He reached up and pressed a knob on one of the sconces and a secret door opened. I followed him through, and the passage led to another door, then things got misty, then I found myself in a hallway running through a long line of cells. Violet was in one of them, crouching. She looked . . ." He stopped, his voice growing harsh. "She was bruised, and covered in filth."

I stared at the table, a slow boil beginning to rise. I glanced up to see Camille staring at me with the same look in her eyes. We'd both been there, we'd both been the victims of freakshow pervs before. Maybe we hadn't been captured to sell off as slaves, but we'd been kidnapped, used, and abused. There really wasn't much difference. Whether the psycho was out to make money on us, or out to just hurt us, the end result was pretty much the same thing. Slavery and abuse.

"There's a lot of the underground to go through." Camille turned to Delilah. "Any way to narrow it down?"

"You said you saw signs, Tanne. Do you remember what they said?"

He inhaled deeply, closed his eyes, and his breath trickled out in a slow stream. "Let me think. I see the sign—it's to the right, broken and off to the side. The words were painted in white, with a faint drop-shadow of red. I glanced at it and the sign read . . . the sign read . . . yes! The sign reads PETE'S BARBERSHOP. And there's a red-and-white barber's pole painted beside it!" His eyes flew open and he sat up straight. "That was it—Pete's Barbershop! There has to be a way we can find out where that sign is located without searching every inch of those tunnels."

"I don't doubt there is." Delilah pulled out her laptop and flipped it open, typing quickly as soon as the screen booted up. As she began to search, Trillian pushed back his chair.

"Anybody want any more coffee?"

"I'll take a cookie, if they have any." Camille held up her latte. "Still good here."

Delilah mumbled something about a brownie, and Tanne gratefully held up his cup. "Refill, please. Cream, no sugar."

As Trillian headed up to the counter, I glanced around the shop. Even this late, it was buzzing. It occurred to me that, without caffeine, the entire greater Seattle metropolitan area would shut down and die an unruly death. Both Seattle proper, as well as the Eastside—just across Lake Washington, where Microsoft and Google roamed free in the sprawl of back-to-back cities.

Camille excused herself and went to the restroom while we waited. Delilah was nose-deep into her computer and Trillian hadn't returned, so I leaned over to Tanne.

"What's the Black Forest like?"

He gave me a long, quiet look, but it was friendly, if reserved. "Your forests here—they are old and wild and tangled, and filled with fern and bracken. The Black Forest is different. We have fir, like you do, in the highlands, but there are vast swaths of beech and oak, and we have wide meadows that open out to catch the sun. The history of my area is rich—but most of it is human history—where here, the mountains grew untouched by most human mythology. Civilization is still new to the lands here, while across the ocean, it was established when there were no inklings that North America even existed."

"I think . . . I think I prefer it the way it is here, but I see how the cultural heritage over there might be a nice thing to have."

"Ah, but it is not my cultural heritage—it belongs to the humans." Tanne smiled again, and once more I was struck by the fact that though he looked very much like any handsome man on the street, his Fae blood crept out to tinge everything he said and did.

Camille returned, sliding into her seat just as Delilah popped her head up from her Internet wanderings.

"I found it. Or rather a reference to it. Pete's Barbershop was located underneath the . . . oh perfect . . . it was on the outer edge of what's now Underground Seattle, near the Greenbelt Park District. We're talking ghost city there."

I perked up. "Not near where Wade and I took out that priest-turned-vampire. Charles, that was his name. I doubt those tunnels have been cleared of rubble yet." The vamp had gone over the edge when he was turned and ended up lobbing a hand grenade at us, which of course, brought down the house. Or the tunnels, rather.

Delilah shook her head. "Different branch of the tunnels but not too far from there. Those were closed off years ago by the authorities, and now only the Supes and teenagers bent on a thrill ride go down there."

"So the sconces on the wall lead to a secret door and that is where Lowestar's operation is stashing their victims." I glanced at my watch. Ten twenty. "We've got plenty of time tonight. I suggest a raiding party. If Violet's still alive and there, we have a chance to rescue her before they sell her off." So much had gone wrong the past week, the chance to save someone—anyone—beckoned like a warm day in the middle of an icy winter.

Camille nodded. "I'm in. We need to go home and change first." She paused, looking at Tanne. "You want to come with us?"

He pushed back his chair, standing. "Of course. I'm handy with fights. I throw a mean punch and have magical abilities you might not have."

Delilah slammed her laptop shut. "Let's roll. Tanne, you driving or riding with us?"

"I'll come with you. I took the bus here."

As we headed out to the car, I couldn't help but think

this was just what we needed. Not only a break in finding Violet, but the opportunity to accomplish something—to be able to actually put a stop to at least one of the bad guys.

By her car in the driveway, I saw that Nerissa had made it home. Chase, too, by the looks of things. But unless the evening had gone badly, he'd be over at Iris's playing with his daughter.

As we walked through the door, I motioned for Tanne to wait for us in the living room, and headed into the kitchen, where I found Nerissa, parked in front of her own laptop, frowning. As she saw me come through the door, she waved me over.

"I'm starting to get e-mail from HotBod24." She had logged into the Supe Matchups website. "He's viewed my video five times already—and there have only been four other views, all from different users. He just sent me an e-mail requesting to meet."

HotBod24 had been obsessed with Violet's video on the Supe Matchups site, and he had been the one to e-mail her shortly before her disappearance, requesting a meeting. Which meant, if we were right in our suspicions, that Low-estar Radcliffe had taken the bait. Here's where it got dicey—stringing him along while we figured out our best approach.

I frowned. "No way in hell are you going to meet him. But for now, just tell him you're not sure. Ask him a few minor questions—get-to-know-you types. Don't make them obvious. Express . . . a little doubt as to whether you're ready to meet or not, but try to phrase it so . . ." I wasn't sure what I was saying.

"Play hard to get but not unattainable." Nerissa glanced up at me as I leaned over her shoulder.

"Right!" I laughed and stroked her back. "I've got to head out. We finally caught a break. We think we know where to find Violet."

She paused. "You're going to search for her."

I knew exactly what she was thinking by the tone of her voice. She was worried. She had a certain lilt, a certain light accusatory tone, that only showed up when we had to head out on a case, and I knew it was her fear talking. She'd never ask me not to go, she knew what we were up against, but the fear was there, and chances were it would never go away.

"We have to." I studied her face. "I wish you could come with us but . . ."

"But I'd be a liability. I'm trained in healing—be it through words or through sex, I'm trained to heal the soul. Not fight. I understand. But please . . ."

"I'll be careful. I love you." And with a kiss, I headed downstairs to change clothes. I was wearing a nice outfit and chances were things were going to get dirty, if not rough. I switched it out for a pair of snug but flexible indigo jeans, a black turtleneck, and a banged-up corduroy jacket. I slid on a pair of motorcycle boots and was ready to rumble.

By the time I returned to the kitchen, Nerissa had finished her e-mail back to HotBod24—a perfect blend of hesitation and promise—and she was eating dinner. Hanna had sliced some leftover steak, added gravy, and made her a thick sandwich.

"Do everything you can to save her," Nerissa said, staring at her plate. "Get her out of that hellhole."

I rested my hand on her shoulder. "We'll find her." I wished I felt as confident as I sounded. But so much had gone wrong, it was hard to trust in anything anymore. "You get some sleep. We probably won't be back till late and I don't want you waiting up like you usually do. Promise me?"

She shrugged, but nodded. "Yeah, I'll try."

Camille and Delilah appeared. Camille was wearing her Emma Peel catsuit, along with a low-slung silver belt. Her kitten-heel granny boots and black suede jacket were both gothy and yet functional for where we were headed. Somehow, she managed to look dressed for clubbing no matter what the circumstance.

Delilah had changed into a pair of camo cargo pants with a green V-neck sweater, and she had her leather jacket slung over her shoulder. Her boots—this time a pair of steel-toed hiking boots—were new, but I knew she'd been breaking them in for a couple weeks so they shouldn't present a problem.

Smoky, Morio, and Roz were waiting for us. Vanzir, Trillian, and Shade would stay home to help protect the place. Even with Aeval's guards, we still were uncomfortable emptying the joint, especially with babies in the mix now. Trillian had headed over to Iris's house to make sure everything was set for the night. Shade gave Delilah a kiss and I heard him murmur a warning for her to be careful as we headed out the door.

"We'll take two cars—Camille, you take Tanne, Smoky, and Morio. Roz and I will ride with Delilah." I preferred taking my Jag when I could, but with it banged up, I didn't want to chance using it much. And we'd be less conspicuous with two cars instead of three.

"What's the plan? Or do we even have one?" Camille snorted. "Not that we usually do."

"We head down in the tunnels nearest where Pete's Barbershop was, follow the trail Tanne did, and . . . well . . . see what we find." I gave her a fangy grin. "That's the best I've got."

"Then it will have to do. Make sure we all have our weapons. I can't use the unicorn horn till after I charge it in a few days—I expended all of its power when Delilah and I were trying to escape from that room during the storm in Elqaneve. So I'm packing silver. And magic."

She patted her hip and I saw she had strapped on the sheath to her silver dagger. Father had given each of us a silver dagger when we were younger. Delilah's had proved to be sentient, after a fashion. I couldn't touch mine now—silver and vamps didn't mix. So it stayed in my lair, on the wall in a display case.

"I'm ready." Roz opened his jacket. As usual, he was a walking armory. Stakes, magical incendiary devices, daggers, shurikens, a mini-crossbow, and gods knew what else were fastened snugly into the folds of his duster.

"You're insane, but that's beside the point. We can always count on you for some sort of destructive fire-power." Morio shook his head, but he was laughing quietly. "I'm ready. Smoky—what about you?"

"I *am* a weapon." That was all the dragon needed to say.

As we headed off into the rain-soaked night, the storm parted for a brief second, but the moon was nowhere in sight, and she was waning to dark anyway. A few stars peeked through, but they were covered over again by another incoming band of dark clouds. October had us by the balls; that was for sure.

Underground Seattle. We'd been there so much you'd think we'd know it like the backs of our hands, but the truth was, the maze of buildings tucked away beneath the city streets was labyrinthine. And with our local crew of denizens who made their home down there, the tunnels were growing—slowly but surely. What had started out being the remains of a major fire that destroyed over twenty-five city blocks of the city back in 1889 had turned into a sublevel of Seattle. An underground haven.

After the fire, the city officials required that all buildings be made of stone or brick, and they raised the level of the growing city from anywhere between ten and thirty feet higher than they'd been, leaving the burned-out shells of stores to linger in the depths below the new city streets.

The official Underground Tour had shifted quite a bit since the Supes had come out of the closet, and the reality of how large the Seattle underground had grown came to light. There were rumors at first, then a few articles had cropped up in the papers, worrying about the stability of the city considering the network of tunnels was growing. But officials were quick to quell fears.

As to what the truth was? I didn't know. And I doubted that *anybody* really did. It was far too chancy to attempt to map out the network, because the FBHs were gradually beginning to realize just how dangerous some of the Supes could be. Chase had mentioned not long ago how much busier the FH-CSI was becoming as the regular police force turned over more and more cases to them. In fact, he'd mentioned that at the last biennium, his department had seen a substantial increase in funding.

All these thoughts and more ran through my head as I called shotgun and slipped into the passenger seat in Delilah's Jeep. Roz and his personal arsenal climbed into the back. He was a one-man army of weapons, and we'd come to rely on him for anything we might have forgotten.

Delilah led the way, with Camille following. They both had the GPS coordinates to the area we were looking for. I wasn't thrilled that we were headed back into the Greenbelt Park district. It was haunted—severely haunted—and while we'd discovered just what had been causing a lot of the intense ghostly activity, and dispatched it—hopefully for good—the spirits would take quite a while to calm down. And by *quite a while*, we could be talking years.

The streets were empty. Seattle was a busy city, with a bustling metropolis, but at night, most of the business districts and a lot of the suburbs were quiet, the activity going on behind locked doors. Oh, in the Broadway District, or the U District, things were different. The streets were filled with students and hipsters, with junkies and hookers, but here it was fairly quiet.

The rain pelted down, hard bullets of water tap dancing against the pavement. The businesses in this district were run-down and shabby, as were the houses. Everything had been let go—and while nothing seemed to be in rack and ruin—nothing actively falling apart—neither were the buildings in great condition. It was as though nobody here cared. There was a feeling of abandonment that permeated the neighborhood.

Delilah swerved to avoid a blown tire in the road, then pointed to a building up ahead. "That warehouse? It's abandoned. It's also got a basement entrance into the tunnels. We can slip in through there."

I frowned. "Anybody using the building that we know

of?" Walking into an abandoned building had never done us any good. There always seemed to be somebody staked out in it.

"I don't know." She laughed. "I guess we pay our money and take our chances." And with that, she turned into the parking lot and swung around back. Camille was following us, and within minutes, we were parked and out of the cars, staring at the back of the warehouse.

The building was three stories high, but we had no clue how far belowground it went. We knew, thanks to Delilah, that there was a basement, but whether that was the extent of the warehouse was anybody's guess.

The place had been a storehouse of some sort, by the looks of the loading docks. The building was brick or concrete or some sort of stone—it was hard to tell what lay under the layers of dirty cream-colored paint. The metal roll-up doors were probably locked, but a regular door stood to the side, and chances were we could pick that lock. This setup seemed to be standard with the warehouses we'd found.

It crossed my mind that it might be handy to have someone like Daniel with us now—he was supposed to be an expert at getting into buildings, and he was used to holding his own in a fight. But then again, how many times had he gone up against a goblin horde? Or a troll? Fighting other humans was one thing. Fighting Supes who were stronger and tougher than you, quite another. Chase had discovered that, all too painfully.

Tanne knelt down by the door. "I know the charm of unraveling. It is akin to the charm of unlocking, but I don't know if it will work." He glanced up at us. "I am a spell singer by nature. I can charm fir and oak. I'm not so handy with metal, but I'll try."

I stared at him. This was a new one to me, but Camille seemed to understand what he was saying.

He began to hum, a low tune—slow and melodic. The sound became a whisper of words in a language I couldn't understand, but I could feel the magic behind them, and the spiral of sound built until I could almost see the shape of a creature emanating from Tanne's lips.

He held out his hand and sure enough, a vaporous form—bipedal and vaguely humanoid—stepped onto his fingers. As he reach out, holding his hand out to the door lock, the creature delicately bent down to touch the lock, and then, in a puff of smoke, it vanished into the keyhole.

We heard the sound of grating, then a faint tumble and click. The door sprang open and Tanne sat back, squatting on his heels, staring at it.

"I can't believe that worked. But then again, the spell of Unraveling is stronger than the spell to charm locks." He stood, letting out a long breath.

I stared at him for a moment. "You aren't nearly as afraid as you should be. Unless you've done this sort of thing before."

Tanne shrugged. "Fear destroys. Fear tears plans and people to pieces. I lived in the ancient forest, where the dark arts are honed to a brilliant degree. My people are not gentle, and neither are the humans who share the forest with us. I brought my skills, and my legacy, here."

"What legacy is that?" It was apparent Tanne was far more than he seemed to be at first notice, but often people with real power were. They didn't need to parade it because it was there, tangible.

"I come from the Woodland Fae, yes. But my people are more than this. People know me as a writer, but my family . . . we are the Hunter's Glen Clan. We've chased down demons and monsters for centuries. Back in the Black Forest, my mother leads the clan. My sisters and I learned from her, and now some of us have emigrated here. We are establishing our own niche."

Camille turned to him. "You really know how to fight, don't you?"

He smiled faintly. "I can hold my own. As I said, I've protected myself over the years in more than one skirmish. And I've destroyed more than one monster. I will tell you more later, if you are interested. For now, let's search for Violet."

"I'm least likely to be harmed by a sneak attack. Let me take the lead." As I moved in front with Delilah, Roz and Tanne swept in behind us. Camille and Morio came next— they worked in unison with their death magic and needed to be able to clasp hands for some of their spells. Smoky played rear guard.

The door led to a darkened hallway. The air was musty, as if nothing had stirred through it for a long time, so I was hopeful we'd make it through to the basement without incident. But we needed light in order to see.

From behind, Morio whispered something and a glowing orb of green light suddenly appeared in the air behind me. Foxfire. One of the youkai-kitsune's natural abilities. It hovered alongside me, lighting our way enough to see a few yards in front of us.

The passageway was like any hallway that had been let go for some time—a feeling of abandonment permeating the air, both in sense and in smell. Our movement stirred up dust from the floor, and the ceiling was covered with cobwebs and spiderwebs. By the looks of things, nothing had ventured this way in a long time, which was a good thing for us. But then again, ghosts didn't stir up dust usually, so I didn't want to get too cocky in case we were surprised by an unwelcome spiritual visitor. The hall ran on for some distance, forking off to the right along the way.

"We want the third hall to the right," Delilah whispered in a falsetto voice. "That should lead us to the basement." She gestured to the next turn. "That one. Turn right."

"Where else would we turn? There is no left turn." I gave a little snort, but turned where she'd motioned to. We were facing another long hall, but it jogged to the right up ahead, after ending at a door. "Is that it? The door to the basement?"

Delilah nodded. "I think so. We'll find out for sure soon enough."

As we reached the door, I stood back to allow Tanne room to examine it. He shook his head. "No lock. Not locked. And I have no ability to tell if it's trapped. That would be one of my sisters' specialties."

Morio took his place. "No traps that I can sense," he said after a moment. "That doesn't mean there isn't one, but if there is, I can't place it."

"Well, here goes nothing." I reached out and turned the knob. As the door inched open, a dark hole appeared and I realized this was, indeed, a staircase leading down. So probably to the basement. But something stopped me before I stepped into the passage.

Get out. Get out now.

"Did anyone hear that besides me?"

"I did," Camille and Delilah said simultaneously.

"Oh fuck. Please, please don't tell me we're dealing with ghosts here." But at that moment, my plea went unanswered because a whooshing sound erupted from the open door as something rushed by on a gust of air.

The next thing I knew, Rozurial was struggling as something was yanking on his coat. He tried to shake it off, but the material was flapping in some astral wind and then—before any of us could do anything—one of those damned magical bombs he carried exploded and the hall was filled with ice crystals, a hail of sleet raining down on us.

Camille let out a shout as Morio stumbled and his foxfire vanished. Behind them, Smoky let loose with a blue streak of cursing.

But before any of us had the thought or time to move, another explosion from Roz's magical bomb stash rocked the air. This time fire ripped through the passage, the magical flames lighting up the corridor with an unnatural glow. The explosion sent me reeling, almost deafening me, but through the ringing in my ears I made out one other sound—the sound of Rozurial screaming as flames consumed him and the hallway filled with smoke.

Chapter 12

❧❧❧

"Fuck! Roz, are you all right?" I scrambled in the darkness that followed the fiery blast. The magical flames had exploded, then burned out within seconds, as frozen rain pelted the hall through the darkness.

"Roz! Rozurial!" Camille and Delilah were calling his name, too, but there was no answer. A moment later and the foxfire suddenly blossomed into view again, lighting the area. Morio was focusing on it, and the flames kept growing until there were several of the lights dancing around us.

"I don't see him anywhere." Smoky raised his hands and the sleet began to die down. "Is he on the ground? Did he fall?"

"I don't know! Did you cause the storm?" Camille turned to him.

"Yes. When I saw the flames engulf him, I did the only thing I could think to do in order to smother them." Smoky was about to say something else when a force slammed past me, into Delilah. She flew back, as if whatever it was had punched her in the stomach. As she landed on her butt, up against the wall of the passage, a low laughter echoed along the hallway.

"That's not demonic. I can't sense demon anywhere." Camille grabbed for Morio's hand. "Ghost?"

I was about to say, "What else?" when Tanne sprang forward.

He pushed us to the side. "I know what it is! Let me through to face it."

Reaching up, he clasped an amulet that was hanging around his neck, and fell into a soft whisper—again, a tune that was as magical as the chant he was invoking. The rush of power that surrounded him was immediate, and dark, and felt like predatory dogs on our heels. In fact, I thought I could hear the baying of a hound—not a wolf—but some large dog, hungry for blood.

"What the fuck—" Camille started, but then fell silent.

Morio stared at Tanne. "I know what you are." His words were soft, but I caught them, and Camille did, too, by the look on her face.

Delilah and Smokey were working their way along the side of the wall, trying to sneak behind Tanne and whatever the fuck it was he had engaged. If they could make it through, they could check on Roz.

Tanne started backing up, but he didn't look afraid. No, he was fishing—luring the thing toward him. As he coaxed the thing toward him, it began to materialize and take shape. What had been a misty field, a ripple in the air, now formed into a dark, winged shape, slowly moving forward. Its wings were arched, oddly reminding me of a spider's jointed legs. The creature looked like a miniature dragon, only bony, murky, and blurred. Its eyes glowed, a neon green that bordered on blinding, and they were focused on Tanne.

He continued to sing—whatever the invocation was, it seemed to be mesmerizing the thing. As he drew it away from the door, Smoky and Delilah were able to slip past and inside.

I glanced at Tanne, wondering if he wanted us to attack,

but until he gave the word, I wasn't going to interfere. Morio and Camille were holding hands, and I had the feeling they were prepping a spell.

As Tanne backed it down the hallway, I glanced over at the door. Relief swept through me as I saw Smoky emerge with a soot-covered Rozurial. He looked a little shaken, but was on his feet. The next moment, Tanne raised one hand and began drawing a rune in the air—his fingers leaving a trail of glowing light behind them as they traced the sigil. I had no clue what spell he was casting but it looked like nothing I'd ever seen before, curled and coiling, with smooth, rounded strokes rather than angular.

A moment later and the creature froze, hanging in mid-air. Tanne held his hand steady, keeping the rune alight.

"Attack now, while it's paralyzed. Hurry—it can be attacked with silver or death magic." His voice echoed through the hall.

That left me out, but Delilah immediately readied Lysanthra, and Roz pulled out a short blade from his duster o' weaponry. But before they could move in, Morio and Camille held out their hands, a purple flame encircling them—they were the hub in a wheel of crackling electrical fire.

They moved forward, hand in hand, until the edge of the flames was just on the outskirts of the creature. Then, with a loud *"Mordente elektris!"* they surged forward, engulfing it with their spell. A loud crackling filled the air, then the sound of shattering as the smell of ozone filled the hallway. A moment later, the winged beast shattered into dust and vanished, as soot showered the floor. The flame vanished, and we all stood there staring at the powder that dusted the hall.

"First things first, Roz, are you okay?" I turned to him, eyeing him up and down. "You hurt?"

He shook his head. "Nothing a little ice and balm won't cure. I was lucky, though. Any more and the rest of the fire bombs I'm carrying would have exploded on me. Then I would be looking at hospital time."

"What was that thing?" Delilah poked at a pile of the shattered cremains.

Tanne shook his hands, as if to shake off excess energy. "A daeflier. The creatures are from the Subterranean Realms, and although they are not daemonic—or demonic—by nature, they are vile tempered and enslaved by daemons and demons to be guardians. It was a sentinel, placed here to guard against anyone going in that basement. They can only be harmed by silver and death magic. Fire—actual flame—will empower them. Ice and water won't faze them. Physical attacks—unless made with silver—just bounce off."

Silver had a natural ability to both harm and repel a number of demonic creatures, including myself. Vampires, incubi, succubi, we were all considered minor demons, and while we hadn't been conscripted to the Sub-Realms along with all the other demons, we were still affected by the essence of the metal. Each metal had an elemental energy to it, a primal force that was considered a god by some people, and each of those forces had its own attributes. Silver hated demonic energy and could bite it. Badly. Just like unalloyed iron hated the Fae.

"Then we are on the right track. If Lowestar is using the tunnels beneath this building and in the area to hide where he's keeping his slaves, then it makes sense that he would use the—you called them daefliers?"

Tanne nodded. "Yes."

"Then it makes sense he would use the daefliers to guard the way. He's a daemon, after all. But . . . do you think there are more, and what can they do to us?" I glanced at the door, nervous. I had nothing to use against these critters. And I had no clue how many times Morio and Camille could cast their spell without draining their energy.

Tanne shrugged. "As to whether there are more, I cannot tell you. It depends on how much he values his operation. I suppose, we have to be prepared for the possibility. Therefore, let me go in front with you. I can hold them. As far as what they can do to you? You saw the blast—that was no trap. That was the daeflier. They can be lethal, and they have claws that can rip open the aura and let the life force bleed out."

"Lovely. Just what we need." I motioned to the others. "Regroup."

We shifted positions, and then Morio cast another fox-fire spell and we headed into the open door.

The doorway led to a stairwell, leading both up and down. We, of course, chose the downward route, though Roz silently slipped up a half a flight to scope out whether anybody—or anything—was waiting on the upper level. After a few tense seconds, he returned, shaking his head.

Tanne and I in the lead, we headed down the steps. They were wide, like most stairwells, and the steps were smooth, concrete, with a solid railing. Each level ran two flights deep, each flight turning back on itself. Unlike a spiral staircase that was open, we couldn't see all the way to the top or bottom.

We'd come in on the main floor, and we descended two floors down without incident to reach the basement level. The door at the bottom, however, made me uneasy. Was another daeflier lurking behind it? Had the one we'd destroyed triggered an alarm that we didn't know about? Any number of possible scenarios flashed through my mind, none of them good.

Morio tapped me on the shoulder. "Let me look for traps. I might be able to find something."

I moved back as he took my place. Tanne knelt by the base of the door. Just what he was examining, I didn't know, but he was intent on something. The others nervously shifted on the stairwell. Smoky stood at the back, guarding the rear. He had a stern, almost alarmist expression on his face.

A moment later, Morio tapped Tanne on the shoulder and pointed to something—I couldn't see what. Tanne scooted over next to him, looked, and then nodded. They stood and Morio motioned us up the stairs.

When we were crowded on the landing above the basement door, Morio let out a long sigh. In a low voice, he said, "No magical traps per se, but we have a security system rigged to trigger if we break through the door. And I sense a similar setup on the astral level if we attempt to gate through the door using the Ionyc Seas or anything else like that. The magical system is set to trigger if the door has not been disarmed. See that panel down there that we uncovered? That's the panel for the Defense One system."

"Oh great. Without the code, we can't get through?" Camille frowned. "And you're certain there's something similar on the magical level?"

Morio nodded. "Yeah. Tanne agrees with me."

"The magical system is bad enough, but the Defense One system? A real bitch." The Black Forest Fae looked unusually grim. "I've dealt with these before and they're bastards to disarm. I know I don't have the knowledge."

"I can take care of simple locks but nothing like that." Delilah leaned against the wall.

Tanne glanced at her. "Somehow I doubt any of us is going to have the know-how to disarm it. Without the code, we're screwed."

"What will the magical side of the alarm do?" Camille stared at the keypad as if she could bore a hole through it with her gaze.

"Think of it this way: If you trip it and don't key in just the right code, it will trigger whatever it's rigged to do. And that could be anything from an explosion to unleashing a hellhound to setting off an alarm."

"Do we have to disarm both?" If we had to not only disarm the physical one, but take care of the magical alarm, we were doubly screwed.

"No. As I said, if we disarm the physical alarm, the magical one should disarm itself—at least that's the way it looks." Morio looked over at Camille. "So what do we do?"

"I haven't the faintest." Camille crossed her arms, frowning at the door.

"Well, there has to be an access panel for the Defense One system—all we found was the keypad but you know it has to be hidden somewhere along the wall." Tanne began searching the wall, squinting by the light of the foxfire.

"Tanne is right." Delilah was holding Lysanthra by the

hilt, the tip of the dagger pressing against her opposite index finger. She was gently twirling the dagger back and forth.

"Do tell." I grinned at her.

"All security systems have to have a setup. Now if this were purely magical, maybe it wouldn't. But since there's an FBH system in place, there *has* to be a panel or something in the wall for the wiring. With some security systems, it's obvious where they are, but Defense One? They put mega-bucks into making it as hard as possible for a thief to find. If we can find the panel, we can probably disarm it that way."

Bingo. That we could work with. "Scour the walls. Just be cautious not to trip off anything."

Morio and Camille joined Tanne in the search. They seemed to be the best bets because of their experience with magic and with traps. After about five minutes, Camille held up her hand.

"I think I found it." She gestured to a place on the wall that looked like . . . well . . . *wall*, to me. But I did notice a slight depression about the size of a finger in the area to which she was pointing.

Morio and Tanne motioned her to move aside, and then they examined the spot. After a moment, Tanne let out a low laugh.

"This is it. Hidden panel leading to the access, I'll bet you anything." He gently pressed a finger against the indentation, and sure enough, a panel slid back to reveal a hole in the wall. A contraption the size of a square dinner plate rested inside, wires feeding into it, then through the wall toward the direction of the door.

"Okay, now we just have to figure out how to take it down. And that's not going to be easy." Morio shook his head.

"Damned straight. Defense One is the top security system in the nation." Tanne cocked his head, examining the panel. "I have dealt with a few of them, but this isn't the best way for me to test out my skills."

A lightbulb went off in the back of my brain. "I know who can do it. But we have to call him fast." I looked at Camille.

She groaned. "You aren't thinking of who I'm thinking of, are you?"

But I already had my phone out. "We have no choice. None of us can take care of this without endangering all of us, as well as anybody locked behind those doors." I punched my Contacts and found the name I was looking for. Within seconds, he answered.

"Hello?" Daniel's voice was easy on the ears; that much was for sure.

"Hey, it's Menolly. Listen, we need your expertise. But we need it *now*—if you have the time. I don't know what we can give you in payment, but we'll think of something." A man like Daniel wasn't prone to philanthropy for philanthropy's sake.

But he just chuckled. "That was fast. Well, you're in luck. I happen to still be in Seattle right now. Where are you, and what am I facing?"

I gave him the address and directions on how to find us. "You need to hurry. And as to what you're facing . . . ever disarmed a Defense One security system before?"

"Yes, and I'm intrigued. I'll be there in ten minutes . . . hold tight. And don't touch anything without me. I have experience with this sort of thing." With that, the dial tone sounded. He'd hung up without so much as a good-bye. But then again, men like Daniel usually didn't engage in chit-chat much.

"Daniel's on his way. Smoky, can you go topside and wait for him?"

"I think you're making a mistake, but yes, I will." The dragon shook his head at me, then turned and swept up the stairs.

We waited. With a little luck, nobody but Smoky would come down those stairs, and nobody would come bursting through that door before Daniel got here. While we waited, we kept quiet. It wouldn't do to attract any unwelcome attention. I was relieved so far to find a distinct lack of ghosts. Though given the choice between fighting spooks or disarming this door, I almost would rather have the ghosties. At least they hadn't ever exploded on us. So far.

Sometimes the universe actually tossed us a break.

Ten minutes later, nothing had happened, we were still in one piece, and Smoky reappeared with Daniel behind him. Daniel must have carried a change of clothes with him, because he was dressed in dark jeans and a sleek turtleneck. He had on fancy sneakers and was silent as a cat. Around his waist, he wore a belt that had a number of gadgets attached. Delilah glanced at me and mouthed, "Bat utility belt," and I did my best to stifle a snort of laughter.

Tanne motioned him over. "The Defense One system is tied into a magical alert system. If you fail to disarm it, and the DO system trips, the magical alarm will also go off, and there's a good chance it will set off something far worse than just a warning system. But we believe that if you can disarm the Defense One system, it will also disarm the magical alarm."

Daniel barely said a word, simply approached the open panel and took a peek in. A moment later and he rubbed his hands together, almost gleefully. "Oh, this isn't so hard. I've taken down systems much more complex than this."

He moved in, pulling a few tools out of his belt. It was hard to see what he was doing from where I stood, but his attention and focus were apparent. Daniel loved his work— that much was clear. And he was also incredibly capable of keeping his mind on what he was doing. Even though Morio and Tanne were watching him intently, he didn't budge, didn't look up. Just worked away.

Ten nerve-racking minutes later, he let out a slow sigh, and then turned back to us. "When I flip this lever, the door will unlock without an alarm. I take it you need to be ready to move in."

"Do you have any clue what we're doing?" I eyed him, trying to ascertain how much he knew.

He grinned. "Only enough to know I don't want to be around when the heavy artillery comes out. I saw the blast marks upstairs. And while I'm still clueless enough to keep me out of trouble, I'll leave you to your work. Just give me a call and let me know you all emerged in one piece."

Smoky was gazing at him, and it was impossible to read what the dragon was thinking by the look on his face. All he said was, "Let me make certain you get out safe." He turned back to us. "I'll be back in a minute."

"You do realize that when I flip this lever, if anybody is right inside the door, they're going to know someone is coming in."

"We'll take that chance. Flip it, and then hightail it out of here with Smoky as we head through." I motioned for him to go through with it.

Daniel lightly reached out and clicked a small lever. A few seconds later, there was a light click from the door and Camille opened it. We were all steeled for whatever might be on the other side, but again, for a change, we lucked out. An empty hall awaited us.

Smoky tapped Daniel on the shoulder and they headed upstairs as I slipped through the open door, followed by Tanne, Delilah, and Roz. We didn't know if the door would lock again or sound an alarm if it was closed and reopened, so Camille held it ajar and we waited for Smoky to reappear. Hopefully keeping it open wouldn't cause problems either. Morio waited with her. But it was only a moment and Smoky returned, and the three of them hustled into the hall. We let the door quietly close behind us. I listened, waiting for the latch to catch, but heard nothing. Maybe we were catching a bit of a break after all.

The hallway was short, and it was brick. Old brick. Near the end of it, on the right side, was a crude archway that looked like it had been formed out of a large hole in the wall.

"It looks like somebody blasted through here and then tried to repair it in order to shore it up." Roz moved to the front. "Let me take a look at it."

I motioned to the others. "Stay here while we check it out."

As we approached the opening, I saw that he was right. The actual stone arch wasn't really smooth—it was jagged.

A wooden trestle, looking to be of polished hardwood, had been fitted into the opening for support. While it was snug, there were plenty of gaps around the edges where the bricks had been shattered in a nonuniform manner.

"Looks like something blasted that hole, and then whoever built this decided to leave the opening but make it safer." Roz reached out, his fingers sliding along the polished beam. "That's hornbeam. Also known as ironwood. It will hold up a lot of weight, and with the opening being only three feet wide, it should last a good long time. I'd surmise the wood has been treated, as well."

"So it seems the actual hole may have been an accident, but the resulting arch keeping it open is deliberate." I pondered this for a moment. "It makes me wonder just who blasted this open in the first place. Goblins are known for coming through these tunnels—remember the ones near Pioneer Square? Somehow they managed to find a rogue portal down in Underground Seattle, and I don't know if that thing is still there or not."

It occurred to me that, in all the chaos of the past couple years, a few things had slipped by the wayside and we really should attend to them. Like rogue portals and who was watching them, and other such little goodies. Knowing we were spacing on things wasn't really conducive to feeling secure, and I wondered what else we'd forgotten along the way.

"Could be. Goblins like brute force; that's for certain. The hole has been around far too long to ascertain what kind of explosives ripped it open. But we should get moving. The longer we loiter here, the more chance we have of being caught." Roz's jaw was set, and he looked unsettled. "There are bound to be bigger and badder things down here than the daeflier. And I'd rather take them by surprise than the other way around."

"Good point." I peeked through the opening.

Sure enough, it led into Underground Seattle; that much was obvious. The tunnel led to the right and left, although to the right was bricked up after about ten yards. To the left, faint lights were affixed to the sides of the walls. I wasn't sure if they were electric, or battery operated. I doubted they were magical. Though down in the underground, it was hard to tell.

There was no one in sight, so I motioned for the others to join us, and Tanne retook the lead beside me, with Delilah and Roz next, then Camille and Morio, and lastly—Smoky. With a dragon holding our guard, we all felt more comfortable.

There was a special feel to Underground Seattle, no matter where you were in it. Passing what had been discarded shops, with their faded signs from the past, served as a stark reminder of how time put to rest all things. People who had lived here were dead, and many—forgotten.

While the city authorities had done their best to block off large portions of the area, both the humans and the Supes who inhabited the underground had opened them right back up, as well as adding new tunnels.

And, of course, the Demon Underground had its own niche beneath the city. I dreaded the thought of a major quake striking the area, which it could easily do, seeing how Seattle was built over a major fault zone. A lot of lives could be lost, as well as an entire subculture of the city.

The passage we were in was narrow. It might have been an alley for the way it looked. The floor here was brick, but there were signs that, once, there had been planking over the brick till somebody had gotten the idea to rip it up. I wasn't sure why, but chances were the wood had eroded away in the dampness.

I looked over my shoulder at Delilah. "Which direction was Pete's Barbershop? I hope it's to the left or we're going to have problems."

She nodded. "Left, it is. About two blocks."

We headed out, as quietly as we could. The bricks seemed to muffle the sounds of our footsteps, but coughs and words reverberated in the silence, and somewhere ahead, the echo of dripping water steadily beat out a cadence. Must have been either a leak in a pipe, or something of the sort.

Along the way, I examined the lights that were affixed to the walls in regular intervals. They were, indeed, electric. Power had been run down through the Underground for years. The soft glow of the forty-watt bulbs was enough to see by, but not so bright that they illuminated every nook and cranny.

"Do you notice something?" Delilah asked after a moment.

"What?"

She motioned to the sides. "No intersecting tunnels. This passage seems to be blocked off from the rest of Underground Seattle. First the brick wall back on the other side of the entrance, then no other exits."

She was right. This did seem to be its own little corner of the world.

"I hadn't noticed, but now that you mention it, you're right. You say we have about another block to go? There should have been other tunnels leading off here—for the alleyways, etc. In fact, I thought we were already *in* an alleyway."

She shook her head. "No. It just feels narrower than usual because it was a side street. However, again—yes. There should be tunnels branching off, with the amount of building and expansion that has gone on down here. But nothing."

By the looks of the tunnel, there had been more than cosmetic work done down here in the past ten years.

"I'll bet you anything, Lowestar had some renovation done down here to give him more privacy. It would make sense when you consider the scope of the operation that he's running. It's probably a multimillion-dollar business. He's not going to jeopardize that—nor is he going to risk being found out. Even if the FBH courts wouldn't know what to do with him, you can bet some angry Supe would do their best to take him out."

Delilah laughed. "I know somebody who would probably love to get his hands on this knowledge. He could make book with it so big."

Camille chimed in from behind. "Are you talking about Daniel?"

"Daniel? No. I'm talking about Alex—someone I met not long ago at the Supe-Urban Café. He owns the Fly by Night Investigations Agency. He and his crew are bounty hunters in a sense. They not only take on paranormal cases, but go after rogue Supes. I'm surprised you haven't met the guy, Menolly. He's a vampire and his IT guy is a werewolf."

I frowned. The name of the agency sounded vaguely familiar. "They're in Seattle?"

"Yeah. I thought of him because his last name is the same as our villain's. Radcliffe. But without the *e* on the end. And there's no connection; that much I can tell you. I checked into it. Alex was originally from Australia." She let out a chuckle. "Not your usual vamp either."

I wanted to ask what she meant by that, but just then, we reached the end of the road. Literally. The tunnel ended at another brick wall. But to the right, we saw a sign. PETE'S BARBERSHOP. And against the brick façade built over the mouth of the passageway were two sconces.

Tanne pointed. "That's what I saw. We're here."

"Then we're close to Lowestar's cells. Did you notice any sort of trap, any other action he took when he came through here?" I gazed at the Fae, hoping to hell he was remembering correctly.

He shook his head. "No, he just fiddled with the sconce and the passageway opened. There's a knob back there, I can see it. That's what he was turning. I'll do it. I just hope to hell we find her in one piece." He moved forward, his lips set.

There wasn't much I could say to that. A woman he loved had been kidnapped and was slated to be sold to the highest bidder. The only thing we could do was pray she was still here, and hadn't been farmed out yet. If she'd been auctioned off, we might never be able to find out where she was.

Behind me, Delilah readied her dagger as Roz pulled out a silver short sword. I could hear Camille and Morio ramping up some sort of spell, and Smoky was, as ever, poised for action. I gave Tanne a silent nod.

He moved to the sconce and reached up, hesitating just a single heartbeat before he twisted the knob. Another heartbeat—I could hear his heart pounding in his chest—and a brick panel slid back.

On the other side, waiting to greet us, stood four armed guards. They weren't Tregarts—think burly biker-demons— but they reminded me of them. And they were fully armed with coldset iron blades—close enough to unalloyed iron in nature that they could do nasty damage to the Fae—and heavy-duty bullwhips. I shuddered. Demons or daemons, there were subsets of both who were so fucking good with whips they could behead a man with a single flick of the wrist.

Then, as they parted slightly, we could see behind them. There, lumbering like a giant three-headed Rottweiler, was a hellhound. He was almost shoulder high to me, huge and with eyes as fiery as his nature.

"Crap! Not hellhounds." Behind me, Camille groaned and I could hear her heart pounding. The monsters had acid in their blood, and, in one battle, Camille had been on the wrong end of it. She still bore the scar.

As the guards pushed forward into the hallway, we fell back, making room for the looming battle. Then, before they could make the first move to attack, I took the initiative and launched myself forward. And once again, the fight was on.

Chapter 13

❦

As I raced forward, I decided to take on the hellhound. He couldn't do as much damage to me as he could to my sisters, and they could probably handle the daemons easier.

The daemons weren't prepared for my attack, and I managed to launch myself off the floor, over their heads, to land behind them. Turning, I shoved them both, forcing them to stumble forward, which would give the others an advantage. Then I whirled to face the hellhound.

The creature was full grown, meaning he was nearly shoulder high to me. Black as night, the three-headed dog had fiery eyes, and each of those heads was rife with teeth that could rip flesh and sinew. I had already decided that one of the best ways to take it down would be to avoid shedding its blood. That way I wouldn't chance the acidic liquid spraying on the others.

One thing about hellhounds—they were intelligent. They were guarded, cunning, and volatile. And they didn't have a lot of patience. When I landed in front of it, there was no hemming or hawing. The hellhound met my aggression, lunging forward, the center head with jaws gaping, ready to bite.

I kicked it under the chin, the force of my foot shoving the freak up off its front legs and skidding it sideways. Before it had time to regroup, I slammed into its side, pushing it farther back, away from the main group. I could hear shouts from behind, and I knew that the fight was on, but I didn't dare chance glancing over my shoulder to see how they were doing.

The hellhound scrambled, recovering its footing as I hit it again. No time to think—no time to plan. I was in out-and-out *beat it senseless* mode. But this time, it was ready for my attack and its right head swung around, the gnashing teeth grabbing hold of the sleeve of my jacket. The monster yanked, and—even though I'd seen it coming, I wasn't prepared for the force of the brute. I stumbled, falling as my arm slipped out of the sleeve, and as I rolled, I pulled my other arm out. But it dropped the jacket the minute it saw me pull away.

As it lunged again, I scrambled to my feet, but the creature landed against me and sent me flying back. Before it could snap at my face, all three of the thing's slobbering jowls looming over me, I managed to roll away, and once again, come up into a crouch. I wondered what the fuck would happen if I tried to drink it down? Would acidic blood hurt me? The acid was corrosive but I didn't know if it would react like fire on me. I decided a sample taste couldn't hurt. Well, maybe not too much.

Leaping on its back, I leaned down and sank my teeth into the skin. Immediately a foul-tasting liquid poured into my mouth, stinging like hell. I spit it out as I felt welts rise up inside my mouth from the corrosive blood. Well, hell, that wasn't going to work, and now the fucker was bleeding from the place where I'd fanged it.

The hellhound yelped and the left head let out a curse in some language I couldn't understand, while the right swung the body around and thrust its muzzle at me, this time latching on to my leg. I yelped—even if I could survive an attack like this, it still fucking hurt.

I brought my hands down, fists clenched, on top of its head with full force, driving them deep into the skull. Bones shattering, the sound of my hands meeting brain was one I never got used to—a sucking, squishy sound that left me nauseated and yet oddly elated.

"One down!" As the teeth let go of my leg and the hellhound staggered, I was on my feet, and this time I grabbed the tail, spinning it around. Heavy as it was, I was stronger, thanks to my vampiric nature, and I managed to lift the creature off the ground a few inches, whirling it like I was Thor, wielding his mighty hammer. As I built up momentum, the hellhound seemed to realize it needed to book its way out of my grasp and began to struggle, so I waited till I was facing away from the group, then let go.

The hellhound went flying through the air, landing against the opposite wall with a massive thud that actually shook the ground, dazing the two heads that were still alive. It was still foggy—meaning, I'd just bought more time.

I moved in again, racing forward to land on its back once more. This time I brought my fists down on the second head, which seemed to be the smarter of the three, and once again, the crunching of bone, the shattering of skull, and another one was down.

As the remaining head howled, I grabbed it around the neck and abruptly twisted, rejoicing in the strength of my body, the elation of the kill, the feel of its life draining away in my hands. Reveling in the bloodlust as my hunger flared, I rose up with a low growl, turning to see how the others were doing. I was in my game, ready for more.

The others were still facing off with the guards, but they couldn't get near enough to fight. The lead daemon had a pair of whips out, going a mile a minute, and he knew how to use them. He alternated sides as the whips became propellers, dangerously lethal. They could take a head off, slice a throat, rend flesh. The crack of the whips echoed through the air with ear-popping precision as he moved forward, his buddies behind him.

Camille and Morio had backed a ways down the hall. They were holding hands, preparing a spell. Magic might be our only hope right now, unless we could get those whips away—but then, I realized, I was facing the back of the daemons. They seemed to have forgotten about me, leaving me to the hellhound's devices. I had the perfect opportunity to narrow the odds a bit. Within two shakes I bounded across the room and launched myself at the one in back, grappling him around the neck and pulling him to the floor with me.

He went down hard—he was big and heavy and his leather armor was stiff to the point of being wooden. I had the upper hand, having surprised him, but I wouldn't for long, so I took full advantage of my position. I grabbed a handful of his hair as I sat on his chest, used it to yank his head off the ground, then smashed it against the floor. He let out a shout as he tried to push me away, but I back-handed him, hard, and his neck snapped to the left with a nasty crack. He wasn't dead, but that had to hurt.

Apparently, one of his buddies noticed the scuffle, because the next thing I knew, I was unceremoniously ripped off my opponent's belly, and I found myself flat on my back to the side of him. As he rolled out of the way, I saw the daemon standing over me bring his whip up, and the next thing I knew, the whistling tip had sliced through my clothing, leaving a long gash on my left side.

The pain made me gasp, but I managed to roll to the side, avoiding his next flick of the whip. Then, I readied myself, and on the third crack, before he could yank it back, my lightning-quick reflexes allowed me to grab the end.

He didn't count on me being a vampire—with the accompanying strength—because when I gave a hearty yank, he stumbled forward, close enough for me to catch the back of his leg with my toe. I pulled, jerking my foot, and he went down in a tumble, falling on his buddy.

With the both of them in a tangle, I shouted for help just as some sort of an explosion went off. It sounded magical by nature, so I could only assume Camille and Morio had let off some spell.

The next moment, Smoky appeared in a shimmer—thank the gods for the Ionyc Seas—and he ripped into my opponents, talons lengthening as he intervened between the daemons and me.

Never anger a dragon. Even in human form, Smoky was a nightmare on the battlefield, and he managed to slice through one's armor, neat as a pin. The other daemon—the one who I'd first attacked—scrambled back, like a crab scuttling along the sand. He was weaving erratically as he tried to get out of the way, and I realized I'd managed to give him a pretty nasty head injury.

Before the prone daemon could lift a finger to protect himself, Smoky let loose with another slash, neatly eviscerating him. As a pile of steaming intestines and other internal organs came pouring through the wide, deep gash, the daemon let out a howl, then fell silent, his head dropping to the side. With one last strike, Smoky slit his throat to ensure he was dead, then turned to the other daemon, who had managed to stagger to his feet, but was still weaving back and forth.

"I've got this." Smoky pushed past me, and within seconds, the other daemon hit the ground, his throat bloody. The sight and scent of the blood stimulated my predatory nature, and I knew that I had to feed, and fast, because both the scent and the rush of the fight were pushing me over the edge.

"Give me space." I stared at Smoky.

His gaze flickered to my face, then he simply nodded and turned back to the others. I fell on the dead daemon, the thirst gnawing in me as I sucked up the blood, licking the wound joyfully.

There was power in the blood, and life force, and it sang in my mouth. I had tasted demon's blood before and it had frightened me with the strength and nasty aftertaste it left behind. But this . . . this was different. The daemon's blood—at least this one's—was sweet, and full in my mouth. Ripe and fruity and sparkling, like champagne. I reeled. What the hell? I'd had reactions to blood before but this was . . .

The room began to spin and I let out a low laugh. I wanted more. Wanted a mouthful, a bellyful, wanted to drain the whole damned river of it that was flowing out of the creature. I fell on him, savaging the corpse, practically rolling in the stuff. Elated, feeling dizzy, I sucked up as much of the blood as I could before I realized Smoky was pulling me off the body.

"Let go! Let me go!" I struggled with him, furious, wanting only to return to my bloody feast.

"Camille—we need you!" Smoky bellowed out as he held me fast.

In my haze, I noticed the other two daemons were down and Camille was running past their bodies. She took one look at the situation and let out a loud command.

"Listen to me!" Her voice rang through the room, and though she didn't have complete control of the command voice, it was strong enough to make me take notice. And in that brief moment, I could tell that I'd been drugged. I struggled for focus, struggled to regain control of myself.

"Can you hear me?" She came closer. Smoky had hold of me, and strong as I was, he was stronger.

"Yes—need to focus. Need . . . control . . ." My sight kept phasing in and out, a bloody blur of lust one moment, and brief glimpses of clarity the next.

"Dilute it!" Roz raced over. "If she gets clear blood, it should dilute the daemon's blood. At least it makes sense to me."

"But who . . ." Camille glanced around. "I'd be too weakened if she fed from me."

"Never—" I'd made a vow never, ever—even in the direst circumstances—to drink from my sisters. And I'd never break that vow, even at the expense of my own life.

Roz quickly stripped off his duster. "I can handle it. She can drink enough from me to hopefully get this under control." And he moved in as Smoky continued to hold me, baring his neck.

I stared at the creamy skin. I'd *fucked* Roz once before but I didn't *drink* from friends. "No . . ." But then the haze came over me, and all I could see was the pulsing of his jugular vein, and all I could hear was the throbbing of his heart.

Grabbing him to me, I sank my fangs in his throat, making it as sensuous and pleasant as possible. He moaned, leaning into me, as I drank, his sweet blood filling my mouth. But because he was a minor demon, like me, it wasn't as sweet as human's blood—or as the daemon's blood had been. I suckled, the rush of warm, sticky fluid filling my mouth, and swallowed deep gulps. A moment later, I realized what I was doing as the raging thirst began to taper off.

Abruptly I let go, pulling my fangs out, and with a horrified understanding of what had just happened, I went limp in Smoky's hands. But I didn't have time to angst over it, because a door I hadn't previously seen opened, and two more of the daemon guards burst through, with another hellhound behind them.

Smoky let go of me. "Just don't drink their blood!" he shouted as he raced forward before they could get their whips out. Delilah was on his heels, along with Tanne, who was flashing a silver blade. Roz must have given him the short sword.

The trio intercepted the guards, but the hellhound came around from behind, making a beeline for Camille. She screamed and let loose with a bolt of her Moon Magic, and this time it hit square center, singeing the hound's center head. It howled and leaped for her.

Morio backed up a step and transformed into his demonic self. He bared his teeth, sharp and gleaming in that vulpine muzzle of his. He was suddenly towering over the hellhound, eight feet tall. He swiped down, his long black talons gashing into the head of the creature.

I decided it was safer for me to help Morio, and so I attacked the hellhound from behind. I grabbed it by its haunches as Morio ripped at the heads, and then I got the idea to get hold of one of its legs and pull. Hard. The sound of snapping bones ricocheted through the air and the hell-

hound let out a howl from its right head, even as Morio
gashed through the throat of the left one. He shouted—a
little of the acidic blood had spilled on him.

At that moment, Roz appeared and he tossed a little
white ball in front of the hellhound. "Scatter!"

As Morio and I obeyed, an explosion encased the creature in ice. It froze, hardening, and then while it was paralyzed, Roz stabbed it through the heart with a heavy spike,
which looked to be steel. The blood that started to ooze
froze as it touched the surface. Roz pulled the spike out and
cautiously wiped it on the hellhound's fur.

I turned my attention to the other two guards but Smoky
and Tanne had managed to take them down somehow. As
we stared at the carnage around us, I realized that the insane
thirst had died down and I was feeling back to normal.

"Well, we know there are probably more of those guards
down here, as well as hellhounds." I looked around, grimly
assessing the situation. "We better have our act together.
All of the guards are wielding cold iron, which means they
are probably guarding whatever Fae that Lowestar and his
groupies have nabbed. They also all seem to have these
handy-dandy bullwhips and they know how to use them.
And the hellhounds are trouble in their own right. We can't
just wing it, because trust me, while I was able to handle a
slash from the whip, I don't think most of you could."

In fact, the welt from the whip had healed over and was
a thin red line now. That was one of the wonderful things
about being a vamp—healing at a highly accelerated state.
But if Camille or Delilah got hit by one of those whips?
They could be healing up for a long, long time, and their
scars would be for real.

"Where the hell are we?" Delilah looked around.

"Oh, yeah." I realized that we'd been engaged in the
battle immediately upon opening the door, before we knew
where we were headed. As I glanced around, I realized
it was some sort of guard post or headquarters room. There
were weapons cases on the walls, with extra blades and
whips in them. Harness hangers, with hellhound harnesses

ready to go. A table to one side held logbooks, but they were in a language I couldn't read.

Tanne took a look at the words. "Daemonic. I don't know the dialect, but I recognize the basic pattern. Look—there are five columns. Single numbers in the first. In the second—can't read, but they're all capitalized and I'm thinking . . . names? The next two columns contain numbers—what appear to be dates or maybe times. Some of the lines have a time or date recorded in one column, but not the next. And the fifth column . . . again, I have no clue."

Roz studied the logbook for a long moment. "I think . . . I think I may have an inkling of an idea. Prisoners. My guess is the column with the longer words—I think those are names. The date they're brought in, the date they're brought out?"

Delilah peeked over his shoulder to examine the papers. "That might be it. If so . . . then there should be five prisoners locked in the cells. There are five that appear to be logged in, and haven't been logged out yet."

"Five." I stared at the desk. "We can't leave the other four and just rescue Violet." A sick feeling swelled up at the thought. We couldn't leave the others to face the slaver's block.

Smoky's voice was gentle as he placed a hand on my shoulder. "We won't. I promise you, if there are five prisoners, we will rescue all of them."

I flashed him a smile, grateful again that he was my brother-in-law. "The door over there must lead to . . . well . . . Tanne, did you see this place in your vision?"

He shook his head. "No, but bear in mind, magical visions are often highly influenced by what we are seeking to discover, and some of them are more metaphorical in nature. I think perhaps I was searching for Violet so I skipped some intervening steps. But because we found the sign and the sconces . . . I want to believe that we're on the right track." He looked a little crestfallen and I realized he thought I was insinuating this was all a waste of time.

"I think you're right. We just need to be cautious moving forward. Those guards are nothing to dick around with, and the hellhounds are deadly."

With a nod, he brightened. "There we agree. We move forward carefully. I wish I could send out a seeing-eye spell to scout ahead but that only works in the forest."

Camille jerked around. "You know the seeing-eye spell?"

He grinned at her then. "Oh yes, I learned it when I was young. You understand what it is, correct?"

"Only too well. It's one I tried and tried to learn but it kept backfiring on me. We need to sit down and have a long talk when this is over, about what you can do, and what spells you know. We might be useful to each other." She pointed to the door. "I think that's our only option. I don't see any other exits."

"We could send Rodney down for us. Send him to check it out. If nobody is on the other side—and we have to hope for that—then maybe a twelve-inch-high skeleton won't be noticed." Morio rolled his eyes. He was back in his human form now.

"Oh gods, do we have to?" Camille grimaced.

"Remember, Grandmother Coyote told you that Rodney may save your life someday." Delilah snorted as she said it, and I had the feeling it was more to get a rise out of Camille than anything else. Although Grandmother Coyote had definitely done exactly that.

"Oh fine. If he can keep his mouth shut and not draw attention to himself." She crossed her arms and moved away. "Little freakshow pervert."

Morio grinned and opened his bag. Within the messenger bag, he kept a skull—which he needed to have near him in order to shift forms. But he found what he was looking for, and pulled out a miniature coffin. Delilah frowned and moved over by Camille. Rodney hadn't made such a good impression on the women of the family. Or the men. Or anybody really. In fact, Rodney was in line for our *least favorite jackass ally* award.

As Morio opened it, there was a slight stir, and then, the

twelve-inch-high bone golem slowly sat up and looked around.

"Hey, bitch-boy, what you up to?" And he was off and swinging.

Rodney could easily have been the love child if Howard Stern and Rodney Dangerfield decided to procreate. He fancied himself a comedian and a hot date—as much as a genital-free bag of bones can *be* a playboy, but he'd managed to come up with some creative—if gross—suggestions.

Rodney reveled in the crude, lewd, and rude. In other words, he was an unwelcome, unlikable companion who happened to be under a geas to obey Morio. And he'd been a present from Grandmother Coyote, which meant no arguing and use him for what we could use him for.

"Shut up and listen." Morio picked him up by one bony arm and set him on the floor. "I want you to go through that door when we open it, and providing nothing blows you to smithereens, you sneak down the hall. Then come back and tell us what you see. *And you keep your mouth shut while doing it.* No drawing attention to us. Got it?"

Rodney glared at him. The light in his eye sockets was disturbingly intelligent. "And what if there happen to be traps on the other side of that door?"

"Then you might find yourself in a dozen pieces. Any other questions?"

"Fox-butt, you've got a hard heart." Rodney turned to see Camille, Delilah, and me standing there. "Maybe I can plead a little sugar from the boobs brigade? A kiss for the road? A ride up the river of your pussy before I go?"

Camille looked ready to beat the shit out of him. Delilah sputtered. I just moved forward and smoothly snatched him up to face me at eye level.

"Maybe we should hand you over to the Maiden of Karask for a play toy? How's that sound, bone-brain?"

Rodney sniggered. "I'd take her on. Skin is skin and cunt is cunt. Give me a willing broad and—"

It was no use. No matter what we said or did, Rodney would be Rodney. I brought him close to my face, but not close enough for him to reach me with his now-flailing arms.

"If you don't behave, we stick you in a dollhouse, dress you in a frilly apron, and make you listen to Martha Stewart reruns all day."

Delilah meandered over. "Or better yet, we'll have a craft marathon and see just how sparkly we can make you. We'll get a Bedazzler and glitter and—"

"Whoa—now, Pussycat, hold on there." Hands on his hipbones, he let out a long, put-upon sigh. "Bitches, you really know how to wound a man's ego, don't you?"

"Oh trust me, we can think of far worse torments." I grinned now, enjoying watching the little son of a bitch squirm.

"Fine! Fine! I'll behave."

And that was that.

Rodney waited by the side of the door as Smoky and Morio prepared to open it. We all tensed, waiting, drawing what weapons we had and thought would be effective against the daemons and hellhounds.

As Morio inched the door open, Rodney peeked through. A second later he popped back in the room. "Nobody out there, Fox-butt."

"Then get your ass down the hall and remember which way you went. Don't take a lot of twists and turns. We're looking for a jail area, with a few Fae locked up there. Or Fae and Supes. Doesn't matter—we're just out to find the cells in this dungeon." Morio leaned down. "Remember—you fuck up, you blow our cover, you're bone dust in a graveyard."

"Or so sparkly you'll make Liberace look Amish." I wiggled my finger at him. "I don't make promises lightly, remember that."

"Remembering!" But as he slipped back out the door, I heard him mutter, "Bloodsucking bitch, I'll give you something to suck on."

I didn't bother responding. Instead we waited, on pins and needles, hoping he wouldn't blow it for us, hoping that the little trash-talking skeleton could keep his fucking mouth shut.

Five minutes passed. Six . . . I was about to suggest we head out without him when he came rustling back with the pitter-patter of little bony feet. Rodney slid inside the room.

"I found them. The cells. And there are four women and one man there. Those bitches look cold and dirty, by the way. Their cells aren't the Holiday Express Hotel, and there's a lot of shit on the floor and, bitch"—he turned to Morio—"I mean that literally."

Morio looked over at me. "We have five people to rescue, then, as Rozurial thought we might."

"One more thing—I didn't see no fucking hellhounds or pretty boys in black leather, but there's something there. I could sense it. Don't even bother to ask what because that is not *my* job. I'm not a pay-for-play psychic." Rodney leered at Camille—and yes, bone golems can leer. "I'd pay to play you, though, Boobette."

Morio swept him up and shook the crap out him. "One. More. Comment. To. My. Wife. Just one more . . ." He set the bone golem down again, and this time, Rodney kept his eyes—or what passed for them—to himself.

Camille snorted as Rodney cracked his neck back into place. "That *something* could be anything. Did you see anything, or just sense it?"

"Just sensed it." Rodney muttered something under his breath but quickly stopped when Morio leaned down to stare at him. "What? I'm not saying nuthin' . . ."

"Precisely. Now grow. We need you full size. There have been too many dangers tonight. We need more firepower and we don't have time to summon anyone else. Chances are we'll never make it in again after they discover the breach in their security. But remember: One misstep and—"

"I'm bone dust. Bag o' bones. Graveyard fodder. Sparkly like a pony. I know, I know." Rodney let out an exasperated sigh.

As we watched, he began to grow to full size. This was

one ability none of us were comfortable with, but there was little we could do about it. So we made use of it whenever possible, or when we could stand to have the freak around.

As he stood there, gleaming ivory bones the size of a grown man, it struck me how odd our lives had become. We were steeped in death—all around us—from losing friends, to relying on perverted bone golems, to fighting zombies, to dealing with our own personal paths. I was a vampire—one of the undead. Delilah was pledged to one of the Harvestmen—a harbinger of death. And Camille was a Dark Moon Priestess and a practitioner of death magic. We'd all strayed down the dark alley so far that there was no going back. And that . . . that was okay.

"I guess then we head out?" I moved to the lead, stopping beside Rodney. "You come up front with me and Rozurial. And no funny stuff, no jokes, no butt pinches or boob grabs. Got it?"

"Color me a rainbow and poop sparkle turds. Yeah, I got it."

"Then, Delilah and Tanne, you take second flank. Camille and Morio, third, and Smoky, watch our backs, dude."

"Will do, Captain Menolly. Lead on." The dragon saluted me, but there was a twinkle in his eye that told me he had no intention of trying to take over. In fact, all our lovers let us lead. They might offer suggestions and sweep in to save the day now and then, but they knew we three were at the foremost helm of this little war, and they gave us all the space and freedom we needed to make our decisions. And for that, I was ever grateful.

"Okay, then. Let's get a move on, and let's go rescue those prisoners."

"I just hope one of them is Violet," Tanne whispered behind me.

I turned to him. "I hope so, too," I said. "I hope so, too."

Chapter 14

As Rodney led us through the hall, it ran through my mind that if the golem could sense a dangerous energy, then whatever it was had to be strong. Rodney wasn't the brightest bulb in the psychic socket, and he'd never been one to be sensitive in any other direction either.

The area we were in looked like it had been tunneled long after Underground Seattle had come to be, but it wasn't new or fresh. I wondered who had originally built it, and why? Had it been Lowestar, or had the original architect been up to some *other* low-life project?

The walls were cool and slightly damp, and they were shored up by a dark brick façade. Whether it was dirt or stone beneath the wall, I didn't know and it didn't really matter. The floor was smooth, and I thought it might be concrete. Lights—electric and dim—ran the length of the corridor.

We hurried, making quick time. We'd been lucky since we killed off the guards back at the secret entrance, but who knew how long that luck would hold up?

As we rounded a corner, Rodney pointed to the passageway that unfolded in front of us. "There are your cells."

Along the tunnel, on either side, were iron-barred cells. They were dank, and Camille and Delilah coughed. I deliberately inhaled, and the smell of feces and urine, of mold and decay, filled my lungs.

"Great Bastus . . . I've been here before." Delilah quickly began to move forward, not touching the bars but looking through them. "I was here when I was in Gerald's mind—when I saw the girl sitting in the cell. And—there she is!"

We hurried forward, but not before I noticed another woman in the cell next to hers. The woman looked up at me, and in the depths of the despair on her face, a hope blossomed. Hell yes, we had to get them all out.

I stared at the iron bars, willing them to break open. Of course, they didn't. But Smoky moved to the front, with Morio beside him. They motioned the rest of us aside, and Morio took his demon shape. Smokey took hold of one bar, Morio took hold of the one next to it, and they pulled, their muscles straining against the heavy iron bars. I wanted to help, too, but the bars were unalloyed iron, pure and harmful to me. Even though I'd heal, it would be a nasty burn to my hands since my half-Fae nature still ran within my veins.

The bars groaned as they bent, resisting the call to open. And then, a moment later, a siren pierced the air.

"Fuck! Alarm!" I turned, readying myself for a fight.

"Enough with this." Smoky closed his eyes and vanished. Within moments, he appeared on the inside of the cell. The woman looked up at him. "Is your name Violet?"

She nodded, speechless, and he broke the chain that tethered her to the wall, gathered her up, and vanished. Roz raced down to the cell next to hers and did the same, only he used one of his firebombs to blow the chain out of the wall. Since he had originally been Fae, he groaned when the iron shrapnel singed his arm. But ignoring the burn, he gathered up the woman in his arms and vanished.

That was all well and good, I thought, but we still had

three prisoners, and now we were down two of our best fighters.

Delilah, Tanne, and Rodney took one side. I took the other, and Camille and Morio stood in the middle, preparing a spell. We had no clue what was going to answer the sound of those alarms, but no doubt, something would.

A moment later, we had our answer. Something swooped in on us. It wasn't a daeflier—that much even I could tell. No, it was translucent and hard to see, except for the concentric circles rippling around it, like stones landing on water in a pond. Whatever it was made no noise, but the next moment, it soared up toward the ceiling and dove for Camille and Morio.

They raised their hands, joined together, and shouted, "Reflect!" and a thin shield of purple covered them, emanating out of their hands. Another second and the creature bounced off it, spun in the air, and came toward me.

I had no clue how to fight it, or whether its attack would even be physical. But that question was put to rest as it slammed into and through me. A rush of icy cold air curdled my veins, making it hard to move. I was fairly immune to the cold, so whatever this was must be damned chill because if it could affect me, I dreaded to think what it might do to the others.

It launched itself at me again, and this time, I tried to fight back—swiping at it as it came near, but my hand hit the rippling air and pain nearly knocked me senseless. I reeled back as it barreled through me again, and this time I could barely move; it felt like my body was frozen.

"What the fuck *is* this thing?"

Tanne ran to my side. "I think I know. I fought one of these in the Black Forest. I'm surprised to see it here!"

"W-w-what is it? H-h-how can we fight it?" I was stuttering, my lips barely able to form words. Every movement was a struggle, like I was sinking in quicksand or molasses.

At that moment, Smoky reappeared, along with Roz.

Tanne motioned to Roz. "A *sichbarmon* is attacking her! 'Invisible ghost demon' is the best translation I can give you.

They are from the Netherworld and they use the power of cold to drain the life force from their enemies. We fight it with fire. The fiery explosives you have? Do you have more?"

"Will they work on a ghost?" Roz hunted through his pockets.

"If they are magical, they will."

At that moment, the creature dove at me again and, once more, blasted a wave of snow and ice and bone-chilling cold through me. If I'd been alive, I'd now be a corpse-sicle. I let out a croaking sound as Camille and Morio fired off a spell at the thing, but their magic bounced off.

The next moment, Roz shouted, "Close your eyes!" and I struggled to obey. I'd no sooner shut my eyes than a wave of warmth and heat spread over me, and a shockwave so loud I couldn't hear a thing after that except for a nasty ringing in my ears.

But the paralysis began to lift and I was able to move a little. Tanne raced in, grabbing me and dragging me to the side, as the sichbarmon dove again. Roz tossed another bomb at it, and this time, the ripple in the air lit up in a brilliant flash, then vanished.

Tanne's mouth moved and he said something but I couldn't hear it. Then he turned to me. I watched his lips. "Are you all right?"

I nodded, slowly dragging myself up to my feet, using his shoulder to balance on. "I can't hear. How long will this ringing last?"

Everybody stopped and turned to look at me. Great, I was the center of attention and so not for a helpful reason. Tanne turned me to face him and pointed to his lips. I nodded and watched as he mouthed, "It will wear off of you quickly, being vampire. But if you were human? Or Fae without the vampire? You'd be dead, as well as deaf."

Smoky and Roz hurried to bring the other three prisoners out. I couldn't make out any of the conversation, but Smoky grabbed two of them around the waist—a man and woman—and Roz took hold of the last woman, and they vanished again.

Delilah grabbed me by the arm and motioned to turn around. Torn, I resisted. We'd come this far—could we find out more? But then the realization of our current state hit me. We'd found Violet. We'd rescued the other four prisoners who were trapped there with her. I was running zero in the hearing category. And we were dreadfully undermanned for a mission of this sort. We'd managed to luck out with some nasty bruises and scars, but who knew what lay farther beyond in this complex. Reluctantly, I nodded, and we headed back the way we had come at a quick jog. The sooner we were out of here, the better.

By the time we reached the secret passage, I was relieved we'd turned around. I was also beginning to hear again. Lowestar would find out about this soon enough, and he'd probably bring an army with him. Morio, Camille, and Tanne's magical signatures were probably all over the place, and no doubt they'd figure out who had rampaged through, killed the guards and hellhounds, and stolen their *merchandise*.

And tonight, I really didn't want to find myself on the end of a pissed-off major daemon.

We made it out without incident, skirting the dead bodies. I stopped and picked up several of the bullwhips by the entrance to the secret passageway. They fascinated me and I thought it might be fun to have them around.

Morio confined Rodney to his coffin again and the bone golem went without so much as a peep.

"We don't have far to go, but the longer we stay down here, the more nervous I get." Camille glanced around. "I have the feeling something is looming and I don't know what, so it's making me antsy."

We sped up, and by the time we reached the door with the alarm, Smoky and Roz were waiting on the other side.

"We figured that you would be on the move, so we decided to wait here for you rather than try to backtrack and find you. Come on—we've accomplished this mission and we better not hang around. Besides . . ." Smoky paused, then drew a long breath. "Trenyth called on the Whispering Mirror. News from the war front. Not good, he says. But he wouldn't tell us till you get home and are there to hear."

Great. Another thing to worry about. But I tried to focus on the positive. We'd rescued five people tonight who would otherwise have been sold into slavery. They couldn't go back to their daily lives, though—too much chance Lowestar would track them down and wreak revenge, or try to silence them before they could give out any information.

In fact, the thought occurred to me that, once he realized they were gone, he couldn't just go back to his SOP. We knew too much about his operation, and so he'd either have to hide it beneath something else, or ramp up some other aspect of it. Suddenly unsettled, I realized that our actions tonight would have far-reaching ramifications. And considering we didn't have a clue as to how powerful he was, or what the extent of his reach was, I wondered just what the fuck can of worms we'd opened up now. But we'd had no choice. We couldn't leave five prisoners there, set to be sold. We *had* to rescue them, regardless of the fallout.

We reached the cars and split up, hightailing it out of there as quickly as we could. All the way home, Delilah nervously watched the rearview mirror, making certain that nobody was following us. I called Camille, and Morio answered.

"Put me on speaker. I don't want to wait till we get home and caught up with whatever Trenyth's news is to tell you what I've been thinking about."

"One sec . . . okay, go ahead. You're on speaker." Morio's voice crackled with the static that speaker phones always picked up.

I spilled out what I'd been thinking about. "I think we may have just escalated whatever this thing with Lowestar is. We threw a nasty monkey wrench in the works, and who knows what he'll do next?"

From Camille's car, Smoky's voice sounded. "If he's truly

trying to raise some ancient, crusty demigod, that might become his major focus. If he knows we're on to his slavery operation, he might decide to bring in the big guns, so to speak."

I groaned, and so did Delilah and Camille.

Camille's voice came over the phone. "Just what we need, but I have a nasty feeling you're right. Okay, good to keep in mind. Don't want to keep it in mind, but we have to be ready for anything at this point."

And with that, I hung up and we drove on into the silent night.

When we reached home, we took a few minutes to clean up and the others grabbed snacks. Hanna had left a message for me—Roman needed to see me. I glanced at the clock. It was two in the morning.

Our rescued prisoners had all been cleaned and bathed and were huddled in the parlor under the watchful eyes of Nerissa, Vanzir, and Shade, who had been gathering as much information as they could without traumatizing them. We'd talk to them as soon as we put out whatever fire Trenyth had for us.

Camille slipped into the seat in front of the Whispering Mirror and activated it. A moment later, the mist cleared and a guard faced us.

"Allow me a moment and I'll fetch Lord Trenyth." His eyes were sober and clear, but something about his expression told me the elf had been through hell. He stood and disappeared to the right, out of our view. True to his word, a moment later, Trenyth slid into the vacant seat.

"I don't have time to linger, girls. But I wanted to keep you updated. Trillian, are you there?" It was obvious that Trenyth hadn't slept in days—deep lines underscored his eyes, and he yawned even as he spoke.

Trillian grunted. "Yes, I'm here."

"The storm has rained its fury on Svartalfheim, I'm sorry to say. The sorcerers did their best to deflect it, and good thing, or the damage would have been worse. But the city is still a smoldering mess. Luckily, they took less damage than Elqaneve, but it's still bad. Several thousand dead, we think. King Vodox managed to survive, but there is much damage."

"And the storm?" I asked. "It is still raging?"

Trenyth let out a long sigh. "What mages survived our onslaught tell me they think it has weakened a bit, but yes, and it marches on toward Gylden, the city of the Goldunsan."

Crap. Gylden was a relatively peaceful city of Fae who lived in the mountains. Reclusive, the Goldunsan were seldom found in cities other than their own. Golden-skinned, they were beautiful in ways that made most Fae glamour seem like a knockoff. But the fact that they had few dealings with outsiders meant they didn't often form alliances. The storm could trash their city to the ground.

"We've alerted them, of course. But now we have a new worry."

And it just kept coming.

"We've received a message from Ceredream stating that there's some sort of activity happening on their borders. But they sat on the fence too long. We have no reserves left to send them at this point. King Gwyfn of the Nebulveori Mountains is closer; he is sending scouts to the City of the East to find out what they can."

"So the dwarves are fully involved." Delilah frowned. "I almost hate to ask but what's happening in Y'Elestrial?"

"They are prepared—they have gathered every sorcerer and witch they can. They're all working on war efforts, both in fortifying the city, and in discovering any weakness they can in Telazhar's army. If we can discover where Telazhar himself is, we can attempt an assassination coup." He paused. "Your cousin Shamas showed up. We've put him to work here—it's too dangerous for him to attempt the roads to Svartalfheim right now."

Camille winced, but said nothing.

"And Elqaneve?" I didn't want to ask, but we had to know. "How are you doing? You look like crap, Trenyth."

He smiled then, wearily, but it was a smile. "You think I don't know that? Of course I do. I haven't slept in days. I've been run ragged. Sharah looks just as tired as I am, but I'm making sure she gets as much rest as she can, given that she just had a baby. Is Chase there?"

"No." Camille started to stand. "Do you need me to go get him? He's probably asleep at Iris's."

"No, let him rest. Sharah misses him terribly. I have a feeling when this war is over, she's going to drag Elqaneve in directions we have been resisting for years. The people love her—what better heroine than a woman who had to choose duty over the love of her life and her child?"

"Then she's told your people?" Somehow I couldn't imagine Sharah keeping her mouth shut.

"Oh, yes. Sharah has a backbone of steel, regardless of that quiet demeanor. Over the past few days, she's made no bones about mentioning that she left her family back Earthside, and I guess that people here are just too shell-shocked to care if her family happens to be a mostly FBH and a half-breed child. I don't know how they'll work it out once the war is settled—may it be settled—but by then, I doubt if any of the former proscriptions regarding heritage will matter." Trenyth looked both pleased and irritated.

I couldn't help but laugh. "Good. And that's the way it should be. We put up with enough crap as children because we were half-breeds. You have to know where *our* sympathies lie."

He laughed in return. "Yes, I most certainly do. And trust me, I understand." After a brief pause, he added, "Camille—Derisa wants to see you as soon as possible. I told her it might not be for a few days, considering what's going on. She said she may make the trip Earthside, given how dangerous it is over here, now."

Camille stared at the mirror, her expression blank. "We are in the middle of something big here. I can't possibly come back right now."

"Oh, she understands that. This war will not go away in the next day or two—whatever it is, it isn't an emergency, though she did stress it's important." Another pause, and then, "And Trillian? We finally received word from Darynal. He and Taath survived, but Quall is dead. They can't make it back to Elqaneve right now, given the chaos happening, so they're headed toward Y'Elestrial."

"From the desert?" Trillian gnawed on his lip. "That means they'll have to travel through the Shadow Lands."

Trenyth nodded, his look matching Trillian's. "Yes. I know . . . but it's the only way. There's so much unrest in the Southern Wastes that they don't dare stay there. If they tried to make it up to Nebulveori, chances are they'd be spotted on the way and killed. The goblins are up in arms, and so are the mountain bogies. The dwarves are picking them off right and left. That leaves the Shadow Lands, if they want to work their way back up north."

"Darynal has family in Svartalfheim. He needs to find out if they are safe or if they perished." Trillian slowly lowered himself to the sofa. "I have to do something."

Camille paled. "But the Shadow Lands—you can't go to the Shadow Lands. Damn it, you know what perils hide there."

Trillian held her gaze. "Of course I know. But you also know that he is my *lavoyda* . . . my blood-oath brother. How can I turn my back on him when I know he's in danger?"

"I *do* understand." She stared back at him for a moment. "If you must go, you must. But remember: We need you here, too."

Trenyth interrupted. "Trillian, listen to Camille. The Shadow Lands are deep and long with history—many who have attempted to pass through their borders are never seen again. For now, Darynal is safe, but if he chooses that route . . . there is a good chance he will never return. And if you go after him, you, too, may vanish."

The Shadow Lands were a valley that separated the deserts of the Southern Wastes from the eastern lands. The valley had been the last refuge of those who fled the great forests destroyed during the Scorching Wars. They raced into the canyons, and there, Telazhar and his armies had hunted them down and slaughtered them en masse. The entire area, including the bordering Ranakwa Fens, were rife with the spirits of the dead—angry and frightened and still missing their homes.

Trillian fell silent, but by the look on his face, the wheels were turning fast and furious upstairs.

"How many sorcerers do you think that Telazhar has gathered, Trenyth?" It was a question we probably didn't want the answer to, but it was important that we knew what we were up against.

"Last report I got from Darynal's group before they disappeared was . . . well over three hundred. Telazhar swept through the Brotherhood of the Sun and gathered up the entire cult. And most of the guilds in the Southern Wastes threw their weight behind him. We're talking an army of magic-wielding psychopaths twice as large as the one he commanded during the Scorching Wars. One sorcerer can destroy a village if he's powerful enough. Three hundred—"

"Can rule the world, especially when they have an army of grunts behind them." We all fell silent for a moment. All it took was one charismatic orator who held true power, and you had the makings for disaster. Put a Demon Lord at his back and a spirit seal around his neck and there was the beginning to the end.

"Right. I need to get back to matters at hand. I'm trying to find out how many villages in Elqaneve still stand, but the going is rough and gathering data is dangerous. There are so many dead here, girls. I don't know . . . the Elfin race will rebuild but I don't know if we'll ever be the nation and people we were a week ago. Telazhar was trying for total annihilation, and he damned near achieved it." And with that, he signed off before we could say any more.

I sat back, sighing. "I guess we should talk to Violet."

Tanne, who had been watching silently, shook his head. "You really are up against the wall. For rescuing Violet . . . any time you need me? I'm ready and willing to go for it. All you have to do is ask."

I realized that Tanne now knew far more about matters than we'd planned. But he seemed like an ally worth having.

"I'm surprised you aren't in there, making sure she's okay." I cocked my head, wondering at how calm and pulled together he was.

"You know little about what I've faced, and the people I've lost. I've learned to focus on the matters at hand, to push everything else to the side, even when it's ripping me up inside. I've learned how to separate my personal life from what needs done. My mother trained us well. The Hunter's Glen Clan has a reputation of being the hope of last resort. People come to us who have tried every other outlet and failed. And we seldom fail." He leaned back in his chair and a shock of his tousled blond hair fell in his eyes. He brushed it back, a faint, arrogant grin on his face. "Living in the Black Forest breeds strength."

"We welcome your help." I glanced at the others. I had a good feeling about Tanne. He was an oddball, but he was one of the good guys. "Before it gets much later, we should talk to Violet and the others. You know, of course, we can't let them go home. We can't chance Lowestar looking for them. He'd probably kill them outright, hoping to keep them from talking. Or out of spite."

"That's going to present its own problems. Where do they go?"

"We'll decide that in a little while. Meanwhile, bring them in and let's find out what we're facing."

By the looks of them, Nerissa had seen that they'd had showers and they were comfortably dressed in clean clothing that she'd scrounged up from our various wardrobes. By now, we were used to lending our clothes to stragglers who needed a change.

But the haunted looks in their eyes told me they'd been through hell. Violet started when she saw Tanne, and she broke into a run, racing into his arms. He held her tight, kissing her brow, kissing her lips, but then he gently disengaged her and pushed her to arm's length.

"There will be time for us later," he whispered. "Now we need to talk to you. To find out everything you know."

Violet let out a long breath, sounding exhausted. "We've already talked to the dragon and Were. They know everything we know, and they wrote it down so we wouldn't lose anything." She turned to us, and a soft smile played over her lips. "Thank you. Thank you more than I can ever express. I didn't think I'd ever make it out of there."

Nerissa stepped forward. She gave me a light kiss before introducing the others. "You know Violet already. Meet Shay, Daisy, Fray, and this is Weaver."

The four of them nodded, looking confused and more than a little dazed. Nerissa settled them onto the sofa, while the rest of us took the other chairs. Violet joined her comrades, looking a little less shell-shocked than the others.

Nerissa turned to us. "Shay was in there over a year. The others have been prisoners for between two and five months. Violet was the last one captured. They told us they've seen at least four Fae and two Weres come through the cells in the past five months. Shay doesn't know how many were laundered through during the period between when she was captured and when Weaver was put in the cell next to her five months back."

"So it's not first in, first out." I frowned. "I wonder what the criteria are."

Weaver spoke up, his voice shaky. "I know. I managed to get one of the guards talking. He said that sometimes the transfer takes a while, and once in a while, a buyer reneges on the deal. Then they have to either find a new one, or they have to work out whatever the problem was."

"The guards—were they all daemons?" Camille shifted to allow Hanna room to bring in a tea tray and some cookies. It was obvious that our housekeeper had been in bed; she was in a nightgown and her hair was braided back.

But she never missed a beat—just like Iris, she was always on call.

"No, there were a few humans, too." Weaver shook his head. "They've got a tight operation. By the way, I have to contact my superiors. You're going to find out sooner or later so I might as well tell you."

Shade glanced up. "He's an operative for the Fly by Night Investigations Agency. A freelancer."

Again with the FBN agency. Twice in one night meant it might be time to pay a visit to the business, especially since it was being run by a vampire. But that could keep.

"What were you doing there?" I accepted the bottle of blood that Hanna handed me. After the experience with the daemon's blood, I thought I might stick to bottled for a while. The whole out-of-control thing had been frightening.

"Searching for Shay. Her family reported her missing, and the last known contacts were through Supernatural Matchups. Alex hired me to do some research. It led to me getting captured. We thought we were dealing with a kidnapper or serial killer—we had no clue the villain was the dating service itself. By the time I realized what was going down, it was too late. I have no idea why Alex didn't come sniffing around—he takes good care of his people. Even those of us who freelance for him."

"We'll try to find out. But here's the deal, peeps. You can't go home. You can't even come out of hiding. If Lowestar Radcliffe—the daemon who runs the slavery operation—finds out where you're at, he'll come after you. He won't know if you've spilled any info or not, but he won't take any chances. If nothing else, he'll try to shut you up. Or he'll kill you out of spite." I shrugged. "You have to stay missing for a while."

"She's not kidding." Delilah waved a cookie at them. "I saw into the mind of one of their now-deceased partners. They're vicious, they're sadistic, and they have absolutely no conscience when it comes to trafficking in people. Or in killing those that cross them. The fact that we rescued the five of you? It's going to go down in a bad way and the last place you want to be is on the receiving end of their anger and revenge."

"Then what do we do? Our families must be worried sick—can't we tell them we're okay?" Daisy spoke up, her voice wavering.

"I'm afraid not. If they find you, they'll try to find out who rescued you before they kill you. And then they'll find out about us. We can't risk that. Chances are they're going to discover it was us anyway, but you don't need to be in the middle of it." I glanced over at Camille. "We need to figure out where to hide them."

"We need to start our own underground railroad, given the number of peeps we seem to be running through lately." Her gaze flickered and I knew she was thinking of the Keraastar Knights.

"We can't keep them here." Smoky leaned against a wall, crossing his arms. "If Lowestar figures out we're the ones who rescued them, we can expect a raid sooner or later, and if they're here, they'll be in just as much danger as they would at home."

Nerissa started to say something, then paused. We all looked at her and she shrugged. "I might know of a place, but I'm not at liberty to say just yet. I'll have to talk to . . . someone . . . tomorrow. For tonight . . ."

"I think I know where we can keep them for tonight. You guys wait here. Vanzir, Smoky, you're with me." Camille jumped up and grabbed her keys.

"You're going out? But you're exhausted." Trillian rested his hand on her arm.

She shook her head. "This won't take long. We'll be back soon. For now, get them down in Menolly's lair. She's not going to bed just yet. I just don't want to chance anything—not with life as precarious as it is lately."

And with that, she was out the door. I motioned to Nerissa. "Take them down below." As she and Vanzir led the Fae away, Tanne gave Violet a long kiss before letting her go.

Meanwhile, I put in a call to Roman. "What's up? You need to see me?"

"Yeah, there's some heavy shit going down and we need to talk."

I glanced at the clock. Three A.M. Realistically, I could get to his place in half an hour, but I wanted to wait until Camille got back safely. Sunrise was about three hours away. "I don't know if I can make it tonight. Is it really important?"

"It's important, but not dire. I know tomorrow night is your Samhain celebration—but afterward, perhaps you can come over?"

I thought about it. It seemed insane to make promises of more than a day now, with so much chaos surrounding us, but we had to keep on the move, keep acting like there was a tomorrow we could count on.

"Menolly?"

"I'm nodding," I said. "I'll be there tomorrow night—I don't know what time, so I'll call you before I leave."

"Good enough. I lo . . ." He stopped, to my relief. And then quietly he said, "Be safe, my love."

I stared at the phone, wanting to say, *"I told you don't fall in love with me. It's dangerous, I'll break your heart if you let yourself love me."* But in the end, all I said was, "I'll see you tomorrow." That was all I *could* say.

Chapter 15

When Camille returned, she had some good news. "Grandmother Coyote will look after them for the night. They can hide in her tree. Vanzir, Shade, can you run them out there? They'll be safe until Nerissa finds out whatever it is she needs to know."

"Great." Delilah snorted. "As if they're not shellshocked enough, they get to hang out with one of the Hags of Fate."

"Better that than if Lowestar finds out about us and launches a preemptive strike." Camille shook her head. "We're in a wartime situation on so many fronts—we do what we have to and accept help from wherever we can find it."

She yawned. "I'm done in. I say we get some sleep. We have to be on top of things tomorrow. We need to find out what Lowestar gets up to. Now that we've disrupted his little operation, you know he's going to be after us."

As Vanzir and Shade took our guests out to an even darker space than they'd been in—albeit with less danger for them—my sisters headed up to bed and, hopefully, a deep, dreamless sleep.

I still had a couple hours before sleep claimed me, and all I wanted to do was cuddle with Nerissa. But she was exhausted, too, and I sent her back to bed after a long kiss and a quick feel of those beautiful breasts.

The house was silent within ten minutes, everyone tucked in for the night. I sat at the kitchen table, looking around the room. We'd worked so hard, and our family had grown. Now everything felt shaky and at odds. Not internally—we were a strong unit—but the dangers looming from the outside. I was tired. We were all tired, and we needed a break.

As I sat there, toying with the tablecloth, a noise startled me and I looked up to see Trillian. He was in his bathrobe, leaning against the door frame.

"Couldn't sleep?"

He shook his head. "Am I interrupting? I can go in the living room if you like."

"Not at all. Come. Sit." Truth was, I welcomed the company. Too long alone with my thoughts wasn't always a good thing.

Trillian put on the teakettle and rummaged in the fridge, looking for a snack. He found some leftover chicken and an apple, and then fixed his cup of tea. Sitting opposite me, he took a long sip of the hot drink.

I watched him eat. "Why can't you sleep?"

"Thinking. A lot on my mind."

I knew what was bothering him. "You're thinking about Darynal, aren't you?" At his nod, I decided to ask something that had been in the back of my mind for a while. "Trillian, do you have family back in Svartalfheim? Are you worried they might be in danger?"

He paused, lingering over the drumstick. After a moment, he set it down on the plate, wiped his fingers on his napkin, and propped his elbows on the table. "Yes, I do have family there, but I'm not concerned. They disowned me many years back—before I ever met Camille."

"I didn't know that." I had never heard him talk about his family, but that didn't always indicate a problem.

"I wasn't . . . they didn't like my attitude. Believe it or not, Darynal and I are considered too philanthropic by our families, if you want to put it that way. You think I'm arrogant—oh don't bother denying it." He waved away my protestations. "I know it's true, you know it's true. I don't care either way. But the fact is, that for my family, I'm considered meek. I care too much about people outside the family, outside the caste I was born into. I mingle with 'undesirables' and had the gall to fall in love with . . ." Here he stopped, and picked up his tea again.

I stared at him. That cast a whole new light on matters. "You think they wouldn't approve of Camille."

"Think, nothing. They found out about us shortly after we met, and blew a gasket. My father gave me an ultimatum. Leave her, or leave the family. They had arranged a marriage for me to one of the higher-ups in the Court. And I wouldn't play along. Now, Vodox—the King—he is the most progressive ruler we've had in centuries. But his rule is still criticized. And my family is old school. They are firmly ensconced in the caste system. Tradition means everything to them."

That was the most I'd ever heard him talk about his background, and by the look on his face, I began to realize just how far away Trillian was from his upbringing, and the sacrifices he'd made to be with Camille.

"And our father treated you like dirt, too." I suddenly felt ashamed that I'd backed Sephreh in his opinion. I hadn't really bothered to find out the man behind the mask. And it was obvious that there was a lot more there than I'd anticipated.

"He was a product of his upbringing. But that only goes so far. Once you discover what someone is like beyond your preconceptions, then it's up to you to make a change in your perception and action. Your father didn't want to change his beliefs." He was treading carefully, I could tell. And I knew it was because of Sephreh's death.

But I understood—probably more than Camille, and definitely more than Delilah. "He was the same about my vampirism. He hated vampires, and was suddenly up against the horror of a daughter of his being turned. It was hard for him. For the first couple years after I returned home from the OIA's year of rehabilitation, he could barely look at me. He was civil, but it was all lip service, and he never once told me he loved me during that time. And after he managed to learn how to treat me with any semblance of respect, I still always knew that I was broken—that I'd been whole and lovable, and then Dredge tainted me."

I seldom dwelt on the past, but some days, the memories swept up as if they were from yesterday. I pressed my lips together, trying to keep from sinking into the mire. It was never a good thing when the quicksand of the past rose up and sucked me down.

"He had a narrow range of acceptability. Look at what happened with Camille." Trillian finished his tea. "I know she's not going to say anything, but it's breaking her up that he wasted time they could have spent together being angry at her. She'll never say a word, but you know it's happening."

I leaned forward, gazing into Trillian's face. "It was always like that. He loved her most, but only if she stayed strictly on the path he approved for her. One misstep and he was yelling at her and calling her names."

A cloud passed over his face. "Oh, I know. After Hyto's attack, a lot of those memories came back and she told us about how strict Sephreh was with her in terms of forcing her to run the household. And how angry he was because she could never do anything as well as her mother. You all had a rough time. I do believe your father loved you, but he had no clue on how to show it."

"He had no clue on a lot of things." I stared at my hands. "I want to apologize. I treated you badly. I didn't look beyond the fact that you are Svartan. I was brought up to consider your people dangerous. And I just accepted it as fact."

Trillian broke out in a smile then, the easy charm giving a warm glow to his otherwise aloof nature. "Not a problem, Menolly. I think . . . if anything . . . the past couple of years have brought us to an understanding and—I hope—a mutual respect." He leaned back and yawned, stretching. "And now, I think I'll head back to bed. Your sister is snuggled warm, and I want to be next to her."

He stood and—without thinking—I rose and crossed around the table to give him a hug. Surprised, he accepted and returned it. Then without another word, he headed back upstairs.

I watched him go, suddenly feeling more at peace. Yes, we were facing danger from all fronts, but we had a pretty damned good foundation here at home, and no matter what, we'd persevere. Another glance at the clock told me it was nearing three thirty. While I couldn't fall asleep early like most people, I could go down, crawl into bed next to my gorgeous wife, and just let my mind wander. And that's just what I did.

The next night, I received a call from Erin. She wanted to take Roman up on his offer, and with both a heavy heart—it suddenly felt like I was losing her in an odd way, like she was "growing up"—and a smile, I told her that I'd contact him and we'd hammer out plans soon. I slowly dressed, my thoughts drifting over the past few years as I thought about how far we had all come from where we started, then, glancing at the clock, I shook away the memories as I headed up the stairs.

I entered the kitchen to find myself in the midst of a bustle of activity. And it wasn't just for dinner. Then I remembered, it was Samhain Eve, and we were scheduled for ritual. As I glanced at the table, I saw an urn sitting there, and I knew what it was before even bothering to ask.

Father's ashes.

Camille saw me staring at it. "I picked them up today. We'll consecrate them in our ritual tonight, then when we head back to Otherworld next, we'll take them with us and scatter them up at Erulizi Falls."

I nodded. "Sounds right. So what are we doing tonight?"

"Ritual down by Birchwater Pond and then a late dinner. Hanna's making ham and sweet potatoes and a green bean and bacon dish. Apple pie for dessert. I'm going to run up to my room and get ready. You should, too. Formal dress. We need to keep some traditions alive." And with that, she bounced off, hurrying out of the room.

Iris and Bruce came crowding into the kitchen just then. Iris was wearing a formal blue gown and her white fur cape. Bruce was dressed in rusts and greens.

"Iris! Are you joining us tonight?" It seemed like it had been forever since we'd all been together. I realized how much I missed having her around the house. But there was no way our house could fit everybody now, and she and Bruce needed their own space.

"Yes, we are. The Duchess is taking care of the babies. Chase will be joining us, too." Iris grinned. The Duchess was her mother-in-law, who had arrived to help out when Iris had her twins a week ago. And she showed no inclination to return home, so Iris was making full use of her to steal moments away from the sudden influx of responsibility twins had thrust upon her. Add wet nursing Chase's daughter, Astrid, to the mix, and she was one tired house sprite.

The men were carrying stuff out into the backyard, and I realized they were heading down to the pond with the odds and ends we would need. As I stepped out onto the steps of the back porch, the wind whipped past. A storm was on the way and we were due for strong winds and heavy rain. The air felt chill, ready for a good blow.

Morio slid past me, dressed in his ritual kimono that he reserved for holidays. He was carrying a box with candles in it, and he gave me a little wave as he hurried toward the path.

I turned back inside, not bothering to ask what I could do. Everything looked firmly under control, so I returned downstairs to my lair and opened my closet. There, in the back, hung two gowns. My usual—black as night and beaded—

covered me fully, from throat to hem, from shoulder to wrist. But behind that, hung one I'd worn before I was turned. It was a pale shade of silver, and it shimmered with beaded embroidery. It was also sleeveless and had a low neck. I hadn't touched it since the last Samhain I had worn it—the year before I was turned. But something pushed me tonight to take a chance. To take a step from where I'd been stuck for the past fourteen years.

Three nights ago had been the fourteenth anniversary of when Dredge turned me, when he killed me. Covered with his scars, I had come back to life as a vampire. The scars on the inside were a long ways toward healing. The scars on my body would never fade, a constant reminder. But maybe, maybe I was ready to face them. Maybe I was ready to let go of the fear of being seen. Seen as ugly, as deformed.

Hesitating, I almost caved and reached for the black gown, but then I shoved it to the side and pulled out the silver one. I slid out of my jeans and shirt, wishing I could see myself in a mirror. But truthfully, I had eyes. I could look down, see the marks on my body, the hundreds of intricate spirals and designs he had carved into my flesh. Everywhere was marked, except for my hands, my feet, and my face. Even my pubic mound bore the letters etching out his name. He had claimed me for all time. But he was dead, and now Roman was my sire. And I was still here, still in control, loved and in love.

Pushing aside the past, I slid into the silver gown. That it was sleeveless wouldn't bother me other than my scars showing. The cold didn't faze me when it was natural weather. I added a silver shawl, and then, before I could talk myself out of it, I undid the perpetual braids that I kept my hair in. I loved the corn rows, but tonight I wanted to be free—free from my usual identity.

I thought about Trillian, how I had categorized him and stereotyped him based on his looks. I'd been trying so hard to avoid showing my scars, that nobody had even had the chance to see the real me. Who I had been—unmarred, alive, pretty without a scar on her body—was forever gone.

Now I was simply Menolly, the vampire. Menolly, the wife. Menolly, the mother of Erin, my middle-aged daughter. Menolly, the warrior and the sister. Menolly, consort of a Vampire Lord. And that . . . that had to be enough for anybody. Including myself.

Laughing, I slipped on a pair of black flats and then, with one last pause, I headed upstairs.

"Menolly? Everybody's gone down to the pond. I waited for—" Camille rounded the kitchen corner and stopped, gasping.

"What? Too much?" Nervous once again, I shifted uncomfortably, my resolve of a moment before starting to slip.

"You're so beautiful. I haven't seen you in that gown since . . ." She stopped. "Oh, Menolly. The last time you wore that was before . . ."

"Before Dredge turned me. The year before. I know. I thought . . . I thought it was time to drag it out again. Do I look okay? I can't see myself in the mirror." I trusted Camille. She'd tell me the truth, even if it was what I didn't want to hear.

But she just smiled, ducking her head. "Better than okay. You look wonderful. And your hair. I miss your hair like that. It was always so curly and pretty. It's hard to see just how much it shimmers when you've got it back in the braids. But whatever makes you comfortable, that's all that matters."

She was wearing her priestess robes—a sheer peacock halter dress, beneath which she wore an ornate demi-bra and a pair of bikini panties. She was carrying the cloak of the Black Unicorn that matched the horn—a gift from the Black Unicorn himself.

Once every so many thousand years, he shed his body like the phoenix and was renewed. The hide and horn were considered great artifacts and some nine or so pairings of them existed. Any sorcerer or magician or witch would slaver to have them, which made Camille a sitting duck should some unsavory and powerful wizard type find out she owned them.

"I have to charge the horn tonight—I exhausted it last week in Elqaneve getting those damned doors open so Delilah and I could escape." She slid the horn into the inner pocket of the cloak. "Tonight's going to be so hard," she said, sinking into a chair. "I have to stand up there and summon our father's spirit among the roll call of the dead. Do you realize how difficult that's going to be for me?"

She didn't say it accusatorily. In fact, the resigned look on her face told me she'd already resolved the fact that—as Priestess—she was responsible for the tough part of the job tonight.

Samhain was the night we honored our ancestors and celebrated the dead. FBH pagans often celebrated the holiday, too, as well as our Earthside Fae kin. It was a night in which to reflect on the nature of death. Unfortunately, when you'd seen as much death as we had, the honor part was often outweighed with the heaviness of loss. But it was our way, and it helped cushion the sense of futility against a force over which, truly, no one had any control.

"I know, and we love you for doing it. I think . . ." I stopped, trying to think of a way to phrase what had been running through my head. "I think it's important that we do this, that we take time for this ritual. It will help us cope with Father's death. Everything has seemed so surreal the past week, and we're just holding on by the tips of our fingers."

"Along for the ride?" She flashed me a smile then, weary as it was.

"That's pretty much it. We've been dragged through the mud and this will give us some sense of continuity. Our home world is in trouble. Let's face it—Telazhar is wreaking terror across the land. We have little left from our past. This gives us a sense of tradition. Of building new traditions, even when it's rough."

I wasn't sure if I was making myself clear but Camille

seemed to get my drift. She pushed to her feet and slid the cloak around her shoulders. "I suppose we should head out there. The others will be waiting."

And without further ado, we exited the kitchen and headed toward the backyard.

Birchwater Pond gleamed under the glow of lantern light. We owned the entire property that surrounded the pond now, and had turned it into a veritable park. Picnic tables, arched poles that held flickering candles encased safely within hurricane lanterns, fallen logs surrounding a fire pit—we'd worked our butts off out here to create the perfect ritual area, and it was a comforting place in which to spend a few quiet hours.

The rain was at a drizzle, but at least it was no longer pouring, and the clouds parted now and then to show the evening sky. The moon, she was nearing her darkest point, and did not turn her face to us. But the stars gleamed through the inky blackness that overshadowed the night. Another gust, and the cloud cover closed once again, bringing with them showers. It was around forty-two degrees, and as we all stood around, I could see everybody's breath.

We were a good-sized group. Camille motioned for us to spread out in a circle. The permanent altar table had been erected—Smoky had carved it out of a large stump, etching a perfect pentagram in it, then he had polished the top to a high sheen, allowing the grain of the massive tree to show through.

The altar was set with candles in hurricane lamps, a chalice of wine, a chalice of blood for me, Father's ashes, and Camille's dagger. She was carrying the yew staff Aeval had given her. It was a little taller than she was, with a silver knob on top, and in an indentation on the knob rested a small crystal ball. Silver webbing encased the sides of the globe, keeping it in place, and the bottom of the staff was capped by a silver foot.

Bruce, who had turned out to be an excellent drummer, set a steady, firm beat on the bodhran, as Camille picked up her dagger. She slowly circled the area, a pale purple light emanating from the tip of her blade. Within the light, sparkles danced—minute faerie lights, shimmering.

As she finished casting the Circle, once again she stepped up to the altar and inhaled sharply in the chill night.

"We gather together, as we have for years on end, to celebrate the day of death and the festival of spirits . . . we gather to bid farewell to friends and family who have passed since last Samhain."

And just like that, I closed my eyes, and was swept back to the first time I remembered celebrating . . . and how much the rite had clung to my memory.

I was around three years old. Or the equivalent to it. And it was a dark night like this one, only we were standing on the shores of Lake Y'Leveshan. I was holding on to Delilah's hand, and we were dressed in warm cloaks over long white dresses. Father was there, but he wasn't paying much attention—he was standing by the shore, staring at the falls as they tumbled over the bluff.

Camille was at the bottom of the Erulizi Falls, on a rock that overlooked the pond at the bottom. The water thundered down, spraying her with mist, as she stared into the depths. Her eyes were wet, but with the water, not tears. During the day I never saw a tear on her face, even when Father yelled at her because she'd forgotten to tell the housekeeper what to fix for dinner or because the gardens weren't in order. But at night, I heard her. She was the oldest so she had her own room, but I could still hear her crying over Mother.

Father was kind to Kitten, and to me. But Camille? He was hard on her, and his complaints rained like bitter drops. Every day it was one thing or another.

He hadn't wanted to come tonight. He'd told Camille to ask Aunt Rythwar to bring us, but she'd talked him into it, begging him to join us. Finally he gave up and agreed. Now he stared into the water, as if he were alone in the world, as if we didn't exist.

After a bit, Camille returned to the altar she had set up. She was studying with the Coterie of the Moon Mother, and they'd assigned her the task of leading a simple rite for the holiday. So she'd laid out an altar with white star-flowers—an autumn-blooming plant, and candles, and a glass of wine. Ginger cookies, made by Leethe, our house-keeper and cook, rested on a tray next to the altar.

"We should start." She watched Father expectantly. He studiously ignored her. "Fah—we should start the rite. Menny's tired."

But he did not turn, did not speak. So she gathered Delilah and me around the altar and, in halting fashion, cast the magic Circle to keep spirits out and energy within. Her knife let out a few halting sputters of energy, but she bit her lip and kept going. And Delilah, with a glance back at our father, resolutely stood at attention. I turned to watch Sephreh. He was alone; he missed Mother. But so did we, and for the first time, I felt like this was the way it would be from now on. The three of us on the inside of the Circle, with him on the outside.

And inside, a swell of anger bubbled up. If that was the way he wanted it, then that was the way it would be. I turned my back on him and focused on Camille, and for the rest of that short, tense ritual, there was no one else in the world except my sisters and me, and the moon shining down overhead, and the memory of a woman with golden hair and a smile that could blind the morning sky.

The Circle cast, Camille took her place at the altar and Morio joined her. They were a matched pair—magic to magic, heart to heart, soul to soul. Smoky and Trillian were also her matches, but the magic—it bound Morio and her in a way she could never have with anyone else in the world. But Camille could never be with just one man. There were too many sides of her. It would be a disaster if she expected one person in the world to understand her inside-out. It would be too much to ask of anyone.

Like me. I glanced over at Nerissa, who wore a cloak as gold as the sun, over a black dress. She matched me well, but I also needed Roman for when my predator wanted out to play. I would never expect just one person to meet my needs. And Delilah? Well, she was more like our mother, but still she had both Shade and the Autumn Lord.

Perhaps that had been the problem. Perhaps Father had turned against his nature, needed Mother too much, and in doing so, denied anyone else the chance to make him happy and whole.

Whatever the case, the past was long over, and now we stood on the side of Birchwater Pond. Instead of our mother, we were here to bid farewell to Sephreh. The formal rites would come later—but for now, we passed the chalice and intoned the prayer of the dead, and focused our energy on Camille as she cut the cords of energy connecting him to our lives. Grieving would take time, mourning would move as it would, but letting go? We had to let him go. We had to let him journey on to find his joy and his future.

We ate our communion cakes—ate the body of the Great Mother. And we sipped the blood of the Harvest God, found in sweet wine, although my chalice contained actual blood. We lit the fires and wandered the shore after wishing Father's spirit—and Chrysandra and Queen Asteria and all those we'd lost over the past few years—well on their journeys.

After we were done, Nerissa and I strolled arm in arm to the water's edge, and once again, I flashed back to childhood, watching the lake churn as the falling water thundered into it.

"What are you thinking about? You look so far away." Nerissa slid her arm around me and kissed the top of my head.

"Memories. Just . . . the past. The first Samhain we bade

farewell to our mother. And how Father was such an ass." I told her about it.

"He was mourning your mother."

"He had three daughters who needed him to man up, to be both father and mother to them. We needed him then, and I swear, he never fully returned after checking out. I just hope Mother was waiting for him. I don't like to think of him wandering alone. For one thing, I don't want him haunting our home."

She laughed, but I was serious. The last thing we needed was the ghost of our father wandering around the house, bemoaning his fate.

"I think you're safe. Wouldn't your mother be there for him? Isn't that how it works in your afterlife?" The way she said it made it sound almost like a disease, but I knew she didn't mean anything by it.

"I hope so. I seriously hope so." We paused by a little bower where Smoky and Morio had built a covered bench. Taking shelter from the rain, we held hands, snuggling together.

"I love the look, by the way. I love your hair down." The way she said it sounded wistful. "You seem more vulnerable . . . less . . . less like nothing matters. Sometimes I think everything just bounces off you, and I worry that anything I say will do the same."

Oh, no. We didn't need angst tonight and this had become a common argument. There was enough pain with remembering our dead, remembering our friends and family who had passed. Especially those who died because of *us*.

"Don't. Not tonight. You know I love you. You know I listen to you—even if I don't say anything. I never ignore you." Apparently I wasn't tuned in enough, or so Nerissa thought. I wasn't entirely sure where her complaints were coming from because I didn't think I did that at all.

"Yes, you do." She let out a long sigh. "But we'll talk about that later. You're right. Tonight is not for arguing. Tonight's for remembering the dead, and letting the past move into the past."

I hated seeing the clouded look on her face and leaned in

to give her a kiss. "I promise—we'll work on this. I may not understand why you're upset, but I see that you are. And I don't want you unhappy. I love you too much for that."

She squeezed my hand. "I know. I love you, too."

And with that, we headed back to the others. Trillian and Morio grilled the meat while Hanna and Vanzir spread out the rest of the food on the tables. Iris was playing with Maggie, who looked delighted to have her first nanny around again. Iris hadn't been able to care for Maggie since mid-pregnancy, because Maggie accidentally tripped her up, and she could be a real handful. But now, she sat, contented, on Iris's lap, leaning against her softly with that wide-eyed innocence beaming up at her.

Trillian picked up a guitar and started to play an Otherworld melody. He'd proved quite adept with the instrument, and Camille had bought him one last Yule. The song was one of loss, and acceptance, and I recognized it right off. I'd learned it when I was a teenager.

I closed my eyes and fell into the rhythm, then started singing softly. I missed singing—I'd been considered talented before Dredge had gotten to me, and I still led the chants and songs during our holidays.

Camille glanced over at me, where she sat between Morio and Smoky, and smiled softly. Kitten stoked the fire, then handed out skewers with marshmallows. Vanzir scrounged up a drum and joined in, and Iris lent her voice to mine. As one song ended, we moved into the next, and then the next, heedless of the light misting drizzle that showered down. Warmed by the fire, we ignored what might be coming tomorrow, as we remembered our yesterdays.

Chapter 16

❧❧❧

Late in the evening—around midnight—we returned to the house. The others were tired, and so I bade them good night and went down to my lair to get ready for my trip to Roman's. I thought about braiding my hair again before I left but then said, "Fuck it," and changed into jeans and a turtleneck, leaving my hair down. Nerissa was already asleep by the time I left. She had a busy day ahead of her at work tomorrow and I didn't want to disturb her, so I left a note on the nightstand and headed out. I decided to take the Jag. It was still rattling, but if Jason said it would make it until next week, I believed him.

The streets were still fairly busy—not only was it Samhain Eve, but it was also Halloween for the general populace, and adult partygoers were reveling. I was headed down a side street when a Hummer lurched forward out of the alley. The next moment, I screamed as the beast's nose drove itself directly into the side of my Jag on the passenger side. Before I knew what was happening, we went skidding across the intersection.

Gripping the wheel, I held on, the sound of metal screeching as I struggled to break my Jag free from the Hummer. But my bumper was tangled up in its bumper, like a chicken on a spit, and all I could do was ride out the attack.

Seconds later, the oncoming brick wall loomed large, and I panicked. I could probably survive this, if nothing pierced me through the heart, but the idea of being wedged between that monstrosity and the building didn't strike me as comforting. I let go of the wheel and struggled with my seat belt.

But it was too late—my Jag hit the building, side first, as metal screeched along metal. The Hummer wasn't braking—it continued its drive forward, like a compactor in a junkyard, shattering the passenger door and window, trundling me into the brick wall before I could get free of my seat belt.

I braced myself for impact as it crunched the front seats, expecting to be mangled at any moment. I knew I could survive the impact, and heal, but only if my heart was protected from anything that might be aimed at it and if my car didn't explode into flames.

But then, as the sounds of a siren echoed nearby, the Hummer stopped abruptly, then pulled away, dragging the passenger door of my car with it. It barreled down the street. I held tight to the steering wheel, trying to get my bearings. Then, panic rising, I ripped off the seat belt and, unable to make it past the jumble of metal on either side, I smashed my fist through the already fractured windshield. Within seconds, I crawled over the hood as the cops came skidding up. I cleared the wreck and stood there, numb, staring at the remains of what had been my Jag. There was nothing left except twisted metal and broken glass.

"Menolly!" Yugi's voice shook me out of my daze.

"Yugi?" I turned, staring at Chase's second in command. "Yugi? What are you doing here?"

"I was on my way back to headquarters when I saw the whole thing." He was Swedish, and an empath, and he was damned good at his job. Now a look of concern spread across his face. "Who the hell was trying to kill you, Menolly? Because from what I saw, that was deliberate."

Twenty minutes later, I was in the headquarters of the FH-CSI, and Roman was there by my side. Yugi had called Nerissa, and she, Camille, and Delilah were on their way down to pick me up. I couldn't have the hot coffee, but Yugi had found a spare bottle of blood and he warmed it up. I sipped slowly, the liquid loosening the knots in my back. While I hadn't been hurt, I'd had one hell of a shock.

"We have to trace the Hummer." Roman was furious. He leaned his hands on the table and stared at Yugi, who was sitting beside me. "You're the policeman. Did you get the license plate?"

Yugi shook his head. "My first priority was making sure Menolly was okay. By the time I saw her, the car had vanished. But we have the make and model, and we have the color. It's hard to hide a Hummer. They don't just blend in with the crowd."

"It's not hard if you have a garage or a warehouse." Roman was pissed. I'd seldom seen him this angry.

"Don't bother. We're pretty sure we know who's responsible. Or at least, who has a hand in it." I reached up, placed my hand on his arm.

"I may have some information that can shed some light on the attack." Rane—one of the Fae officers who worked the night shift—entered the room at that moment. She was holding my purse. "This is yours, right?"

I nodded. "Right."

"There was a tracer bug in it. I caught the little bugger when we were clearing out your car before the tow truck showed up. It was trying to crawl out of the bag as I picked it up. I managed to catch the critter." She held up a jar. Inside, a tracer bug was fluttering around.

A lot like beetles, tracer bugs were from Otherworld, and they did a remarkable job of acting like a tracker—a biological GPS, so to speak. While not intelligent, they could easily be used by anybody who was good with a seeing-eye spell, or any sort of spy spells. Usually, sorcerers used them to track their rivals.

I stared at the thing. They were good at camouflage. I seldom pawed through my purse other than looking for my wallet or my keys. It could have easily hidden there for any length of time.

"When's the last time you fully cleaned out your purse?" Yugi stared at the bug, then motioned for Rane to place the jar on the table.

Thinking back, I tried to remember when I'd last looked through the handbag. After a moment, I knew. "Two weeks ago. I emptied it out to find Nerissa's chocolates she'd tossed in there."

"Can you think of any time in the past two weeks that you haven't been around your purse, other than at home? I doubt anybody there would have bugged your handbag." Yugi jotted something down in his notebook.

"Damn it . . . there have been several occasions." I propped my chin up with my hands. "I can't believe this— my Jag's destroyed. The first accident was bad enough but this one? I can't believe I've been in two wrecks in less than a week. They can't be coincidence."

Roman rubbed his chin and looked at Yugi. "You know who's doing this but you aren't telling us. Don't you think it's time?"

Yugi stared at him for a moment. "Menolly, was your purse unattended during the first accident?"

I frowned, thinking back. "Yeah, actually. It was . . . I left it on the seat when I let . . . whatever her name was— I can't remember it right now—sit in my car to warm up while we waited for the tow truck."

"And she vanished, right?"

"Right. And her insurance information turned out to be fraudulent."

Yugi flipped through the file folder, and I realized it was the same one that they had created for the first accident. "We have here that you told us her name was Eisha te

Kana. Here's the information she gave you for her phone and address, but it says that her info checked out as fake."

"Right. She disappeared, and nobody ever contacted me to tell me if they'd found her."

"We didn't. She just vanished into nowhere." Yugi looked up as Nerissa and my sisters entered the room.

They flocked around me like a group of mother hens, crowding Roman out. I was too rattled to hear what they were all saying, so I held up my hands.

"One at a time. Please." Suddenly feeling as if all the wind had left my sails, I drooped. "I'm tired. I know vamps aren't supposed to get tired, but I am. I'm weary and stressed and shaky."

Camille motioned to the chairs. "Everybody, sit down and shut up. Let Menolly take the lead. She's all right, we can see that much, so back off and give her some space."

Grateful, I waited till they had sorted themselves out. Nerissa vanished for a moment and brought back a box of doughnuts. Camille and Delilah each accepted raspberry-filled pastries, while Nerissa bit into a chocolate-covered cake doughnut. As they listened, I told them what had happened. Recounting it didn't take any of the horror away, nor did spelling out the connection we thought there might be with Eisha te Kana.

"So is your car totally trashed?" Delilah winced as she asked. She knew how much I loved my Jag.

In answer, I pulled out my phone and showed her the pictures I'd taken before driving back to headquarters. The crumpled metal, crushed in on itself, was shocking. That I'd been right in the middle of it was worse.

"Oh, great gods." Delilah motioned to Camille, who peeked over her shoulder. "If it had been Camille or me, we wouldn't have walked out of that alive, I think. Oh, Menolly, your Jag."

"I damned near didn't walk out of there. A dozen spears of metal could have skewered me—or the gas tank could have blown. The only reason my attacker fled was because of the sirens."

At that point, Yugi got a call. After a moment, he hung up. "I'm betting she left the tracer bug in your bag."

"If she left that, did she leave anything else?" Now I was worried. "And why an accident?"

"Maybe because you aren't always accessible? We speculated that one before. It's hard to sneak up on a vampire. But a wreck? Can conceivably kill one. And that night—Eisha may have been armed to take you out another way if the accident didn't work, but you had already called the cops. Do you think she was driving the Hummer?" Delilah flipped open her laptop and began tapping away.

"I don't think so, but I have no idea." Pausing, I frowned and turned to Nerissa. "Can you ask Yugi about whatever it was you wanted to talk to Chase about? For our unexpected guests?"

She blinked. "I hadn't thought of that, but yeah, I might as well. Yugi?"

He glanced over at her. "Yes?"

"Can I speak to you in private for a moment?" She led him out of the room.

I slid back in my chair, stretching out my legs. "I have to buy a new car." That was the first thing that crossed my mind. Then, "If I was bugged, have you guys been targeted, too?"

Camille and Delilah immediately emptied their purses and sorted through. Delilah's was easy—keys, compact, candy bars, phone, and notepad. Camille's was like the jumble from hell. But she went through everything and, finally, shook her head.

"Nothing in mine either. I wonder why they tried the same tactic twice."

"I wasn't expecting it. Puts them at arm's length—a safer place to be with a vampire. This time, they used a bigger vehicle. And it probably would have worked if the cruiser hadn't spotted it and put on the sirens."

Camille set down the rest of her second doughnut. "I have a theory."

"Wait till Yugi gets back. I'm too tired to rehash things over and over."

We sat in silence until he returned, followed by Nerissa. By the look on her beaming face, whatever the conversation was, it had been successful.

"Yugi can hide our guests. Don't ask where, but he and Chase can squirrel them into hiding for a while." She winked at me. "See, I'm good for something!"

The comment was in jest, but it still stung. I winced. "I never, *ever* have implied you aren't."

"I was just joking." She stared at me, then both of us dropped our gazes. Too much stress, too little sleep, and some unresolved nebulous issues made for a volatile combo, and not one to dive into when we were in our current states.

I decided to skirt the issue. "Where? Or can you guys tell us? If you can't, that's fine."

Yugi started to shake his head but Delilah interrupted.

"I know! It's that hidden floor here, isn't it? Chase hinted there was a hidden level to the FH-CSI, and I always thought there might be one." She paused and—at his startled look—laughed. "Don't answer. I know you can't. But that's my guess."

I grinned. "I think you may be onto something, but we'll leave it to Chase whether or not he can tell us. Meanwhile, Camille, you had a theory?"

She nodded slowly, worrying her lip. "My guess . . . this Eisha woman? She was tracking you before this. And I'm betting it was since you refused to sell the bar."

"What? How could she?"

"I don't know, but think about it. The same scenario— she was waiting for you, pulled out at just the right time. Which meant she had to know you were on the way. How? Because she was already following you."

"That fits," Yugi said, and we all stared at him. "While Nerissa and I were outside talking, I got word that the boys found a second tracer bug. It was still alive and in the trunk of your car. And that would fall right in line with Camille's supposition."

"Another one? Fuck." I slammed my hand on the table, shaking it. "Then why the second one? Why bug my purse . . ."

"Easy. While it's not difficult to target your car with a tracer bug, whoever was responsible probably thought ahead. Why not have a second bug ready to go, just in case you survived the first wreck? What if you walked away but your car was totaled? Or needed some extensive work? Why not ensure they can still follow you? Slip the tracer bug into your purse for good measure?"

It all made sense. Lowestar had been targeting me for a while. "Fuck, put security on Shikra of the Utopia Club. Don't ask why; just do it. If I was a target, she'll be a target."

He nodded. "Will do. Meanwhile, be cautious. I know there's more going on here than you are telling me. So be careful, Menolly. Be careful, all of you."

Yugi sent two squad cars to pick up our guests. Violet and the others were exhausted, and they didn't protest as the cops took them away. She asked me if I'd tell Tanne where she was, and I made a vague promise—one I doubted I could keep, since I didn't know the answer to that myself.

Roman followed us back to the house, although I made him stay outside. As much as I liked him, and regardless of the fact that he was my sire now, I refused to give him access to the house.

He waited outside while I said good night to my sisters and Nerissa before they climbed back in bed. Nerissa gave us a narrow look before heading downstairs, but I kissed her long and hard, hoping to reassure her that everything was all right. I had to figure out what I was doing that bothered her. No way in hell did I want my wife pissed off at me like this.

I led Roman over to the porch swing and we sat under the rainy night, as the misting rain whipped past us. I had brought a blanket out, because I didn't want to get wet more than for any other reason, and we huddled beneath it.

"I'm not very chatty." I forestalled his attempts at small talk. "It's not that I don't appreciate our conversations, but so much shit has gone on that I just don't have the energy to keep up chitchat."

"You'd better find a way to do so with your wife. I heard what she said back at the FH-CSI, and I saw the way she looked at you before you entered the house. Nerissa's feeling neglected, and I don't blame her. You have a way of shutting out the world when you don't want to deal with emotion, Menolly. You shut out the people you love—the people who are your friends."

I brooded on his words for moment. And then, in a moment of clarity, they hit home. He was right. I knew I did that, and yet it wasn't something I could help. *Or do you just want to avoid facing it, so you tell yourself you can't help it? Is that it perhaps?*

The thought ran through my mind and I tried to brush it away, but it wouldn't budge. Maybe Roman was right. Was I, after only six months' worth of marriage, already neglecting my wife? I'd been avoiding Roman lately, too. And this past week, I'd tried to avoid my feelings on what was going down back home, focusing instead on what needed to be done.

"All right. I'll give you that one. I'll work on it. But what did you want to talk to me about? What's going down?"

He sighed, leaning back and draping an arm around my shoulders. "First, we've figured out that at least seven of the vamps on the missing-persons list were placed at the Wayfarer the night it was torched. They haven't been seen since, and I think we can safely assume they were dusted."

Seven more victims, for a total of fifteen so far. My stomach lurched. "Oh." I couldn't think of anything else to say. *I'm sorry* didn't cover it.

"We know the Utopia Club fire was arson, as well, and we got the report on what went on down there when you and your sisters went to help. Do you have anything you want to tell me since you last talked to me?"

It was time to come clean. "We know who's behind the fires." I told him about Lowestar then, and the connections between the letters and the threatening phone calls, and what we'd found out about Suvika and why Lowestar was trying to raise him. "We think he's first trying a power grab for Seattle's supernatural businesses. Then we think he might branch out to co-opt the FBH financial district."

Roman coughed. "You mean he's looking to become a supernatural business magnate?"

"It would seem that way. And our worry is, should he manage to raise Suvika, there's a little matter of a prophecy that Suvika's brothers will rise with him, which means three demigods of lord and vice running around. But you cannot start a war with him—I can't let you. Too much rides on secrecy."

"I don't like making promises like that but . . . for you, I will. For now." Roman let out a low whistle. "What have you managed to find out about how far along Lowestar is with his plan?"

"That's the problem. What with everything going down back in Otherworld, and losing our father, and the Way-farer and finding Violet before she could be sold off, we haven't had the chance to look. I guess that's on the agenda for tomorrow. Just please, don't mention we found the prisoners alive. On the off chance that Lowestar doesn't know, we don't want him finding out. It's too dangerous for them and their families."

He nodded. "Got it." After a moment, he leaned back. "So you think Lowestar is responsible for your accident—or rather, accidents?"

"Yeah. I think it's a punishment for not selling the bar."

"Well, the other bit of news, remember that my lawyer wants to talk to you about the lawsuit. We think we can get them to drop it outright, but he needs some information from you first. As soon as you can make arrangements to see him, the better."

And with that, he draped his arm around my shoulders and gathered me in for a long, slow kiss. Roman's lips were soft. They were cool as death, cool as my own, and I lingered, letting his tongue play over my lips.

I moaned lightly into his mouth, realizing just how much stress I'd been under. As he pressed against me, the thirst—the bloodlust—began to wake, whirling up like a rising storm. I let out a little growl and he responded.

"Come, love. Let us go out in the woods. You need me and I need you. You have to release some of the stress, and you know that I'm the best antidote for that. I'm your cure, your remedy, your vaccine against the pressure that you keep pushed down day after day."

My heart lurched at his words and I wanted to cry. He was right. The pressure was absolutely insane, and I worked so fucking hard to keep it in check, to keep the tight rein over my predator that allowed me to exist within society without being a menace.

I nodded, standing. "Lead me, my liege." For he was. He was my liege, my sire, my consort in blood sport.

We slipped down into the darkness, away from the house, toward Birchwater Pond. The slow beat of the forest rippled past, echoing with the autumn storm. But the rain and wind were of no consequence, and as we began to run, to chase through the trees, they became so many blurs. I tagged Roman on the shoulder.

"You're it."

He laughed. "Try as you might." And he was off and running.

I gave him a five-second start, then began to race through the forest, hunting him, seeking him, following his trail. I could smell him on the wind, taste the bloodlust that surrounded his wake. He was fast, terribly fast, and cunning—the perfect apex predator, and I was one of the few that could follow him where he was going. I stalked him, peeking behind tree and bush, picking up his scent, lust bubbling up in my veins like slow fire.

The woods were a cacophony of sound, of tree branches sighing in the wind, of leaves swirling in the darkness, rain pounding through leaf and bough and needle. The animals were silent—they knew we were out, they knew we were hunting, and fear trailed their retreat. But we weren't out for them—we weren't out for fresh blood. Not tonight. Tonight we were both hunter and hunted, and our focus was solely placed on each other.

And then, as I paused by a boulder beneath a large fir tree, a noise from above startled me. Roman landed in front of me from where he'd been hiding up in the branches. His eyes were on fire, and he was laughing as he tapped my shoulder.

"You're it. Go."

And, my cunt tightening, I turned and raced into the night. I was his prey, only this time I wanted him to catch me. I wanted him to find me, to take me down—but I couldn't make it easy. If he found me, it would be because he could match me, not because I gave him any quarter.

I passed through brush and fern, barely skimming the ground, and then, in the way he had taught me, fueled by his blood in my veins, I closed my eyes and, in the next moment, was gliding into the night on bat wings.

Spiraling up and out, into the storm, I reveled in the currents that tossed me from side to side. The storm was blowing up a gale now, and I let it carry me on, giving in. Tired of fighting, I let the wind carry me willy-nilly, and then, spotting a good place to hide, I spiraled down to land on a branch of a tall fir. As I shifted back into my normal form, I wondered how far away Roman was. I stood up, holding on to the tree for balance, trying to scout out the area, but I couldn't see him. Secure in my lead, I lightly stepped off the branch and slowly levitated to the ground. There I began to run through the trees again.

The exercise was doing wonders for my mood—the stress coming out in the movement. I began to laugh, not caring if he heard me. For the first time in days, I felt free. If I were still alive, I'd say I was able to breathe.

And then, as I rounded the corner of a stand of cedar, there he was, waiting for me. Roman was leaning against a cedar, a smart-assed look on his face. I skidded to a halt as the mood shifted in a fraction of a second. My hunger grew strong, my thirst burning in my throat. As he began to walk me back against a tree as big around as a car, I locked eyes with him, watching him cautiously.

His icy gray gaze swept over me, and I felt naked. The next moment he lunged forward and had hold of my hands. I found myself back up against the tree, as he thrust my arms over my head and caught my mouth with lips soft as silk, sweet as blood and wine. His fangs began to descend and I moaned, wanting him. Wanting to dive deep under his skin, to taste the blood rise to the surface, bubble into my mouth with its foaming crimson warmth.

Blood. It was the only part about him—the only part of me—that retained any heat. Blood, the life force. Blood, the passion and the pain. Blood, the crimson flowers that stained the snow, that stained alabaster skin, that stained sheets and clothes and bodies. Blood, the drink of the damned—and I wanted it, wanted Roman's blood so badly I screamed.

"Feed me. Drink me. Taste me. Fuck me."

He laughed, low and sultry, and his arms enveloped me, holding me tight. "Can you moan for me, pretty one? Can you beg for me? Because I would beg for you—I'd beg for a taste of your blood, to fuck your cunt, to fill you up and drive you deep into the night."

I shifted, exposing my neck, and Roman leaned his head back, fangs gleaming in the shock of lightning that flashed overhead. He reared back, then with a low moan of desire, of lust, he plunged deep into my skin. I felt the blood begin to flow, and the ache of his bite, the pain of his fangs, drove themselves deep into my heart.

"Hurt me, make me bleed, make me feel." I begged him, pleading for the pain. Pleading for the sensations that reminded me I was still here, still existing.

He made it hurt for me, made it ache, driving me under with a wash of bloody tears and searing pain. And in the pain, I began to weep. Weeping for my father, for my sisters, for the thousands who had died in Elqaneve. I wept for the victims who had been caught in the fire at my bar. I wept for Nerissa, who was stuck with loving me—who deserved so much better.

As the tears stained my face, Roman began to murmur something, and the next thing I knew, we were standing in the middle of a brilliant shower of blood, in a waterfall of energy—red and gold and burning orange, and all around was the scent of copper, the copper of blood, the cloying wash that gave the creatures of the earth their substance. Blood was life. Blood was power.

And there, under the Crimson Veil, under the watchful eyes of the great Mother of Vampires, Roman took me to the ground. He ripped at my shirt, and tossed it to the side. I unzipped my jeans, pushing them down as he removed his smoking jacket. Then, unzipping his leather pants, he pushed them down and moved between my legs.

I looked up at him, the hunger gnawing deep. "Take me. Make me feel alive. I need to feel alive."

With a rough laugh, he flipped me over. "I will make you feel alive in every way I can. As long as that's what you want."

"Do it. Do whatever you want to me."

Roman let out a low grunt as he stuck two fingers up my cunt, and my body responded. I groaned as he pulled them out and lubricated my ass with them. Instinct took over and I tightened my butt cheeks, but he wouldn't stop. He parted them—surprisingly gentle in his movements—and then, inserted one finger up my ass. I shifted, moaning as the surprising notes of pleasure swept through me.

"You like that?"

I nodded. "More?"

"As you wish, my consort." And then, he pushed his cock against my ass, slowly driving forward, easing himself inside, fraction by fraction of an inch, until he let out a satisfied grunt. "Head's in. Now, love, are you ready? I'm going to fill you up, take it to the hilt. Beg me."

Responding to the passion behind his words, to the absolute feeling of being desired and wanted, I obeyed. "Fuck me. Fuck me hard."

And so he drove in, and again the mix of pain and pleasure sent me reeling. I squirmed as he slowly thrust in to the hilt, till I could feel his balls pressing against my butt. And then, he reached down between my legs and began to finger my clit. As I fell into the rhythm, and began to soar—rising higher, letting out little cries—he abruptly stopped and pulled out.

He reached down and grabbed me by the ankles, flipping me over on my back. With a quick wipe of his cock, he lunged between my legs, plunging deep into my cunt.

As he shifted, penetrating deeper with each thrust, his eyes never leaving my face, all that existed was his cock inside me, the sensation of being full, of not having to be the one in charge. Of not having to worry about hurting him.

I fell into his stare as around us the veil of blood continued to flow. The energy of the Veil began to absorb us into it, and I realized that I was fucking the essence of the blood, fucking the soul of every vampire that had ever walked the world. Their passion, hunger, drive roiled around me in vast clouds of thirst and joy and hunger and pain.

Finally, when I could stand it no longer, I let go of my pain, of my fear, and gave it up. And as I did so, I came, losing myself in an orgasm that spiraled me into the fire. Into the blood. Back into the core of myself.

Chapter 17

❧❧❧

When I came to, Roman and I were snuggled up at the base of the tree. Exhausted, I closed my eyes as he wrapped his arm around me. I was shirtless, but my jeans were buttoned and the softness of his jacket against my skin felt welcoming. He kissed the top of my head.

"Better now?"

I nodded. "I needed that." Pausing, I took stock. I felt refreshed. Tired but like a whole fuckton of stress had gone bye-bye. The sex had been fantastic, but it was more than that. "I feel renewed."

"That's because of where we were." He leaned forward, brushing a spider off his leg.

"Were we in . . . the Veil?" I'd been in the Crimson Veil only once, when his mother, Blood Wyne—Queen of the Vampire Nation—had sent me there. And within the Veil I'd learned more about my true nature, about the nature of vampires, than I had ever known even existed. The Crimson Veil was the core of the hunger—of the bloodlust. It was the source of vampirism, created by Mother Kesana, who had melded her soul with a demon to become the first vampire to walk the earth.

"Yes, I took you to the Veil. You were exhausted and weary. You've had some great shocks lately. The Veil is a place of renewal and regeneration. And you so dearly needed both." He stood then, pulling me to my feet. "I have business to attend to before the rest of the night is spent. But Menolly . . . thank you. Thank you for letting me help you. And remember what I said about Nerissa. You need to give her more of yourself. You can't just take on a title of wife and expect that wearing it will be enough. You have to *live* the part."

And with that, he grabbed my hand and we raced through the forest at a blinding speed. He stopped at the bottom of the porch steps, kissed me once more, and then vanished into the night.

As I headed up the stairs, I realized that for the first time in a long while, I felt rested and ready to face whatever might be coming. Inside, I glanced at the clock. It was going on four. Mourning my Jag, but feeling oddly content, for the rest of the night, I watched old movies, curled up in the living room.

The next evening—or rather late afternoon, considering how early the sun was setting—I woke up to a relatively calm house. Hanna was washing dishes, and it looked like dinner was over. Maggie was playing in her playpen, Delilah and Camille were poring over the documents Carter had given us about the Farantino Building. The guys were busy outside cleaning up after the storm. Though I hadn't noticed it the night before while in the throes of wild hot monkey sex with Roman, the wind had been blowing up a gale, and now branches littered the yard.

As I picked up Maggie out of her playpen and snuggled her for a moment, Kitten gave me a resigned smile. But at least, it was a smile. Maggie yanked on my hair—which hurt like the devil—as I cuddled the little gargoyle.

"Camille, can you braid my hair? I've decided that, while it's pretty down, I don't want to keep it loose in case of a fight. Too much chance to have it used against me." With how curly and tangled my hair was, much safer to leave it braided up. I tucked Maggie back in her playpen and crossed to the table.

"Sure." She stood, arching her back. "Where are the beads?"

I handed her the box I'd picked up off my dresser. They contained a bunch of new beads that Nerissa had bought for me and I had pretty much ignored till now. "Here, why don't you try some of these?"

They were pretty—greens and blues and gold. I'd been hesitant to change them because . . . well . . . now I wasn't sure what my reasons were, but this seemed like the first step to letting my wife know how much she meant to me. She'd mentioned once or twice how I wouldn't even consider some of her suggestions when it came to hair and clothes.

Camille smiled softly as she picked up the box. "I helped her pick these out, you know. She asked me what you might like."

Now I *did* feel like a heel, but I chose to ride over it. "I have to buy a new car. I don't want to buy a new one, but there's no help for it. Mine's trashed. So what say we go down to the dealer and see what we can find? Roman will front me the money, so no worries on that count."

"We can get one hell of a good deal. We did before." Camille snickered as she began brushing through my hair and parting it into sections. She used a mister to moisten the curls and smooth them down as she braided them.

"What kind of car are you thinking of getting?" Delilah pushed aside the files she'd been looking at. "Another Jag?"

I frowned. "No . . . too many associations now with being almost pulverized twice. I'm thinking I might get a Mustang. I thought about it before the Jaguar and now . . . well . . ."

"Why don't we build it online and then order it?" Delilah brought up the website, and within seconds, we were building my new car. I wanted the royal blue color—or that's what I called it—and as we added up the options, I grimaced at the price tag. But Roman had said to get what I wanted and I could take as long as I wanted to pay him back. Of course, he'd also said I didn't have to pay him back but that wasn't going to happen.

Delilah hit the final update button and then a search. "Looks like you can have it in three days at the Belles-Faire dealership. Forty-one thousand and some change."

I grimaced but texted Roman. Within minutes I had a return text to forward the information and the check would be delivered to the dealership, so that I could pick up the car without worries when it came in. And that was that. No muss. No fuss. No hours spent listening to the dealer trying to sell me something I didn't want.

"Is Nerissa home yet?" I wanted to talk to her. Wanted to start mending the fences before they fully broke.

"Not yet, but she should be soon. Now hold still while I finish your hair." She made quick work of the rest—by now she'd had plenty of practice—and I had shiny new beads in my cornrows.

I suddenly wondered why I'd been so hesitant to change them before. The new beads were pretty, and they didn't do anything but spruce up my hair. Why had I been so resistant? Pondering the question, I barely noticed when Camille's phone rang and she answered. But the next moment, I sure as hell noticed her conversation.

"Holy fuck. Right! We'll get right over there. Thanks, Carter." As she punched the End Talk button, Delilah and I looked at her, waiting.

"You don't want to know. But we have to go out tonight and we'd better get our butts in gear. Carter wants to see us *now*. And he said come prepared and with a full crew, which I'm translating to *'be ready for a fight.'*"

We scrambled. I scribbled off a note for Nerissa, while Delilah hurried outside to alert the men. Camille raced upstairs to change clothes. Within ten minutes, we were armed and ready to go. Because Aeval's men were guarding the house, we decided that Roz and Trillian should stay behind, while Morio, Smoky, Shade, and Vanzir would go with us.

"Morio, Smoky, Menolly—you come with me. Shade and Vanzir, ride with Delilah." Camille barked out orders as we crowded out of the doorway. As we split off to the two cars, a streak of lightning split the sky and rain thundered down. It was definitely the night for a fight, all right.

Carter was waiting for us. He hurried us in, out of the rain. Tea was waiting, and cookies—you could always count on Carter to provide refreshments and hospitality, even if the situation was dire. And by the look on his face, the shit was about to hit the fan.

We filed into his living room and gathered around the coffee table, where he had what looked like some architectural plans scattered around. He took his seat, and without chitchat or even his usual niceties, he dove right in.

"I think Lowestar will try to wake Suvika tonight."

Crap. None of us had expected to hear that. We stared at him, silence thick as pea soup.

"What the hell did you do to spur him on like this? It had to be you—only a major disruption in his plans would force him to move this fast. He's slow and steady; otherwise he wouldn't have flown under the radar all these years." Carter bit into one of his cookies and cocked his head, a quizzical look on his face.

I glanced at the others. "We may have freed all his potential sex slaves."

"You *may* have? Or you *did*?"

"Well . . . did. Or at least all of them we could find. We have them in hiding—if Lowestar finds them, chances are he'll either kill them or worse. He's not the type to take this sort of behavior lying down." I scuffed my foot against the carpet. "By the way, do you know of a Fae woman named Eisha te Kana?"

Carter did a double take. "You're friends with a paid assassin? Of course I know who she is."

It was our turn to spit-take. "You mean you actually know her name without checking up on any files? Then she didn't give me a false name?"

He slapped his palm to his forehead. "If you've run afoul of her, consider yourself lucky to still be alive. Eisha's well paid, but not because she's terribly discreet. No, she's willing to take risks—put her own life on the line to go after her target. What the hell happened?"

I shrugged. "I think Lowestar hired her to kill me after I refused to sell my bar. That didn't work, so she planted a tracer bug on me and another goon—maybe her, too—came after me."

Carter shook his head. "Probably right on that. She's never out to get anybody on a personal level, but the woman will do anything for money. Chances are she was paid well to make a hit. And now that she's failed to kill you twice? She'll probably be long gone before whoever took out the contract can catch up with her and take her down for failure. I doubt you'll ever see her again."

I leaned back. That was reassuring, yet not. She was still out there. Gun for hire. Or in this case, SUV for hire.

"Meanwhile, back to Lowestar and Suvika. Word has filtered through the grapevine that he's performing the ritual tonight. So I did a little more research—I paid dearly for this information so I hope you appreciate it. The ritual to waken the demigod must take place during the first three days after the dark of the moon, in the autumn-tide. So it's perfect timing."

Carter tossed a dossier on the table. "Here's what I could gather. I think there must be a temple complex beneath the Farantino Building. And I think that's where they will be performing the rite. To do so takes blood. Human blood. The fresh, warm, sticky blood of a virgin girl and a strong young man."

He sat back, taking another cookie.

I picked up the file and opened it. Then as Carter motioned to the blueprints, Delilah scooped them up.

The file was a treatise on how the ritual to Suvika went. It was written in a foreign tongue, but had been translated to English. I skimmed through the rites and charms to get an idea of what we were facing, and it wasn't pretty.

"Okay, we have ritual bloodletting as part of the offering. The defloration of virgins. Throat cutting of young virile men. The offering of gold and silver. A little torture, a little tickle . . . the whole ball of wax. Suvika must be friends with Jakaris." Jakaris was the Svartan god of vice and torture, and I had the feeling that they'd have a fuckton of fun together.

Delilah held up the prints. "It seems the Farantino Building is definitely hiding more than we thought. In the basement, there is a passage that leads to a stairwell going down."

"Not back into Underground Seattle." Camille groaned.

"No, but into the depths of a temple. From what I can tell, there's a way to get into the temple through an old sewer line that runs there."

"Great. What you want to bet he's filled it with alligators?" Camille put her cookie down, looking vaguely nauseated. "The last thing I want to do is tramp through a sewer."

"It could be worse. Maybe they've figured out a way to hook up electric lines through the sewage. One good turn of the switch and bingo. Crispy critters via electrocution. Crispy critters that *smell*." I hadn't meant to sound flippant, but it came out that way. "Oh, don't give me those looks. You all know what I mean. And if that's actually the case, better we plan on it in advance and be happily surprised if it doesn't happen."

"You make a good point." Vanzir frowned. "So what—we go in there tonight and invade their temple room? Very *Conan the Barbarian*."

"Very *Indiana Jones and the Crystal Skull*," Delilah countered.

"Very likely to get us killed but who the fuck cares?" Camille let out a short burst of laughter. "We've faced worse before. Gulakah was a full-fledged god, not just some sleeping demigod. And Lowestar is a daemon. We've fought *demon generals*. But what do we know about his body guards other than he seems to have a penchant for hellhounds and Tregart-like thugs? Does he have any secondary priests—because I assume he is a priest of this god?"

"He is, indeed. I managed to scrounge up a few details about the ritual. Not many, but enough to give us a rough guideline. First, it requires that the rite be performed at four hours before midnight. Meaning eight P.M. It's almost six now. Second, they need a virgin to sacrifice. Old school, but apparently Suvika gets into the kinky stuff. And third, they must have a virile and muscular young man—I wasn't able to translate the reasons for that except it involves throat cutting. Lastly, the priest attempting to wake Suvika and become his favorite must offer a basket of gold and a basket of silver up to the demigod."

"Virgin. Jock. Gold and silver. Got it." I shook my head. This was starting to sound like a bad B-grade horror flick. *Satan's Schlong for Girls* or some such movie. "So what goes down during this horror show?"

Carter repressed a snicker. "Well, they kill the virgin, which means you have to save the girl first. Then I'm not sure what they do with the jock, but the money is poured into a fire hot enough to melt it. After that it gets muddy and hard to translate, but the best I can read it, Suvika wakes up, the priest gets rewarded, and then . . . whatever happens, I have no clue. But it can't be good."

"No, it can't be good." You just didn't wake up a creaky old perverted demigod and expect fruity joy to follow.

"So we go in. We stop Lowestar. I assume that means killing him because you know that if we do anything else, he'll be back, worse than ever." Smoky slid his hands into his jeans' pockets and leaned back in his chair. "Our actions yesterday precipitated this, but there was nothing else we could do. We couldn't leave the prisoners there. And they're in danger until Lowestar is put out to pasture."

"I have a question." Morio leaned forward, resting his elbows on his knees. "What the fuck do we do if he does manage to summon up Suvika? How do you fight this demigod?"

I wanted to say "perish the thought," but the truth was, we did need to think about the possibility. "Carter, what do you know about Suvika's vulnerabilities? The information I found earlier stated that if he's summoned incorrectly, all hell will break loose and he'll be totally free. Which indicates that he might be under some form of control if Lowestar manages to perform the rites correctly."

"Suvika is one of what we call the ancient gods. They predate the Greeks and Romans. My father, Hyperion the Titan, is from that time-before-time. While some of the world had written records—Egypt, Sumer, Babylonia— there were great civilizations that you know nothing about because all record of them was lost to time. Atlantis is one of these. Predating Egypt, it was an island nation that did, indeed, sink beneath the waves when the massive volcano that was at the center of the island erupted, causing a huge quake and tsunami. There's very little in the way of proof that it ever existed, but it was there."

"I found evidence that he is thought to be either an ancient Mongolian or Finnish deity—at least from that area." I frowned. "But there's not much to go on."

"That's because those cultures were passed down through oral tradition. So much has been lost over the years, especially when you go back that far. But if he is from that area, then we need to find his weakness, and find the proper name of his enemy—be it iron or whatever."

"That sounds like something Tanne was talking about. He mentioned knowing the name of . . . oh . . . some metal." Camille quickly told him about Tanne's part in rescuing Violet and the others.

"Black Forest Fae? Then he may be useful in helping you with this. Call him and see if he'll go with you. Meanwhile, I'll see if I can find anything at all on Suvika's weaknesses while you start looking over these plans."

As he took to his computer, we studied the blueprints, figuring out what was where. Camille put in a call to Tanne, who agreed to meet us outside the Farantino Building at around six thirty.

Carter returned as we were trying to trace a route into the building. It appeared there *was* access via the city sewers.

"I found very little, other than Suvika loves metals. Therefore, I doubt if any one metal in particular will harm him. However, from what I could tell, he didn't like the outdoors very much and spent most of his waking time in temples, where yew was banned. Perhaps yew can harm him?"

"My staff is yew." Camille frowned. "But I forgot to bring it."

"Great. We're all armed up and he likes metal." Delilah pulled her dagger out of her boot and began toying with it.

Carter reached out. "May I see that?"

She paused, then handed him Lysanthra. As he touched it, he laughed, and the dagger let out a melodic chime that echoed through the room and began to glow with a pale yellow light. We'd all seen the energy around the sentient dagger before, but never like this. It began to hum and vibrate, and then with a flash, the silver took on a softly burnished glow.

Delilah gasped as he handed the dagger back to her. "What—what . . . oh, great gods. What did you do? I can feel her so much more—she's . . ." With a soft awe in her voice, she whispered, "She's beautiful. I've never heard her sing before."

Carter cocked his head to one side. "I didn't realize you had one of the daggers of Luciél."

"Luciél? And . . . this is one of a matched set of three that our father gave us." Delilah glanced over at Camille, who pulled out her own dagger and presented it to Carter.

Carter stroked the metal and smiled softly. "Your dagger is still sleeping. I cannot waken it, just make it more aware once it has chosen to rise and shine. The third, I assume, would be Menolly's?"

I nodded. "I can't touch it, though. Obviously."

"The daggers of Luciél belonged to three Fae sisters—they were full Fae, make no mistake about that. And they ruled one of the barrow mounds Earthside before the Great Divide. They were warrior women and great lovers. Not much is known about them, save for bits and pieces in song and legend. They stood together, bound by blood and honor, and I believe . . . they died together during a great battle." He stared at Delilah and Camille's daggers, a somber look on his face. "You bear the weapons of warrior women. Do not disgrace your legacy."

"I wonder if Father knew what these were. I don't know where he got them, but one day he brought them home and said they were for us. Many years back when we were just starting out with the YIA." Camille hung her head. "I doubt we'll ever know now . . . how much he understood of their nature."

I cleared my throat, not wanting to let the mood fall into a melancholy state. "We have work to do. We can reminisce later."

And so, fueled by cookies and pot after pot of tea, we spent the next hour planning out our strategy. It felt odd, having an actual plan of action, and part of me wondered how much our luck relied on our haphazard and chaotic nature. Well, we were going to find out. That much was for sure.

By the time we headed out for the Farantino Building, it was six twenty. We were cutting it close. We had an hour and forty minutes until Lowestar decided to play Keymaster-Gatekeeper; only this was real and not *Ghostbusters*.

The plans had shown that the way in was via a secret passage located in a broom closet. It could also be reached from a passage in Lowestar's office. The broom closet was our likelier target, given that the daemon probably kept his office highly warded. I had visions of bombs destroying the building if we barged in without an expert.

I'd suggested bringing Daniel in on this, but Camille and Delilah nixed the idea immediately as too dangerous for him. He was, after all, FBH. And they also refused to call Chase to tell him about our plans.

"He's risking enough with his regular job, now that he has Astrid. With Sharah gone, he's the only guardian that baby has and we're not about to put him in any form of danger if we can help it."

For someone who didn't want kids, Camille sure had a protective nature toward them. But then again, she'd been our protector when Delilah and I were little, and she'd never grown out of it. I had the feeling she never would.

"Okay, but I have to tell Nerissa where we're going. And Hanna and Trillian and Roz need to know, too."

They agreed with that, so while we were on the way over, I called home. I got hold of Roz and asked him to get Nerissa for me. When she came on the phone, my heart leapt at her voice.

"We're on our way in to try to stop Lowestar, love." I told her what had gone down at Carter's. "We don't have a choice. It's move tonight or risk him succeeding. We have no idea whether he can actually manage this, but we don't dare take a chance that he can."

Her voice was shaky. "I understand and I'll tell Trillian and Roz. Promise me you'll be careful? Promise me you won't do anything stupid?"

I didn't want her to cry. I didn't want to scare her. I was about to tell her to man up, but then, I realized that maybe she was scared because she loved me. Maybe she needed to feel what she was feeling and not repress her fear.

I sought for something that would tell her I loved her. Words alone just weren't enough at times. And then I knew. "Honey?"

I could imagine her perfect pink lips mouthing the word *yes* as she spoke softly into the phone.

"I'm wearing the beads. I had Camille braid them into my hair. I love them—they're perfect. And so are you." And then before I could stop myself, I choked on my words, and dashed away the threat of a tear, stoically ignoring the looks Smoky and Morio were giving me. Camille didn't glance over her shoulder, though I knew she was listening.

Nerissa started to cry then and I felt both helpless and a little gratified. "I am *not* perfect, and neither are you. You don't listen to me, and you try to protect me when I don't need protecting. You turn yourself off—you shut down when I cry or get upset. But I still love you, damn it. Even though you put me on a pedestal, which you *know* I hate, I love you!"

I bit my lip, my fangs descending as I tried to find the right words to defuse the situation. But then I realized I was doing it again. I was shutting down, falling back on logic, sidestepping her emotion.

"I know. I'm sorry. I do that. I really do. I'll try to do better—but you have to understand how hard this is for me. I spent years cultivating my self-control, and I'm afraid that if I lose that, if so much as a crack appears, I won't be able to control my predator!" Again I glared at Morio. And Smoky, who was looking over his shoulder at me.

Nerissa paused . . . I could hear her heart through the phone, it was beating so loud. She cleared her throat. "I never knew that you were afraid of that. I didn't know . . . I thought you just were uncomfortable expressing emotion."

"Only because I'm afraid that if I let myself go, I'll . . . *really* let myself go and then I'll hurt somebody. And if I hurt you, I'd never, ever forgive myself. Listen, love, I have to go. We're almost at the Farantino Building. Tell Trillian and Roz what we're up to, and we'll talk when I get home."

She laughed, just a little, but it was enough. "Be careful, you beautiful, sexy vamp you. You're my wife. And you're the only woman in the world for me."

I could hear the relief in her voice. "And you . . . you're my heart's desire. I'll see you later. Don't wait up."

"Right. That's a good one." And then she hung up and I

leaned back. At least I had cleared the air. Now we could start to work on strengthening our relationship.

But first . . . first we had to take a walk through Lowestar's nightmare ritual. And we had to stop a demigod from regaining consciousness. Oh yeah. No pressure. No pressure at all.

Chapter 18

❧❦❧

While the building looked dark when we got there, we knew better. I glanced at the car clock. Six thirty-five. Not quite ninety minutes. While we had the plans, and we knew basically where we were going, the trick would be, first, to break into the building without setting off any alarms, and second, to find our way into the temple without alerting any guards. And there were bound to be guards. There was no doubt of that in any of our minds.

We parked in the lot across the street, and as we stepped out, Tanne slipped out of a nearby archway that led into the building there—it was some sort of wholesale distributor.

He held up a wand. "I brought yew, like you asked."

"Are you sure you're up for this?" I studied his face. He didn't have to throw his lot in with ours. "This is going to be dangerous, you know."

"I have lived with danger all my life. Remember what I do?" He grinned then. "Actually, I'm rather looking forward to a good showdown. I haven't done much in the way of hunting since I've been in the States, and it's time I got things organized and set up for the Clan to migrate. My sister, Silber, will be moving here soon."

I nodded. He did seem more alert, more vibrant, than when we'd first met him, and I had a feeling he thrived on adventure. "Well, good. We don't know if yew will affect Suvika, and hopefully we won't have to find out. But just in case, I'm glad you brought the wand."

Camille wanted to see it, of course, but I shook my head. "You two can ooo-and-ahh over magical tools all you want later. Right now, let's get a move on. Every minute that slips by is a minute closer to the time when Lowestar is scheduled to perform the ritual. We're at six forty-five, and that gives us a little over an hour. And we still have to brief Tanne, here, on our plans."

As we ran them down for him, he listened carefully.

"The plans show a tunnel leading from the sewers up into the basement. Prepare yourself for a *delightful* stench." Not for the first time, I was grateful that I didn't have to breathe. Though some smells were strong enough to notice without bothering to inhale.

"I can't wait for this. *Not*." Camille grimaced as we headed for the manhole cover. "I just have no stomach for this kind of thing."

"You can blast an enemy with death magic and blow their brains out. You can impale the Black Unicorn with his own horn. You can mix up potions using the damndest ingredients, but you can't stomach a little stench?" I was teasing her, of course, to take the edge off the tension, but she just flashed me one of her *"you have to be kidding"* glares and I backed off. Sometimes jokes weren't the ticket.

"Speaking of, I left the horn at home. It's still recharging." She flashed me another look, daring me to argue, but I wasn't about to.

Smoky yanked the manhole cover off with two fingers. The dude was strong. He was big and strong, and I was damned glad he was on my side. Nothing like having an angry dragon breathing down your neck.

Time to establish marching order.

"I'm going first. Smoky—you're up front right behind me. Then Vanzir, Delilah. Camille, and Morio. Tanne and Shade in the back, please." As everyone lined up, I cautiously lowered myself into the manhole tunnel. The rungs of the ladder going down were steel rather than iron—which made good sense, considering the propensity for rust in damp quarters.

The sewer tunnel was brick or stone—it was hard to tell in the dark, and with only a flashlight hanging from my belt to shine light down, I wasn't really taking a close look at the walls. The fit was fine for me, but I was glad I wasn't Smoky—he managed it, but with his six-four frame, it was a snug squeeze.

As I scrambled down, I didn't really expect to meet any problems along the way. It wasn't like Underground Seattle, where creatures routinely made their homes, other than rats and cockroaches. I couldn't see Lowestar worrying too much about sewer traffic, considering how dank and nasty it was.

The climb wasn't terribly far, but when I reached the bottom, I realized that the sewer tunnel itself was only around five feet tall, and narrow. Very narrow shoulders lined the sides, while water and debris rushed through the channel in between them. Thank gods, we didn't have far to go, because—if I didn't have claustrophobia coming down here—I could easily see how fast I might develop it.

I hurried south, in the direction of the Farantino Building, grimacing as I gave up trying to balance on the thin, slick bricks forming the side ledges and just walked in the muck.

The smell was rank, it filtered into my nose, into my mouth, and I heard Smoky behind me let out a garbled sound as he bent over, trying to fit through the passage. He was bent double, and it occurred to me that—if anything did live down here and wanted a fight—we were in a shitload of trouble. At that moment I stepped in what seemed to be a steaming pile of crap, and I groaned at my unintentional pun.

The temperature was bad—it was like a muggy, clammy day, and I hurried ahead, not wanting the rest of them to be caught here. Breathing would become a problem if we were down here too long, and even though we were all resistant to so many FBH diseases and infections, that didn't mean we couldn't suffer from other issues brought on by the sheer amount of bacteria that must be roaming the water, walls, and air.

Camille's voice echoed from behind. "Fuck . . . this is bad! Hurry up."

"I'm pushing through," I called back. "We don't have far to go, but be careful. It's slippery and nasty." Though truth be told, if somebody started to fall to the side, they'd land against the wall before they landed on the ground. There really wasn't anyplace to fall.

"This sewer tunnel isn't used much anymore," Vanzir said. "I had a long look at the plans. If it was, we'd be in a hell of a lot of hurt right now. This one is old and only a few buildings make use of it."

"Small favors, huh?" I shuddered as I leaned out to brace myself against the wall and a swarm of roaches fluttered over my hand. Shaking them off, I tried not to shriek. "Roaches coming up—lots of them. Try not to touch the walls too much."

"Any signs of viro-mortis slime?" Delilah's question was a good one.

"Stop and I'll look." I pulled my flashlight off my belt and shone it toward the walls. A flurry of movement startled me—*a murmuration of roaches*? Not quite as pretty as starlings. Beneath the roaches, as I glanced along the tunnel, I could see layers of fat built up. Enough to make me gag. For once, I was grateful I couldn't eat. And then, ahead to the left, yes—some green goo oozing along the wall.

"Affirmative on the viro-mortis slime. Be very careful about where you put your hands. I only see the green kind—which is the less aggressive type—but that doesn't mean that there isn't some indigo slime hanging out and that would be harder to see."

I wondered how many sewer workers had been harmed by the stuff—it seldom appeared in areas without high ectoplasmic activity from the Netherworld, or from ghosts in general. But then again, we were near a ghost-ridden area of town, and the spiritual activity here was extremely high. So it was no surprise that viro-mortis slimes were showing up.

Delilah let out a garbled reply. She'd been on the receiving end of their attentions before. The slimes acted a lot like the Blob—growing to encompass the host onto whom they attached themselves, and then they set about devouring—or rather absorbing—the creature. The thought that maybe they'd take care of the cockroach problem soon ran through my head, but I shook it away. Random thoughts could be dangerous, especially when we needed to focus.

Another moment, though, brought me to a ladder heading up. The tunnel continued, but the plans had shown that the first ladder south of where we entered the tunnel should take us up to an old manhole that was there when the building was built. Michael Farantino had simply built over it, agreeing to give city workers access to the tunnel through the basement if need be. Apparently back then, the city planners had been willing to agree, probably for a good-size sum of money, no doubt.

Grateful, I stood up. Even I'd had to bend over in here, and my back groaned a little as I reached up and grabbed the rungs, swinging myself up and onto the ladder. Within another minute, I was at the top, cautiously listening for any sound that might be coming from the basement. Here was where we were taking a big risk—we had no clue if anybody might be on the other side. But given the ritual was set for tonight in the underground levels of the building, my guess was they wouldn't be guarding a lone manhole cover in the basement.

Carefully, inch my inch, I eased the cover up and to the side, then peeked out. The basement was dark, and I heard no breath, no sound of movement. Relieved, I swung myself up and out of the dank tunnel.

Within minutes we were all standing there, albeit dirty, grimy, and reeking like overripe sardines. Except Smoky, that is. As usual, his duster was sparkling white, his clothes were clean, if a bit damp, and he smelled like his usual musky dragon self. I wanted to smack him. It wasn't fair.

Camille let out a long sigh, staring at her boots—which were ruined. There was no way to save suede after that little walk through the muck. Delilah didn't look too happy either. Neither did the others actually. On the bright side, being in a grumpy mood might just make us fight harder and better.

Nobody spoke—we didn't want to chance giving ourselves away—but we already knew what we were going to do. The broom closet that led to the hidden levels was one floor up, not on the main floor but a subfloor. We headed up to level S-1, taking the stairs rather than the elevator. There was no telling if the elevators had hidden cameras in them, and now was not the time to find out.

Level S-1 had an employee break room and several conference rooms on it. And the maintenance room. But . . . there to the right of the janitor's closet was a narrow door. And that was our goal.

It was locked, of course. I just hoped nobody else was running late and would catch us in the act. From everything we knew about rituals—and Camille and Morio had performed a lot of them—most large-scale operations required an extensive setup period. Which meant, we were hoping, that everybody who needed to be downstairs in the temple room was already there.

Tanne motioned us back. He leaned over and began whispering to the lock. Again the incantation sounded like a low trill as he persuaded the lock to release and open. Another moment, and a soft *click* sounded, and the door sprang ajar. He quietly pushed it all the way open, and we were looking into a small, square room. No stairs. No nothing.

But Morio motioned for me to move to the side, and he stepped into the room, said something—he, too, barely whispered the words—and the outline of a door appeared. There was a handle, but no obvious lock.

"I'm not sensing any traps." Morio reached for the handle. "I'll bet if there were any, he had to disarm them to make sure nobody who was supposed to be down there set one off by accident."

That made sense. But I stopped him.

"Let me go first. And Smoky. You get back with Camille and start prepping whatever spells it is you guys prep."

"We can encircle the group with protection, but that would mean we'd have to take time to regroup if we need to fight." He glanced around at the others. "You all willing to go in without our force field?"

"Better to have you guys on the offense, rather than worry about a little defense." Vanzir held up his sword. It was a wicked little number, and it was barbed. When it thrust into someone, the barbs slid in smoothly, then flared out at the push of a button, making the return damned nasty.

With a deep breath, I looked at Smoky. He nodded, and I opened the door.

We found ourselves staring at a steep, spiral stairway. It wasn't metal—but simple, concrete, spiraling down a pale cream-colored passageway. Brightly lit, it wasn't at all what you would think of in terms of a hidden passage leading to an underground temple. But then, Lowestar was a pretty classy daemon when it came to style. I doubted he'd want anything remotely gothic. No cobwebs, no dust, no doom-and-gloom stone walls dripping with slime and moisture.

But the trouble with concrete stairs in a stairwell? They're going to echo, no matter what you do. Still, we did our best to silently make our descent. By what the plans had shown us, there were three flights leading down to the temple area. A level above was used for . . . well, we didn't know what the rooms there were used for. But the temple itself was the bottom, and that was where we were headed.

We passed the doorway leading into the floor above the temple, and I paused to press my ear against the door. There were muffled sounds on the other side—not a comforting thought. But we didn't have time to explore. We were already running near seven thirty. We had half an hour to stop Lowestar from waking up Suvika.

Could he even do it? The question hung in the back of my mind, but the fact was that we just didn't know. And since we didn't know, we had to go on the assumption that he probably could. Better to overestimate someone than underestimate their abilities.

And then, turning the bend in the stairwell, I found myself facing a door. It was metal, and had ornate designs etched into it. I stood back, motioning for Morio and Tanne to step down and take a look at it. After a moment, both shook their heads—they didn't have a clue—and returned to their places in line.

So this was it. According to the blueprints, this door led directly into the temple. And once I opened it, we'd be out of the frying pan, into the fire. And I'd had enough of fire to last me a lifetime.

A soft swish accompanied the opening door. Ready to pounce on the first sign of trouble, Smoky and I took in our surroundings.

The temple was lush—ornate. Marble lined the floor, and the walls were also marble, likely a façade but still beautiful. Ivory with veins of gold, the gleaming stone shimmered in the light of what looked like a thousand candles. I quickly realized they were flameless—no chance of using them to burn up the silk and velvet curtains that lined sections of the walls.

Columns were evenly spaced, Corinthian in design, with coiling, curving metal vines creeping out from their sides. Lush plants—ivy and fern and trailing jasmine—hung from the metal scrollwork, and the air here was vibrant and perfumed, as intoxicating as the sewers had been nauseating.

Near the back of the spacious hall, a tall throne carved in marble sat, its seat lined with what looked to be velvet cushions in gold and brown. Marble benches lined the walls, and an offering font sat in front of the throne, next to a giant altar stone. On the stone, chained with silver chains, lay a woman. Blond hair streamed over her shoulders and she looked still relatively young.

"Were. She's Were." Delilah's whisper met my ears and I nodded. She had to be our virgin. At least they wouldn't have abused her, needing her virginity intact for the ritual.

Next to the throne stood another marble slab—this one upright. Again, silver chains restrained a muscled young man. He was obviously Fae, and his hair was long and as platinum as Marilyn Monroe's had been. Only his was natural.

They said nothing. No screams, no pleas, no begging for release. By the expressions on their faces, it was a good bet they were doped up. Here and there, figures in long red robes scurried around, but there was no sign of Lowestar.

Behind the throne, though, was a marble statue. On a plinth that had to be seven feet tall in itself, the statue was life-sized—a very tall man, with streaming hair and wearing what looked like some sort of tunic and trousers.

Before we could be spotted, I motioned for us to move off to the side. We hid behind a nearby column, waiting. For once, we'd gotten in on time, rather than bursting in during the middle of the ritual.

A drumbeat caught my attention and I pulled back even farther, hoping we were all well out of sight, as the doors started to open. Into the room filed two rows of robed figures, all in crimson.

As they passed by, they didn't seem to be aware of our intrusion, which could mean one of two things. We'd done well in hiding ourselves. *Or* they knew we were here and they were biding their time. Given the stench we were letting off, I decided that opting for the latter was safest and prepared myself for any sign they were going to attack.

It was then that I noticed something—or *didn't notice*, as the case may be. The stench from the sewer had vanished. I couldn't smell a thing—not even Smoky. Confused, I glanced around. Tanne was near me, and his eyes were closed and he was whispering something below his breath. *Magic.* He was working magic. And whatever he was doing had absorbed the odors we were giving off. I wanted to hug him, but that could come later.

As the last of the ritualists filed into the room, they took their place in a semicircle around the throne, behind the altar and font. Damn, they were blocking our view of the girl—we'd have to work quickly to avoid somebody stabbing her, or whatever they were planning on doing. But I wanted to wait until Lowestar was there. If we moved too quickly, he could escape and then we'd just have one more nasty enemy in the wild.

We didn't have to wait long, though. As the drumbeat came to a halt, a door near the back of the hall opened and a figure dressed in brown and gold entered the room. He pushed his hood back, revealing that yes, it was Lowestar, with his closely shaved head and brilliant shining eyes. He was a handsome daemon, and that was part of his danger.

As he approached the throne, I tensed, motioning for the others to get ready. We had to make this surprise attack run like clockwork. I leaned forward, ready to take a running leap over the heads of the ritualists, when Lowestar raised an ornate gold baton.

"Rise now, from the depths of your slumber, oh mighty god of fortune!"

Wait—it wasn't 8 P.M. yet! Frantically I looked around. They weren't due to start for another ten minutes—but here Lowestar was already beginning the incantation to wake up Suvika.

Frantic now, I burst out of my hiding place, followed by the others. I went barreling directly toward the group and—as they turned in unison—started to sail over their heads, only to go thudding right into a force field.

I slid to the ground against the invisible wall, landing in a heap on the floor. As I did so, Lowestar laughed and resumed his incantation. His followers, however, turned and pushed back their own hoods. *Fuck*. They looked like businessmen—not daemons—but it was impossible to tell whether they were FBHs or not. We couldn't just outright slaughter a bunch of humans, could we?

Smoky sent a blast of winter their way, the chill wind freezing against the ground, running below the force field to drive a blinding wall of snow toward them. The men seemed confused, at least most of them, but a couple broke away from the pack and moved to the front, their eyes now glowing.

"Daemons—at least the ones in front are!" Camille's voice echoed through the hall.

At that moment, Morio managed to find his way around the force field, moving to the side. Ah, so it wasn't all-inclusive. I raced to the other side and, sure enough, found myself in the fray. Vanzir was on my heels, and it looked like Morio and Camille were cooking up something. As they cast their spell, a purple bolt shot forth, striking the heart of the force field, and then—all hell broke loose.

"What the hell—" Delilah's scream was cut off as thunder split the air and the marble statue behind the throne began to fracture, cracks racing through like windshield glass shattering after a cold snap.

Lowestar's voice rose, his incantation deep and reverberating now.

"Stop him—focus on Lowestar!" I pushed through the force field where Morio and Camille had broken through. Little sparks of lightning still flared out from it, but I ignored them, driving on. The men behind the field scattered, save for the two that were daemonkin, and now they cast off their robes and turned to face me. I leaped between them, leaving them for the others. I was after Lowestar.

The statue continued to fracture, and beneath it, I could see the form of someone—crap. Was that where Suvika had been sleeping? Was this his *tomb deep in the ethers*? Or was this just his new godform, waiting for him as he broke free from his slumber?

I managed to reach the girl on the altar before Lowestar turned on me. He held out his hand and a flash of light drove out, aiming for my heart. I dove for the side. Screams behind me told me that the others had engaged the dae-mons and the good ol' boys' club.

The streaming light hit somebody, because I heard a shriek and turned as I came back to my feet. One of Lowe-star's cronies had a gaping hole in his chest, burned through and cauterized at the same time. A look of surprise on his face, he toppled face first to the floor.

Lowestar grabbed for a staff that was lying on the altar stone next to the girl. He brought it up as I did a spin kick, aiming for his chin. He met me with the staff, but I man-aged to break it in half and a crack of light burst out of the broken ends. He tossed it aside as I met him, hand to hand.

Lowestar was horribly strong—I hadn't counted on how strong the daemon might be, and he managed to get hold of my neck. Aha, he didn't know I was a vampire. He could break the vertebrae but they would heal. I let him pull me close, then flashed him my fangs.

"Oh, so that's how you want to play?" His eyes flashed and he let go of me with one hand to reach for the broken end of the staff.

Fuck—makeshift wooden stake!

I thrust myself forward into his arms. Caught off guard, he wasn't able to stop me. As I sank my fangs deep into his neck, he let out a startled shout and dropped the staff. I took him down, feeding so fast and deep that the blood was making me dizzy.

I was sucking him in, drinking him deep, when a noise shattered the chaos in the room. Glancing up as a shower of dust sprayed over me, I saw the rest of the marble on the statue crack and fall away as a tall, gorgeously handsome man leapt off the dais.

"Suvika!" Camille's voice echoed from behind me. I pulled away from Lowestar and began to back up as the demigod turned my way. No way did I want to get caught in his grasp. I glimpsed the mayhem that had been going on—both daemons were dead, and the FBHs were scat-tered, cowering against the floor as if hiding their heads was going to save them. Turning back, I noticed the girl was gone—as well as the young man. They had vanished from their chains.

Lowestar turned on his belly and began to crawl toward Suvika. The demigod's hair was glowing black, long and luxurious, falling against a well-muscled chest, and a thin Mandarin mustache accentuated the sharpness of his chin. He truly was glorious in looks, and I found myself magnetized by the gleam in his eyes.

He looked at Lowestar, who—weak from my attack—dragged himself one inch at a time toward the god. A fire began to burn in my belly, and I realized the daemon blood was starting to have an effect on me. I wanted to touch the god, to feel that chest under my skin. Maybe have a taste of—

"Menolly, get back!" Vanzir had hold of my arm and he was dragging me away. I struggled but he was as strong as I was, and the next thing I knew, he had those damned neon feeding tubes emerging from his hands and he fed them straight into my mind.

I screamed—the feeling of being mentally violated was sickening. Now, I understood why Camille had done what she did—why she had offered him her body instead of her mind. But then, just as I started to beg him to stop, the horrible intrusion vanished and I could think clearly again. Vanzir had left my mind.

He gave me a wan smile. "Sorry, but you needed to come down from that high, and fast."

I nodded, then turned back to see the demigod approach Lowestar. Would he heal him up? Stand him as his general? But Suvika cocked his head, staring at the daemon, then lifted his foot . . . and crushed Lowestar Radcliffe's skull with his boot with a simple, light step.

"Fuck! Get the hell out of here!" Delilah was backpedaling toward the door.

"The yew wand ain't gonna do shit against that freak." Vanzir backed away. "He's big and he's bad."

"The girl—" Camille lunged forward.

Smoky caught her. "Shade got her! He moved through the shadows and I saw him taking her and the boy upstairs.

Now get the fuck back from there. Can't you feel how powerful this creature is? Suvika could bring this place down around our heads."

Even as Smoky spoke, Suvika looked over at us, smiled, and raised his arms. The temple floor began to shake, rolling under our feet. All too close to what had happened in Elqaneve for comfort.

I turned to the others. "Get out. Get out of here now. We can't stop him. He's just too powerful. We need to know more before we take him on." Even as I spoke, I was pushing them toward the door, Smoky helping me.

We raced out of the temple and to the stairs, running as fast as we could up the spiral case. As we cleared the broom closet, we didn't bother going back to the basement or sewers. Smoky rampaged right through one of the plate glass windows and we made our way out. Another rumble and we crossed the street, heading for the parking lot. Five seconds later, the entire structure imploded, and a roiling storm billowed down the street, in clouds of dust and debris.

As we turned, staring at the destruction, a light rose from the chaos, and streaked into the sky. *Suvika*. He was awake and free, and who the fuck knew what that meant?

Chapter 19

❧❧❧

As the pile of dust and debris settled, Shade came up beside us, the two captives with him. He'd given the girl his duster to cover her nakedness. The young man had been wearing a loincloth. Both looked shell-shocked and dazed.

"They're still drugged. I found out her name is Sealy, and his is Grynald. She's from Siobhan's pod—a Selkie—and Grynald is a water nixie. For some reason, Lowestar decided to pick on the water Fae for sacrifices."

Why? We would probably never know, but there had to be some reason.

"What the hell now?" Delilah stared up at the sky. "Suvika . . . he could be anywhere."

"I'm hoping he decided to hike it a long, long ways away. But it's been a while since he's been in the world. Look at how much money there is flowing now . . . look at the corporate greed. He's not going to go far, I think. Not with all the bright shiny toys to attract him."

In the distance, sirens wailed as the fire department and the cops responded to what had to be an avalanche of 911 calls. The noise must have been heard around the city for miles. You don't just explode an entire building without somebody taking notice.

"Let's head back to Carter's." I couldn't think of any-where else to go. We'd killed Lowestar—or rather, Suvika had—and considering a good share of his cronies appeared to have been with him, I had a feeling Supernatural Match-ups was going down the toilet, as well as their slavery oper-ation and a number of other sideline businesses.

We'd done a bang-up job . . . but everything felt surreal and I wondered if the others felt as confused as I did.

Slowly we headed to our cars. As we pulled out of the parking lot, the first-responders were starting to sift through the rubble. I called Nerissa to let her know we were safe. All in all, the night was turning out to be one hell of a clusterfuck.

Carter was waiting for us. I'd called ahead to let him know we were there. But he wasn't alone. A woman was just get-ting ready to leave. She was tall—Delilah's height—and she had long hair that tumbled down her back to her butt. Multicolored, it was dark brown with streaks of purple and blue running through it. She was muscled, sturdy, and busty, and there was something about her that struck me as odd. She seemed familiar. Something about her eyes struck me. They were brilliant blue, and flashing. She was wearing a pair of black jeans and a V-neck tank, which showed off the muscles in her arms as well as her impressive cleavage. A silver belt wrapped the low-riders, ending in a knotwork buckle.

"I'd like you all to meet Shimmer, my date." Carter introduced us one by one, and covered in dust and blood, we shook hands as if nothing were out of the ordinary.

She gave us the once-over, a smile playing on her lips as she came to Smoky and Shade. "Well met." She curtseyed, which seemed odd enough, but Smoky's response was even odder.

Smoky let out a little harrumph and he inclined his head in acknowledgment. "Well met, Shimmer."

Shade cocked his head, a smile creasing his face. "Well met yourself."

Before we could ask what that was all about, she slid on her coat and vanished out the door. As the door swung shut, Smoky turned to Carter.

"Since when are you dating a dragon?"

Immediately Camille and Delilah turned to stare at him.

"For a week or so now." Carter motioned for us to have a seat. "But we'll talk more of her later. Now sit and tell me what happened."

And so we did. We told him about Lowestar and Suvika, and we introduced him to the Selkie and the nixie. "They need to go back to their homes. They're drugged, and we have no clue with what."

Carter nodded, then let out a long sigh. "All the records are gone then in the destruction. We can't ever begin to realize the full extent of Lowestar's holdings, or who he might have partnered with, or how many of the Fae he ran through his slavery operation."

"I can't see how, unless we can find the people he was working with. Even then, I think we're running on empty with this one. But he's gone. His precious demigod gave him a present for waking him up, all right. A crushed skull."

I couldn't find it in my heart to give one fuck for Lowestar's fate. He'd been cruel and ruthless, and he deserved every bit of what he got. "I have a feeling there won't be any more fires now, at least not like the one that destroyed the Wayfarer and the Utopia Club. I'm pretty sure we will find that Vistar-Tashdey Enterprises was one of Lowestar's holdings. And most likely, the lawyers behind it were among the group of ritualists that went down for the count."

"So where does that leave us?" Camille wearily accepted a muffin from Carter's maid.

"I'll do what research I can to figure out where Suvika might turn his sights next, but I'd say, for now, there's nothing you can do. Lowestar is dead—the Fae you rescued can come out of hiding and go back to their lives now. And you . . . I suggest you go home and rest. Be with your loved ones. Take a moment to breathe because you know what's happening in Otherworld is going to need your attention soon."

"There are two spirit seals running loose now. And Shadow Wing has three. We have to intensify our hunt for the one that disappeared from Benjamin's body and the one that was already still missing. Whoever took his hasn't handed it over to Shadow Wing yet, that we know of. Which means it could be someone keeping it for themselves. And that will draw Telazhar's attention. He's good at picking up on things like that." Morio looked as dragged out as the rest of us.

"I have to visit Derisa. She's supposed to come Earthside to talk to me." Camille glanced over at me. "Maybe we can ask her to take Father's ashes back with her and give them to Aunt Rythwar."

"I'd like that." Delilah toyed with the hem of her jacket. "I know it's dangerous, but right now, I wish we could see our home again. We may not have a home to go to if Telazhar brings the war to our city."

"I want to see home, too." Why, oh why, did I have the feeling we were making our good-byes? True, Otherworld would be there, even if Telazhar razed the land. But if war came to our home, if war came to our city . . . then our childhood memories would fade in the ashes.

Camille gave me a bleak look. "I think Trillian still plans on going to the Shadow Lands to look for Darynal. I want to go with him, but I can't. I know I'm needed here. But if he goes . . ." She fell silent and we all knew the end of that sentence.

Carter stood, hands on his hips. "These are dark times, yes. But this is why you must fight against them. I have watched centuries of human history go by. I have watched countries rise and fall. And during every great unrest one thing held true: Those who survived always looked to their victories and not their losses. They focused on winning, not on defeat. If you ever expect to make it through the coming fray, you have to do this. And I know you can."

We stared at him. Camille was the first to laugh. "Okay already. I hate it when you're right. But you are. We will pick up, and go on. We did get rid of Lowestar; that's a major victory."

"And his slaving operation. And we rescued not only Violet, but five others," I chimed in. My natural inclination to pessimism had to go by the wayside, if for nothing more than rallying my sisters.

Delilah shrugged. "Seven, if you count Sealy and Grynald."

Smoky pulled Camille onto his lap, his hair trailing around her like gentle fern fronds. "Don't forget—we all survived. None of us died."

That was best of all. And with that, we headed for home. There was nothing more we could do here tonight except speculate on what was going to happen with Suvika, and somehow, that thought didn't seem all too appealing.

As we trudged to the cars, a break in the clouds allowed the light from a single star to shimmer down. I stared at it, thinking about how much it had seen, and how much time had passed since the light first started to travel. A star's lifetime—how long was that?

Not understanding where my mind was going with this, I got in the car and leaned against the back of the seat, just letting my thoughts wander. Sometimes, *not thinking* was the best medicine of all.

Chapter 20

❧✦❧

Nerissa was waiting up for me, as were Trillian and Roz. We told them what had gone down, and now we all sat around the table, just staring at one another.

"A little shell-shocked, I'd say." Hanna bustled over, in her nightgown again. She put a pot of tea on the table. Trillian brought the teacups for her, and Vanzir handed Delilah some milk. I declined the offered blood, but it felt so good to just lean back in a chair, around our table, where the sounds of everyday life were going on. Maggie had woken up and she was sitting on Smoky's lap.

The rest of us were back to reeking—Tanne's spell had worn off before we dropped him off at his house. Hanna sniffed, and a scowl crossed her face.

"Where in Hel's great world have you been? You all smell like an outhouse. Except Master Smoky." She grinned at him. She'd finally gotten over her fear of the dragon.

"We might as well have been in an outhouse," I grumbled. "Hanna, we're all tired and worn out and a little bit confused by this evening. Don't mind us. We aren't meaning to stink up the kitchen. And we don't mean to be grumpy to you."

She pshawed away my apology. "Girl, you don't have to apologize for anything. I've lived with monsters before. You? You . . . you all have become my family." Her eyes crinkled as she spoke, and that in itself was enough to reduce Camille and Delilah to tears.

"We love you, too, Hanna. We love you, too." Roz slid his arm around her, and for the first time in front of the rest of us, he kissed her soundly on the lips. She rested her head on his shoulder—the staunch Northwoman had a tender side and we knew it. We also knew they'd never be any more than good friends with benefits, but sometimes that was the best you could hope for, and far better than the other options.

Finally, with nothing more to say, I pulled away and, after a tired good night to the others, headed downstairs with Nerissa. I stood under the shower for twenty minutes, scrubbing the stench off me. It was still early, around midnight, but it felt like it was reaching toward dawn.

As I came out of the shower, Nerissa was there, holding a towel for me. She dried me off, then tucked me into a velour robe and guided me to the bed. I propped myself up against the headboard and she curled up next to me, her head in my lap. I stroked her hair, smoothing the tangled tawny locks.

"I meant what I said, you know. I don't mean to ignore you, but I obviously do and I want to change that."

She glanced up at me, her eyes deep and rich in the glow of the lamplight. "I suppose we still have to find our rhythm. But I love you—and I know you love me. And while love isn't enough, we're talking, and that's the most important thing. I had no idea you were so afraid that letting down your guard would open you up to your predator."

I ducked my head. "Neither did I. I had no clue I was building walls between us."

A beat. Then, "Do you love Roman? I know you can fully be yourself with him." And there it was. I could hear the fear in her voice. The fear that Roman would win me away because I could take out my darker nature and instincts with him.

I placed one finger against my lips, then lowered it to hers. "No, love. I don't love Roman. I enjoy him. I like him. And yes, I can play hard with him—far harder than I ever dare play with you. But . . . being with him allows me to love you. It gives me the freedom to open my heart to you. Oddly enough, he might just be what makes *us* possible. At least in the long run."

"I hadn't thought about it that way." She stared up at me, the soft rise and fall of her breast a mesmerizing sight. The woman was the incarnation of sheer beauty, and I couldn't look away. "I have to tell you something."

Freeze frame. I hated those words. They never preceded anything remotely good. After a moment, I forced myself to ask, "What is it?"

"For a while I was thinking of . . . asking you to turn me."

Her words shattered my heart. An unexpected wash of pain rolled over me and I leaned forward, searching her face. She stared at me steadily.

"Why? Why would you say such a thing? Think such a thing?"

"I thought that maybe then I could be in your world. I could be with you in the ways you can't take me now. We would be a good match." She smiled then, and shook her head. "And after I thought about it, I realized that I can't do it. I will never ask that of you, because then I wouldn't be who I am. And Nerissa . . . the werepuma? That's who I am. I made up my mind that, if I'm not enough for you, then that's the way it will have to be."

Hanging my head, realizing how much my silences and aloofness had put her through, I began to cry. The blood ran down my cheeks, falling on the crimson sheets to blossom out, tone on tone stains.

"Nerissa . . . listen to me." I made her sit up, took her by the shoulders, and stared into her eyes. "You are enough. You are perfect the way you are. You are the woman I want. If I wanted to be with another vampire, I would already have found someone before I met you. I love playing with Roman, but at the end of the day? He doesn't make my heart skip a beat. And he can't make me cry."

And with that, I pulled her into my arms, and drew the sheets up over us. Life was harsh. War was an ever-present reality. And sometimes the battles landed squarely in our laps. But there were some battles that talking could resolve. And sometimes what we thought was a solid defense ended up being a wedge.

As I kissed her, the warmth of her body pressing against the coldness of my own, I knew that those walls had to come down. It was time to let someone fully into my heart. Because there were too many wars, too many battles, waiting ahead. And even when it meant taking a risk, we couldn't deny our feelings. Because life was all too short to throw away the love offered up to us.

CAST OF MAJOR CHARACTERS

The D'Artigo Family
Arial Lianan te Maria: Delilah's twin, who died at birth.
  Half-Fae, half-human. Wereleopard who lives in spirit
  form in Haseofon, the temple of the Death Maidens.
Camille Sepharial te Maria, aka Camille D'Artigo: The
  oldest sister; a Moon Witch and Priestess. Half-Fae,
  half-human.
Daniel George Fredericks: The D'Artigo Sisters' half
  cousin; FBH.
Delilah Maria te Maria, aka Delilah D'Artigo: The middle
  sister; a werecat and Death Maiden.
Hester Lou Fredericks: The D'Artigo Sisters' half
  cousin; FBH.
Maria D'Artigo: The D'Artigo Sisters' mother. Human.
  Deceased.
Menolly Rosabelle te Maria, aka Menolly D'Artigo: The
  youngest sister; a vampire and jian-tu; extraordinary
  acrobat. Half-Fae, half-human.
Sephreh ob Tanu: The D'Artigo Sisters' father. Full Fae.
  Deceased.
Shamas ob Olanda: The D'Artigo girls' cousin. Full Fae.

The D'Artigo Sisters' Lovers and Close Friends
Astrid (Johnson): Chase and Sharah's baby daughter.
Bruce O'Shea: Iris's husband. Leprechaun.
Carter: Leader of the Demonica Vacana Society, a group
  that watches and records the interactions of Demonkin
  and human through the ages. Carter is half-demon and
  half-Titan—his father was Hyperion, one of the Greek
  Titans.
Chase Garden Johnson: Detective, director of the Faerie-
  Human Crime Scene Investigation (FH-CSI) team.
  Human who has taken the Nectar of Life, which

extends his life span beyond any ordinary mortal, and has opened up his psychic abilities.

Chrysandra: Waitress at the Wayfarer Bar & Grill. Human. Deceased.

Derrick Means: Bartender at the Wayfarer Bar & Grill. Werebadger.

Erin Mathews: Former president of the Faerie Watchers Club and former owner of the Scarlet Harlot Boutique. Turned into a vampire by Menolly, her sire, moments before her death. Human.

Greta: Leader of the Death Maidens; Delilah's tutor.

Iris (Kuusi) O'Shea: Friend and companion of the girls. Priestess of Undutar. Talon-haltija (Finnish house sprite).

Lindsey Katharine Cartridge: Director of the Green Goddess Women's Shelter. Pagan and witch. Human.

Luke: Former bartender at the Wayfarer Bar & Grill. Werewolf. One of the Keraastar Knights.

Maria O'Shea: Iris and Bruce's baby daughter.

Marion Vespa: Coyote shifter; owner of the Supe-Urban Café.

Morio Kuroyama: One of Camille's lovers and husbands. Essentially the grandson of Grandmother Coyote. Youkai-kitsune (roughly translated: Japanese fox demon).

Nerissa Shale: Menolly's wife. Worked for DSHS. Now working for Chase Johnson as a victims' rights counselor for the FH-CSI. Werepuma and member of the Rainier Puma Pride.

Roman: Ancient vampire; son of Blood Wyne, Queen of the Crimson Veil. Menolly's official consort in the Vampire Nation and her new sire.

Rozurial, aka Roz: Mercenary. Menolly's secondary lover. Incubus who used to be Fae before Zeus and Hera destroyed his marriage.

Shade: Delilah's fiancé. Part Stradolan, part black (shadow) dragon.

Sharah: Elfin medic; Chase's girlfriend. New Queen of Kelvashan and Elqaneve.

Siobhan Morgan: One of the girls' friends. Selkie (wereseal); member of the Puget Sound Harbor Seal Pod.

Smoky: One of Camille's lovers and husbands. Half-white, half-silver dragon.

Tanne Baum: One of the Black Forest Woodland Fae. A member of the Hunter's Glen Clan.

Tavah: Guardian of the portal at the Wayfarer Bar & Grill. Vampire (full Fae).

Tim Winthrop, aka Cleo Blanco: Computer student/ genius, female impersonator. FBH. Now owns the Scarlet Harlot.

Trillian: Mercenary. Camille's alpha lover and one of her three husbands. Svartan (one of the Charming Fae).

Ukkonen O'Shea: Iris and Bruce's baby son.

Vanzir: Was indentured slave to the Sisters, by his own choice. Dream-chaser demon who lost his powers and now is regaining new ones.

Venus the Moon Child: Former shaman of the Rainier Puma Pride. Werepuma. One of the Keraastar Knights.

Wade Stevens: President of Vampires Anonymous. Vampire (human).

Zachary Lyonnesse: Former member of the Rainier Puma Pride Council of Elders. Werepuma living in Otherworld.

GLOSSARY

Black Unicorn/Black Beast: Father of the Dahns unicorns, a magical unicorn that is reborn like the phoenix and lives in Darkynwyrd and Thistlewyd Deep. Raven Mother is his consort, and he is more a force of nature than a unicorn.

Calouk: The rough, common dialect used by a number of Otherworld inhabitants.

Court and Crown: "Crown" refers to the Queen of Y'Elestrial. "Court" refers to the nobility and military personnel that surround the Queen. "Court and Crown" together refer to the entire government of Y'Elestrial.

Court of the Three Queens: The newly risen Court of the three Earthside Fae Queens: Titania, the Fae Queen of Light and Morning; Morgaine, the half-Fae Queen of Dusk and Twilight ; and Aeval, the Fae Queen of Shadow and Night.

Crypto: One of the Cryptozoid races. Cryptos include creatures out of legend that are not technically of the Fae races: gargoyles, unicorns, gryphons, chimeras, and so on. Most primarily inhabit Otherworld, but some have Earthside cousins.

Demon Gate: A gate through which demons may be summoned by a powerful sorcerer or necromancer.

Dreyerie: A dragon lair.

Earthside: Everything that exists on the Earth side of the portals.

Elqaneve: The Elfin city in Otherworld, located in Kelvashan—the Elfin lands.

Elemental Lords: The elemental beings—both male and female—who, along with the Hags of Fate and the Harvestmen, are the only true Immortals. They are avatars of various elements and energies, and they inhabit all realms. They do as they will and seldom concern themselves with humankind or Fae unless summoned. If asked for help, they often exact steep prices in return. The Elemental Lords are not concerned with balance like the Hags of Fate.

FBH: Full-Blooded Human (usually refers to Earthside humans).

FH-CSI: The Faerie-Human Crime Scene Investigation team. The brainchild of Detective Chase Johnson, it was first formed as a collaboration between the OIA and the Seattle Police Department. Other FH-CSI units have been created around the country, based on the Seattle prototype. The FH-CSI takes care of both medical and criminal emergencies involving visitors from Otherworld.

Great Divide: A time of immense turmoil when the Elemental Lords and some of the High Court of Fae decided to rip apart the worlds. Until then, the Fae existed primarily on Earth, their lives and worlds mingling with those of humans. The Great Divide tore everything asunder, splitting off another dimension, which became Otherworld. At that time, the Twin Courts of Fae were disbanded and their Queens stripped of power. This was the time during which the Spirit Seal was formed and broken in order to seal off the realms from each other. Some Fae chose to stay Earthside, others moved to the realm of Otherworld, and the demons were—for the most part—sealed in the Subterranean Realms.

Guard Des'Estar: The military of Y'Elestrial.

Hags of Fate: The women of destiny who keep the balance righted. Neither good nor evil, they observe the flow of destiny. When events get too far out of balance, they step in and take action, usually using humans, Fae, Supes, and other creatures as pawns to bring the path of destiny back into line.

Harvestmen: The lords of death—a few cross over and are also Elemental Lords. The Harvestmen, along with their followers (the Valkyries and the Death Maidens, for example), reap the souls of the dead.

Haseofon: The abode of the Death Maidens—where they stay and where they train.

Ionyc Lands: The astral, etheric, and spirit realms, along with several other lesser-known noncorporeal dimensions, form the Ionyc Lands. These realms are separated by the Ionyc Seas, a current of energy that prevents the Ionyc Lands from colliding, thereby sparking off an explosion of universal proportions.

Ionyc Seas: The currents of energy that separate the Ionyc Lands. Certain creatures, especially those connected with the elemental energies of ice, snow, and wind, can travel through the Ionyc Seas without protection.

Kelvashan: The lands of the elves.

Koyanni: The coyote shifters who took an evil path away from the Great Coyote; followers of Nukpana.

Melosealfôr: A rare Crypto dialect learned by powerful Cryptos and all Moon Witches.

Nectar of Life: An elixir that can extend the life span of humans to nearly the length of a Fae's years. Highly prized and cautiously used. Can drive someone insane if he or she doesn't have the emotional capacity to handle the changes incurred.

Oblition: The act of a Death Maiden sucking the soul out of one of her targets.

OIA: The Otherworld Intelligence Agency; the "brains" behind the Guard Des'Estar. Earthside Division now run by Camille, Menolly, and Delilah.

Otherworld/OW: The human term for the "United Nations" of Faerie Land. A dimension apart from ours that contains creatures from legend and lore, pathways to the gods, and various other places, such as Olympus. Otherworld's actual name varies among the differing dialects of the many races of Cryptos and Fae.

Portal, Portals: The interdimensional gates that connect the different realms. Some were created during the Great Divide; others open up randomly.

Seelie Court: The Earthside Fae Court of Light and Summer, disbanded during the Great Divide. Titania was the Seelie Queen.

Soul Statues: In Otherworld, small figurines created for the Fae of certain races and magically linked with the baby. These figurines reside in family shrines, and when one of the Fae dies, their soul statue shatters. In Menolly's case, when she was reborn as a vampire, her soul statue re-formed, although twisted. If a family member disappears, his or her family can always tell if their loved one is alive or dead if they have access to the soul statue.

Spirit Seals: A magical crystal artifact, the Spirit Seal was created during the Great Divide. When the portals were sealed, the Spirit Seal was broken into nine gems and each piece was given to an Elemental Lord or Lady. These gems each have varying powers. Even possessing one of the spirit seals can allow the wielder to weaken the portals that divide Otherworld, Earthside, and the Subterranean Realms. If all of the seals are joined together again, then all of the portals will open.

Stradolan: A being who can walk between worlds, who can walk through the shadows, using them as a method of transportation.

Supe/Supes: Short for "Supernaturals." Refers to Earthside supernatural beings who are not of Fae nature. Refers to Weres especially.

Talamh Lonrach Oll: The name for the Earthside Sovereign Fae Nation.

Triple Threat: Camille's nickname for the newly risen three Earthside Queens of Fae.

Unseelie Court: The Earthside Fae Court of Shadow and Winter, disbanded during the Great Divide. Aeval was the Unseelie Queen.

VA/Vampires Anonymous: The Earthside group started by Wade Stevens, a vampire who was a psychiatrist during life. The group is focused on helping newly born vampires adjust to their new state of existence, and to encourage vampires to avoid harming the innocent as much as possible. The VA is vying for control. Their goal is to rule the vampires of the United States and to set up an internal policing agency.

Whispering Mirror: A magical communications device that links Otherworld and Earth. Think magical video phone.

Y'Eírialiastar: The Sidhe/Fae name for Otherworld.

Y'Elestrial: The city-state in Otherworld where the D'Artigo girls were born and raised. A Fae city, recently embroiled in a civil war between the drug-crazed tyrannical Queen Lethesanar and her more level-headed sister Tanaquar, who managed to claim the throne for herself. The civil war has ended and Tanaquar is restoring order to the land.

YIA: The Y'Elestrial Intelligence Agency. The original agency from which the OIA sprang, once the portals were opened between Otherworld and Earthside.

Youkai: Loosely (very loosely) translated as Japanese demon/nature spirit. For the purposes of this series, the youkai have three shapes: the animal form, the human form, and the true demon form. Unlike the demons of the Subterranean Realms, youkai are not necessarily evil by nature.

PLAYLIST FOR *CRIMSON VEIL*

I write to music a good share of the time, and so I always put my playlists in the back of each book so you can see which artists/songs I listened to during the writing. Here's the playlist for *Crimson Veil*:

AC/DC: "Back in Black"

Adam Lambert: "Mad World"

Adele: "Rumour Has It"

Agnes Obel: "Close Watch"

Air: "Napalm Love," "Moon Fever," "Playground Love"

AJ Roach: "Devil May Dance"

Alice Cooper: "Go to Hell," "I'm the Coolest"

Amanda Blank: "Something Bigger," "Something Better," "Shame on Me"

Android Lust: "Saint Over," "Here and Now," "When the Rains Came," "Dragonfly"

Arcade Fire: "Abraham's Daughter"

Asteroids Galaxy Tour, The: "Out of Frequency," "Sunshine Coolin'," "The Sun Ain't Shining No More," "Bad Fever"

Awolnation: "Sail"

Bangles, The: "Walk Like an Egyptian"

Black Angels, The: "You on the Run," "Manipulation," "Vikings," "Indigo Meadow," "Twisted Light," "Phosphene Dream," "Haunting at 1300 McKinley"

Black Rebel Motorcycle Club: "Shuffle Your Feet"

Blondie: "I Know but I Don't Know"

Bravery, The: "Believe"

Bret Michaels: "Love Sucks"

Broken Bells: "October," "The High Road," "The Ghost Inside"

Buffalo Springfield: "For What It's Worth"

Cat Power: "I Don't Blame You"

Chris Isaak: "Wicked Game"

Commodores: "Brick House"

Crazy Town: "Butterfly"

Cul de Sac: "The Invisible Worm"

Cure, The: "Charlotte Sometimes," "The Hanging Garden"

David Bowie: "I'm Afraid of Americans," "Without You," "Let's Dance," "Sister Midnight," "Rebel Rebel," "Golden Years"

Depeche Mode: "Blasphemous Rumours"

Eagles: "Life in the Fast Lane"

Eastern Sun: "Beautiful Being"

Fatboy Slim: "Praise You"

Feeling, The: "Sewn"

Foster the People: "Pumped Up Kicks"

Garbage: "Queer," "I Think I'm Paranoid," "Bleed Like Me," "Sex Is Not the Enemy," "Blood for Poppies," "I Hate Love"

Gary Numan: "Down in the Park," "Are Friends Electric," "I, Assassin," "Metal," "Stories," "War Songs," "My Shadow in Vain," "My Breathing"

Gotye: "Hearts a Mess"

Julian Cope: "Charlotte Anne"

King Black Acid: "Rolling Under," "One and Only"

Kinks, The: "Destroyer"

Kraftwerk: "Pocket Calculator"

Kyuss: "Thong Song," "Thumb"

Lady Gaga: "Poker Face," "I Like It Rough"

Ladytron: "Predict the Day," "Black Cat"

Larry Tee & Princess Superstar: "Licky (Vandalism Remix)"

Low: "Half Light"

Lynyrd Skynyrd: "Sweet Home Alabama," "Saturday Night Special"

Mark Lanegan: "Bleeding Muddy Water," "Phantasmagoria Blues," "Miracle," "Pentacostal" (with Duke Garwood)

Men Without Hats: "Safety Dance"

Oingo Boingo: "Weird Science"

People in Planes: "Vampire"

Screaming Trees: "Gospel Plow," "Where the Twain Shall Meet," "Dime Western"

Scorpions: "The Zoo," "Send Me an Angel"

Shriekback: "New Man," "Dust and a Shadow"

Stone Temple Pilots: "No Way Out," "Glide"

Talking Heads: "I Zimbra," "Slippery People"

Thomas Dolby: "She Blinded Me with Science"

Thompson Twins: "Watching," "Love on Your Side"

3 Doors Down: "Loser"

Wang Chung: "Everybody Have Fun Tonight"

Verve, The: "Bittersweet Symphony"

Yoko Kanno: "Lithium Flower"

Zero 7: "In the Waiting Line"

Dear Reader:

I hope you enjoyed **Crimson Veil**, *book fifteen of the Otherworld Series. I love writing this world, it expands and grows with each book, and I see so many possibilities ahead for the D'Artigo sisters.*

Next, stay tuned for the last book in the Indigo Court Series, **Night's End,** *coming July 2014, in which Cicely and her friends face the final battle against Myst and the Indigo Court. Turn the page for a sneak peek at the first chapter.*

While the Indigo Court Series will be wrapping up, the Otherworld series will not! **Priestess Dreaming** *(a Camille book) comes out in the fall of 2014, and there will be more books from Otherworld after that. I am also starting a spin-off series set in the Otherworld altaverse—same time frame, different characters.*

*The first book in the Fly By Night Series—***Flight From Death**—*will be out in 2015. This series will not take the place of the Otherworld Series, but will run concurrently! It's exciting for me to have the opportunity to bring you more stories from the Otherworld.*

For those of you new to my books, I hope you've enjoyed your first foray into my worlds. For those of you who have followed me for a while, I want to thank you for once again revisiting the world of Camille, Menolly, and Delilah.

Bright Blessings,
The Painted Panther
Yasmine Galenorn

I stood on a hillock near the barrow. The land was covered with snow and ice, the horizon stretching out in a vast panorama of winter. It was like the perfect picture: The snow gleamed under an overcast sky, sparkling with the cold. Here and there, patches of ice glistened the faint blue that winter ice tends to take. Evergreens—firs and cedars—stood cloaked in white blankets, the snow weighing down their limbs to touch the ground.

My breath was visible in the icy chill of early dusk, a cloud of white every time I exhaled. But the pristine chill that made the very air shimmer barely penetrated the white feathered cloak I wore. And even the cold that *did* make it through had ceased to bother me over the weeks. For I was the Queen of Snow and Ice now, and cold was no longer an enemy.

As I surveyed the land around my barrow, I was aware that, not ten yards away, Check, my personal guard, kept watch. Beside him stood Fearless, who had recovered from his wounds. The Cambyra Fae had healed quickly, even from the severe wounds he had sustained from the Shadow Hunters, and while he had been in great pain for several weeks, now he was back in action. As an interesting side effect, I sensed his attitude toward me had shifted. Where before, he had been doing his duty, now there seemed to be a loyalty in place that I hadn't expected.

I listened to the slipstream carefully, searching for information. The realm of Snow and Ice might be mine to command, but it was vulnerable, and Myst was still out there. While I trusted the scouts and my advisors, I had begun to realize that my awareness had heightened since the coronation, and I could—if I listened carefully—sense Myst when she was around. After all, in a lifetime long before this one, she had been my mother and I had been her daughter Cherish, the hope of the Indigo Court, until I betrayed both her and my people.

Ulean, my wind Elemental, swept around me. She was stronger here, the winter kingdom agreed with her. While she'd always come through clear to me—ever since being bound to me when I was six years old—here, in this frozen realm, I had become even more aware of her.

At times, I thought I could catch a visible glimpse of her. Strict, my advisor, had told me it was one of the side effects from taking the crown—one in a long line of shifts and changes that I had been going through. Some days, I looked in the mirror and wasn't entirely sure of who I was.

Cicely, there is danger close by. A looming shadow. I believe Myst is on the rise again. Ulean swept past me, swirling snow in the gust of her wake.

It was only a matter of time. We knew she was regrouping. I've been hoping she would hold off until Rhiannon and I are more settled in our positions—that it would take her more time to re-strengthen her forces, but I don't think we have that leeway. I'm afraid we'll be fighting sooner than we'd hoped.

Shivering, I pulled my cloak tightly around my shoulders. The owl feathers used to make the cape had been gathered one by one, gifted by my Uwilahsidhe brethren. I was half magic-born, and half Uwilahsidhe—a branch of the Cambyra Sidhe. We were the owl shifters. I'd only discovered the latter half of my heritage less than six weeks before. The cloak had been a wedding gift from my people.

We will do as we must. If we fail, Myst will extend her reach. She will take control of this realm and drive the eternal winter into the world to blanket the land with ice and snow. She will loose the ravenous appetites of her Shadow Hunters on anyone who stands in her way. We cannot let her win, Cicely, or everyone—the magic-born and the Weres and the yummanii—they will all be so much prey for the Vampiric Fae. Even the true vampires, Lannan and Regina's people, will fall to her fury if we don't stop her.

I reached out, trying to sense the danger she'd mentioned. It was like stretching a new muscle—one that wasn't in body but within my spirit. Focusing, I sent out feelers, probing the landscape, creeping like vines through the slipstream. *There*, I could sense an arctic fox, and *over there*—the hare it was stalking. A ways beyond and I felt the chill of a group of Ice Elementals passing through, their focus so distant and alien that I couldn't have deciphered their intent if anybody paid me to. But the creatures were my subjects, they were aligned to me, and so I simply touched their energy before I passed on.

Beyond the Ice Elementals, I came to a treeline, and the dark sentinels of the woodlands whispered rumors in my ears. There were creatures in the woods—creatures who did not belong here, even though they, too, were born of winter and hearkened to the dark months of the year.

I softly began to move forward, my attention drawn by a familiar presence in a stand of snow-covered bushes nearby. As I approached the Wilding Fae—I knew who she was—Check and Fearless flanked my sides.

Ulean laughed. *Your friend. You have won the hearts of the Wilding Fae, and that is a double-edged blessing.*

The Wilding Fae were dangerous, a breed unto themselves. Ancient even by the standards of the Cambyra Fae, they were feral, belonging to themselves, aligned with no one. But they had chosen to live in the realm of Snow and Ice when I took the throne. Bargaining with them could prove dangerous, but once they'd accepted my rule, they knew better than to try to trip me up with their deals. A good thing, too, considering my lack of bargaining skills.

I paused by the juniper bush. As I stood there, waiting, a figure stepped out from behind the laden branches. She was dressed in a ragtag patchwork of a dress that swept the ground. Her hair was matted into clumps, draping to cover her shoulders. A withered roadwork of lines crossed and crisscrossed her face. Gaunt, her limbs were long and lean, her fingers jointed and gnarled with what one might think of as age. But to be honest, I had no clue of her age. The Snow Hag might be old as the world for all I knew.

She flashed me a cunning snaggletooth smile—one of her teeth curving up from her upper jaw to rest against her bottom lip. She did not kneel, but neither did I expect her to. The Wilding Fae, while they might now live in my realm, were still to be feared and respected.

"A queen might be listening for danger but looking in the wrong direction." She cocked her head.

I stared at her. Apparently we were dispensing with the niceties today. Usually there was a set format—a pattern with the Wilding Fae, that held sway even when discussing nearby dangers.

"It would be helpful if a certain Snow Hag could guide a Queen—who is, in fact, seeking the source of danger on the wind."

I didn't have the full rhythm down, but Chatter—my cousin's husband and the new King of Summer—had been drilling us. He was adept at bargaining with the Wilding Fae, and right now, I wished he could be here to help me. But I had to learn at some point.

"There is a learning curve and a queen might be making good progress, however, she might also be tripping over her words. If a certain Wilding Fae were less scrupulous, there might be trouble brewing, but luck will out. Though, sometimes, luck has nothing to do with it and desire, every-thing. And there is desire to see the new rule continue."

She gave me a wide smile and laughed, and once again, I could feel her power, down to my very bones. They were a crafty, cunning lot, the Wilding Fae, and were dangerous enemies to have.

I thought over what she had said and tried to pinpoint my mistake, but right now the thought of danger lurking in my land preoccupied me and I was having a hard time concentrating.

After a moment's silence, the Snow Hag broke a small branch off the tree. "Looking into the distance often leaves a queen ignoring what is directly below her nose. Danger can be alluring and beautiful, and seemingly, the best of friends. Danger might also throw a cunning glance, speak a misplaced word, and usually, such hints will be visible if one chances to look for them."

That didn't sound good. "A spy? You're saying that I have a spy in my midst?" When she remained silent, I rephrased it as best as I could. "One might think, by your comment, that a queen might have a spy in her court, as eyes and ears of Myst."

And with that, the Snow Hag cackled. "One might think the Queen of Snow and Ice is growing into her throne and learning to listen and understand the Wilding Fae. One might think the Queen of Snow and Ice is on the right trail." And with that, she vanished back into the bushes.

Hell. The last thing I needed was one of Myst's people hiding in my court. And the Snow Hag had said the danger was right under my nose. I glanced back. Check and Fear-less were standing back, as they knew to do, and I didn't think they'd heard me. This information meant I couldn't trust anyone, and while Check had been nothing but atten-tive, and Fearless now seemed more than willing to protect me, when I thought about it, I really didn't know them. I'd have to talk privately with Grieve, my husband, when I returned home.

As I made my way back to the guards, a sudden shift in the wind alerted me as Ulean slipped in.

Cicely, move. Fly. Get out of reach!

Without hesitation—Ulean, I could trust with my life—I closed my eyes and, arms shrinking as they spread into wings, body shifting, I was aloft and on the wing in my barred owl shape. Until recently, I'd had to remove my clothing in order to transform but again, one of the perks of becoming a Fae Queen.

As I spiraled up into the chill evening air, I looked down to see something racing out of a nearby bush—and then, a shimmer and another figure appeared out of thin air. Shadow Hunters! And they had gotten in via some way other than the entrance to the realm. As I watched, Check and Fearless engaged them.

I wanted to be down there, fighting, but I was the queen and I wasn't allowed to fight my own battles. At least, not unless there was no other option. It felt more and more that my life had been shoved into a box, even as it had broadened out in so many other ways. I chaffed at the restrictions even though I understood the reasoning for them.

As I watched, the two Shadow Hunters—Vampiric Fae who were members of the Indigo Court—launched themselves at my guards. They were twisting, morphing into the great cerulean-colored beasts they became when they aimed to destroy, to rip muscle and sinew away from the bone, to devour the flesh and—in some cases—the life force.

Check was engaging with a jeweled sword as Fearless toppled back. He'd just recovered from a similar attack, and my blood began to rise as I watched my men struggling to keep the Shadow Hunters' slobbering jaws and great bared teeth from latching onto them.

There was no way I could survive should I set down on the ground—not even my queen's dagger could deflect the attack of one of these monsters, but then, I knew exactly what I could do. It was a dangerous choice, but I couldn't fly off and let the Shadow Hunters ravage my guards.

I spiraled up to the nearest tree and landed on the first bare branch I could find big enough to support myself when I changed back into my normal shape.

I balanced on the limb, making certain it would be wide enough to support my weight without breaking. I grabbed hold of the trunk as my cloak almost threw me off balance when I transformed back into myself. But I caught myself and managed to stand at the crotch of the limb where it met the trunk, putting my weight back against the tree.

I closed my eyes and summoned the winds. A shiver of delight raced through me. It had become more and more dangerous for me to call in the gale force winds, to stir up a tornado, but it was also a gift that could save both Check and Fearless and I wouldn't hesitate to use it. As I glanced at the ground below, the blood channeled across the snow in a delicate wash of rose that spread over the the blanket of white. Whether the blood belonged to Check, Fearless, or the Shadow Hunters, I didn't know.

The breeze started small, but quickly sped up, rushing through me. They went beyond the winds of the cold Winter realm. They were from the heart of the primal Wind Element. A boreal wind sweeping directly out from the plane of air. The gusting currents buoyed me up, filled me with a delicious sense of power, as I rose to my tiptoes, balancing precariously on the branch.

I raised my arms, no longer needing the support of the tree trunk, as the winds lifted me into the air and spun me aloft, carrying me on a bank of mist and whirling snow. A whispered *Gale Force,* and the winds turned into a storm of hurricane proportions, only instead of driving rain along in front, the fury picked up the snow and used it as a weapon.

Sleet and snow pelted against the Shadow Hunters, blinding the Vampiric Fae as they struggled against the biting wind. Check and Fearless fell back, Check shouting something to me that I couldn't hear through the raging storm, but I understood his gestures. He wanted me to drop the storm, to fly back to the barrow.

But the winds held me in their mania, and I couldn't break free. Each time I used this power, it was harder to rein myself back in. Each time was a step closer to me being enslaved by the chaotic forces driving the wind across the world. One day, I knew I might not be able to free myself.

Today, they summoned me, cajoled me to dive headfirst, to give myself over to them.

But then, shouts from below caught my attention, and I saw a handful of other guards wading into the fray. They must have seen what was going on and rushed to help. Armed, they pushed forward to attack the Shadow Hunters, even as Check and Fearless rejoined the battle. They were too many and Myst's pair couldn't stand up against them.

In that moment of clarity, I released the storm, and as the Shadow Hunters fell under the wave of my guards, I transformed back into my owl form, and returned to the snow field below.

I sat on the edge of my bed, letting Druise, my personal maid, help me change clothes. She bundled me up into a clean, dry pair of black jeans and laced my royal blue corset snugly, then brought me dry boots, and a spider-web thin black cloak embroidered with silver threads. As she draped the cloak around my shoulders, she was careful not to touch the crown that circled my head. A diadem of silver leaves entwining on either side of the circlet, the vines met in the center to embrace a glowing cabochon of black onyx, and below that, a sparkling diamond teardrop.

I sat on the bed, sipping tea and eating a cookie.

The huge, four-poster bed was made from yew wood, the headboard intricately carved. Piled high with under-blankets and sheets, the indigo comforter matched the pattern of the carpet. Covering rows of cobblestones, the rug was a sweeping panorama of swirling patterns set in indigo, eggplant, and silver.

On the ceiling over the bed, the pattern continued, only in inlaid gems of iolite, sapphire, amethyst, and quartz. The rest of the ceiling was jet-black, and the gems shimmered with an inner light that picked up the glow from the lanterns, setting to a slow, sinuous dance of movement in light and shadow.

"How long before you have to be at your meeting?" Druise refilled my teacup and I inhaled the rich aroma of peppermint, grateful as it cleared my head. I glanced up at the clock—time worked differently here in the realm of Snow and Ice but I used a clock to keep me on track *within* the barrow. The familiar touch from the outer world made me more comfortable as I adjusted to my new way of life.

"An hour. They're conferring now, but I needed a little while to think." Actually, what I had needed was a chance to decompress from raising the winds.

I inhaled slowly, my breath grounding me back into my body. After I finished my tea and cookies, I stood, sighing. Time to face the reality we had all been dreading. But we'd known it was coming. Myst was out for my blood and bone.

It had been a month since my cousin Rhiannon and I had taken the thrones of Summer and Winter. A month since I had married Grieve, and she had married Chatter. Since then, Rhia and I poured intensive study into the language of our new people, the customs of our courts, as we desperately attempted to learn what it meant to be Fae queens. The whole concept that we were effectively immortal was still too much to deal with, although truth was, we could be killed. But if we avoided accidents and murder, and no one found our heartstones, we would live into the mists of time until we were ready to let go and lay down our duties.

Gathering up the messenger bag I carried within the barrow, I made sure my notebooks were in it, along with pens, chewing gum, Epi-pen, and everything else I would need when out of my chambers. With one last look around the bedroom, wishing I could just curl up in the chamber and hide, I pushed open the door. Check was waiting on the other side to escort me to the council room.

The council room was a dark chamber, lit by the ever present lanterns that lined the Eldburry Barrow. The lights within, pale blue and violet, were young Ice Elementals, indentured into service for a time before they were set loose into the world. They did not mind their service—in the Fae world, in the world of Elementals, human rules and emotions didn't always apply. In the Marbury Barrow—in the Summer Court of Rivers and Rushes—the lights were fueled by young Fire Elementals.

Strict was waiting at the table, along with Grieve, my Fae Prince-turned-King. Also waiting were Check and Fearless, and several other advisors and guard leaders. As I entered the room, they stood to bow. Once again it hit me that I was the end of the line. No matter what everyone else did, it all came back to land on my shoulders.

I took my place at the table and nodded for them to sit. A servant brought over a tray filled with roast beef sandwiches, bowls of hot chicken soup, and the ever present tea. I was weaning them onto coffee, but they would drink their tea.

The barrow kitchen had experienced culture shock when I banned all fish and shellfish products. If people wanted to eat them in their own homes, fine, but for me and my staff— no seafood. I was Epi-pen allergic, anaphylactic, and even though I didn't like thinking about it, the fact was it would be an easy way for an assassin to get to me. That I even *had* to think about things like that still sent me reeling, but I was quickly getting used to it.

Once we were settled in with food, Grieve leaned over and placed a kiss on my lips. He was my love, the heart of my heart, and I wore a tattoo of his wolf on my stomach that responded to his feelings. Grieve had been crown prince of the Summer Court—the Court of Rivers and Rushes—until Myst had overrun the Marbury Barrow, killing hundreds of the Cambyra Fae. But Grieve, she had turned, and even though he had control over his nature now, he was still feral and wild. But he was my love, and that's all that mattered.

"Myst is on the move." Small talk was all well and good, but right now wasn't the time for it. I told them about my encounter with the Snow Hag. "Check and Fearless would have bought the farm if backup hadn't come. Luckily we weren't far from the barrow, or we would have been in a fuckton of trouble."

Strict winced. My slang still bothered him, and we were speaking in English because I didn't know enough Cambyra to make myself understood. I was learning, but it was a complex language and slow-going.

"Bite me, Strict. When I speak my own language, it's going to be in my own way." I flashed him a smile.

He laughed. "The Cambyra are definitely being dragged into a new way of life thanks to you and your cousin. As to Myst, do we know if she's within the realm of Snow and Ice yet?"

I shrugged. "Dunno, but I don't think so. When I was flying overhead, in my owl form, I saw the second Shadow Hunter shimmer into view. It was like watching someone appear through a portal, though we know there is no portal there. So it stands to reason that Myst used some form of magic to transport them over here. Which would indicate that she isn't here in our realm. Yet."

"Not necessarily, Your Majesty." Check tilted his head slightly. "She could be here. She might have sent them ahead as scouts. Just because they traveled via magical means doesn't mean they came from outside the realm. We shouldn't assume anything."

He made a good point. I leaned back, wondering whether it was safe to tell them what the Snow Hag had told me. She had said danger was under my nose rather than in the distance, and I didn't think she had been talking about the Shadow Hunters we'd encountered. If I did have a spy, could it be Strict, Check, Fearless? Or one of the other members of my staff gathered around the table with me? Or even . . . beautiful and alluring, my own sweet Grieve?

But then I wiped away the last thought. I knew my love, inside and out. I knew that even though he was a member of the Indigo Court, he had broken the connection with Myst. He would always be wild-eyed and feral, my wolf-shifter husband, but he loved me and would lay down his life for me.

After a moment's thought, I motioned to him. "We need to talk. Alone."

He followed me into a private chamber just off the council room.

Ulean, keep watch and make certain nobody is listening at the door. Warn me. And listen to what they are saying—I want to know.

I will, Cicely. But the Snow Hag is right. Danger lurks here. Not necessarily in this room, but the barrow feels uneasy, and I think there is treachery to be found here. This edge was not here yesterday—I only notice now because I am looking for it, but I think, had it been here before, I would have sensed it. I could be wrong on that, however.

I shuddered and Grieve noticed. He pulled me into his arms. His long platinum hair shimmered against the dim light, and his olive skin was warm and musky. He smelled like cinnamon and autumn leaves, like the dark half of the year on a rainy, chill night. Like the blackness of stars against the snow. He held me close, kissing my hair, kissing my forehead.

"What's wrong, my Cicely? What gives you grief?"

In soft tones, so as not to be overheard by any prying ears, I laid out what the Snow Hag had told me. "Someone is playing spy for Myst here . . . and I don't know who. Now I can't trust anybody. My father told me I could trust Strict before he and Lainule left for the Golden Isle, but can I really? Do I dare trust anybody?"

"Trust is a relative word. We can't take a chance telling them what we know—if one of the men in there happens to be in the service of Myst, then she'd find out we're onto her plans." His gaze flickered to the ground and he moved back, holding me by my shoulders. "I know you aren't going to like this, but there is a way to find out. We have to be cautious about how we go about it so word doesn't get around, however."

I knew what he was talking about and he was right. I didn't like it.

The Shamans of the Cambyra Fae had a procedure. It was painful and intrusive, but allowed them to delve into someone's mind, to root through their thoughts and feelings and secrets. Essentially a form of mental torture, it was a real mindfuck. But it got the job done. And everyone in the barrow had been through it before I took the throne, so either someone new had joined us, or someone's loyalty had been turned after the fact.

"I don't want to order that." Even as I said the words, I knew that I was fighting a losing battle. There was no other option. Simply going around asking, *"By the way, are you working for Myst now?"* wasn't going to get me anywhere and I knew it. "It's mind-rape," I whispered.

"Perhaps so, but it might also save our people. You let a spy from Myst loose in this barrow and she'll have a good chance of sweeping through here again. And this time, she won't leave *anybody* alive. If she gains entrance, you can be assured the barrow will be slick with blood and bone and gristle."

"And she'll turn everyone who she can use. And the rest . . . food for the Shadow Hunters." I hung my head. "I don't have a choice, do I?"

Grieve slowly backed away and knelt before me. "You are the Queen of Snow and Ice. Wear your crown and wield your power."

And so, reluctantly, I whispered, "Then how do we go about this without word getting out?"

"We tell no one else. Not Luna, not Peyton or Kaylin." The warning in his voice was clear—our friends couldn't know what was going on. "We visit the Shamans. They alone can be trusted. They are chosen from birth for their discipline and power." He rose, staring into my eyes. "And first, they put me to the test."

"You?" Startled, I began to shake my head. "Not you—"

But Grieve took my hands and gently brushed my wrist with his razor sharp teeth, leaving a thin red weal as blood welled up. Even as I responded, melting under his touch, he shook his head.

"Remember, my love. I belonged to Myst for a time. I carry her blood in my body. She turned me into one of the Vampiric Fae and while I have gained a modicum of control, as Queen, you cannot be complacent. You cannot trust even me without knowing for certain."

And so, my heart heavy, we returned to the main chamber and told everyone to sit tight. And then, Grieve and I made our way through the barrow, to where the Shamans lived. To where I would order them to torture the truth from my beloved husband and the rest of my people.

New York Times bestselling author **Yasmine Galenorn** writes urban fantasy, mystery, and metaphysical nonfiction. A graduate of Evergreen State College, she majored in theater and creative writing. Yasmine has been in the Craft for more than thirty years and is a shamanic witch. She describes her life as a blend of teacups and tattoos, and lives in the Seattle area with her husband, Samwise, and their cats. Yasmine can be reached at her website at galenorn.com, via Twitter at twitter.com/yasminegalenorn, at facebook.com/AuthorYasmineGalenorn, and via her publisher. If you send her snail mail, please enclose a self-addressed stamped envelope if you want a reply.

FROM *NEW YORK TIMES* BESTSELLING AUTHOR

Yasmine Galenorn

HAUNTED MOON

AN OTHERWORLD NOVEL

There's a new Fae sorcerer in town—Bran, the son of Raven Mother and the Black Unicorn—and Camille is the unwilling liaison between him and the new Earthside OIA. With cemeteries being ransacked and spirits being harvested by a sinister, otherworldly force, Aeval sends the D'Artigo sisters to rescue the missing wife of a prominent member of the Fae nobility. Their search leads them to the mysterious Aleksais Psychic Network and, ultimately, to face the Lord of Ghosts. There, Morio and Camille must undergo a ritual that will plunge them both directly into the realm of the dead.

"Yasmine Galenorn is a powerhouse author; a master of the craft."
—*New York Times* bestselling
author Maggie Shayne

galenorn.com
facebook.com/AuthorYasmineGalenorn
facebook.com/ProjectParanormalBooks
penguin.com

M1312T0513

Don't miss a word from the "erotic and darkly bewitching"* series featuring the D'Artigo sisters, half-human, half-Fae supernatural agents.

By *New York Times* Bestselling Author
Yasmine Galenorn

Praise for the Otherworld series:

"Galenorn creates a world I never want to leave."
—*New York Times* bestselling author Sherrilyn Kenyon

"Thrilling, chilling, and deliciously dark."
—Alyssa Day, *New York Times* bestselling author

facebook.com/AuthorYasmineGalenorn
facebook.com/ProjectParanormalBooks
penguin.com

*Jeaniene Frost, *New York Times* bestselling author

M192AS0513

FROM *NEW YORK TIMES* BESTSELLING AUTHOR
YASMINE GALENORN

◄**THE INDIGO COURT SERIES**►

NIGHT MYST
NIGHT VEIL
NIGHT SEEKER
NIGHT VISION

PRAISE FOR THE INDIGO COURT NOVELS:

"Excitement at every turn…a great read."

—*Night Owl Reviews*

"Lyrical, luscious, and irresistible."

— Stella Cameron, *New York Times* bestselling author

galenorn.com
facebook.com/AuthorYasmineGalenorn
facebook.com/ProjectParanormalBooks
penguin.com

M1254AS0213